Duncan Fallowell was bor[...]
travelled a good deal and co[...]
is his second novel. He is [...]
places. He is also the a[...]
Paladin).

DUNCAN FALLOWELL

The Underbelly

PALADIN
GRAFTON BOOKS
A Division of the Collins Publishing Group

LONDON GLASGOW
TORONTO SYDNEY AUCKLAND

Paladin
Grafton Books
A Division of the Collins Publishing Group
8 Grafton Street, London W1X 3LA

Published in Paladin Books 1989

First published in Great Britain by
Macmillan London Ltd 1987

Copyright © Duncan Fallowell 1987

ISBN 0-586-08742-7

Printed and bound in Great Britain by
Collins, Glasgow

Set in Bembo

to Von

'. . . We may have to wait for years – we may have to wait for ever, if we wait until life is safe.'

H.G. Wells, *Love and Mr Lewisham*

'Black holes clearly create very unusual large-scale effects in the universe, but strangely, they need not bring about any unusual local events. We could all be living inside a black hole now without noticing anything amiss . . .'

Barrow and Silk, *The Left Hand of Creation*

'It was appalling. And reminded me so much of myself!'

Una Prestonpans, *A Bitch Has Her Seasons*

'When I bring suffering into another human being's life by interfering with it, I justify my action by blaming the character of the other.'

Theodore Lessing

'. . . life is lived forwards but understood backwards.'

S. Kierkegaard

'At this the Pope raised his hand, carefully made a great sign of the cross above my head, and said that he gave me his blessing and that he forgave me all the homicides I had ever committed and all those I ever would commit in the service of the Apostolic Church.'

Benvenuto Cellini's *Autobiography*

'He who grasps the whole automatically grasps the parts – but only the parts can be uttered. He who grasps only the parts can utter them too.'

Jervys O'Jimminy, *Here To-day, Gone To-morrow*

'Only in the distance the sound of heavy firing continued, so far off as to give a sense of peace . . .'

D.H. Lawrence, *England, My England*

'I always feel unsafe, as if I'm in the presence of superior possibilities.'

C. Jung

'. . . the ancients were not decorous; they did not, as we make our moderns do, write for ladies.'

George Meredith, *The Egoist*

'So one must have this total discontent – but with joy. Do you understand?'

J. Krishnamurti

Contents

Part One

It was tea-time. The telephone rang. She put her ginger nut biscuit back in the saucer, hauled her heels off the pouffe, placed both hands on the arms of the chair and, summoning slackened energies, pushed herself onto her feet – feet which, having begun to take their ease and indulge a sense of fatigue, had swollen slightly; feet which now carried her with puffy reluctance into the hall; feet – always her Achilles heel . . .

It was Gordon. 'I'll be a bit late to-night,' he said. On receipt of this news a small region inside Pam's ribcage flinched slightly – she was ashamed of this flinching. 'A client is coming over at 6,' he went on. 'Sorry, pet.'

'Will you want anything to eat?'

'Put something aside for me.'

'All right.'

Pam replaced the telephone. It was the third time this month – back a bit late . . . She didn't mind really. Gordon was a solicitor. He had an office a mile or so away on the Hogarth Parade. This sort of thing happened when you were your own man. Except that it hadn't happened before. Back a bit late – this was a recent development. Gordon had previously been rather particular about drawing the line at 5.30 p.m. Home just after 6, a sherry, dinner just after 7. That was the way it was – unless they'd done something else . . . Pam rubbed a dirty thumbmark off the receiver of the cream telephone. She looked about her, fiddled with the daffodils in Gordon's mother's vase – Crown Derby, old, beautiful, it made its surroundings seem by contrast shabby. This struck her all at once. The hall needed redecorating. A moment ago she'd taken the hall for granted. Now however the wallpaper had a furry look, an old people's home look. Pam shuddered. The hall should be stripped – stripped! – and given a pale wash, light,

3

clean, airy. Lemon. She could probably do it herself, she would get round to it. Then the wind picked up and it leaned over and swooned dolorously against the walls of the house, swept sheets of prickly rain against the windows in erratic gusts.

Outside was gloom – then the orange streetlamps began glowing into life. There was one near the entrance to their drive. It was faulty – instead of waxing into the full orange, it jammed at a strawberry throb that was dreamy – Pam could stare at it and be carried away. When, on heavy overcast days, these lights came on too early, she would find herself thinking of Time, its cruelty.

Above the manmade gleam of the street, filthy rainclouds rolled, huddled, scurried onwards like flocks of distracted sheep. Different greys moved desperately across the sky, crowding each other, overtaking each other, driven by a wind which shaped the sharp March air into cold spurts. She pulled aside the net curtain in the bay of the sitting-room window and looked out into a watery slur. A car door banged far away – a mother and child returning from school. In so far as she could see beyond the privet hedge, the street was empty, its trees lifeless sticks. The front garden was sodden, brown, soiled green, except where clumps of daffodils fought against the conspiracy of dinge, wind and rain with trumpets of heretic yellow.

– Spring, spring! Is it spring yet? she wondered.

Pam climbed the staircase and paused on the landing, a quiet carpeted space into which direct light was filtered by net curtains. The doors of all the rooms were closed. The atmosphere was refined, secret, with the tension created by a closed door. 4 bedrooms and a bathroom – all the doors closed – why? To keep out the dust? She opened the door of Mark's bedroom – where was Mark now? This room was always kept just as it was. Model soldiers on the window-sill. A 20-year-old calendar on the wall – Gordon said he liked the pictures, the great steam trains, the photographs were too good to throw away, not good enough to frame. Pam dusted off the calendar every so often – except when Irish Mary dusted. Irish Mary came twice a week. Pam liked to look after the house herself but it was too big to do this without a sense of effort. And Pam liked the company. And she liked the status to which Irish Mary, sliding in under her 2 days a week,

4

lifted her up. Pam was not a snob – but she was a human being. She'd never had a career – but she wasn't afraid of work, wasn't afraid of a filthy suite or a muddy floor. But Irish Mary twice a week allowed Pam self-possession, completed her sense of gentility. However the suite had never attained filthiness and the floor was rarely muddied – a mental barrier at the outer doors prevented ingress of muddy shoes or boots.

Mark, where are you? He worked for the Government on chemical weapons. 'I wish he wasn't doing that,' Gordon said. Sometimes Mark wrote, sometimes he telephoned, always there was remoteness. Pam never felt, when she thought of her son at a particular time of day or night, that she knew what he was doing. And when she thought of him a great fogginess filled up her head and invisible fingers pinched painfully at her heart. This pain was connected to longing, and also to guilt. Mark's bedroom as she entered it, was a box of dark-bluish light. The green silk curtains, very grand for a boy's bedroom, were always closed. His clothes still hung in the wardrobe. There hadn't been any more children after Mark. On his way out of her body he had grabbed her tubes and done something funny to them. Gordon became less passionate, she thought, after Mark was born. Perhaps he felt less sure of her with the baby around. Not that Gordon anyway was the very passionate type. Not like, say, Bob Dashman. Well, not like how, in her odd thoughts, she imagined Bob Dashman might be. She had been an excellent mother – always worried when Mark went out in bad weather insufficiently clothed, always worried when he came in wet, always worried when he had a funny expression on his face – tried not to worry too much – failed in that. She noticed the wardrobe door ajar. Irish Mary must have left it open. Pam looked in. She smoothed down Mark's cream cricketing flannels hanging there, smoothed them down several times with the flat of her hand, then closed the wardrobe door, left the room and closed the door with a hot shiver.

Mark's room was at the front above the garage – Pam now went into the bedroom at the back next to the bathroom. This was the guest room: a double bed with walnut headboard and a green silk counterpane; a big old wardrobe in matching walnut with a large mirror set into the front of the central door; and a big old dressing table, also to match, on which was mounted a 3-part

5

mirror, large one in the centre and 2 small side mirrors on hinges, like a triptych for an altar. Pam crossed the room, walking round the bed, and looked out of the back window. The rain had stopped; the dripping, sucking water crackled in the back garden. Here and there the cloud had thinned and broken. Unexpectedly the sinking sun shot forth horizontal rays of gold light in a belated violent protest. The daffodils in the back garden caught the burst of sunlight and for a moment appeared to throb with tumescent heat, a yellow rich and buttery as if blood might have been a vivid yellow fluid engorging them. The bark of the trees was wet and black. These trees at the bottom of the garden merged with others on the far side of the fence to form a small woodland along the back of the houses. On the far side it was owned by the Local Council and known as the Spinney and soon gave way to the Recreation Field. But from the bedroom window it had a rural look, as if it might lead to fields and cows, an impression strengthened by the Victorian gothic spire of St John the Divine rising up behind and which could be descried between 2 elms because of the death of a third elm between them. The spire was topped by a golden cross which gleamed wetly now and again, according to the erratic beams of sunlight, and this gave to the prospect an exotic, almost Byzantine feature which warmed her because at the same time she knew she was at home.

– Why don't I go to church? she thought. Presumably because I don't believe in God. But I do believe in God. It is just that believing in God doesn't mean anything to me any more. It is an amorphous, impersonal belief, a mass of grey. I believe in God; I believe in a bottle of milk; I believe in lots of things . . . Perhaps if we lived in a village I'd go to church – there would be more point, there'd be people to see – reverberations, implications, consequences. When Gordon retires, shall we move a little further out? Not too far out. Not so far out as not to be able to go shopping in town occasionally, but just beyond the suburbs perhaps . . .

The thought of moving didn't attract her. It was like believing in God – the notion became lost in a heaving greyness (a greyness which was itself her mental and emotional response to the expectation of effort). Much less grey than her belief in God was her belief in the paranormal. It wasn't a cranky belief – it scarcely amounted to more than reading the horoscope in *Woman's*

Monthly – but she knew that the truth of life was unfathomable and could spring surprises. She felt, sometimes (usually when alone) (but not always), she felt the cold wind of a tremendous mystery stir in the distance and lift itself and begin to move towards her. This always left her 'strange' for the rest of the day, occasionally for the rest of the week, but she would say nothing, the cold wind having passed by, having merely brushed her with the extremity of disturbance. She didn't like to look too far into these things, lest what had merely brushed her should propagate by feeding on the attention she gave it and overwhelm her if not with madness, at least with a sensation so profoundly inconvenient as to make life impossible, at least that particular life which she chose to lead (or imagined she chose to lead). Once Pam had read that one should always sleep with one's head to the magnetic north in the northern hemisphere, and in the southern to the south, because there are currents flowing from pole to pole which facilitate the realignment of physical and psychological disorders and the elimination of impurities. This kind of precept struck her as true in an obvious, common-sensical way. And so she asked Gordon to help her rearrange their bedroom, without telling him precisely why. 'Just for a change,' she said. She could never have slept athwart the N/S axis after reading this notion – the idea would have grated constantly. So there was stubbornness in Pam. But she didn't bother with the beds in other bedrooms – so there was selfishness too.

As the sun hit it, the cross on the spire of St John the Divine shot out a solid ray of gold – late afternoon sunshine struck her face with amber – she shuddered again . . . she should do her exercises. On the video. She was funking it – she wasn't in the mood – she should do it anyway – if you always wait for the mood you never do anything. Marilyn Dashman had said 'Classes are better' but Pam didn't like classes, didn't like romping about in a gang. She wasn't anti-social, it's just the way she was. Her individualism and sense of decorum got in the way. Certainly she could let her hair down when she had to, of course she could. She could let her hair down watching Wimbledon tennis and swear like a trooper. That was one of her things – Wimbledon Fortnight. It was a long, drawn-out emotional experience for Pam, with none of the disadvantages of most drawn-out emotional experiences: it was at a distance, a switch away. If she physically attended the Tournament, she found herself crushed and distracted by other people, many of whom perspired odoriferously in the summer heat or were nerve-rackingly young. Also Wimbledon was a sexual experience for her, although Pam would never have confessed it. But she knew the experience was more complete if experienced alone. It was fun to have friends in to watch from time to time but even with others present she experienced it basically alone, in a realm of passion, despair and exultation that was private. Quite often she would be sunbathing in the back garden but would have to come in when it began on television. Pam had missed much brilliant weather watching Wimbledon. And she would have been ashamed to have explained how watching the tennis affected her, watching the men.

Pam decided to put the workout on the video, the warm-up section anyway. She had a track suit in powder blue and white pumps. Putting on the gear always made her giggle. She felt it was risible – and yet it made perfect sense: health. The exercise *always* voomphed her up, improved her sense of well-being, her aliveness. So why always this reluctance beforehand, this sense of being ridiculous? Were such feelings just another of the burdens of having been brought up British? And the blissful comfort of the track suit, undreamt of in her mother's day . . . loose . . . loose . . . the bliss of being loose . . . . . She kept it in a tallboy in the guest room as if it were not properly part of her wardrobe but an item apart, an item to be disowned if necessary. Gordon had said 'I think you look rather good in that thing . . .' She'd had it over a month before showing herself in it. Changing her clothes now, she caught her body in the wardrobe mirror. Seeing her body in this way was like one of those unpleasant things that swoop up to you in dreams.

– Scrawny, dear, you look scrawny – you used to be almost chubby – no, never chubby – but with a fuller face, fuller lips, curving hips – now scrawny. I always look good in clothes though – I'm upright. [She ran a finger over one of her yellowish breasts.] Never anything to crow about, your boobs, dear, your boobs – now there are vertical creases in them, like the marks of forks dragged through clay. How wonderful it was to be young, how wonderful . . . it was.

Pam went to the window. Eunice Chivers was pottering in the back garden next door. She was in Wellington boots and bending over with her great bottom in the air, stabbing at a dark squelchy flowerbed with a handfork. She wore a green silk dress with large pink tulips on it and a big woolly jumper over the top. The dress trailed in the mud in front and showed her long cream cami-knickers behind. Every so often she would stand up straight, or as straight as she could manage (which was considerably off the vertical), and look about her through pink-framed National Health spectacles Sellotaped across the bridge and with a piece of pink Elastoplast across one of the lenses.

– Oh God, thought Pam, what a neighbour . . .

Actually there were 2 of them living next door, the Chivers Sisters, Eunice and Sybil, but Sybil was never out of doors. Plus a third female, one who now waddled into sight, Jennifer, an old black labrador with distended dugs which almost brushed the garden path as the venerable bitch hauled herself along in a half-hearted attempt to approach her mistress.

Pam heard Eunice say 'Stay there.' Jennifer didn't need telling twice and collapsed into the mud in a geriatric heap and looked around with glazed eyes. A while ago Pam had read in the newspaper the case of an old lady who died. This lady's daughter, going through the effects, had come across a battered suitcase at the back of the wardrobe. On opening it, she found, wrapped in crumpled newspaper, a dead baby, all rotted and withered away. In her mind's eye, Pam had flashed up an image of Eunice in the role of the old lady – so quiet and mild and ineffectual. Sybil, also unmarried, had more guts. You could have a row with Sybil. In fact it had been quite difficult avoiding it years ago when Pam and Gordon first moved in. The Chivers sisters had been born in the house and Sybil especially loathed change, such as implied by new neighbours. But you knew where you were with Sybil, you felt the rise and fall of an active personality behind her words. She meant things, she intended things, did Sybil. But one never saw her any more. From what one could gather, she kept almost entirely to the upstairs front bed-room.

Scrawny – Pam ran her hands lightly over the surface of her body. A resistance in her gave way somewhat and softened and

9

stirred in her like warm caramel. Then she lost it; she felt silly in front of the wardrobe mirror with no clothes on. She felt her shoulders hunch a little as the curve of shame stiffened across her back. But she shook herself, standing up straight like a naked adult. Who are you in that mirror? How did you get there? She grinned at this interrogation, and the grin reflected in the mirror was like the opening of a fissure into another dimension – it was heartless, alien, paganly old, older than familiarity, older than home, and older by far than herself. She was horrified, turned away and sat on the edge of the bed where a light chill crept over her as if she'd been overrun by an army of ants. Pam returned the track suit to the tallboy, put her ordinary clothes back on, straightened the counterpane, left the room, closing the door very quietly as if someone ill were lying within, and went downstairs. She stopped and thought for a moment at the bottom of the stairs with a knuckle up at her mouth, then went and sprinkled some fish food into Gordon's aquarium.

It was hot. It was very hot. It was in fact repulsively hot. The very air seemed endowed with malign motive – its molecules shot directly at Gordon's skin. Purpose? Heart failure . . . He couldn't go on much longer sitting in this heat. How much can a man take? How much can Gordon take? A terrible faintness swished through him. He hovered on the verge of collapse. His skin, though running with sweat, burned. His heart – was that his heart banging? Bloody loud noise . . . The dizziness was dispelled by a stiffening of the spine which was both metaphysical and actual but this had the side effect of causing a small contraction across the brow – he felt a tightness in the head which was manifested externally by a frown. He rubbed the frown, tried to rub it away . . . His shoulders were heavy, drew him downwards. He felt his head was about to topple forward – and it did, sinking slowly like a boulder through mud. Eventually it came to rest when his chin struck his breast bone with muffled coruscations – and there was rest until the muscles at the back of the neck, unusually elongated, became aware of this fact and began to complain in low murmurs. With eyes closed, he slowly lifted up his head and gave out a deep long saintly sigh which drew up and expelled redundant vapours from his deepest core. So thorough an exhalation left him short of breath and he now sucked in oxygen in a number of short, conscious operations of the lungs. His heart returned to his attention. He was vaguely panicky – very very vaguely . . . . it resembled the frantic barking of dogs on the opposite side of a valley . . . . .

Sweat fell down his cheeks in cataracts. There was a rank odour all but masked by eucalyptus – and then no odour at all because a smell decays in the consciousness in 4 minutes – but he'd been inside a lot longer than 4 minutes, surely? What did that mean? That, olfactorily speaking, he was abnormal? He stretched out lengthwise on the pine slats, lay back and stared upwards. His mind swam. He accepted it – the barking stopped . . . He was aware of his body yet, at the same time, not aware of his body. That is to say, his mind wasn't aware of his body – but his body was aware of his body. This was a satisfactory state of affairs. This struck him as how things should be. It left him with an awful lot of space and a great deal of time. Time for what? . . . Time, that's all, just time . . . As for his mind, he couldn't focus it in the usual way. Somehow it was already focussed, but independently of him. His mind was no longer gripped in the body by anxiety. He wasn't the victim of thoughts. He was blank. His thought faculty rested, like a faithful patient powerful dog, ever ready, undemanding. Only intention gave significance to thoughts, which might then arrange themselves intelligently, like iron filings round a magnet – otherwise they were useless and noisy, random and silly. But he had no intention. He was blank. His mind had gone. He saw his mind a great way off, bobbing in the distance like a sponge on the waters of consciousness. How terrifying. How fabulous. Waves of heat went through him slowly the way waves of motion pass through the body of a serpent. Then a blast of cold air, followed by a crash. Gordon raised himself up on one elbow. Someone had left the sauna cabin. He hadn't realised there was someone else in there. And now they had left. His skin went prickly in patches. His head dropped back again. His eyes flickered and closed. In his mind's eye, he saw 2 massive white breasts, the quintessence of 'curve'. They were hanging over him. Full, firm, weighty with milk, and smooth-surfaced. The nipples were stretched as by a pressure from within

11

and the teats stood out. The fullness and distended ripeness of that pressure within was pushing towards him; and he in reciprocation felt a magnetic force enter at his neck, at the muscles which support the head, and his mouth was drawn up towards the large brownpink nipples – but slowly, as if the great magnetic force were only *just* in excess of a contrary gravitas. The 2 mighty pallid breasts hung there, and very slowly the slumbering heaviness of the head was drawn up by the tensing, pulpy compulsion of its mouth which wanted above all things to suck at the left nipple, by a tingle in its jaw which wanted to chew the nipple and suck blood there, and by the amorousness of its face which wanted to bury itself between the breasts and nuzzle wantonly there. Blast of cold air. Crash of door. Someone entered the cabin. Gordon lifted his head – slightly – he had an almost complete erection! Ghastly consternation – a thousand gales shredded his peace. Awkwardly, in a private terror, he adjusted his towel. His heart beat jerkily. The other man gave him a casual sideways look. Gordon knew what this man must be thinking – bloody perverts get everywhere, he was thinking. I'm not a pervert! Gordon wanted to say this but instead he sat up, wrapped the towel round his waist and said to cut the tension of his embarrassment 'Very hot.'

'That's the general idea,' said the man, who was large and burly, with a beard, and a small penis all but lost in a forest of black pubic hair.

Gordon fancied the air in the cabin congealed like glue, congealed with unpleasant meaning. He left awkwardly, stubbing his toe on the wooden bar of the threshold. He turned the shower-control to cold and showered painfully. Cold! It's very . . . cold . . . He wanted his penis to shrivel to the smallest possible dimensions. It had begun to escape from him – it had to be beaten back into its narrow cage, the thing must not escape, the inconvenient damn thing MUST NOT ESCAPE . . . He bit his lip under the cold shower until the flesh burst and blood leaked into his mouth, while inside the sauna the other man lay on his back, scratching his bollocks, drifting off in the heat, not giving a damn about anything – except perhaps how it would be nice to have a decent sized chopper like the bloke who'd just left the cabin.

Gordon patted his body with the wet towel and then went to ask for a couple of fresh ones from the attendant, Miss Wimbush, who wore a tee-shirt and sports shorts, and knitted jumpers in her large booth situated between the separate entrances to the Gentlemen's and Ladies' suites. She handed him the folded towels, plump and warm like bread from the oven. He tucked one round his waist and drew the other across his shoulders and stretched out on a white plastic chaise-longue in the television lounge. He was alone in there – it was Monday and Mondays were always quiet. Multicoloured images flitted on the screen but he took nothing in. He was aware of a potted palm on the floor to the left of the screen and found the plant irritating, wanted to rip it up, rip it apart (not realising it was plastic and all but indestructible). Gordon examined his hands and feet. They were bleached round the edges. Quite bloodless. White, dead skin. And puffy. Leprous. A victim's hands and feet.

– Whose breasts were they? he thought. Those great things – impending – imminent. Whose were they? For they were surely things possessed. They weren't Pam's – they weren't Pam's style at all. Were they Mother's? Mummy's mammals? Was I breast-fed or bottle-fed? I always meant to ask Mother before she died. Now there is no one who can tell me. Is it important? Yes, it is important to me. I suspect I was bottle-fed. I can't see Mother pulling her dug out for anyone. On the other hand, child-bearing does funny things to women, reveals unsuspected aspects of their characters, and emotions stronger than self-consciousness. After Mark was born, Pam became a bit stand-offish, as if we really shouldn't be doing it any more now there was a third pair of eyes in the house. Also, since we couldn't have any more children, perhaps it struck her as an unseemly indulgence, sex without even the possibility of conception. I wonder what the Roman Catholic teaching would be on such a point. The other thing I wanted to ask Mother was – what time of day was I born? I haven't the faintest idea. The reason I wanted to know – it was Pam and a horoscope thing she was fiddling with, you needed to know the time of day of your birth to establish the rising sign, but I couldn't tell her – and now I can never know – not that I give a damn about the rising sign – and I'm surprised Pam does, she's so bloody down to earth about everything. But a man should know when he was born. I'm not sure why it seems important, but it does. Perhaps it is that it's not important when you know it, but not

13

knowing it, that makes it important, because it implies an ignorance in a vital area; it is indicative of that general, squeamish ignorance of the intimate, true self. There's lots of things like that. They are not important in themselves – but their absence is crucially important. Money, for example. I never cried when Mother died. Should I have done? The Big Guilt that surfaces when a parent dies – I had it for Father but not for Mother. I wonder why. It seems the wrong way round. Sometimes I feel guilty about not having the Guilt for her! When I think of my childhood, no warmth flows towards me. Pleasure when it came was always the pleasure of escape, not of embrace. I remember Bertram Mills at Olympia on Boxing Day. I remember Baker Street Tube Station, the gateway to Regent's Park and the Zoo, Selfridges, Madame Tussaud's, the Planetarium and the stars . . . Baker Street Station, Gateway to the Universe! . . . . .

Anyway, they can't have been Mother's breasts – I'd never have had an erection. Were they my secretary's, Ms Harding's? Pretty girl, good worker. There aren't many perks in a solicitor's office – a pretty secretary is one of them. She came straight from the Comprehensive School 8 years ago to work in the outer office, and when Mrs Vale left Ms Harding moved up. Never regretted it. I like the way she calls me Gordon. It's not a bit presumptuous. She attracts me but I don't want to have an affair with her – Christ, that would ruin everything! But it's good to have her working there, it lifts the adrenalin, boosts the morale, tunes up the hormones. Pam is a frigid cow! I could do with a cup of tea.

Miss Wimbush in the booth supplied the free cup of tea which came with the ticket. Gordon sipped it pensively. It was a good strong cup and it stimulated thought the way cigarettes once had. Gordon hadn't smoked for 6 years now – and he didn't even want one! No, he just didn't want one! So there, all you smart alecs who said he couldn't do it! 40 a day from the age of 18. And now – none – nothing – nothing . . .

What did he still do that was vicious? This line of thought led Gordon to a blank wall. And as he contemplated this wall, a sensation of great feebleness overcame him. He felt trapped in a solidifying mass of inconsequential sludge. And this physical lassitude, it dawned on him, was not only a sensation. It was also an opinion – his opinion of himself.

14

– I'm old, he thought. My birthday – Pam's threatening to have a party this year to celebrate my gathering decrepitude. Oh God, perish the thought! I hate parties! But I'm not an old man. I've got another 10 years of work in me – *at least*. More like 15 years. Er . . . 15 years is quite a slab of time. What am I going to do with such a slab? Spend it talking to friends? Doing the garden? Reading books? I expect I shall spend it working . . . but what for? And what friends? Peter Fowler's gone. Drowned at Cowes. Not a friend but a good partner – we worked better for not having much to do with each other out of office hours. And Jack . . . I miss Jack . . .

Jack had been Gordon's best friend. He'd had an accountancy practice at the other end of the Parade and they'd enjoyed each other's company for many years, finding a deep reassurance in it that was humorous and easy. Jack had died from a heart attack just over a year ago – his secretary had gone in to take some dictation and found the body slumped forward across the desk – Jack had knocked over a plastic cup of black coffee and it was dripping off the desk like dark brown blood. Jack dead. Just like that. Gordon always had his tea or coffee out of a proper cup & saucer, but Jack was quite happy having his brought up in a plastic cup from the automatic machine in the Laundrette beneath his office. Jack who'd been to a good school, Jack who liked to linger over a bottle of good claret, Jack with his expert knowledge of geology and fossils, Jack who'd been divorced early, Jack who was having an affair with a geography mistress at the local girls' school . . .

– What are my vices? Gordon thought. No vices . . . not a single one . . . I'm not sure this is a wholly admirable state of affairs.

Despite all ethical teachings, despite the fathers and sages of cultures, despite everything that a decent suburban upbringing could do to affirm that man's noblest objective was goodness, a strand of cells in Gordon's head, as it cooled in the balmy air of the television lounge, could not accept that this was the whole story. Why were naughty people so attractive? Even evil people were sometimes attractive – and always fascinating. Gordon had no vices – why was *nobody* impressed by that? What do people really admire? . . . Success. Yes. But not always. Only that kind

15

of success behind which lies . . . courage. What people really admire is courage. Humility, goodness, obedience, these elicit no response. The paralysing virtues! The paralysing virtues lead nowhere. Were such virtues not the product of, at best, laziness, and at worst of fear and lack of imagination? But courage, that was it, a certain kind of nerve, fibre, integrity, trueness. But not any old nerve or trueness, not mere daring. Who dares wins – this is as true for the mugger, rapist, terrorist, criminal as for anyone else. Who dares wins – here is the voice of terror, destruction and cruelty, the philosophy of violent abuse. But courage, a certain kind of trueness – what was it exactly? . . . Gordon experienced a twitching in his right thigh muscle as mentally he struggled with this essential problem. Twitch . . . twitch/twitch . . . twitch . . . It annoyed him. Maybe he should have a massage. But on the question of massage he was also rather indecisive. On Mondays Miss Wimbush did it. Miss Wimbush – she wasn't pretty but she had something. She had that name for a start. What if he got an erection mid-massage? It would be so damn humiliating. It wasn't like him to be worried about getting erections. If he was to worry at all, it was about not getting them. – What's wrong with me?!?!

Gordon had read in a newspaper recently that 44% of married men in England claimed they had no close male friends. He was staggered by this finding. What was a close friend? One with whom you didn't maintain the façade? One you could be your real self with, discarding the coat of human vanity? Now that Jack had gone, he supposed himself to be among the 44% and this supposition, coming as it did with ruthless unexpectedness, shocked him. A wave of self-pity, deriving from fear, flowed through him. It began as a vague muscular uneasiness at his extremities and grew to a dull ache across his torso, blotting out the pictures of his mind, and when it left him he felt tired and reduced. Bob Dashman barged into his thoughts. As Dashman's solicitor, Gordon occasionally felt himself drawn into things against his better judgement, felt himself slipping off familiar territory. Drawn into what? Don't know . . . but a sense of vertigo would accompany it, a drowning helplessness, which wasn't yet sufficiently acute to oblige him to revise their relationship but . . . not feeling 100% clean, and therefore vaguely threatened, this was similar to the distress which insomnia caused him. Insomnia – he'd solved it with sleeping pills. It wasn't the perfect solution but it was a solution. The price of insomnia was too high – he had to be well-slept to face the day's work – he'd compromised with his principles and gone for sleeping pills – it was one problem solved – he could give his attention to other problems – Gordon wished however that he'd not been obliged to resort to narcotics. The nightly sleeping pill has replaced the morning brimstone & treacle. An obsession with regular sleep is perhaps no more reasonable than an obsession with regular bowel movements – we hanker after perfect rhythms in our life, smooth rewarding routines, but nature is not so smooth, and the regime must be imposed artificially. One should not insist upon the regime, it only produces tensions, frustrations, a constant failure to be perfect. On the other hand Gordon had to be at the office at 9 a.m. every weekday morning and this very fact produced a recalcitrant alertness in him the night before. Insomnia – Gordon found that insomnia led to a loss of discrimination between the sleep and awake states. And a loss of discrimination between these 2 states led to a loss of discrimination between all phenomena. Such discrimination is the mark of a clear mind – and a clear mind is a peaceful mind. The tendency to allow phenomena to flow into each other, in conformity with the ultimate truth of the transience of all phenomena, is nonetheless an idleness of the brain and a symptom of mental disease. Differentiation in all things is as necessary as correspondence in the pursuit of sanity and accomplishment. A man who sees beyond differentiations into a matrix of archetype, force and chance must still respect integrity. Otherwise a man divorces himself from the circle of humanity, and all true knowledge is rooted in this circle. The spirit of integrity is honesty in the moral sphere and a man must not allow himself to separate from it. A man connects here by respecting the object. Don't let your thoughts interfere with the object. Don't waste mental energy and knot yourself up by letting your thoughts run into places and things where they have (and can have) no business. Thus Gordon had thought it out.

The man with the beard and small penis walked by. 'Had enough?' asked Gordon. In the sauna he often talked to other men with ease and intimacy, as if he'd known them forever. But if he

17

met them on the outside, in the street, they'd hardly be capable of saying anything to each other – the wraps would be on again, differentiation exerting its divisive power.

Gordon followed him into the changing-room. 'Do they do a mixed sauna here?' asked the bearded man.

'No,' said Gordon, unlocking his locker, 'because they have separate suites.'

'Shame,' said the bearded man, rubbing his belly with circular motions of his towel. 'I went to a mixed sauna in France, in Nice. You wouldn't believe what went on. Mind you, it wasn't a Council sauna like this. Privately owned. But big. They're more relaxed about that sort of thing in France.'

'Yes, I expect they are,' said Gordon, sorting through his clothes.

'Another dose of punishment then,' said the bearded man, and he took himself off through the archway towards the heat and water, while Gordon turned towards a mirror and started combing his hair.

– I think I'm as bald as I'm ever going to be. I don't think I'll get any balder, will I? he wondered. He played with the arrangement to minimise his receding hairline without going to the preposterous extremes of camouflage which some men go in for. He had a receding hairline and a bald patch at the back and his hair was greying mouse. He could handle that. Many men go through hell on account of falling hair but Gordon still had enough to be going on with. He towelled himself vigorously. His skin tingled. He looked at his body in the mirror. Peculiar shape. A short body with long legs. Like a radio on top of long tripod-type legs. His only serious oddity was a dark brown patch about the size of an oakleaf on his lower right back from which hair grew in a weird tuft. He was thin – ribs and kneecaps very much in evidence – funny little pot belly in evidence like a small football under the skin – silly penis hanging down, rather shrivelled now, white and loose – he smiled at it, chuckled lightly, feeling good, a feeling which was modified somewhat when, on his way out, throwing his used towels into the large plastic drum and returning his locker key, Miss Wimbush said to him 'Isn't it terrible about all this nuclear bomb business?' There had been a major nuclear summit in Vienna and the headlines on the front of the *Evening*

18

Cry, underneath her elbow, read *Still No Deal*.

Gordon glared at her. 'It's not just the nuclear threat,' he said. 'It's all the biological and chemical weapons too. Nobody ever thinks of these!' And as he left the Sports Centre and faced the brisk outside, his physical well-being was oppressed by a needling sense of exasperation.

It was still light, having brightened at the very end of the day, and Pam thought as she stared into the back garden from the kitchen window – The evenings are drawing out – it's getting milder. She wasn't going to cook for Gordon – she'd rustle up an omelette when he chose to show up – she'd had enough of putting plates of stuff aside. If he didn't want an omelette he could go back to the Parade, to the Chinese Takeaway, where the proprietor had a habit of always saying 'Funny wevver for de time ob year', or the Fish & Chip Shop instead where she always found the chips too greasy by half. Soon, she could see it, they'd give up using the dining-room altogether and start eating in the kitchen. *For convenience.* Is that what modern life was about? Convenience? Finishing as quickly as possible with this thing so that you could get on with the next thing and then dashing hell-for-leather through the next thing so you could get on with the bloody thing after that . . . but what for? To what was it all leading? It had been a cold drizzly day – she'd been going to bake Gordon a pudding, a Hollygog Pudding, a golden syrup roly-poly baked in milk which only takes 40 minutes.

– I'll be damned if I'm going to bake him a sodding Hollygog! He can finish off the sherry trifle in the fridge!

Pam went upstairs to run a bath and have a good soak. She went into their bedroom and was fiddling about in there when she saw through the net curtains a large black limousine slide slowly past the house. So slowly was it travelling that she thought this hearse-like creation was going to halt at her gates and call. But it slid on along the road and paused at the entrance to the Dashmans' drive, then turned and went in through the open gates to the circle of gravel in front of the front door – which was opened by Bob Dashman – was that Marilyn behind him? Pam couldn't see – the house was just too far away in the dusky light to be comfortably within the scrutiny of the naked eye. Pam went and found Gordon's field glasses in the cupboard on the landing and whooshed back for an in-depth probe. The first thing to roll into focus (and it did so quite suddenly) was a mass of billowing black. It was a most curious phenomenon, resembling what in her mind's eye she fancied a soul in torment must look like. But as she began to get a grip on the scene, she realised that she was looking at the tribal dress of an Arab woman who'd clambered from the car and was struggling across the gravel through the March vespers to the Dashman door. An Arab man had also emerged from the car (which she now noticed had gold fittings) and 2 Arab children in western clothes of blue and pink respectively. The man was in a western suit – only the woman, in her sinister cloud of wind-blown black, brought with her the odour of camels and the hiss of sand-dunes. Pam was fascinated. She'd never seen such a thing in Wildwood Rise before. Certainly all sorts of people visited the Dashmans – they were like that, the allsorts type. Actually Pam was ambivalent about the Dashmans. She was interested and faintly sneery – and in fact rather liked them whenever she found herself in their company which was occasionally. Their house was Georgian, with additions. That is – *real* Georgian. It was all that remained of whatever community had existed on this spot before the long winding avenue of Wild-wood Rise was built. It was the grand house of the road, detached in large grounds, and whoever lived there was always thoroughly aware of this fact. The Dashmans had moved in 5 years ago when the Gibbons family – known as the Gibbonziz – sold up and moved to Devon. Gordon had done the conveyancing on the property, then called The Wood House and surrounded by many beautiful trees. Bob Dashman rechristened it Rorke's Drift after seeing a film called *Zulu*, and chopped down many of the trees at the front so that the house would be more visible from the road. Pam and Gordon had gone in for drinks – it was being done up in Nylon Georgian Repro – very comfortable but everything brand new and clicking with static electricity. Marilyn Dashman had said 'Come into the lounge, er, drawing-room. I can't bear secondhand stuff, can you? It reminds me of old people's homes.' Their young daughter Cordelia, a beautiful child, brought round nibbles to eat. 'Have a nibble, Mrs Drake. Cordelia, give Mrs Drake a nibble. We have a son too,' said Marilyn, brushing back a long lock of hair. 'He's called Ward which is short for Hereward. He's just started as a dayboy at Harrow and doesn't get in until late. I think we're going to be *so* happy here. Aren't we, darling? And Albert already *adores* it.'

At this point Albert looked up from the fluffy nylon rug in front of the pretend-log gas fire and seemed to grin. He was an Alsatian puppy of 6 months and had joined them at their previous home, a deluxe flat in Maida Vale. Albert was finding himself very attracted to the concept of garden.

'What a strange name for a dog,' said Pam.

'We named him after Grandaddy,' said Mrs Dashman. 'My grandfather was Raven Master at the Tower of London – which means he was a Yeoman of the Guard which is the oldest military corps in the world. Isn't that interesting?' Mrs Dashman always told people this at the earliest opportunity. She wasn't an incorrigible snob and you didn't have to be anybody with blue blood to become Raven Master but she felt the fact linked her to the incomparable sweep of British History – just as her mother's Jewish blood had tended to separate her from this sweep. Marilyn had a natural tendency to emphasise the non-Jewish side of her family. Not that she was anti-Semitic or anything. God, no. Or guilty. Or ashamed. God, no. It was simply that somehow . . . well, it just happened . . . without her realising it usually, unconsciously, it just happened that she identified with the non-Jewish side more, the Talbot side; she just felt it in her bones that the Talbot side was more *her*. In fact when she'd married Bob she'd said 'Let's hyphenate!' In an excess of upwardly mobile zeal they'd done so. Marilyn Dashman-Talbot. She thought it the most beautiful name in the world. But as Bob's kitchen gadgets company prospered he had been teased by colleagues and he let the extra barrel fall into disuse. Marilyn fought a valiant rearguard action on behalf of the world's most beautiful name, but even she came to feel that insisting they keep it up against his increasingly contrary wishes was perhaps desperate to the point of being *déclassé*. She couldn't use the hyphenated name unless they *all* used it. If she did, it would seem phoney – and nothing kills beauty deader than phoniness. Bob knew he'd come a long way. 'If the classes have survived in England,' he would often say, 'it is because they are not watertight.' To kitchen gadgets were added electronics and then property and with success came self-affirmation. Bob Dashman he was born, Bob Dashman he would die.

Now, as Marilyn looked over Bob's shoulder at the Arab family approaching across the gravel, she fixed a bright smile to her face and prepared to back up her husband to the hilt by being his gracious and solid support in whatever funny business was afoot.

Having eaten his omelette and trifle on the kitchen table, Gordon thoroughly blew his nose into a handkerchief. He was the type to blow his nose without restraint in public, although on this occasion he was alone. He saw no reason to repress or even moderate the snorting out of 2 nostrilsful of snotty mucus into a piece of white linen just because others were present – which trait reflected the more robust aspect of his upbringing. Then he took his coffee into the dining-room to finish off some paperwork while Pam sat in the sitting-room with her feet up, searching for a television programme to get lost in. A play called *Juice* about a fruit-seller in Helsinki and his affair with his father's mistress – Pam couldn't get into it. She flicked the remote control. An advertisement. *So come and buy one of our magnificent carpets at prices normally associated with total shit.* The language they used in ads these days – Pam winced and flicked. A programme about baby battering and family violence – a zombie said 'I couldn't help it, I didn't mean to' – apparently he'd killed his baby son by holding the boy by the feet and repeatedly dunking him in a pan of boiling water. Pam went all funny and flicked. A news report on leakages from a brand-new leakproof nuclear power plant in the Cotswolds was coming to an end and the commentator said 'And after the commercial break we take a look at a subject of increasing interest to many of you: dioxin poisoning.' Pam sipped at her coffee and flicked. Trees, green trees, the camera panned across an endless vista of green trees, wonderful, soothing, sublime, and immediately she began to wallow. Her obsession with choice vanished, her sense of time, and of missing something elsewhere, vanished.

She settled into the green trees, peaceful, blissful . . .

Gordon's paperwork failed to grip him so he decided to join her in front of the box which was showing this fabulously photographed programme made in conjunction with Polyprog of West Germany and Télévision La Gloire of France about the destruction of the tropical rainforest in South America.

'It's terrible what they're doing,' said Pam.

'Yes, isn't it terrible what they're doing,' said Gordon.

'Do you want any more coffee?' asked Pam.

'Er – no, I won't, not now.'

Pam moved her eyes from the screen – they seemed to make a popping sound like suckers being pulled off glass – and let them rest on a bronze Mercury 18″ high on the coffee table. She thought – We haven't given a party for ages – I remember I felt a bit funny during the last one – not quite with it – it was my birthday.

And she'd felt a bit funny after the party too, lost, imprecise, acidulous, until it had dawned on her with a pang, long after everyone had left and Gordon was stacking the dishwasher in the kitchen while she sat in the sitting-room among the detritus, that this funny feeling was a feeling of being unloved – and that she had the need to love someone, actively, as a conscious activity, not as an assumption. To hug. And be hugged. She loved Gordon – she always said so. But it was a sluggish sort of love which became apparent only when something violent was done to it . . . . .

To-night Pam was first in bed – as usual. A lamp with a yellow fringed shade cast a trapezium of light upon a page of a paperback novel, *Pumpkins at Midnight* by Anthea Lately; not brilliant, but a change from Mary Yodel. Pam sometimes managed a few paragraphs before lights out. Paragraphs had become pages by the time Gordon clambered in – later than usual. She put away the book and the room went black. There was space between their bodies. It was customary – Pam could handle the noise of his snoring but not the vibrations. To-night he softly touched her breast which he sometimes did as his sleeping pill came on. She was lying on her side facing the wall. Now she turned half onto her back and said 'Do let's have some people in.'

'What for?'

23

'Gor*don*.' She knew he knew what she was talking about.
'Why not . . .' he murmured.
And Gordon fell asleep.
And Pam drifted off half an hour after.

Part Two

Part Two

A comedian was telling a joke. '*Why did the man who raped the deaf & dumb girl break all her fingers?*' Silence. '*So she wouldn't talk.*'

– Bastard, thought Doll, and she flicked.

'*So shut your fucking cakehole!*' It was a contemporary drama. Doll flicked.

Matter, buff-coloured, with disgusting lumps in it, dripped from a spoon and a gravelly overdubbed voice said '*Yum-yum. Yum-yum. Pure goodness from Synthoglop. Buy some now and give the kids a treat.*'

– That looks tasty, thought Doll. She waited for the advertisements to end and the programme return.

'*To-night we report on a subject of interest to everyone: baby-battering. If you aren't a battered-baby yourself, you are bound to know one who is. They're everywhere. Howling, bleeding, bruised, burned, all wrenched out of shape and punched in. To-night we look in depth at this brutish pastime to see if—*'

– Bastards, thought Doll, flicking.

Clip. Clop. Clip. Clip. Clop. Clip-clop . . . Clop . . . . . Clop! Applause . . . . International tennis – Doll flicked.

Boom. Banga-boom. Banga-boom. Banga-boom. Banga-boom. Banga-boom. A pop diva, dithyrambic, blue in the face, was vomiting lyrics at the screen through throbbing bass pulses and waves of sonic tinsel.

Doll scrutinised the picture for a while, then said aloud 'And I thought I had problems.' She flicked a few tabs and buttons on the set, picked up a cartridge and slotted it into the video player, settling down to watch her film where it had left off earlier in the day. As she started painting her fingernails she felt something warm and moist slide out of her centre.

– Damn, my period, it's early, and I've just got ready.

Doll was fat but shapely – not yet one all-purpose blob. Therefore she was sexy. Derek came in.

'You're late,' she said.

'Late for what?'

'Have you eaten?'

'Not much.'

'There's fish fingers in the fridge. I got you your Liquorice Allsorts.'

'What's this?'

'Aren't you going to thank me?'

'Thanks, Mum. What's this?'

On the screen 2 painted people sat in an upmarket plastic environment. The painted man said to the painted woman 'Your mouth was made for the madness of kissing.' The painted woman's mouth pulsated and opened but nothing came out of it – she'd won an Oscar for this.

'It's my film from the video club. *Miss Faust.*'

'. . . . . It's diabolical. It's American. Did you get my film?'

'What film?'

'*Hammersmith Is Out.*'

'No, I got you Liquorice Allsorts.'

On the screen, the painted man stood up and went to a large window. He stood with his back to the screen, expressing the crisis of the moment by clenching his buttocks a few times. Miss Faust's mouth opened and closed a few times in sympathy, in close-up. She arose and rustled to the opposite end of the room where tenderly she stroked the back of a chair.

'Really, this is dead pathetic,' said Derek.

'Go and eat your fish fingers,' said Doll. She blew irritably on her fingernails, then went into the bedroom to find a tampon and change her knickers. 'Switch the bloody thing off if you like. I'm going out in a minute. What've you done with my hairbrush?'

Derek was bored by American films – except space ones. His passion was for British films (and lately French and Italian ones) of the 1960s and early 70s – any of them – they had a kind of . . . He didn't know what it was exactly, but they made life seem immediate, adventurous, amusing and free.

Derek is 17 years old, the indivisible age.

Not child, not adult, Derek can be both and is loyal to neither. He struggles between. He has black hair, curly, cut well at a barber's with money given to him by Auntie May who is not his real aunt.

Derek would like an adventurous life – the word 'adventure' itself had a wavelike motion which excited him and made him frown. Often had he dreamed over the bright artificial brochures from the Moonlight Travel Agency, dreaming of faraway places, beautiful impossible women, beaches, starlight, drama, beautiful impossible events in unheard-of archipelagoes. The names of the streets around him exploded like fireworks in a wasteland of council flats – Swedenborg Gardens, Henriques St, Artichoke Hill, Sly St, Rampart St, Back Church Lane, Blue Anchor Yard . . . . . Pop told him about the good old days when the place was filled with the fruits of empire, boats moored at the end of streets and looming above you in lights as you walked on flagstones through the night to the pub, when the place seethed with vitality, smells, shouts . . . Oh, the suppurating nostalgia and despair! How refulgent it was then, how golden! Pop took him down the Lane to look at the puppies, an entire alleyway of puppies on sale in Petticoat Lane. Pop talked of the horses which drew barges along East End canals, the horses which drew the carts of rag & bone men – it seemed that in those days the place was full of animals. Pop said hullo to many many people on these walks to the Eel & Pie Shop, to the Vapour Baths at York Hall. He often bought Derek a bar of Tiffin, saying 'This is what they eat in India'. Pop, as a little boy, waited on the steps of the Turk's Head in Wapping while his father sold soused fish from a basket to the drinkers inside. Pop, as a little boy, looked up into the sky which was filled with the intersecting ropes of ships silhouetted from behind by the setting sun . . . Pop said 'Sing me that song, dear.' And Derek sang the song he learned at school.

> See how the snowflakes are falling
> Falling so softly and white . . .

Pop told him about the shell during the war in Flanders, the shell which came straight for him out of the night, the brilliant golden comet of death coming straight for him – but it stopped in its tracks a few feet from his forehead, screeched to a halt and blazed there, mesmerising him, paralysing him. He always knew that the comet of death stood off his brow by only a few feet and this distracted him from life, enthralled him in a deeper spell, so that he didn't do very much and played the piano between times, until, 65 years (during which there was another war) later, the shell decided to complete its trajectory, shot forward onto his brow and Pop, an old man, was dead. Pop was gone. The bomb sites were gone. Much was gone . . . Now, so little adventure stirred in the place; the only adventure was the adventure of memory or the adventure of destruction; no raucous jollity sparkled in the streets; and the little boy Derek stands on a street corner, looking this way, looking that way, failing to recognise anything, the familiar marks gone, indifference on all sides, towering blankness in a seedy silence. He shouts and nothing answers in the concrete world, not even an echo, and the little boy is lost on the street corner, crying for his mummy, shedding sentimental tears.

Doll's nails at last were dry. So she applied another coat. And when that too was dry, she said 'Do you want to come to the pub? I'll get Tracey to let you in – just one beer, mind.'

They sat in the lounge of the Britannia Pub, Doll sipping her vodka & orange, Derek sipping his pint of bitter. She lit a cork-tip cigarette. Derek said 'Can I have one?' and Doll said 'You can't afford to smoke. Go on then. Just one, mind.' This seemed to be her basic philosophy, that one of anything was OK (viz. Voltaire: once is experience, twice is sodomy).

It was early, quiet. At the bar 2 solid-looking men with rubbery faces were discussing a boxing match. One said to the other 'We know what resuscitation is. But what I want to know is – what's suscitation?' Pop music came through from the saloon while darts went intermittently thunking into a dartboard. The pop song grew loud in Derek's ears.

Someone
Touch me

30

Doll rubbed the back of her neck, adjusted a lock of hair there, and said 'Now if I see a man and he takes a liking, you're not to get funny.'

'Do you fancy one of the geezers over there?'

'I mean – in general. I wouldn't mind having a man in my life again.'

Derek didn't mind either. He often wondered why his mother didn't just get on with it, instead of all this advance fussing for the male who was to lift her life into amplitude, this male who never arrived. Derek wasn't funny about the prospect – it might relieve him a bit. Doll imagined he was, but he wasn't. Well, he was a bit, but not in the way she supposed. He worried about the territory. He and his mother lived in a flat above a Betting Shop and he felt this wasn't big enough for 3. But he wasn't afraid of a man stealing his mother. Let the man try, ha! . . . . . Doll knew where to get her sanity-making fix of love & affection when she needed it – she occasionally had men in for the night. Derek heard them grunting, creaking and gasping through the wall. Doll always said it was because she didn't like waking up alone. But Doll was far from being anybody's and always held at least 2 parts of herself in reserve, the part that was always for Derek and the part which would be given to the right man.

Derek said 'A woman went into the doctor's surgery with a frog on her head. The doctor looked up and said "Can I help you?" And the frog said "Yes please, I've got something sticking to my bottom." '

Doll laughed and shouted across 'What would you do with him, Tracey?'

'What?' shouted Tracey back.

'Can I have another?' asked Derek, emptying his beer.

'Why don't you treat me for a change?' Then she shouted across to the bar 'Can he have another, Tracey?' One of the solid-looking men glanced across at Doll and smiled.

'Honest, Doll, I mustn't, you'll get me shot. Come back when you're 18, Derek.'

'Tracey has spoken,' said Doll. 'Run along now. Come here a

31

moment.' She ran her fingers through his hair, smoothing it back from the forehead, tidying it. 'You're getting so handsome,' she said in a slightly strange tone, with an odd Mona Lisa smile that was loving, predatory, knowing and inquisitive all at once.

In the street outside Derek bumped into Dougal Gupta who said 'Wotcher, Derek. Haven't seen you in ages. Do you want to come with us Friday?'

'Where?'

'Nowhere special. Up the Hearts of Oak, Dock St. Meeting Maurice and Dudley there. 8 o'clock.'

'Will they let us in?'

'Yeah. There's a new bloke runs it.'

'OK. See ya then.'

They parted and Derek went to the Fish & Chip Shop which was far away since the one nearby had been demolished.

'Anything with it?' said the girl behind the counter with bad acne and red scrubbed hands.

Derek pondered. Mushy peas or curry sauce? Examined his change, pondered.

'Come on,' said the girl, wiping her red raw nose with her sleeve. 'There are other people, you know.' But Derek was the only customer.

'Curry sauce,' he said.

In the Laundrette, Derek watched the washing recede to infinity. And when he wasn't doing this, he was watching a girl out of the corner of his eye. She looked half English and half something else. She looked at him occasionally and when she did so he looked away. He thought he'd seen her somewhere before. He had an erection in his cotton trousers – he was glad they were baggy and made from heavy cotton because this both concealed it and enabled him to play with the tip of it by putting his hand in his pocket. He took his hand out of his pocket and sat forward with his elbows propped on his knees. She was taking her washing out of the machine. He looked sideways at her, she caught his eye, and he said 'Diabolical weather'.

'Really?' she said, smiling. Then she picked up her washing and left.

The cord of resentment was pulled nastily inside Derek. He felt rejected. Why had he taken so long to open the conversation? What did she mean by 'Really?'? . . . What a rude person . . .

There were 3 others in the Laundrette but they were so mute, passive and thoroughly nondescript that had you clapped a hand over Derek's eyes and asked him 'What sex are they?' he would not have known. Had they stories too? Or were they the background sludge necessary for making a story visible? Derek stopped thinking this way and thought another way, namely that everyone was a passenger on a high-speed train but that the majority sat with their backs to the engine so they could see only the landscape which had passed, were not in a position to see the landscape ahead. Those few who sat facing the engine, among whom Derek counted himself, often had a difficult time of it because the majority regarded them as preposterous or dangerous or simply ignored them altogether: those who sat facing the engine were not often esteemed. Derek did not feel esteemed and didn't quite know how to go about getting esteemed. And what did Derek see as he sat facing the engine, staring out of the window? He saw . . . he saw . . . . for a start, he saw himself – and this so terrified him that he looked up with heart beating, palms sweating, and said to the bag of clothes on his right 'Got the time, please?' A face puffy and ancient, covered with tiny broken blood vessels, and tiny coloured lumps (grey, blue, purple, red, yellow) scattered under the wizened skin, turned on him a gaze so deep and vacant that it appeared to focus on an object 100 light years beyond Derek's head. It said 'Don't ask me. How'm I supposed to know? I'm blind. I'm just sitting here for company. But there's a clock on the opposite wall. Can you tell me what it says?'

Derek knew there was a clock on the wall. Of course there was a clock on the wall. The question of the time wasn't the important thing. When he'd asked it, it was because of a need to communicate with another in order to reassure his perception which had been unpleasantly rocked by a picture of himself rattling away into a black hole on an out-of-control railway train getting faster and faster and faster and faster . . . . . He wasn't in the mood for talking to the blind, but he said 'It's 9 o'clock.'

'Cor blimey. I must've fallen asleep. Will you help me to the door, please? I've got to get home. Where are you? Where's the door?'

Derek did his duty and the blind person left, although the clock read 7. Derek chuckled. He sat down again and found himself on board the train facing the engine but the moment of panic had gone, the train was behaving, it was the Flying Scotsman or perhaps the Golden Arrow, and by and by a curious thought occurred to him – Why did all the books on sex, all the official mores on it, assume that the function of sex was confined to reproduction when sex itself so obviously did not confine itself to this function? In other words, why did Mankind suppose that the sex drive in Nature was only for reproduction when Nature herself supposed no such thing?

Derek cogitated awhile and came to the following conclusions:— The essential purpose of the sex impulse is to draw the species together, human bonding, human consciousness. This is the umbrella purpose of which reproduction is the most visible effect or by-product. Sex is the all-embracing integrating force for our species in its earthly state. It is to humans what the force of gravity is to matter, to planetary systems, to galaxies. And like gravity it can often be violent and surprising in its operations. But it is always symbiotic. What is the anti-gravity in human life? Individualism: freedom, purpose. Any healthy society must allow for the play of both these forces.

– And another thing, thought Derek. When people talk about sex among themselves it is nearly always in terms of pleasure, but when they write about sex it is never in terms of pleasure – why? A Martian reading an earthly sex manual would assume that this was a rotten penance laid upon mankind by a Universal Mover given to making sick jokes.

– This iron bar straining at my groin, is that pleasure? thought Derek. It is definitely sex.

– No, thought Derek, it's lack of sex.

– Ah, but lack of sex is sex too, thought Derek.

– It's all sex.

– And what's love?

On his way back from the Laundrette, Derek turned into Burslem Street. He looked down the dull length of it and was arrested by seeing at the end, in orange lamplight, 2 eighteenth

34

century doorways. He was astonished, he came this way often, why had he not seen them before? There they stood, with a vividness that was hallucinogenic, but with the certainty of self-possessed facts. One had a flat cornice lintel supported on 2 pilasters, the other a triangular pediment on 2 pillars, and both came as a fabulous surprise that was to his mind almost Chinese in its elegance and exoticism. The windows above these doorways were black, punched out of the brick like eyes put out. The buildings were derelict. Above them floated a moon. Derek could hardly believe what he was seeing – there shouldn't be anything like this round here! And as he stared at these 2 crumbling and forgotten doorways making an outlandish delicacy at the end of Burslem Street, as if 2 date palms had suddenly been spotted growing on the banks of the Thames, the moon turned bloodred and a constriction clasped his throat.

Dragging itself slowly towards him on hands and knees, Friday finally arrived – he was going out with the boys. They'd all been at school together up the road. Maurice Hampton, whose family was West Indian, was still there, spending most of his time in the school gymnasium working out with weights. The others had left. Dougal Gupta, whose family was Indian, helped his father in the grocer's shop. Dudley Dennis, the oldest of the 4 (and older than Derek by a couple of months), hadn't found a job. For a few weeks he and Derek went looking together, but the strain was too much and now, if they looked at all, they looked separately. Dudley, Dougal and Maurice lived in Harold Wilson House, a tower of graceful proportions which wobbled in high winds. Its concrete flanks had discoloured and the prefabricated panels on its façade had warped and sometimes they fell off, descending to the ground in a manner which was dangerous to passers-by. A heavily pregnant woman had once been decapitated thus (but the baby lived). Derek in the small flat with his mother above the Betting Shop lived comparatively close to the earth and this made him feel different from the other 3, though he couldn't have specified the nature of this difference.

What had they done as boys? Played space outlaws through the streets. Showed each other their willies. Hung around, got dirty, laughing. Later they started going to the football match. They had fights. Derek once had a fight with Dudley outside Central Buildings in Southwark Street. They'd been visiting Dudley's grandmother in Guy's Hospital (a man tried to commit suicide by jumping from the penthouse in one of the Barbican towers – the wind was so strong up there that it blew him in through the open window of a flat lower down where the daily was doing the cleaning – the daily, lost in the noise of her hoovering, looked up to see a man flying in through the window and had a heart attack – the daily was Dud's grandmother). It had been over the question of which is further south, the Tropic of Capricorn or the Equator? Dudley said the Equator. Derek said the Tropic of Capricorn. Derek found a public library and dragged Dudley into it. On checking it out, Derek discovered that he was correct. He hadn't been absolutely certain and with the swagger of a man who has gambled and won he called Dudley a silly pillock. Dudley then called Derek a fucking wanker. It came to blows outside the Hop Exchange. Hair was ripped from scalps. There was blood. A woman screamed. Clothes were torn and cheeks grazed the pavement. Dudley was fat and greasy, bull-necked, narrow-eyed, furious, but Derek was lighter, quicker, concentrated and cool-headed in his rage: an even match. Finally the landlord of the Southwark Tavern pulled them apart and the boys went home by different routes because each was in tears and didn't want the other to know. Not long after this incident, which qualified but did not terminate their association, they started to carry knives. The *gemütlichkeit* of childhood had begun to smoke, sending up wisps of doubt as if what merely smouldered might at any moment, by a capricious change of wind, flare up and altogether annihilate itself, leaving them naked, defenceless. For Dudley this process of distrusting life began earlier – his mother had vanished when he was 8 years old. The boys were not especially suspicious of each other – they more or less had each other's measure now – but of the world about them, a world which grew larger, more incomprehensible and venomous and ludicrous with every step they took into it, a world in which they felt more comfortable if armed. And being creatures of very limited experience, this arming took the form of knives.

Derek soaked in the bath with the radio on . . . *and I'd like to dedicate this song to Marion of Manchester Surgical Goods and thank her for her support* . . . currently Number 3 in the Hit Parade:

> *The day begins with a thud –*
> *Then it*
> *Starts to*
> *Chew you*
> *Slowly*
>
> *Spots of anxiety in*
> *Front of*
> *My eyes*
> *Drifting*
> *Zig zag*

Steam gathered on the bathroom walls and slipped down in droplets to the linoleum where it formed small pools. Derek stared at his feet beneath the taps and sighed. He'd once imagined they were football feet. Now he accepted that they weren't. In which case, what sort of feet were they? He was suspended between 2 life phases and this was experienced as being stuck merely in the present: no school, no job; no childhood, no adulthood. He lived day by day. Every so often there would be an ecstatic, unaccountable leaping of the heart as he *almost* glimpsed a WONDERFUL . . . what? . . . Just beyond his fingertips, just beyond knowing, then it was gone. He looked at his legs propped up in the bath. They were hairy and the wet hair divided along the shin bone in dark streaks on either side. He looked down at his plump cock and peeled back the foreskin, washing it thoroughly, giving himself beautiful tingling sensations – he didn't want to get cancer of the knob . . . and he didn't want to get smelly. You never know, luck can strike at any time, and he didn't want to put off any prospectives by being stinky down there – front or back. After shitting he always wiped and then cleaned his bottom with lavatory paper soaked in water and was always angry at finding himself in a closet with no wash basin for this purpose. He'd started doing this after noticing a bidet in *Un Homme et Une*

Femme and finding out what it was for. He felt sure that none of the boys in Harold Wilson House cleaned themselves in this way and he wondered if he were a bit weird. On the other hand he'd once or twice caught a whiff of Dudley – not nice, old smegma . . .

Derek climbed out of the bath, avoiding the bath mat and heaving water onto the floor. He dried off, donned vest and pants and Pop's old dressing-gown, and went into the lounge to iron his shirt. The flat was cosy and dilapidated. The lounge, kitchen and bathroom were immediately above the Betting Shop, and on the floor above them were 2 bedrooms. When Doll moved in years ago it had been advertised under 'lettings' in the local paper as a maisonette, but she could never bring herself to use this word. She wasn't house proud – probably because she'd never had a house – except as a girl. She dimly recalled their little East End house, 2 up, 2 down, the door to the parlour always closed, and occasionally she had bravely poked her head in there to discover an embalmed attempt at gentility forever unused. Presumably Doll's stepmother thought that the King & Queen might drop in for a cup of tea without warning and this small fusty chamber had to be held permanently in reserve for the supreme occasion.

Doll had had a period of going to the Bermondsey Market, looking for antiques and always ending up with junk. Everything in the flat was wrong, had been invalided out of normal service and then rescued by Doll. Cracked plates in the kitchen. Knives and forks which didn't match. 2 armchairs and a settee in black plastic with studs in the back (but half the studs missing), green and blue and orange nylon cushions, gimcrack ornaments, some plastic horses, even a gilt picture frame was plastic, old magazines, half empty tins, knick-knacks salvaged from Christmas crackers, plaster rubbish from visits to fairgrounds when Derek was small and now preserved like holy relics. Everything was chipped or undone, torn or incomplete. The red second hand had fallen from the face of the electric clock on the wall and lay supine at the bottom of the glass cover. On the sideboard stood 5 tall drinking glasses with emerald green and ruby red frosting up the sides and wavy gilding round the rims, and one beautiful cut lead crystal goblet but there was a tiny segment out of its base.

Beside them was an old record player which didn't work – anyway Derek preferred listening to tapes in his bedroom where the most arresting object, however, was not his radio cassette player but a large globe of the world in painted tin. Derek thought he was lucky to have his own bedroom and as long as he kept it stink-free his mother stayed out of it. Recently Doll's preference for damaged goods had begun to annoy her son. Perhaps it was his age. Doll told him she salvaged – but others said she scavenged. Even Phyllis, the cat they'd had for 3 years, was broken and pieced together again, having been run over in the Commercial Road. 'That *bloody* road!' said Doll. 'That's all it takes, Derek, one hit; for God's sake, be careful . . .' When she cooked, the food was left swimming in grease or water – vegetables she never drained properly, an invisible force prevented her from completing the appropriate movement. So she rarely cooked. They lived on tins, boxes, frozen boxes, dehydrated packets, coloured ready-to-eat matter in transparent boxes, takeaways: convenience foods. And on picking up the steam-iron one *knew* that from the steamholes would issue black stuff, the result of having not used distilled water, and sure enough, here it comes, black smears right across Derek's clean white collar fresh from the Laundrette, across the collar for maximum visibility.

'For God's sake, you've done it again! You've buggered this iron again!' he shouted with tremendous fury. Doll was eating a bacon sandwich in the kitchen, greasing the pages of a newspaper she was reading. 'You've ruined my shirt! Can't you get anything bloody right?'

Doll came into the lounge where Derek's face hung fretfully above the ironing-board and she slapped him round the head. 'Don't speak to your mother like that! I've told you before.'

'But I got you the special water. I went out and *got* it.'

'I forgot.' Funny thing was – Doll worked in a Dry Cleaner's.

The Betting Shop phoned up to complain about water coming through onto their ceiling *again*. Doll had the ritual row with the manager and slammed down the phone.

'You've soaked that bathroom floor again, haven't you?'

'Sorry,' said Derek, staring at the telephone receiver upon which a number of bacon-grease fingerprints shone in the soft lamplight.

Derek walked sulkily along and arrived at the Hearts of Oak Pub in Dock Street 20 minutes later than he'd intended. It was crowded but he found the 3 occupying a curvaceous corner with a table in it.

'Wotcher, Derek.'

'Wotcher, Maurice, Dougal, Dudley.'

Dudley wiped froth from his upper lip and said 'What you having, Derek? This round's on Dougal.'

'OK, I can handle it myself,' said Dougal pulling a face, pushing out his eyeballs.

'I'm sure you can, Doog,' said Dudley, 'and judging by an uncanny pallor that's bleached your complexion I'd say you've been handling it a bit too much lately.'

'He doesn't grow up, does he?' said Dougal to Derek. 'I'll get you a pint, shall I?'

Derek nodded. Dudley sat sweating in his chair with an inane grin on his face. He was wearing a sky-blue polyester jacket with tomato sauce stains beneath the breast pocket. It was buttoned up, creasing horizontally across his gut. 'As I was saying before you joined us, Derek – what is it coming to, what *is* the world coming to? Now I've no objection to Mr Honeybunch Gupta going into property now he's left school, or opening up a chain of supermarkets across the Isle of Dogs, or whatever he plans to do – so long as he doesn't become *selfish*. Ain't that right, Maurice?'

'I thought it was just about whithky,' said Maurice who, though a big black boy, had a lisp and a gentle tranquillity as if his soul were a smooth inland lake with untroubled surface. But this calmness hadn't done him much good; examiners got the impression he was asleep, whereas he was in fact a natural Buddhist waiting on the quay of life for death to come by and pick him up, and meanwhile he was open to suggestions.

'Dudley demanded a double whisky,' said Dougal returning, 'and I'm afraid I can't afford it.'

'Can't afford, can't afford?' said Dudley with a preposterous frown. 'That's not a phrase I like to hear on the lips of an ambitious young man. Where are the peanuts? You didn't bring any peanuts.'

'Fuck off,' said Dougal.

Dudley pulled his lips tight and said 'I'll pardon your French. But do us a favour, Doog. When you do open those supermarkets on the Isle of Dogs, try not to let them smell of armpit odour. Know what I mean? I don't know how you people manage it but they always smell of armpit—'

'It's called cumin. It's a spice,' said Dougal.

'You're no fucking rose,' said Maurice to Dudley.

'Er, Maurice love,' said Dudley, 'you are treading on dangerous ground here. Walking on eggs, one might say. Which is not something you should do. What's got into you boys to-night? You used to be so' – Dudley searched in the air for the word – 'so *easy*. I'm surprised at you, Maurice. I thought you was a natural Buddhist, waiting on the quay of life for the repatriation boat back to Trinidad.'

'It's not Trinidad,' said Maurice.

'Where is it then? Timbuctoo?'

'I don't know. Nowhere in particular. I've never been to the West Indies. It's here I thuppose. Yeah – here. Harold Wilson House is the only home I've ever known.'

'Really?' said Dudley with a lugubrious expression. 'I think that's the saddest story I ever heard.' He finished off his beer and said 'You're sitting very quiet, Derek. Would this be your round? And a bag of peanuts, there's a good boy.'

Derek, whose nose was in his pint, mid-swallow, just held up 2 fingers. 'Seen someone you know,' said Dudley turning to look over his own shoulder, adding 'Do you mean I have to buy another round already?'

'You haven't bought one yet,' said Dougal.

'Doog, you're wrong there. I bought the first one. It's not my fault if you boys turned up late and missed it.'

'The rules are – one round each – then we club together,' said Maurice who had virtually no money at all.

'Relax, Maurice, it's Friday. Now look, boys, never say Dudley Dennis don't care for you. I'm gonna teach you some-thing. Can't sit here taking my cue from a bunch of tight arses, no time for that, I'm the expansive type, I like to plunge ahead. Pints all round? Good! And let this be a lesson to you in how to live right.' With a Neronian swagger, Dudley pushed through the crowd towards the bar.

'What happened to that girl you was going out with, Maurice?' asked Derek.

'She got too demanding,' said Maurice.

'I thought that was the idea.'

'Financially demanding,' said Maurice, flashing the whites of his eyes.

'I don't want a relationship. Not yet,' said Dougal.

'I'd like to have several,' said Derek. 'Multiple ongoing relationships – that appeals to me.'

'Yeah, that's what I meant,' said Dougal.

Dudley came back from the bar in a sweat. 'I'm financially embarrassed,' he said. 'A few bob short. Who'll lend me? Watcha got there, Derek? Yeah, that'll do.' With podgy fingers Dudley delicately plucked a golden sovereign from the number of coins in Derek's warm uplifted palm.

'Don't you want the rest?' asked Derek.

Dudley shot him a glance and said 'Oh, er – thanks.'

But Derek had returned the money to his pocket. 'Too late,' he said.

Dudley staggered back with 4 pints pushed together in a bunch between his hands. 'I like the look of that,' he said, nodding in the direction of a Wagnerian blonde with massive bosoms under a silk blouse and a huge crimson mouth full of artificial teeth.

'She'd have you for afters,' said Maurice to Dudley who'd blushed.

'He's gone all red,' said Derek.

'That means I'm healthy,' said Dudley, squirming.

'Remember Sharon Bassett?' said Dougal.

Several years ago, a girl called Sharon Bassett stood on the corner of Pinchin Street and Back Church Lane, undulating against a backdrop of beautiful black bricks, a black girl in a woollen bobble hat, lumberjack shirt and grey jeans.

The black girl said 'I know somewhere interesting', and via narrow deserted streets she led the 4 boys to a derelict house. Inside, the air was rank and wet. Green and dark grey mould had broken out across a faded torn wallpaper of orange flowers. 'This was what they called the parlour,' said the girl, 'and that's a rose,' pointing to a circular moulding of leaves in the centre of the room where a light had once hung. 'My name's Sharon.' She turned her large dark eyes on them and they drowned helplessly in her eyes. The floor was littered with broken plaster, broken glass, a number of empty cigarette packets and ancient beer tins. Several balls of screwed-up newspaper quietly stank in a corner where a vagrant had shat. 'I'll show you somewhere else,' she said. They moved to the sound of crunching underfoot and followed her up a fragile narrow staircase. Small pieces of plaster fell on them in puffs of dust. They were terrified. The very walls trembled and the staircase seemed about to collapse. Upstairs she said 'This here was the main bedroom. What they call the master bedroom.' Inside on the floor was an old mattress in striped cotton studded with fluffy nodules. Its innards ruptured out through rips in the cotton. It smelt damp and funny in there. Wallpaper had unpeeled onto the floor. The windows were thick with dust and a light the colour of pale tea seeped into the room from the afternoon outside. She looked at them, a great wide look which scooped everything into itself, sat down on the mattress, removed her shoes, undid her shirt, exposing her large dark breasts to the cooling moist air, unzipped her jeans, pushed them down over her plump sleek hips, lay back with her heels drawn up against her buttocks and knees wide apart. A rich salty, fishy fume came from her. They all had a go, one after another, trembling in their legs, dry mouths, salivating mouths, hearts thumping, thumping, thumping . . . . . Afterwards she said 'I've got a terrible disease. Now you've all got it.' Never before had the deep cold terror gripped them so. Death leered and sniggered in every cloud, every cup of tea, every television programme. They went to the Special Clinic – she'd been lying – but it made them circumspect . . .

What ever happened to Sharon Bassett?

She was a snapper.

They divided girls into snappers and squelchers, tight down there, loose down there – not that they'd had much actual experience.

'*You lot* – OUT!!'

'Whadyamean?'

'You heard me. *Out.*' It was the landlord.

'Whadyamean?'

'You gonna give me trouble?' He looked comfortable with

43

trouble. 'You're under age. So OUT.' Another big bloke came alongside the landlord and looked down at them with punching lust.

As they went out the door, Dudley turned round and shouted 'Wankers!' They ran into the rain and went swaggering off down Dock Street, kicking a metal dustbin, making a hell of a noise and spilling its decomposing contents along the pavement, shouting 'Wankers!' At 17 Derek – and of course his companions – was in the thick of wristed love.

The 4 of them slunk towards the Thames in sullen mood, their shadows flickering along the sides of satanic buildings to where the remaining warehouses at the riverside reared up in glossy grandeur through the drizzle and silence. Converted with panache and a great deal of money, lit opulently within, these great buildings were filled with the chatter and glitter of several hundred smart Friday night dinner parties. Outside in the rain 4 shadows skimmed over the black shiny cobbles and drew in at a doorway which was the iron-barred entrance to a compound de luxe.

'This ain't no fun,' said Derek. 'My clothes are wet.'

'And mine aren't?' proposed Dudley.

'Look at that,' said Dougal. He pointed to a large lavender-coloured Jaguar which glistened along the kerbside nearby. They stared at it, communicated their desire to it in a silence of pregnant depth. The Jaguar, very composed and self-possessed, ignored them; their adoration slid off its shining surfaces like insult off confidence.

'Oooo – very . . . . . swish . . . . .' intoned Dudley, walking slowly round the motor car with his head cocked to one side. 'This would definitely get me from A to B. Watcha think, Derek?'

'Ace,' said Derek quietly and he was about to add a more specific observation when Dudley without warning made a curious pirouette.

'Oops!' said Dudley. 'Oh dear me, look what I've gone and done. Such a clumsy lad. What a shame.' He'd taken out his knife and gouged a small hole in the door of the car. Now he walked slowly round and round it with his arm held straight down and the knife in his fist sticking out at a right angle cutting a thin line in the paintwork. Slowly, round and round he walked, desecrating the body. 'Such a shame,' he said sardonically. 'Let me see if I can even it up.' He sliced coolly across the bonnet with the point

44

of the blade, then across the boot, then ran half a dozen lines across the roof. 'Does that look better, boys?' The boys didn't say anything. They grunted in a peculiarly abstract way while an emotion circled and glowed inside them. They were hypnotised and excited. They stood there while the emotion, circling inside, grew hotter. Dudley joined them in the doorway. He was *looking*. His eyes flicked everywhere with astonishing rapidity. The boys stared at him. Then he found what he was looking for. Inside the barred doorway lay some old – or was it new? – copper piping, left over from the Great Conversion. Dudley stuck his arm between the bars, selected a piece about a yard long and pulled it out. He leaned it at an angle against the wall, stamped on it, breaking it in 2, and picking up one of the pieces he examined it, matter-of-factly. Suddenly he changed – the cool had gone – everything about him tightened and twisted – Dudley trembled with a ferocious malevolence. A scream of demonic concentration issued from his trunk and mouth, as he brought the bar down with all his force against the Jaguar's windscreen. So violent was the blow that Dudley was lifted into the air by it and a fountain of glass exploded in all directions. He took off along the street, smashing in frenzy at car windows to left and right. Derek, picking up the other piece of pipe, followed him in a wild sprint, smashing where Dudley had left unsmashed. Dougal and Maurice dashed after them, picking up odd bricks and throwing them wherever a smash seemed likely – groundfloor windows for example (which the other 2 hadn't thought of). Screaming and smashing down Wapping High Street, it was as if the boys ran through water because shimmering splashes of shattered glass marked their passage. Derek ran the Great Run! Smashing with glee! With a high colour in his face, with the pure passionate movement of his spirit through Time and Space and Matter, he streamed down the street as a tremendous surge of power marking its full, expressive line through life! Oh, we are here to fly thus!

The sound of a police car broke upon his ecstasy. A loud, droning, negative noise – like a donkey braying through an amplifier – the sound of stupidity – a sound which is activated only by the actions of others – the donkey sound of the parasite – ee/aw – ee/aw – ee/aw. This raucous klaxon of stupidity follows him up the street, reaching for his back, getting louder, gaining

on him – an alley opens at his left – he dashes into it! – along –
dash left again! – along its serpentine length on desperate, pranc-
ing legs – a wild rush of nothing in the ears – a clamour of nothing
within – fly! fly! fleeeeeeeeeeeeeeeeeeeeeeeeeeeeeeeeeeeeeeeeeeeee
. . . . stop. Where is the noise? Run, run, run, run, run . . .
Heaving of the lungs, legs trembling out of control – frenzy
undermines co-ordination with exhaustion . . . stop. Shoot down
another alley to the right. Stop. Where is the noise? A roar of
emptiness in the ears . . . . . blood pounding in the ears. Now a
real noise. The klaxon cruises close, moving with the considerate
slowness of a shark, eyes searching to right and left, a moving
noise that does not halt. It passes along a street a distance away –
along . . . . up the street . . . and beyond . . . . . it passes by
. . . . . by slow quivering degrees of tormenting intensity,
the   noise   passes   away,   passes   away   into   silence
. . . .

The rain had stopped. Derek leant against an old brick wall in a
side alley. Small plants grew in the broken brickwork and
between the broken stones of the pavement. His hands were
sticky. His heart banged like a school desklid. 3 small trees over-
grew the wall from the other side and occasionally dropped
miniature pears of rainwater upon him to cool his head. A small
streetlamp, converted long ago from gas, threw a meagre light
across the pathway. And in this almost rustic place, and out of
the clamorous nothingness of his brain, grew terror. At any
moment he expected the silence to be ripped open by his pursuers,
fanged alsatians jumping at him from the blackness . . . But the
silence only grew and deepened as wave upon wave of silence fell
across the cityscape hushing it and soothing it to an immense
stillness which was made only more profound by the occasional
ooze and click of the wet earth and its plants. Panic, fear, violence
swam out of him, and he began to grow in this spot. A grace,
strong and triumphant, grew in him, steadying in due course his
pulse, and bringing an abundance to his heart, while his brain
recognised completeness, a completed day, a day not wizened and
lost but filled, fulfilled. He let his head sink into the wall. A
tremulous warmth, originating beneath his feet and stealing up
his legs, growing warmer in the thighs, engorging his penis,
soaking upwards through his trunk, warmer and warmer, burst

46

gloriously across his face in a wide, divine smile. . . . But his hands were sticky. Very sticky. He edged carefully into the light. Both his hands were cut, the left one deeply. Big drops of blood hit the ground, making red stars.

'Where the *hell've* you been? What the *hell've* you been doing?' Doll's face was horribly clenched. 'You idiot! You bastard!' She'd returned to the flat to find Derek attempting to bandage his hands. He looked a mess.

'You been in a fight?'

He said nothing, swallowed, stared at the floor.

'Have you got a knife?'

'No.' He lied. But he felt he didn't lie because the knife, his knife anyway, had not been involved in the evening's events.

'I'll kill you if you've got a knife. Come here, let me do it. Do you need stitches?'

'No. I cut myself on some glass.'

'You bloody liar! What happened? Oh God . . . If your father were alive now, he'd turn in his grave.'

– Why does she bother? he thought. Why does she keep up the pretence? She doesn't even know who my father was.

Doll finished tying the bandages and lit a cigarette to help herself hold back the tears.

'Can I have one?' he asked, lifting his head.

'No. You little bleeder . . . What are you doing to me? Oh . . . go on then, take one. . . . Don't get hurt, that's all I ask.'

Derek looked at his mother. Her anger had gone – she looked worn out. Her hair needed brushing. Her shoes needed drying out.

'I'm sorry, it was a bit of fun.'

The phone rang.

'It's that pig Dudley,' said Doll. 'Was he involved in this?'

Derek went out to the small landing where the phone sat on a blue plastic table.

Dudley said 'They got Maurice. He won't say anything. Don't you say anything.'

'You think I would? Poor Maurice.'

'He'll get a suspended. Nothing too drastic. They'll put it down to booze, high spirits, and social deprivation. It's all very well throwing iron round the gym, but Maurice must learn to run faster – and run in the right direction.' Dudley, despite his grossness, could vanish in seconds. He had no stamina for the long race but could always produce the crucial burst.

When Derek came back in he caught his mother's face in the cracked mirror – not only worn out, but old. He'd never thought of her as old before. She'd been drinking in the pub most of the night, not getting drunk, this wasn't her way, but having a good time. And now, coming home to this, she'd sagged when confronted by the basic unalluring facts of her existence, and then the drink had pulled her right down. She stood up in defiance. He went up behind her, said 'I'm sorry' with more feeling than before, and put his chin down on her shoulder, which he'd been able to do since 12 years old, and put his arms round her waist. She turned. He felt the weight of his mother against him and she hugged him and Doll cried quietly against her son, some tears at last squeezing through the narrow chink created by her loss of vigilance and surrender to emotion, by her surrender to love.

Sunday. The Drakes' home in Wildwood Rise. The back lawn was getting its first mow of the year. The small electric mower had been difficult to start but was now flowing back and forth with disciplinary zeal. There were many muddy patches but few weeds; the lawn would soon start breathing and growing. Earlier in the day he'd absorbed the big newspaper, the *Sunday Zoo*, and as he held the 2 handles and walked comfortably up and down he thought – I'd like to read that book they reviewed, *Notes on Secrecy* by James Thorne – sounds interesting – they call him one of the Comic Philosophers . . . *an aphoristic style reminiscent of Nietzsche's but drier, lighter, without that drag of 19th century portentousness . . .* I'll ask Pam to get it from the library.

He didn't normally read philosophy books – this was more Major Playfair's thing. But the title attracted him. He was feeling secretive himself – and he liked the feeling. He wanted secrets. He wanted to do things which demanded of him the ability to keep

48

secrets. Secrecy implied a life of dramatic eventfulness. Secrecy implied a depth and complexity, a past and present and future, an existence in which the possible was becoming actual – this excited him. The bare branch of a small apple tree caught him by surprise as he careered along and struck him painfully on the side of the face – the tree was one of several which grew out of the lawn towards the bottom of the garden. Gordon angrily crashed about the base of it, trying to reduce the grass there, but the bulk of the mower prevented him. He would have to get the clippers out after lunch. 'Bloody trees!' he said aloud, rubbing a crimson stripe on his cheek.

'Drunk again,' said a face (more generally red) over the garden fence.

Gordon looked round. 'Good morning, Major Playfair. No, I'm not.'

'No, I mean, I am,' said Major Playfair. 'Just come from the Vicar's. He wants me to do a spot of bell-ringing but I don't think I want to do that, do I? Why can't he get an electric machine, like everyone else? He's a member of the Green Party, you know.'

'I've never met him,' said Gordon.

'Well, not drunk exactly. Tiddly. Sherry always does that to me. I can drink any amount of whisky you care to give. I like a good single malt – there's nothing safer. But after 3 or 4 sherries . . . Your lawn's extreeemely muddy. I'm going to leave mine a few more weeks.'

'I can't remember the last time I was drunk,' observed Gordon, emptying a bin of grass in a corner near the Major's head.

'More the other way round with me,' said Playfair. 'Except I don't start before lunch. Except on Sundays – and there's something about a Sunday which makes me feel a bit groggy and pissed anyway. Look, I'm going to pop in now for a bite to eat. I've got a young man coming round this afternoon to look at my old Riley and I'd like to be awake for that. Says he can make it go. Incidentally—' The Major beckoned Gordon closer to the fence, looked to left and right, stood up on tiptoe to glance over Gordon's shoulder, and said 'I saw *her* earlier to-day.'

'Who?'

'You know, the, er, funny one.'

'You mean—'

'Yes. Sybil. *Her*. She was shuffling about near their shed. Looked very odd, in a big shawl and red Wellington boots. And a big hat on, straw, black, frayed round the edges. *Very* frayed. More of a veil. It must be the first time she's been out this year. Can't be much of a life,' mused the Major. 'Cooped up indoors. What does she do?'

'Beats me,' said Gordon. 'But Eunice is always very sweet and chatty and says Sybil is busy.'

'Eunice does everything. I think she's much taken advantage of.'

'Oh we don't know what goes on, do we. But do you know anything about James Thorne, Major?'

'Yes. Thoroughly first rate. Poor chap was blown to bits in a terrorist outrage. Look – I need some stodge. I'm standing on an orange box and it feels damn unsafe. Cheerio.'

After lunch and before dinner (which was 'supper' on Sundays), while Pam was getting to grips with the ironing, Gordon played *Tod und Verklärung* by Richard Strauss in laser sound (Herbert von Karajan conducting the Berlin Phil-harmonic). Chords of music penetrated him painfully like the bolts of St Sebastian. Waves of music climbed over each other in shuddering climaxes. It was glorious, agonising, that hunger for resolution and release – Gordon tingled at the threshold of a state he could not comprehend, a realm that was dangerous and desired.

A weekday evening. They were eating chops in the dining-room and Gordon said 'The shop next door had its window smashed last night.'

'On the Parade?'

'Mmm.'

'It'll be that disco.'

'That's what I told the police. There was never any trouble there until that dam' place opened. Do you know what they call it? The Psychoplasty. I ask you. It's in the basement of the old dairy.'

'Can't you get it closed?' asked Pam with a purposeful frown.

50

'Possibly. The problem is – it makes money.'

'Yes, that's the problem. Go on, have the rest of those potatoes.'

'You're trying to make me fat.'

'Gordon, the chances of your putting on any weight are very slim. Oh God, I've made a joke!' They both chuckled but Gordon looked strained. 'I've been thinking, Gordon.'

'Oh dear,' he said.

'We should do something with Mark's room.'

'Here we go. Such as?'

'I don't know. But it seems wasted.'

'I wish he'd get a different job,' said Gordon.

Pam didn't pursue it and the subject of Mark's room lapsed. It came up and lapsed about once a year. They saw Mark at roughly the same intervals. He worked so hard – and travelled so much, to various poisonous places. So much of his work was secret. Mark had been in the 17th/21st Lancers (motto: Death or Glory; insignia: Skull & Crossbones) which was Major Playfair's old regiment. The Major had got him in: 'They run a pretty good show, Mark, and they have a banquet once a year at Belvoir Castle which is very acceptable.' Mark had then found himself on a scheme which combined regular service with a degree course at the Imperial College of Science and Technology and this led to research into chemical warfare. 'Look, Mum, I can't talk about it,' Mark had said, 'and anyway, even if I could, it would only upset you.'

Pam stared at the potatoes, to which adhered small squares of parsley congealing in butter, and thought – I wish I had grand-children. Mark had married a girl called Veronica who was in computers. Pam had found that if she didn't try too hard she could quite like Veronica, but they never saw enough of each other for familiarity, let alone intimacy, to have arisen. Veronica hadn't showed the slightest willingness to swell up and produce – and then Mark and Veronica were divorced, so that was that.

She went into the kitchen and came back with a dish of bananas baked in brandy and brown sugar and a small jug of real custard. The bananas were sliced lengthwise and Pam served 3 slices to Gordon, 1 to herself. They ate.

'You're in a funny mood to-night,' said Pam. She was piqued because Gordon hadn't polished off the potatoes.

'Am I, pet? I don't think I am.'

Gordon went into the sitting-room, switched on the electric fire with imitation glass coals, switched on the television, and had another look at the *Daily Zoo* crossword – impossibly tortuous – he'd filled only half a dozen lights, he couldn't concentrate. He was in a funny mood. Among other things, a phone call from Bob Dashman had done his peace of mind no good at all. Dashman was up to something.

Pam came in with the coffee and said 'What's this?', addressing the screen where a religious discussion was under way in front of a studio audience.

One man was saying *'God, you see, is torpedo-shaped.'*

'Oh no, that's wrong. God is heart-shaped,' said a second.

'Do you think so?' said a third. *'Personally, if there's any God at all, which I very much doubt, then the only possible shape he can be is gob-shaped. That is – shaped like a gob.'*

'Oh look,' said Pam, 'there goes that car again.' The black limousine with gold fittings slid past. Pam noticed it through the bay window in the light of the streetlamp.

'What car?'

'A quite over-the-top car. Full of Arabs. It visited the Dashmans last week. And I've just seen it go past again. We really must get one of those gas fires with logs like the Dashmans have. Are you sure you're all right, dear?'

'What do you mean? Of course I am.'

'You seem a little preoccupied.'

'Do I? Well, I'm not, that is, I—'

'Yes?' Pam looked concentratedly.

Gordon pursed his lips and thought for a second, then said 'But there's something I should tell you, Pam.'

Pam went cold, squared her shoulders, and looked him dead in the eye. Gordon's lips stayed closed. 'Well?' she said drily.

He looked at her. 'I've—'

'Oh God – what!?' she pressed. She suddenly felt weak, nervous, had stopped breathing.

'Well . . . I've been visiting a sauna,' he said.

Saturday Night In (a week and a day after the Wapping offensive). Derek watched *The Electric Courgette*, one of his favourite programmes. Then the 9 o'Clock News came on – nations were attacking each other, terrorists with strong principles were blowing people up, men in uniforms were torturing people, the Sovereign was off on the Royal Yacht for a State Visit to Leningrad and Moscow, more oilfields have been discovered in the Arctic, money was worth less but there was more of it about; the world was going round, a point on the equator continued to move from left to right at, when viewed from the Sun, an ascending angle of 90°; to-morrow there'd be showers and sunny spells. Doll came in. She was going out.

'I'm going to the Britannia. Are you staying in?'

'Yeah. The boys are coming round. Dougal's got a video.'

'I've told you, I don't want that Dudley here. Derek, do you hear me?'

He didn't move his eyes from the screen where an advertisement for paradise was under way.

It would be a blue video – a sex video – titties and dickies and bottoms and juices and goings-on – oh how terrible. Dougal had access to his cousin's video collection (which the cousin let out to people on the Council Estate) and often borrowed one when his cousin wasn't looking. They'd had their first collective viewing and wanking session about 10 days after the Sharon Bassett incident.

'Look at Maurice's great dong beside Dougal's little stabber,' Dudley had declared.

The Asian boy and the West Indian boy smiled weirdly. Dougal would have liked a larger penis, more whitemansize, more sahibsize, less fine a thing, less of a little stabber. And Maurice was faintly ashamed of his, as of something too overtly animal and gross, would have preferred it smaller, less bendy, more whitemansize, more bwanasize, less of a DONG.

'Did you thay thomething?' asked Maurice, exaggerating his lisp which for him was rare and a sign of aggression.

'That was an aside, Maurice. You're not supposed to hear an aside,' said Dudley.

'A what?'

'An aside. You get them in Shakespeare.'

'Derek's the only left-hander here,' said Maurice, moving the attention of the group elsewhere while continuing to ply his cumbersome meat. Now all 4 got seriously down to it, staring straight ahead at the slurping screen, locking into their capsules of fantasy, 3 right forearms and a left one going like the clappers. Dougal came – he was always the first – spattering his golden tummy with snowdrops. Derek and Dudley, flashing rapid glances at each other's progress between gulps of the screen, came more or less at the same time. And Maurice came last – he usually did – he was having a girl and found this wanking scene a bit limited, but eventually he forced out a large volume of white matter.

Then as suddenly as these wanking sessions had started they stopped. These days they just watched – and did whatever else they did, elsewhere.

'I don't want you taking any drugs,' said Doll, teasing her hair in front of the cracked mirror above the sideboard. 'You don't take drugs, do you?'

'You're always asking that.'

'*Do* you!?'

'Oh for Christ's sake . . . No, of course not.' He did actually. But not much. Only playfully, curiously, now and again, here and there, this and that. He wasn't the type to get swallowed up by a drug or indeed by any *thing*. 'Why are you so nervous tonight?' he asked.

'What d'ya mean? Me, nervous? Whatya talking about? Stupid kid . . .' She was nervous because she was meeting a man, not *the* man, a man only, but it was rare enough for her, despite appearances.

'Are you meeting a man?'

'Of course not. I'm meeting Joy and her sister.'

'Where's *my* bloody sister? That's what I want to know.'

'Derek, don't start all that again.'

'But I want to know.'

'She's somewhere where she's happy. So don't start, OK?'

Derek's baby sister had been fostered a few weeks after she was born. Doll thought the little girl would have a better chance in another place, with a proper family – but the guilt was always

54

there, pumping dark and strong. In a few years when she'd got things straightened out a bit, she'd have Clare back. Certainly. But she couldn't tell Derek where the girl was – he'd go off and get her – there'd be endless complications . . . . .

When the Boys turned up, Dudley said through a mouthful of chocolate bar he was eating 'We passed your mum in the street. She looked furious. She said to me "Don't be there when I get back". What've I done now?'

'Wotcha got, Dougal?' asked Derek sourly.

'I couldn't get anything. He was watching me like an eagle.'

'Maurice wouldn't come,' said Dudley. 'He's full of self-pity. I must say, I don't think self-pity gets a bloke very far.'

'It's all right for you,' said Dougal. 'He's the one that caught it.'

Dudley said 'I'll personally see to it that Maurice gets all the moral support he needs. But it won't do any of us any good to hang around that courtroom when the great day arrives.'

'I got this film on video,' said Derek. '*Hammersmith Is Out*. It's brilliant. We can watch that.'

'Is it one of those British films from the 60s?' asked Dougal.

'Yeah, I'll put it on.'

'It says here,' said Dudley examining the box, '*United States 1972.*'

'Does it?' said Derek. 'But it counts as British. It's directed by Peter Ustinov.'

'Who the fuck's he? Sounds like some Russian pillock. Your mum got any beer in her fridge?' said Dudley.

'Get your own beer, you ponce,' said Derek.

'Charming,' said Dudley. 'Have you stopped taking the pills or something? So it's your beer, yours and Mummy's, how sweet.'

'Drop dead. Just because – yeah – well, we know . . .' Derek let his voice trail away. He couldn't say the truly hurtful thing. Dudley had no mother, only an old granny. Not that Derek was over-the-top on the question of mothers. He knew his own neglected him in many ways. But it wasn't easy for her, he understood that too. And she wasn't one of those mothers who don't even teach their children how to use a knife & fork. They exist, but Doll wasn't one of them. Derek knew how to eat properly and all that. And she touched Derek a lot and loved him and he knew that too, even when she made him mad or upset, so

55

that he felt safe at home. And it did no harm to learn to look after himself sooner rather than later. In some ways he was quite grown up. He missed things of course. But she didn't smother him and he valued the freedom and the trust implicit in this. So all in all he loved her and was aware of loving her. But 2 days after this irritable little Saturday evening, Doll was walking back from work at the Dry Cleaner's when she was knocked down by a car. She died in the ambulance on the way to hospital.

Wrapping the dressing-gown more closely about her chill body, Pam Drake descended yawningly to the hall, picked up the post on the mat, and went into the kitchen to put on the kettle. She was up early this morning, hadn't slept too well, and so Gordon would get a cup of tea in bed. She opened the back door to say hullo to a blue cat who was sitting on the small terrace but the animal vanished down the garden. Her head was tight, numbing her mind somewhat – it was going to be one of her wuzzy days. She gulped the air – it tasted tinny – and came back into the house. The sun was shining.

One of the letters was addressed in writing that was strange to her. She and Gordon didn't often receive personal letters and very rarely from an unknown hand – and never to herself alone. Yet this letter was to herself alone. She slit it open with a small fruit knife. It was from a place called Callaghan Heights, presumably a block of flats, in Whitechapel.

Dear Mrs Drake,
I'm writing because I thought you'd want to know that Augusta Love [for this was Doll's name] *died 2 weeks ago run over by a car. I've taken it upon myself to look after her affairs because there's no one else. She mentioned you once or twice and I found your address in her things. Since you are her only surviving relative I wanted to invite you to the funeral but I'm sorry that was last week. I didn't find your address until yesterday. Her son Derek is staying with me for the moment. He is 17 and it's harder on him than he lets on. I think he would appreciate a letter if you could write something nice. I'd like to apologise again for not being able to contact you until*

56

now. Augusta didn't leave a will, so everything went to Derek but that's not much. Don't hesitate to get in touch if you need to know anything else.

Yours sincerely,
May Holloway

There was no telephone number. Pam stared concentratedly into space. Wuzziness had vanished. A tall plume of steam was gushing from the kettle and planting a wet disc on the ceiling. Pam made the tea, sat down again on a kitchen chair, and when it had brewed she sipped a cup very slowly. She was thinking very fast, very efficiently – the process caused a soft flush to bathe her cheeks. It was excitement. Then she poured a cup for Gordon, took it up to him, and sat on a corner of the bed.

'Gordon . . .'

'Yes . . .' he murmured among the pillows and sheets. She could only see the ragged tufts of grey hair on his balding head.

'Gordon, do you remember Augusta Love?'

'No . . .'

'Yes, you do. She was a distant cousin of mine who lived in the East End.'

'Vaguely . . .' He slid deeper into the bed.

'Gordon, don't let your tea get cold. We didn't see each other. I don't think I've seen her since I was a young woman . . . Anyway she was killed recently, knocked down by a car. But look, she had a 17-year-old son. He's got no one. No one in the world . . . except us. What I want to say is – I think he should come and live here for a bit, don't you?'

Gordon sat bolt upright.

Part Three

– Violets, lovely violets! There don't seem to be violet sellers any longer in Piccadilly Circus, hub of the Empire, London, 18th century/Victorian/Modern city founded by the Romans, hallucinatory city – the phantasmagorical quality of its architecture, its vitality and endless inventiveness, every façade different, streets of individual buildings, strange higgledy-piggledy dreamland of architecture – so much smashed away – not only through philistinism but also for relief – relief from the oppression of such endless creative riot – oxygenate the city with horizontal and vertical caesurae – the modern buildings are places for the eye to rest, cool down, recover, dream for itself – cool elegant glass spaces in rioting individualism – London, a series of planets – it is a kit, it supplies all the components for creating any life you want – there is no edge to London – it goes on and on and on – grows out into the suburbs and the suburbs when you reach them are old: mediaeval hearts with Tudor and 17th century skeletons, 18th century flesh, 19th century dress, modern accessories – the suburbs drift into fields, woods, hills – Chinese boxes – worlds within worlds – London is curved like the Universe – it is unknowable like the Universe – these thoughts were passing through Derek's head in less verbal form while he sat on top of a bus jammed in Piccadilly Circus, staring out of the window from the front seat of the upper deck, paying extraordinary attention to his city, his head ablaze with the luxuriant plenitude of it, the infinite detail and surprise of its inner and outer ornateness. He was also wondering what sort of life he was moving towards, inch by inch in the constipated traffic. He thought about getting off the bus – right here – drowning in the anonymity of unlimited opportunity – but he didn't – he felt terribly alone and was afraid of surrendering his sense of having,

61

albeit provisionally, a destination. He was hot and nervous. A large grip sat on the floor and he had his feet on it. There was a second on the seat beside him. 'You'll have to take it off the seat if someone wants the seat,' said the conductor. But the bus wasn't quite full. And the traffic was jammed. Derek grew jittery. He didn't want to be trapped here with himself and his thoughts and his agitation. But he didn't move. The bus didn't move. The traffic didn't move. All was paralysed. Nothing happened. It was suffocating. Nothing was happening. He felt extremely ill-at-case, short of breath. Then the bus jolted forward.

The doorbell rang. Pam jumped. But it was only the milkman who wanted paying. He went round collecting his bills in the late morning without the float. He said it left his hands free. Pam thought this very suspicious. She settled up and returned to the kitchen to think about cooking dinner. She was making a special old-fashioned suet pudding. She had to do something to quell her nerves. This evening a boy was coming to live with them – which didn't happen every day. They hadn't even met him. They'd only spoken on the telephone.

'Hullo, is that Derek?'
'Yes.'
'This is Auntie Pam.'
'Oh.'
'But just call me Pam.'
'OK.'
'And just call Gordon – Gordon.'
'Who?'
'My husband.'
'Oh.'
'He's here. He'll have a word with you in a moment.'
'Oh.'
'Is everything all right? Can we do anything?'
'No. Er, yes. I mean the other way round.'
'But about the letter I wrote to you – do you think it's a good idea?'

'Dunno.' Derek was still a long way from being able to dis-
criminate between good and bad ideas. He was still numb.

'Would you like to?'

'Dunno.'

'Well – why not give it a try?'

'Yeah?'

'Yes, give it a try. Come and stay for a few weeks. And if you
really find us terrible, you can go back to Auntie May. I expect
we're pretty terrible in some ways.'

He didn't laugh. She wondered if she'd said the wrong thing.
Then Derek said 'OK.'

'Truly? You'll give us a try?'

'OK, if you like.'

'That's wonderful! You've made me very happy. Could I have
another word with May?'

Derek passed the telephone to May without saying good-bye.
He wasn't being surly, just absent-minded. And while this
changeover was taking place, Pam thought – He can have Mark's
bedroom – we can put Mark's stuff in the boxroom.

'Mrs Drake?'

'Mrs Holloway. It's settled then. I'm so glad. When shall he
come?'

'Hang on.' May returned to the phone and said 'He says
Saturday week.'

'Right. We'll expect him in time for dinner, will you tell him
that?'

'I think it's very kind what you're doing, Mrs Drake. I'm sure
Derek'll really appreciate it too – you know, when he's more
himself.'

'Shall we come and collect him?'

'Wait a mo.' May had a conflab with Derek which seemed to
Pam to go on quite a long time, then returned to the phone and
said 'He says he'll find his own way by himself.'

'Really? Are you sure?'

May was off the phone again for a while and then came back,
confirming that she was sure. Derek would take the bus from the
East End to Oxford Circus, another bus to Baker Street, then the
tube from Baker Street into the suburbs of Northwest London. 'It
seems he's already worked out the route,' added May.

'Really?' This made Pam think – but she didn't know exactly what she thought. 'Er, I'll say good-bye now, May. Let us meet in a few weeks' time and I'll let you know how it's all going.'

May said she'd like that and they both rang off. Pam realised that Gordon, who was stuck behind a newspaper somewhere, hadn't had his word with Derek.

– Will they get on? she wondered. You know what men are.

– No, I'm not sure what men are, she thought again. Will Derek be a boy or a man? Derek – and his friends! Oh God, at 17, they have friends, don't they! Hell, what've I done?

Now, on the appointed Saturday, Pam was in the kitchen, up to her elbows in suet pudding, trying to forget that in a few hours the bell would go and . . . A nice old-fashioned suet pudding, packed with steak & kidney – there was plenty of distracting work in that. She'd said to Gordon 'Guess what, I'm going to make a *real suet pudding*.'

'What a terribly good idea,' said Gordon who, in his soft gentlemanly way, always knew exactly what distinguished a good idea from a bad one. He knew for example that their son working in chemical warfare was a thoroughly bad idea.

Gordon lit their new imitation log fire in the sitting-room and Pam was about to take the weight off her feet and have a cup of tea when she became aware of a rattling noise at the front gate. She looked through the net. A young man was having problems with the latch on the front gate and looking helplessly towards the house.

– Oh God, he's here already! she gasped to herself and shouted upstairs 'Gordon, he's here!'

– Oh God, I'm not ready! she thought, taking off her pinafore. She went into the hall, fiddled with her hair in the mirror, aware of her heart thumping, thumping, fixed a nervous welcoming smile to her face, and opened the front door.

Derek, bending over the gate, raised his head, startled, his face flushed, his thoughts in turmoil. He stopped fiddling with the gate, stood upright and stared straight at Pam.

Pam's first thought was – Oh God, he's beautiful – he's a beautiful young man.

She hadn't known at all what to expect. She hadn't thought about what he might look like – in her mind's eye she'd sort of understood that he would look like Mark but here he was looking

64

like someone else altogether. Derek was standing opposite her on the other side of the wrought-iron gate. He was wearing white trousers, a grey pullover and a green canvas bomber jacket, and all she could think of was – He's beautiful, handsome. This shocked her deeply.

'The fing's stuck,' said Derek in a Cockney voice.

'Let me help you.' She walked down the path to the gate and in her consternation played with it wrongly, likewise failing to open it, and aware that the young man was standing looking at her with intense interest. She shook the gate but the bloody thing wouldn't open. She stopped and said 'This is silly. Well, hullo, I'm Pam, and you're Derek.' They shook hands over the gate, both embarrassed, Pam smiling, Derek trying to smile and failing. At which point the gate coquettishly opened all by itself, swinging against Pam's tummy.

'Look at that,' she said.

'Weird,' he said.

They paused a moment, captured by this little mystery, then Pam said 'Let me take one of your bags.'

'Nah, it's OK.'

'Please.'

'Nah, really, it's OK,' and picking up his bags, he followed her up the path and into the house thinking – There's lots of trees round here – it's like the countryside.

Pam meanwhile had seen Major Playfair wave and disappear from his front room window.

'I'm Gordon,' said Gordon, coming down the stairs.

'Derek,' said Derek.

'Leave your bags in the hall for now. I'll put the kettle on, Pam.'

'Don't worry, dear, I'll do it. Derek, you go with Gordon into the sitting-room and I'll get the tea. Gordon, take Derek into the sitting-room.' She was glad to retreat into the kitchen to compose herself – Gordon had wanted to do the same but she wasn't having that. She hadn't known what to expect and now she still thought – Is he a boy or is he a man? In a matter of seconds, everything was different. . . .

Meanwhile back in the sitting-room Gordon was saying 'Did you have a good journey?'

'Where?'

'You know – to here.'

'Oh yeah,' said Derek. 'No. The tube's on strike. There weren't many running.' Unawares, Derek was speaking in a heavier Cockney voice than usual – it gave him a sense of security in this alien world.

'Really? I didn't know that. They want more money, I suppose.'

'Dunno.'

Gordon thought – Is he thick?

'Cor, a real fire,' said Derek.

'Not quite,' said Gordon; that it wasn't a real fire rankled with him.

Pam swung in with the tea things and said 'You're nice and early, Derek.'

'Am I?' he said. 'I thought I was late.'

'The tube's on strike,' said Gordon.

'Are they?' said Pam. 'For more money presumably.'

'We don't know,' said Gordon.

'I thought I'd get here at 1 o'clock coz I know you wanted me here for dinner so I'm sorry if I messed you about. Whatsit now, about 3?' Derek thought – What the *fuck* am I doing here? I feel bad . . . . .

'Oh, I see, now, well, er, dinner for us,' said Pam colouring, 'is the evening meal. The midday meal we call lunch.'

'Oh lunch, yeah,' mumbled Derek.

– Goodness, what about lunch!? thought Pam. They'd been going to grab a sandwich. She'd only brought in a plate of biscuits.

'Have a squashed fly,' said Gordon.

'What?' queried Derek.

'That's what we call them,' explained Gordon, proffering the plate of round thin biscuits with scalloped edges and currants squashed in them.

'I think the proper name is – er, what *is* the proper name, Gordon?' asked Pam. 'It says on the packet and I always forget to look.'

'Not very good weather,' said Gordon, striking into new territory. Pam was relieved – she'd somehow got stuck in the Biscuit Question.

'Nah,' said Derek. 'But that's England innit. I don't expect brilliant weather in England.'

'Have you been abroad much?' asked Pam, forcing a bright attentive sparkle into her otherwise very jumpy eyes. It was all rather nerve-racking, this. The bright attentive sparkle became fixed in a scrutiny of the boy's face.

'Not really,' said Derek.

'Where've you been in fact?' asked Gordon.

'Nowhere abroad.'

'Have another squashed fly,' said Pam. 'Gordon, more tea.'

'Yes please.'

'I'll top up the pot.'

Pam swung out and Gordon said 'We were both very sorry about your mother.' It cost him an effort but he knew it was the right thing to say. The reason for Derek's presence had to be acknowledged, no matter how uncomfortable this felt. Derek didn't reply. Pam swung back in bearing before her in the air a full pot, like something she'd just scalped back in the kitchen. 'Plenty of tea,' she said inanely.

'I was telling Derek we were both very sorry about his mother.'

'Yes,' said Pam peremptorily, because she felt tears welling at once.

'It can't have been easy for you,' Gordon continued while Derek stared dreamily into the glowing fireplace, 'but, well, we hope you can stay with us for – for as long as you want to. There's a sports field over the back of the house.'

'I used to play football for the school.' Derek's voice was dry as dust.

'I think there's a local team plays on Saturday afternoons. We can walk over and have a look. Do you still play?'

'Nah. I left school, didn't I.'

Silence. They slurped. Pam felt an intense desire not to have silence. It was a rigid silence. Absolute torture. She blurted out 'Would you like to have some sandwiches? We have a big meal this evening.'

'No thank-you.' Derek felt choked.

'Would you like a bath?' she asked.

'No thank-you. I had one before I left.' He had an ache in his throat. It was like balls-ache only round the Adam's apple. He felt totally adrift. And in pain. Sinking pain.

'Right,' said Gordon. 'Let's take your bags upstairs and show you your bedroom.'

– Thank God, thought Derek who had been worrying about where he was to sleep.

– Good idea, thought Pam. Gordon's being *marvellous*.

They showed him Mark's old room which had been cleared of everything. Pam had said 'If it's going to be Derek's room let it *be* Derek's room.' As they transferred Mark's childhood effects to the boxroom it was Gordon who felt the filaments of guilt, of regret, in a generalised mushy sadness, especially when he took down the railway calendar. Pam felt a filament of guilt too but this was almost at once succeeded by an air of renewal, an excitement, a cleansing, and a great expectation.

'Right, Derek,' said Gordon, 'would you like some time to unpack? Here's the bathroom.'

'I'm a bit tired.'

'You have a rest then, dear,' said Pam. 'When you're ready come downstairs and you can help me set the table if you like. Are you sure you wouldn't like a sandwich? All right then. Just come down when you're ready.' Ready. She'd been using the word a great deal to-day. As in 'not ready'. Is one ever really ready? And ready for what?

'Thanks, Mrs Drake.'

'Pam,' said Pam with a sweet smile and closing the bedroom door behind her she descended to the reassurance of vegetables and the chopping board.

Within, Derek sat on the edge of the bed. Not thinking. Looking. Feeling bad, in pain. Stranded on a strange shore. With no one. He lay back on the bed and gazed into the ceiling. There was a greenish tinge to the light which entered the room from the street and this calmed him a little. He lay like this for over an hour, gripped by utter loneliness and desolation. Then he unpacked. All his mother's stuff he'd sold off through a friend of Auntie May's who had a junk stall in Petticoat Lane. He'd kept Doll's photograph album and his personal things – but not all. Only the major items: radio cassette player, clothes, the globe, Pop's fountain pen . . . He fitted the 2 halves of the globe together, fitted it into its frame, and stood it on the small desk beneath the window. He had a choking lump in his throat. Then he took out his radio cassette player, plugged the earphones into the side and put them over his head, put in a cassette and played it at full volume.

But he didn't hear it. He didn't hear anything at all.

The special old-fashioned suet pudding, full of steak & kidney, sat on its plate in the centre of the table, steaming faintly in the unattractive light of the dining-room. The pudding had the colour and greasy texture of human flesh that has never known sunshine. And when Pam ceremoniously cut into it with a large knife, a rich dark diarrhoea oozed forth. It tasted wonderful – Gordon said so, adding that it wasn't every day one had something like this. Derek had never had something like this, never eaten a suet pudding before. Derek had heard of suet puddings; he'd heard them mentioned on television in soap operas set in England's great days. And Pam had been talking about this one as if it were a sublime and exotic sin. 'Oh I shouldn't, Gordon – but I will!' she said, grabbing seconds. Yes, Derek had heard of it. But he couldn't eat it. He couldn't eat any of it. The very first mouthful jammed at his teeth and could go no further. The first course had been no problem. Avocado pear with prawns in the middle and a shocking pink sauce squeezed round the edge in a wavy pattern – he'd gone into the kitchen and seen Pam squeezing this shocking pink stuff out of a tube like toothpaste. He liked prawns. And he liked avocado – he'd had it once before, yes; no, he couldn't remember where. It tasted interesting. And nourishing. But the suet pudding – he didn't mind kidney, he didn't actually *like* it, but he didn't mind it, but to-day a whiff came off the kidney which locked shut his entire eating and digestive apparatus. He couldn't get anything down – no suet pudding, no carrots with onions, no broccoli, a little mashed potato, and it was real mashed potato, not the shit powder Doll used, but after a couple of desultory forkfuls he seized up on the potato too. He wanted to say 'I'm very sorry but I can't eat any more' but he couldn't say it, the muscles wouldn't work, he just couldn't say it, so he did the next best thing and quietly put his knife and fork together as at the close of eating, and sat there staring down at the plate but not seeing the plate. He wanted to cry. But his eyes were hot, dry and prickly.

There was silence. First Pam stopped. Then Gordon stopped.

'It's all right, son,' said Gordon. 'If you've finished eating, that's all right.'

Derek continued to stare at his plate. He felt an appalling tension in his face.

'Do you want any pudding, Derek?' asked Pam. 'You know – dessert.'

'Maybe he does, maybe he doesn't. Just bring it in, Pam,' and Gordon poured a little more red wine into Derek's glass. But Derek didn't want to drink any more. Suddenly he felt wobbly inside. Not drunk; he'd hardly drunk anything. But jellylike. As if he wasn't capable of being softened up any more without altogether dissolving. He didn't want to dissolve. He wasn't going to dissolve. He needed any rigour he could lay his hands on. He'd have to sit tight, sit this one out.

Pam brought in the pudding which was blackberries in syrup with cream and vanilla ice-cream. 'The blackberries are from last September, Gordon. Do you remember? We picked them at Chorleywood. I put some in the deep freeze and when they defrosted they produced this *yummy* syrup. The ice-cream is from Marks & Spencer. It's so creamy – and they do a lovely caramel one too. I'll get some next time I'm in Marks. And they do a lovely—'

While Pam was singing her ode, Gordon thought – Jeeesus! Is there life beyond Marks & Spencer? This ice-cream's too sweet. All the sweet things from that shop are too sweet. Pandering to the British addiction to sugar, of course. Normally Gordon would have said as much – had said as much, although Pam always ignored what he said foodwise – but to-night would not be the night to question the sweetness of the ice-cream, especially as Derek's appetite seemed to have made a partial recovery and he was now eating his pudding, if not with alacrity, at least with something more than distaste.

When they'd finished Gordon was about to say 'That was delicious'. But he thought he wouldn't put Derek on the spot

70

by doing so and changed his remark to 'I'll switch on the telly'.

Without being asked, Derek helped Pam take the dinner things into the kitchen.

– How nice. How terribly well brought up. He's not a slob, she thought.

'Leave them there, dear, and I'll stack them in the dishwasher. Do you know how a dishwasher works?' Derek nodded in the negative. 'Then I'll teach you.' Pam looked at him, swallowed deeply, and said 'I'm so glad you decided to come here.'

Derek mumbled 'Thanks'. He didn't know why he'd said it, he hadn't wanted to, it was a silly reflex – what did he have to thank them for? Nothing.

'Go and watch a bit of television. Gordon's in there. I'll bring the coffee.' Pam pottered in the kitchen, paused to contemplate the half-eaten suet pudding, and said aloud but not loud enough to be heard 'Poor kid'.

In the sitting-room Gordon was sitting in Gordon's chair to the right of the fireplace and Derek was at one end of the sofa, sitting stiffly with his hands in his lap. They were watching *Question Time*, Gordon truly, Derek ostensibly. On the screen a woman professor of physics from a university in the North of England was saying '*The great question facing everyone now is how can human society continue to develop without destroying itself and the planet too!*'

'Exactly!' expostulated Gordon.

Derek looked at him and Gordon smiled back. The boy looked out of the window. On the screen the Shadow Minister of Culture replied to the professor. '*No, no, no! The great question, the fundamental question, remains what it always was, and that is: What is Intelligence and where does it come from? Because the answer to this question will answer your question. But the answer to your question won't answer my question.*'

'*Oh but it will,*' returned the professor, '*and I'll tell you why—*'

'*I don't for a moment doubt that you will,*' said the Minister with a snigger. The audience laughed.

'Good stuff, eh?' said Gordon.

Derek blinked at him then stared out of the window at the streetlamp and at what he could discern of Wildwood Rise, wondering what went on out there. Television didn't interest him

71

unless it was a good film or a very special broadcast like the Olympic Games – except when the Olympic Games *had* been on last time, he'd hardly bothered to watch, it seemed so plastic, so unreal, the occasion for lots of advertising and propaganda crap.

Pam came in and said 'Gordon, you haven't drawn the curtains'. She drew them against the gusty night and Derek was sealed off from the world, shut in here. He glanced at Pam pouring the coffee, at Gordon lost in the television, and Derek's pain turned to fatigue in front of the fire. What was the time? 9.30, 10.30 p.m.? He'd lost his grip on time. Gripping time was never one of his big things but now – it could be any time – any place – anyone . . . His head went slowly round. The fire seemed to drug him. He loved the fire. Then he felt giddy and disliked the feeling and spoke out to steady himself. 'What's that?'

'It's Mercury,' said Pam. 'He was the Roman god of – what was he the Roman god of, Gordon?'

'He was the messenger of the gods,' said Gordon. 'Some people call him Hermes.'

They were in Mark's bedroom. The bedside lamp with its red shade was on, the curtains were closed, and it was cosy.

'Here are your towels. And the laundry basket is out on the landing. Put all your washing in there. Are you all right for pyjamas?'

'I don't have any,' said Derek.

'You can have a pair of Gordon's. There might even be a pair of Mark's you can have—'

'I mean, I don't wear them.'

'Ah, yes, oh . . . well, what about a dressing-gown?' She'd seen the old one he'd hung up behind the door.

'No, it's OK.'

'Because if you'd like another, there's one Gordon's never used and—'

'No, I've got a dressing-gown, thanks.'

'Would you like something before you sleep? You might be hungry later. I'll bring something up in a few minutes. I'll knock first.'

10 minutes later there was a soft knock on Derek's door. He'd undressed and was in bed, with the bedclothes half way up his bare chest. The central heating had gone off but the room was still

warm. Pam entered and could smell him, a faint sweet musky smell.

'Would you like the small window open?' she asked.

'Not now,' he said.

She set a cup of Ovaltine and 4 fig roll biscuits on the bedside table, smoothed back his hair and kissed him on the brow. 'Good night and God bless,' she said.

'Good night.'

The moment she'd gone he devoured the biscuits, then the drink, burning the inside of his mouth. What had he done to find himself in this strange place? That must be it – he was here *because* it was strange. Escape. To remain in the surroundings which resonated to his mother's spirit had become intolerable to him. He had to go somewhere *else*. And here he was. Where was Auntie May? He could almost hear her breathing in the next room – only last night it really had been in the next room – May and the budgie which occasionally woke up in the middle of the night and said 'Who's a pretty boy then?' – Auntie May said 'Be a good boy and here's £20 and I'd like you to use some of it to—' Fuck! I forgot. 'Use some of it to buy Mrs Drake a nice box of chocolates' – she's probably got hundreds of boxes of chocolates stashed away in the garage – or in the fucking guest bedroom – shopping for chocolates down the Roman Road Market – I should've – Who's that geezer? – He's coming to get me! He's pointing a big black gun at me! I'll fly down the alley – fly, fly – I feel hungry but this chicken's rubbery – great black towers rise above and turn in the starry sky – Who's this horrible old fart? – all their windows are blacked out – there is no one – where've they all gone? – empty, empty, I feel sick, hungry, alone, sad – I don't know these towers – the moon turning bloodred – violets, lovely violets! – it's the old man, no, old woman who comes up to me and says 'You don't want any of these silly flowers, do you? Denial of the self only increases one's obsession with oneself.' 'Well said, my good woman. Have a coin.' 'Lawks, guvnor, thanks everso.' Hungry and they say Marks & Spencer do an everso – I'm flying above the great city and looking down at the great wheel of lights, I see violence and panic spread across it like condensation across a window, clouding vision, enabling confusion, shutting off the lights – giant marble statues, the gods of the Roman city, whirl across the starry sky making a cackling noise – the males have erections, the females drip their invitation – they shatter and crunch in orgy – marble turns to rubber turns to flesh . . . Derek tossed and turned. He couldn't sleep. He couldn't even dream. He drifted hotly, erratically. He had a hard-on like a bar of marble. He switched on the bedside lamp and his eyes were flooded with custard-coloured light that poured out beneath the red shade. It was painful. He shielded his eyes, screwed them up, as elements of the room flashed and rocked in and out of position. It was too much. He switched the light off again and climbed out of bed, went across to the curtains and peeped between them. The wind had dropped. He opened the small window. The street was quiet and leafy. A gentle rosy silvery light came into the room from the streetlamp and moon. Derek looked around and found the towels. He picked one up, masturbated into it, tucked it away in the back of his wardrobe, closed the curtain again, returned to bed, and fell asleep.

Pam woke up early and her first thought was – What now? She stared weakly at the ceiling. This thought remained with her and when Gordon awoke, about an hour later, she said 'I suppose we should find him a job. What do you think he's good at? In the meantime, how much pocket money should we give him?'

'Not now, pet,' said Gordon. He turned over, pulled the sheet up round his ears to grab another 15 minutes. Pam was irritated by this. Not that she begrudged Gordon his 15 minutes if he could find them. But she thought – He's going to leave it all up to me – he's not even interested.

Gordon had 25 minutes and at breakfast he said 'I'm late, Pam. We'll talk about it this evening. Is he up yet? I must rush.' He disappeared at once out of the house and out of the road.

Pam stood in the kitchen, looking into the back garden. Early spring had become middle spring. Easter had been early and had gone but no suggestion of summer had arrived. A drizzle came on and a cold wind ricocheted about the garden in gusts. She was gearing herself up to say Good Morning to Derek, whenever that might be. The radio was on and innocuous pop music supplied a soft blockage to more complex circuits of thought. Her thought

74

was – I wonder when he'll get up.

Meanwhile upstairs in the small bedroom, Derek was lying in bed with the horn. It was one of those erections in which the 2 side channels of erectile tissue are locked full and the third on the underside of the penis is less so. It was like a piece of wood fixed to his front. It could be transformed into full sexual awareness but was not of itself that. It was associated more with a terrific desire to pee. He was lying on his back, held fast by the secure and warming embrace of the bed but knowing that very soon he would have to steel himself to confront this new household, – through the necessity of confronting this new bathroom. He disengaged gingerly from the bed, clothed his nakedness in Pop's old dressing-gown, and quietly opened the door. He listened.

The pop music drifted idly up the staircase. He heard a disc jockey's voice say *'Our guest this morning is Rowena Clamp, author of* The Erectile Woman. *If lesbianism leaves a nasty taste in your mouth, Rowena will help you to—'*

Derek padded across the landing, locked himself in the bathroom, pulled up the loo-seat and peed. Because of the stubborn tumescence, to direct his urine properly into the pan and avoid splashing the wall, he was obliged to tilt his whole body forward at the hips with his bottom sticking out ridiculously. Even so he still had to push the stalk down uncomfortably. His first pee of the day was usually effected in this ungainly manner. In Nature there would not be this problem of angle. You'd shoot the water joyously into the air and it would land in the grass, but in Civilisation . . . As he padded back across the landing, the erection subsided, the foreskin reclaimed the plum, and he began to orientate himself for the next thing. A voice came up the staircase: *'Look, get me straight – I've got nothing against men. Nothing at all. It's just that they're so full of shit. Strutting about in that moronic way. And most heterosexual men are pathetically limited to their role. They never look at it, question it, develop it, therefore they never understand it. They are pathetic creatures, with their pathetic little willies, going round trying to find a place to rest, like bits dropped off women. Believe me, I feel fucking sorry for men with their silly futile bollocks hanging down, scraping the bristle off their chins every day, hobbling about looking for a place to rest. Women are at home in the Universe, but men have been dealt the card which can never sleep. Men are fucking tragic, fucking—'* At this point in Rowena's sermon, some music cut in with a footling fa-la fol-de-rol fol-de-rol. There was a new policy at the BBC to limit the use of the word 'fuck' and its forms during daylight hours.

Derek stood at the top of the stairs listening and almost jumped out of his skin when a voice called up 'That you, Derek? Tea or coffee?'

'Tea,' he called down weakly. The word vanished as he swallowed in the middle of it, so he said it again, then went to the bedroom, threw on some clothes, quickly made his bed. Pam started to prepare his breakfast, made a fresh pot of tea, took a yoghurt out of the fridge (she was going to keep him company), was startled by a noise behind her, turned quickly, and with a shock saw a big boy standing in the kitchen doorway staring at her.

Pam thought – There's a big boy standing in my kitchen doorway – feet planted firmly on the floor. What am I going to do with him? He's staring at me. He's full of potential.

She survived.

And that evening Gordon said privately to her 'I've been thinking, Pam. We should give him a few weeks to settle in before we tackle the problem of a career.'

'I'm not talking about a career,' said Pam. 'Come down to earth, Gordon. I'm talking about a job. He's going to be here most of the day – I feel I ought to be entertaining him or something.'

'Relax, pet. It'll be all right.'

'But I can rely on you to broach it, can I, at the proper time? What Derek is to do with his life, you'll broach it, won't you? I can rely on that, can I? Because it's very important, it's perhaps the most important thing we can give him, some guidance, so I can rely on you, can I? I mean—'

'Oh, Pam. For God's sake.'

When, on the following day, the subject of pocket money was raised, Derek said 'It's OK. I can get the dole.'

'Well, that's one problem solved. See you to-night,' said Gordon, pecking Pam, winking at Derek, and he left for the office.

A minute afterwards Derek said 'But I've got to re-register, Mrs Drake. So—'

Pam was thinking that Gordon's wink was perhaps a bit forced, she hoped Gordon wasn't going to force the bonhomie, it never worked, but on the other hand, it was sweet that he was trying, even though trying was often utterly counter-productive, although sometimes one did have to try because very often things didn't simply *happen*, and one's life might grind to a halt if one occasionally didn't throw oneself forward by *trying* something, so she said 'Now, Derek, listen. I'm Pam. I want to be Pam to you. I know you are only being polite but I don't want to be Mrs Drake. When you call me Mrs Drake I feel like a school-mistress. And I'm not a school-mistress. Please, please, it's Pam. Now you try it. Say Pam. Go on – say P . . . a . . .m.'

He blushed bright red and said nothing.

The blush reached Pam's heart and made her feel very tender. She said quietly 'Do you know, Derek, you're already looking more relaxed than when you arrived. Go on. Call me Pam. I dare you.' She gave him a soft little nudge with her elbow. He smiled – just faintly. Something amused and lovely tried to express itself at the corners of his mouth. But he didn't say anything. 'Where do you go to register for this dole?' she asked.

'Social security,' he said. 'D'ya know where it is?'

'No. But I'll get the phonebook and we'll soon find out.'

They hunted everywhere in the phonebook but couldn't find the damn place. 'What on earth is it under?' Pam addressed the vacant space in front of her and plunged back into the fog of the mystifying tome, getting nowhere. 'I can never find Government offices in these things. Do you think they do it on purpose? I'll ring Gordon.'

She offered to accompany Derek to the Social Security but he wanted to do it by himself. So she arranged to meet him out-side Sainsbury's afterwards. She did most of her shopping in bulk at the Cash & Carry, using Gordon's office discount card. 'But if we go to Sainsbury's I can show you the Hogarth Parade which is near it and where Gordon works but we won't go in.'

When Derek met Pam he was looking brighter, as if cleansed of a worry. He had money in his pocket, his own money.

Pam said 'Let's go to the butcher's. We'll have to queue but it's worth it.'

In the queue a voice struck out. 'Where've *you* been? Haven't *seen* you for ages?' It was Marilyn Dashman. She was wearing a red fox jacket to match her reddish, brownish hair, and blue jeans tucked into cherry red high-heeled boots. She was shorter and younger than Pam, and more emphatic in appearance, especially round the eyes and lips which were cleverly painted. She was vivacious and curvacious, not fat but with the fuller figure. Her face had a girlish prettiness, almost chubby, her manner was a touch teasing, and she must have been in her mid 40s. 'Why haven't I seen her for ages?' she asked Derek, touching the bonnet of her hairdo. As she did so, 2 expensive rings flashed upon her fingers.

'We've been so busy,' said Pam. She had developed a corn on one of her little toes and it began to throb – she moved her foot around in her shoe to ease it.

'So've we!' said Marilyn. 'The busiest ever! And we went to Sardinia for 10 days.' Marilyn knew that 10 days was chic. A fortnight was common and a week simply not enough; and if you wanted more than 10 days it had to be at least a month – 3 weeks was too tantalising for words. 'Just for a break. Bob knows some people there. It poured with rain the entire time. And *nothing* to do of course. Unless you're a fisherman. I can't recommend Sardinia.' She pronounced it to rhyme with gardenia.

'This is Derek Love,' said Pam. 'He's living with us. Derek, this is Mrs Dashman.'

'God, call me Marilyn *please*,' said Marilyn to him. She turned to Pam and said 'Why's that then?'

Pam didn't know what to say at first. Then she said 'He's my nephew.' And glancing at Derek's face she knew she'd said the right thing. He went red. He hadn't thought of himself as a nephew; his thoughts had not presumed to this degree, and something which had been imprecise and burdensome and like an invisible irritation, now settled: he had his role. Nephew . . .

'I didn't know you had a nephew,' said Marilyn, perhaps hinting at a dark secret to be explained. 'Such a big strong nephew too. How long are you with us for, Derek?' asked Marilyn with the slightly proprietorial air she adopted *vis-à-vis* goings-on in Wildwood Rise.

'Don't know yet,' said Derek, looking away from her down the street.

'You must meet my son Ward. He sometimes pops home at week-ends with a couple of chums. He's boarding at Harrow now, Pam. It's not what I wanted but now he's in the 6th Form he said it's distracting coming home every night. I do miss him but Bob said the boy's old enough to decide for himself and Ward was standing right *there* so I couldn't argue with that, could I? 2 big men against little me – no chance, Pam, no chance at all. He's doing so well – mathematics – he wants to go to St Andrew's University. I said why not Oxford? And he said no, it had to be St Andrew's. They have such funny ideas at that age, don't they? Pardon me, Derek, but you young men, can't get to the bottom of you sometimes. Oh God, these queues, they eat one's life away. I've just spent weeks queueing at Plummer's for a chocolate gateau. I had to have that gateau. I'm developing *such* a sweet tooth in my old age! [Marilyn had some months ago read the following in *The Times* and it had taken the wraps off her inclinations: *Researchers at the Hebrew University in Jerusalem have discovered in experiments with rats that sexual activity can be 'greatly enhanced' by feeding them sweetened liquids. They believe that a constituent in the sugar triggers the part of the brain which controls the sex drive. The brain is known to contain a chemical PEA, which acts as a stimulant and is supposed to be responsible for the 'falling in love feeling'. There are also very small quantities of PEA in chocolate which could explain why they are so popular as a gift from those with amorous intentions.*] Normally I have everything sent to the house or I go to the Cash & Carry and buy in bulk. You can't beat buying in bulk. But one thing I will always queue for is *meat!*' She flashed a brilliant white set of teeth on Derek. 'A good piece of meat is worth anything. I simply don't trust them, Pam, to send up a decent cut. I mean they might do to begin with, then plop! Old boots the night someone *special's* coming to eat. He does a wonderful sausage here, Pam.'

'I know,' said Pam.

'Makes them himself with herbs and stuff, and they're absolutely – oh sorry, Mr Tibbs, my turn, is it? Right. Show me some *killer* steak?'

79

The complaint – the disease! – that there's nothing we can do – that we are all caught in the ineluctable sweep of history – that nothing anyone does can make any difference – nonsense! Everything anyone does is of importance. So stop complaining – do something!

Death or glory – bless my soul, 'tis the Prince of Gloucester – How strange his skull is, all bone, all bone, and the eyes 2 dark tunnels receding to infinity. . . . .

I cannot agree with the previous speaker. The West says that the East is fatalistic. But the Hindu law of karma, which upholds that everything one does is important, is the opposite of fatalism. On the other hand the western idea, the Marxist belief – that we are indeed caught in the sweep of history against which individual effort is powerless, therefore meaningless – this surely is Grand Fatalism!

Hi, Gloucester! See you at Belvoir Castle for the Great Thrash! To which Merlin replies: I see in the sky made of lead a great skull & crossbones made of cloud! Tis very dangerous! But the greater the danger, the greater should our courage be. Look out, look behind you! . . . it's Death . . .

Sorry. Can't agree with either speaker. It seems to me that to say everything one does makes a difference and to say that nothing one does makes a difference is, in effect, to say the same thing. Both propositions make life impossible, both make man a victim of circumstance, and it seems to me that the only hope out of all this is to – At this point the speaker blew a loud raspberry, the audience applauded, and the chairman said '*Right. The next question is from Mr Maundy of Clitheroe. Does the panel have any ideas on what to do about pimples on the bottom? Over to you, Crispin, who holds the chair of Ismology in the University of Cornwall.*'

'*Well, if you ask me,*' said Crispin, '*a pimply bottom should be exposed to fresh air at frequent intervals. Any chance you get – give it an airing. Why, I remember, not so long ago . . . so long ago . . . the* twin curves of the bottom . . . the smoothly curving bottom . . . a whistling sound jets out from between the buttocks, a whistling whoosh as if one of the sky gods blew a raspberry, his cheeks inflated like a trumpeter's, and from his lips there came a whoosh, a rigid jet at whose extremity whorls formed. Is it a mouth or is it an anus? The riddle of Merlin this. To which the answer is: As above, so below! Oh what a wonderfully curving bottom! Young and furry. Pimpleless. Divine. The curves of holy flesh. Whistle at the holy flesh! What is that whistling? . . . What . . . . Wake up, Major, before the whole street wakes up! You have been dozing off, Major, with the radio on. Dozing off, Major, with the kettle on. And now the kettle's whistle is too much even for you – and the Major rouses himself and says 'Good grief' to the walls. He shuffles out to the kitchen which is a mess. Irish Mary calls in once a week. It's not enough. The kitchen is messy, smelly, and the whole house has a damp fusty old bachelor pong, as if an old dog lived there – but there is no old dog, nor an old cat, nor indeed any other living thing apart from the Major, dozing between the radio and his thoughts and the screaming kettle – and now, finally, he is making a pot of tea in the kitchen, and as he does so he hears this: 'I'm not gonna stay here and get fucking rained on!'

The voice was hard, strong, and followed by the noise of a banging door. The Major trotted from the kitchen through to the front of the house, heard another bang which was the front door of the Drakes', and saw that boy next door strut down the garden path and run off down the street. The boy had left the front gate open and it squealed slightly in erratic gusts of wind.

This is what had happened. Firstly, Pam had gone upstairs to tell Irish Mary not to forget to do behind the pelmets in the sitting-room. Pam had then opened the bathroom door, gone in and found Derek there naked. They both uttered a little gasp. He was preparing to shave, which he almost needed to do every other day, his back was to the door, and he blinked at her in the mirror above his white Santa Claus beard of shaving foam.

For the tiniest, barely discernible fraction of a second longer than one might have supposed, Pam is held there. Derek feels this. Her normal Pavlovian response under such circumstances, the powerful rectitude of an English upbringing which effects immediate withdrawal and an apology, is overridden by a dreamier response which, momentarily, follows the initial shock and interrupts the reflex. Then the reflex of course comes into play and she closes the door again. But instead of saying sorry as she does so, she says in a flat disengaged tone 'Keep the door locked when you're changing, Derek.' Now she feels angry with herself for having said this – confused and hurt – as if she had been destructive, made complexity where there should be simplicity. She feels a collar of heat about her neck and puts distance between herself and the event by tripping primly down the stairs, walking to the sitting-room window, and gazing over the privet hedge.

After the bathroom door had closed on him, Derek had giggled in embarrassment at his own reflection. He thought – I should've flashed my chopper at her, given her a real thrill. And started to scrape away the shaving foam. He had forgotten to lock the bathroom door. The bathroom in Doll's flat hadn't had a lock and they never seemed to overlap bathroomwise anyway. But here, at the Drakes' house, he was particular about locking the bathroom door. It gave him a sense of security in new surroundings. But today, for the first time, he'd forgotten, after nearly two weeks.

Secondly, Derek (now dressed) had gone back into his bedroom – which coincided with Irish Mary finishing the guest bedroom and wanting to get into his. Having been invaded in the bathroom, he stuck his ground in the bedroom and refused to leave it. It should be said that Irish Mary's job wasn't the greatest job on earth. She managed to get through it by not thinking. And not-thinking meant doing things in a certain order. It wasn't a job made any easier by having to cope with the versatile spontaneity of an alert mind. So when in her schedule she came to Derek's bedroom, this meant it was time for Derek's bedroom to be cleaned. But he refused to budge.

'You're always doing this, young Derek,' she said resentfully through her loose dentures.

'No I'm not,' he replied pugnaciously.

'You are too! This is the third or fourth time.' As she said this her dentures shot forward out of her mouth but were immediately drawn back in again by sleight of lip and tongue. It all happened very quickly and gave the impression that she was constructed from mechanical parts.

Also, being Irish, she pronounced it 'turd or fart time' and Derek murmured 'Turd or fart off'.

'What did you say, you young blackguard?'

'Go away.' He felt it was crucial to hold onto this bedroom.

'I'm going to get Mrs D.'

82

Pam was obliged to come upstairs again. She was still discomfited by the earlier incident and said 'Derek, don't be difficult.'

Derek looked at her angrily and said 'She's got the hump. It's not me who's difficult. It weren't *my* idea to come 'ere.'

He went noisily downstairs. Pam found him standing in the kitchen eating biscuits from the biscuit barrel. A young man standing in her kitchen. 2 feet firmly on the floor and a scowl on his face. A shiver went through her. In one sense she and Gordon had been drawn closer together by the arrival of Derek. In another they had been obliged to move apart to create a space for the newcomer. Sometimes it was as if the boy were pushing them apart with the 2 flats of his hands, needing more space as he grew. Sometimes it was as if she were losing sight of Gordon altogether and had to try and catch his attention over the top of the black curls on Derek's head. Sometimes she felt more alone than before.

She said 'You must let Mary get in there to clean, Derek. It's only twice a week.'

Derek turned to her in a passion and said 'I'm not gonna stay here and get fucking rained on!' He dashed out of the kitchen slamming the door, and out of the house slamming the door. Irish Mary came into the kitchen and said 'There's insolence for you, Mrs D.' Pam looked away. There'd been tears in Derek's eyes. Pam felt only her own cruelty and insensitivity. A longing to comfort him, soothe him, swelled in her.

Derek wandered about feeling acutely sorry for himself, then went to the local swimming-pool. He didn't have his trunks and towel and so hired them. He swam up and down but there was no vigour in his strokes. His anger had been followed by despair. Then a few hot tears actually squeezed out, ran down his cheeks and eased him a bit. He wandered along to Hogarth Parade, found himself outside Gordon's office, and decided to go in. It was less impressive than he'd expected and this made him happier. In the outer office the 2 clerks stared at him with objective interest, as if he were a crossword clue. Ms Harding adjusted her cleavage and said 'Wait here. He's got someone with him.' Eventually a woman with blue hair came out saying 'But I still don't understand it. I simply don't understand it.' She said it to Gordon, she said it to Ms Harding, and she turned a long, deeply disappointed face onto Derek and said it to him too. Then she left, leaving behind a faint drift of Shalimar by Guerlain.

'This is a surprise,' said Gordon. 'I'm going to have a sauna bath this evening. Would you like to come with me?' Pam phoned and Gordon said 'He's here with me. Yes, he's OK. We're going to the sauna. We'll pick up a Chinese takeaway. Do you fancy that?'

The sauna was quiet. A Pakistani or Indian man was ahead of them in the changing-room and left as they began to undress.

'Did you see him?' said Derek. 'Have you noticed that smell in their shops? Sort of sweat mixed with old plastic.'

'I think it's the spices,' said Gordon.

'Yeah,' said Derek. 'Bet the curry just *pours* out of him in the sauna. I've never been in a sauna before. I went to the York Hall Vapour Baths a couple of times. That was near where I was. How long do we have to stay in? I don't want to overdo it, don't want an 'eart-attack or anything. Didn't think you'd have Pakis and blacks up this way. But they get everywhere, don't they?' The last sentence was spoken very non-committally.

Gordon replied 'We have a great imperial past. We had the greatest empire the world has ever known. It would be extraordinary indeed if there were no evidence of this in our capital city. Next time you see an Indian or a Negro, take pride, and remember that it is because not so long ago we ruled the world. And think how *mean* London would be if there were only English people in it. It's a great cosmopolitan city, a place where all the elements of life intersect. Where would you like to live? Oslo? Would you like London to be like Oslo? The Romans made citizens of the alien peoples they conquered. And in doing so they prospered. We're only doing the same. Belatedly. Perhaps if we'd done it before we'd still have the Empire, a great federation of races and interests, but as it is—'

'Don't get me wrong,' Derek interrupted. 'I was just making an observation about their funny shops. Got nothing against them personally. One of my mates is an Indian. His name's Gupta which is Indian which is Hindu. The Pakis are Moslem and have

84

names like Singh. But they all look the bloody same to me! Do you know any?'

'No, I don't,' said Gordon. 'You must invite him round. Now what we do is have a shower, then a sauna, then a shower, then a sauna, and so on until you've had enough. It's not a competition, so if you've had enough heat, come out and shower and have a rest.'

'There's no steam room then?'

'No.'

'Oh. You've got a funny hairy patch on your back.'

Afterwards they had a cup of tea and Miss Wimbush said 'So you've got somebody with you this time. That's nice.'

Gordon smiled oddly.

Showering afterwards, Derek said 'You're OK, you're not fat, you got long legs, you'll make old bones.'

'No, I never get fat,' said Gordon. He looked at Derek as the shower shot onto the boy's head and the water ran down his body. From the small of his back downwards, Derek was a series of elegant curves where the muscles were strong and tight beneath the skin. These curves were echoed all over his body but here especially formed a wonderful swinging descent from buttocks down the backs of the thighs and the calves to the small curve of the heel. He was shorter than Gordon, more compact.

As he sudsed his hair, Derek said 'You worried about the Bomb, Gordon?'

'It's not just the nuclear threat,' replied Gordon. 'There are all the chemical and biological weapons too. Has everyone forgotten about those?'

'Diabolical innit.'

'We'll get some Chinese takeaway, eh?'

'Yeah,' said Derek. 'Listen. A man in a Chinese restaurant said "Waiter, this chicken's rubbery". And the waiter said "Aw, fanks vewy much".' Derek laughed. It took Gordon some moments to get it.

Eating their takeaway in front of the television, Derek said 'The sauna was good, but I think the vapour baths is better. It said on the notice you mustn't use it if under the influence of alcohol or if being prescribed drugs. You on drugs, Gordon?' asked Derek with a cheeky grin.

Gordon laughed and said 'Sleeping pills are about as far as I go.'

'Really?' said Derek surprised. 'You really take sleeping pills?'

'It's nothing very special.'

'My mum says drugs and all that stuff's really terrible for you.'

'And your mother was absolutely right,' said Pam. 'Any more of that chicken and cashew?'

– Pam's never objected to my sleeping-pills before, Gordon thought.

They sat in front of the television but weren't absorbed by a programme on a locust plague currently laying waste large parts of Africa. Each was detached and, curiously, each was aware of the other's detachment. It wasn't a telepathic state exactly, but each was aware. Then Derek left the room; just walked out.

Pam said 'Let's go for a drive to Chorleywood this weekend . . .'

Gordon said nothing, stared blankly at the locusts.

'So he enjoyed the sauna then?' she essayed again 5 minutes later.

'Oh yes.'

'He seems to be coming out of himself,' she mused. 'Sometimes you'd never think he lost his mother a few months ago.'

Gordon looked at her and sighed. 'They're very resilient at 17.'

'I think they're more resilient at 7,' she said.

'Don't you want him to get over it?'

'Of course. I want him to be happy. But I hope he doesn't bury his feelings, become too thick-skinned, bitter even, that's possible, by hiding it. Yes, I want him to get over it – but not too quickly. Does that make sense?'

'We never get over these things,' he said. 'We learn to live with them.'

'Gordon, everyone knows that. But what I mean is – well, I hope he doesn't become cold in order to survive.'

'He's a fine boy, Pam.'

'Oh, I know, I wasn't saying he wasn't. It's just that . . . perhaps I'm being silly.'

They both returned to the locusts. Which turned into the News. And Pam said 'I think we should turn Mark's room, I mean Derek's, into a second bathroom. And give Derek the guest room.'

'But what if he doesn't stay? We haven't adopted him.'

'I think he'll stay. Anyway it would increase the value of the house.'

'I'm not sure losing a bedroom would do that.'

'Oh it would. 3 bedrooms and 2 bathrooms is very convenient for many people.'

'That's what I mean. A 3-bedroomed house is not particularly anything. But a 4-bedroomed house, a man can feel satisfied with that. I'm satisfied with our 4-bedroomed house. And where would the guests stay?'

'Once in a blue moon, our guests. It is the fourth bedroom after all. You could clear your junk out of the boxroom. Or we could buy a sofa bed, stick it in the dining-room, you are ridiculous at times.'

'I just don't see why we need 2 bloody bathrooms. There's lots of people in India with no bathroom at all.'

'Don't start on that. Mankind has to push on where he can towards making a better world. And round here, a better world is 2 bathrooms. And I'll add that the Indian or African or South American peasant stands a much better chance of having a bathroom if he'd control his population. They breed like rabbits, then turn their big dreary eyes onto the rest of the world for a handout.'

'That's not fair, pet.'

'I don't know whether it's fair or not. But it's the truth. Where did Derek go?'

'Search me.'

'Gordon, isn't there anything better on than these locusts?'

Derek came in later and Pam said 'Where did you go?'

'I was with Major Playfair. In his garage, helping him.'

'So you've met him then. He's a sweet old thing is the Major.'

'He don't seem so old,' said Derek. 'No older than Gordon.'

Gordon looked peeved and said 'Oh he is, he's older than me.'

'He was very good to Mark,' said Pam. 'Wasn't he, Gordon, good to Mark?'

'He got Mark in with the army, if that's what you mean,' said Gordon. 'And do you know what astonished me most? The emblem of their regiment was the Skull & Crossbones. Can you believe it? I thought only Hitler's SS wore that. But no, a British regiment wears it too.'

'Gordon's parents were pacifists,' said Pam.

'They were Methodists,' said Gordon. 'Can't say I'm a Methodist though. It's a cruel outlook in many ways – especially for the children.'

Derek went out again.

A late-night comedy soap opera called *The Blighters* came on and Gordon said 'Do you want this?'

'No,' said Pam.

'I think I might try to do without my sleeping-pill to-night.'

'Yes, why don't you,' said Pam. 'That's a very good idea.'

She felt uneasy about the day. A discomfort in it had not been resolved. She went in search of Derek and found him sitting on the end of his bed with his back to the door. She intruded and asked in a gentle voice the great question: 'Would you like some Ovaltine?' He didn't stir. Pam looked about with lips tightening, not knowing whether to advance or retreat. Her conditioning suggested that when not in-the-know, retreat was wisest, leave alone, don't interfere, keep oneself to oneself, act as if there were no problem at all and she was about to go away again when the very act of turning caused a fine connection to tug and this roused her character which lay deeper from conditioning. She turned back into the room, moved forward and touched Derek's right shoulder. His head moved down and away to the left. She stroked the soft curls of his hair. He shuddered, turned slightly towards her. Pam placed the back of her hand quietly against his cheek and said almost in a whisper 'Let it go . . .' He turned away again, in slow motion. A little moisture was left on the back of her hand and she knew he was crying. An ache passed through her whole body and she drew his head against her. As she did so, Derek put his hand up as if to stop her. But it was a token gesture only, the last grain of pride dissolving in emotion. His hand was trapped softly between his cheek and her breast. He hardly realised it, but Pam realised, she felt a powerful current there as she drew the head more firmly against her body, felt the strength of Derek crying against her, a very private part of him that was revealing itself. Her head curved over his. Her lips were drawn down and she kissed his head, feeling reassured and strengthened as he sobbed and sobbed and sobbed against her.

10 red nails, still sticky – blow on them – phoooooooooh! – it's amazing how long nail varnish takes to dry, isn't it? – you blow on them and blow and twiddle your fingers about in the air and they take for *ever* – God, I've got an itch on my bum! – can't scratch it, not now, not with wet nails – God, it's a bore being a woman, all this fiddle and fart! – is that Bob? – *please* be Bob! – this itch is driving me CRAZY – yes, it's Bob, thank God, hurry up, you slob, I'm in *agony* . . . hurry, hurry . . .

'Bob!' said Marilyn, rushing into the hall as the key turned in the front door. 'Bob, quick, I've got this dreadful itch on my bottom, my nails are wet, thank *God*, no, the other side, up a bit, left a bit . . . a bit more, too much, right a bit. Stop! Urghhhh . . . . urrghhh . . . . . God, bliss . . . arrrrghhhh, urrrrrghhhhh . . . .'

Marilyn was on her hands and knees in the hall with her head thrown forward, propping herself up with one hand on the telephone chair and her fingers sticking out starfishlike to avoid marking it with red varnish, in a condition of total gasping surrender to the ecstasy of having an intense itch scratched by another. 'Harder, harder! Claw my flesh off!' Such are the joys of living in pairs. At this moment the phone went.

'Let's ignore it,' said Bob leaning across her back as he scratched her bum, and dribbling in her ear.

But Marilyn could never ignore the telephone. It would be like trying to ignore Christmas. Any form of approach stimulated her. Picking up the phone was *delicious* – like gateau – like a sneeze – like a bum scratch – like lighting a cigarette and the first puff – but like the cigarette, the phone was often downhill all the way after that tingly anticipatory *frisson* of picking it up and saying hullo. A few sticky fingernails weren't going to deny her that pleasure. Marilyn was not often denied her pleasure. And pleasure, with a big P or a small p, was the thing she most enjoyed in life. She was not one of those tiresome restless souls who can find pleasure and satisfaction only in supreme experiences. Marilyn was gifted with the ability of finding pleasure all over the place. At the same time hers wasn't a vague, diffuse personality.

Quite the contrary. For example, she liked sex, did Marilyn. 'Making love' she called it. She was a woman who let very little come between her and her orgasm – least of all a mere man. If Bob wasn't in the mood, she'd pull him about until he was, or anyway until she'd got her own rocks off. And if he was in the mood – so much the better. That's how it had been. Until lately. Until the last year or so. She'd always liked getting as close to him as possible when they were in bed. But now the reason was different. She got so close that their heads welded together and more than this, so that she passed right through him and out the other side, so that somehow he was behind her and by looking ahead she wouldn't see him. In this way Bob ceased to be there, became just a man, a fucking man with a fucking woman; because otherwise, if she didn't get close enough not to see him, if her face were a little way off and she looked at him, she would be forced to see that although she liked him a lot, she didn't love him any more, and perhaps never had loved him, and seeing this would make her sad and perhaps even congeal her passion into a mood unsexual. What did it mean? she asked herself. Was it a phase merely? Was it the first sign of the menopause?

The red-tipped starfish stretched out unsteadily, closed over the receiver and lifted it to her ear. 'Rorke's Drift,' she said, while Bob slaved at her hind quarters.

'Oh Marilyn, it's only Pam. We're taking Derek up to Chorley-wood on Sunday. I wondered if Cordelia would like to come.'

'That's very sweet of you, Pam. You mean as company for Derek?'

'Well, you know, he should meet more people his own age. From round here. But I just thought she might like to.'

'It's very sweet of you, Pam. I'll tell you what. She's not here at the moment. But when I see her, I'll ask her. And if she's coming I'll get her to ring you.' Marilyn, who was still on hand and knees, wriggled, trying to throw Bob off her back. He'd moved on from scratching her itch to feeling up her sundries.

'While I'm on the phone,' said Pam, 'can you come to Gordon's birthday party next month? The 29th.'

'Get lost . . .'

'What?'

'Sorry, it's – it's the dog. Yes, I know we can come because it's Bob's mother's birthday on the 28th – and we're not going there.'

Bob had rucked up her skirt and was sniffing and licking round her buttocks doggy fashion.

'Oh good, well, will you ask Cordelia to give me a ring?'

'Certainly, Pam. It's very sweet of you. 'Bye.' Marilyn replaced the receiver, threw her head forward, and turned 2 large eyes round to her husband and winked at him. He wasn't so bad, for a husband . . .

Later in the drawing-room – which Bob frequently called the lounge which drove her wild with rage since it destroyed at a stroke all their social pretensions – 'There are some things which just can't take polish, Bob, and *you're* one of them,' she'd say – later in the evening, in the drawing-room, she said to him 'We don't do our drives to Chorleywood any more . . .'

'We didn't go that often. Only when the kids were small,' said Bob, not looking up from the pages of *Electric Future*. 'That's so like a woman,' he went on, looking up, 'to try to make every little thing a routine. We take the kids up to Chorleywood a few times and we've got to *keep on* doing it, again and again and again, every week, same day, same time, for years and years and years, for ever and ever until the end of the world, until we all bloody choke to death on Chorleywood!'

'Oh, stop exaggerating,' she said.

Bob returned to his magazine. Marilyn muttered 'Slob' and went into another room and fiddled with some silk flowers in a vase. She liked artificial flowers. She put them everywhere, little bowls of them here, big vases of them there, hanging in dinky baskets from arches, sprouting promiscuously in corners and on landings. It wasn't just that they were convenient, didn't drop, didn't smell (as in nasty smelly brown water gone off!), lasted for ever with a quick rinse now and again. She *positively* adored the fact that they were artificial, weren't real. Reality, she wasn't frightened of it exactly – God, she'd known REALITY in her day, God yes – there'd been times, especially in the early days, when she'd had SODDING REALITY COMING OUT OF HER EARS!!! Oh yes, no, it wasn't fear of reality itself, but distaste; that is, fear of the state of affairs which might allow reality back in again. Poverty, of course. No chance of poverty now – Bob had all that buttoned up – even if the Company failed they had plenty put on one side. But reality rather disgusted her as though it belonged to an improper mode of life. Reality had a way of decaying, smelling, falling apart, reappearing without permission, and moving about. Yes, that was the trouble with reality: *Reality moves about too much.* Silk flowers *waited* to be moved. And yet looked everso real, EVERSO real – ha, but weren't! And they were that most wonderful thing – washable. Washable flowers. But not plastic, never plastic. Silk. Silk is tasteful. In fact silk is one of the most tasteful things you can have. Although . . . if Marilyn were shatteringly honest with herself, she'd have to admit that she still harboured a secret love for manmade fabrics. It was conceivable that in her heart of hearts Marilyn's paradise was a thing made wholly of nylon: washable, immutable, eternal.

However, there was in her a sweeter need not catered for by silk flowers and nylon carpets and it was this need which expressed itself in a desire to go to Chorleywood – that would be nice, in spring, now. God, Bob was so *boring* these days. She'd go by herself; no, take Cordelia; commune with Nature awhile; and come back and have a good long soak in the bath with her gorgeous Floris bath oils – all the woodland in a soap bubble! . . . . . Meanwhile, Marilyn 'forgot' to pass on Pam Drake's invitation to her daughter.

Gordon had had an appalling night. He hadn't slept a wink until 5 o'clock when, dazed by clarity, he'd finally swallowed a sleeping-pill – too late! At the office now he couldn't wake up, his head swam, and Bob rang.

'Who owns the freehold on Hogarth Parade, Gordon?'

'International Pink.' Gordon picked up a paperclip and started to fiddle with it. 'The leases come up for renewal next year – mine included.'

'I'd like to buy it. It needs redevelopment. I think I can get that one past the Council. Can you arrange a meeting with International Pink?'

'I should think so.'

'Don't tell them what I've got in mind.'

'Of course not. But it doesn't need redevelopment.'

'Don't you worry about that.'

Bob rang off. Gordon hadn't the foggiest idea what he was

setting in motion but he phoned a broker and obtained a quotation on International Pink – not very good, maybe they would be in the mood to sell off uninteresting properties. He phoned up another broker and found out something unpleasant about the Chairman. And after a morning of swimming about with a phone in his hand, he'd filled a jotter with incomprehensible figures, and had a frightful headache. Finally he phoned International Pink and arranged a meeting with someone of theirs, and Bob Dashman, and an Arab friend of Bob's with *superloot*, and himself. An exploratory meeting. Then Gordon put the phone down and said 'Argh!' He looked down to discover that he had been gripping the paperclip so hard that it had deeply pierced his fingertip, drawing blood.

The room was unexpectedly light. One felt exposed sitting in it.

'I can't stand lace curtains,' said the Major.

'My mum likes lace curtains,' said Derek. 'Pam has lace curtains. Most people have lace curtains, don't they?'

'I don't! Can't stand 'em!' repeated the Major with a degree of vehemence one would have thought lace curtains incapable of arousing. 'They remind me of – of – of soiled underwear. That's it exactly. *Soiled* underwear.'

'What an imagination you got, Major. That comes from all this reading.'

There were books everywhere in the room – in bookcases, on the floor, on tables, tossed down here and there, old ones, new ones, torn ones, the room was a soup of books.

'The gaffer's a book man,' continued Derek. 'Only mostly it's business books and newspapers.'

'I like Charles Dickens,' said the Major. 'But I get them all muddled up! *Great Chuzzlewit*, *Our Mutual Expectations*, *Hard Copperfield*, oh yes definitely *Hard Copperfield*! How about a whisky?'

'Bit early in the day for me.'

'You did a great job on my lawn. You any good at cars? My Riley's stuck in the garage. Daren't take it to a professional – they'd wreck it. Go on, join me in another whisky.'

'I haven't had one yet, so I can't have another.'

'That's logic. But it's not drinking. Where did I put my spectacles? Look, what I wanted to show you in the reading line was *this*.' The Major took a book from beneath a pile of others, knocking a number of things onto the floor, including an empty glass which smashed. 'Damn and blast! Here we are, awfully good, Tatlock's *The Legendary History of Britain*. Extreeeemely interesting. When I was a boy we used to stay at Tintagel in the summer, where Camelot and all that stuff is supposed to be. At the King Arthur's Castle Hotel. Great place on the cliff edge. I believe it's all quite ruined round there now. Holiday shacks and what-have-you. Won't go back, I simply won't. It's in Cornwall.'

'I've never been to Cornwall,' said Derek.

'Don't go. You'll be saddened. Where have you been?' asked the Major with an interrogatory twist of the eyebrow.

'I've been – not much. I went to Brighton – with the school once. I went to Clacton with my mum. That was great. And . . .'

'Doesn't sound like extensive travelling experience to me. We must get you off somewhere before long, yes, get you off. Look, give this one a try, Geoffrey of Monmouth's *Historia Regum Brittaniae*. It's old – don't let that deter you. Abridged by Alfred of Beverley. Full of lies, naturally. And fun! Travel – let me think. Yes, there is a book you might like, I don't have it, I lent it, it never came back, don't lend books now, but you can get a copy – *Here To-day, Gone To-morrow* – a study of death, wanderlust, the psychology of change and movement, totemism, iconoclasm, freedom. It's funny. *Damned* funny. Do you know this new school of philosophy, the Comic Philosophers? No, well, it's by one of them. Chap called Jervys O'Jimminy, Trinity College, Dublin. Starts out as an attack on Bishop Blennerhassett's *Heaven in my Rucksack*, but turns into something *much* meatier. Look, there's a box of orange juice at the back of the fridge. Go and get some. Can't stand you sitting there without a glass. You look naked. Do you smoke?'

Derek took one with an air of familiarity and the Major said 'Should be ashamed of yourself. Scragging up your lungs at your age. What *is* your age?'

'17.'

'Stay 17 as long as you can. Coz after 17 it's hellish!' And the Major rolled a long loud laugh between his belly and his throat.

Then he lit the cigarettes, bending forward in his chair with a lighter. 'Are they treating you all right?'

'What?'

'Pam and Gordon – are they treating you all right?'

'Oh. Yeah. Course. They're really nice.' Derek coughed lightly as he expelled smoke. 'He gets a bit serious sometimes.'

'He's a good man is Gordon,' said the Major, pursing up his face in such a way as to suggest that good men were a race apart and had to be treated as one might treat geriatrics or young children.

'Yeah. Course. I think she'd like me to have a job.'

'Don't you want a job?'

'Yeah. Course. But not any old job. Something interesting. With possibilities.'

'Clearly you are a most ambitious boy,' said the Major, flicking ash on the carpet. 'To-day it's lawns. To-morrow the sky. But what about the bit in between, that's what I'd like to know, the bit *in between.*'

'The bit where?' asked Derek.

'In . . . between . . .' said the Major slowly, bringing his finger forward and touching the point between Derek's eyes.

Derek smiled and said 'You'll make me boss-eyed.'

'I got their boy into the army, you know. Mark. Into my regiment. Death or Honour! That was our motto. He transferred to Defence. And is now doing extreeemely important work on chemical warfare.'

'You never got married then?'

'Me, Derek, got married?' echoed the Major. 'Yes. And do you know what happened? She left me. I was hopping mad at first. *Hopping* mad. Then I adjusted. A long time ago now. She couldn't have kiddies. I think she left me out of shame. The ability to drop calves, you know, is all tied up with a woman's sense of worth. What she left me *for* I couldn't say. There was a note. And that was that. Damn nuisance . . . . . I have a sister in Devon who said she ran across my wife 15 year ago. In Birmingham. The Bullring Shopping Centre. Outside a shoe shop. Recognised her immediately. Maureen – that was her name – my wife's, not my sister's – my sister's called Venice – yes, damn stupid name, but our parents had just come back from there and that's where she was conceived – I was conceived in Bognor, would you believe – jolly good job I wasn't called, well, anyway Venice recognised Maureen immeeeediately because Maureen had been in a car crash as a young woman and had a sort of built-up face on the left side – she said "You're Maureen, aren't you?" and Maureen said "You're Venice. How is he?" and Venice said "He's very well" and Maureen said "Oh", you know, as if she were disappointed about that, that's what Venice said anyway, and well, since then – nothing.' The Major swallowed a good inch of liquor, blinked deeply, and said 'What about you?'

Derek blushed, explaining in a jokey way that he wasn't married, had no one in mind to marry, didn't even have a girlfriend yet.

The Major replied 'No, no, no, no, no, I wasn't talking about *skirt*. I meant generally, the future, why not go into the army?'

'Yeah, I've thought about it. The navy actually. Can I go and get that orange juice?'

'And rejected the idea I suppose.'

'I don't like the idea of being sprayed with chemicals.'

'Good grief, man, we have to defend ourselves!'

'But I like the uniforms,' Derek shouted from the kitchen.

'Do you? Do you really?' the Major shouted back. He nodded thoughtfully and buried his mouth in the glass. When Derek returned he said to him 'Would you like to see mine?'

'You're what?'

The Major tutted with mock exasperation and said 'My *uniforms*.'

'Wouldn't mind.'

'He wouldn't mind . . . Well, they're in the wardrobe upstairs. Follow me.'

At the bottom of the staircase Derek hesitated. Going upstairs in these houses was like ascending to a new level of intimacy. There was an invisible gate at the bottom, passing through which was a rite of passage. Derek looked down at his dirty boots.

'Oh, don't mind them,' said the Major turning on the half landing. 'Take them off if it makes you happier. Come on up.'

The back bedroom was barely furnished with wardrobe, large plain bed, 2 chairs; it had no carpet. The Major rummaged in the wardrobe, sending billows of camphor into the room. 'Try this one,' he said, bringing out the half dress uniform. 'You're about my size. My size *then*. I've shrunk a bit.' The Major removed the jacket and trousers from the hanger and told Derek to take off his jumper and trousers. 'You've got good legs,' said the Major as Derek slipped into the trousers.

Derek eased on the jacket and said 'Got a mirror?'

'All that sort of thing's in the bathroom.'

The house was a reverse copy of the Drakes' and Derek went to look. He liked what he saw and said 'You're irresistible' to the mirror.

'Damn fine,' said the Major beatifically, coming in behind. He took a tooth mug from the glass shelf, swilled it under the tap (an old razorblade span out of it), and poured himself a slug of whisky from a bottle he kept in the laundry basket, for he maintained supplies both up and downstairs. He hid the bottle in the laundry basket not from a sense of shame because shame was not part of his character but to prevent guests from swigging it uninvited – the Major's guests would on the whole have done so without a second thought. 'Now let's try the battle dress.'

Derek changed into the battle dress.

'And the boots,' said the Major. 'The boots are important with this one.'

The uniform was too small for him and the boots very uncomfortable – also too small and age had hardened the leather.

'It's too tight,' said Derek, having popped into the bathroom for a look.

'Nothing wrong with it *at all*.' The Major offered him a cigarette.

'And there's a couple of buttons missing on the fly.' Derek sat in one of the chairs, banged the boots up and down on the floorboards, grinned and smoked. The heavy cloth of the trousers stretched tight across his thighs. The Major was very pleased.

'Have you got a gun?'

'No. I had to give that back. But I've got a beret.'

'That's not the same.'

The Major stood on the other chair and rummaged through the shelf above the clothes rail, saying 'Where is it? Where's the blasted thing?' He was creating quite a disturbance up there. There was a plop as something fell onto the floor.

'Oh,' said the Major.

97

'What's that?' asked Derek. He picked up the Sainsbury's plastic carrier bag and peeped inside.

'Nosey parker. Go on then. Fish 'em out.'

Derek found himself holding 3 pornographic magazines. One featured young naked women in erotic postures, splayed legs disclosing moist orifices, curving bosoms and buttocks, painted lips, half-closed eyes, hair flung carelessly about the head or sprouting around juicy pink holes. The second was of a white girl being gang-banged by 4 black boys with huge cocks in inventive, choreographed positions. The third was undraped male poses in a derelict warehouse.

'Ya dirty bugger,' said Derek jokily, but his head swam as he lingered among the pages with the Major at his side slurping from the tooth mug. '. . . This is giving me the horn,' said Derek. His voice had gone funny – croaky and far-away. The Major slid his hand over the bulge in the battle trousers, pushed apart the cloth of the unbuttoned fly, and with a neat manoeuvre freed Derek's trapped penis which sprang hot and damp into the air. As the Major massaged the thing with expert finesse, a long soft groan issued from the boy's throat and he fell dreamily into the sex photos which oozed across the warm clouded surface of his mind in oleaginous trails of multicoloured slime. The magazine was held in such a way as to shield the operations of the Major's hand from Derek's eyesight. But now he put the magazine aside, stood up, and undid the button of his waistband to allow the Major greater access. He began to weaken at the knees, gripping the Major's shoulder for support; then his head pressed hard onto the shoulder and he dribbled into the cloth of the Major's shirt. White jelly jumped out of the pink knob onto the bare floorboards.

Downstairs the Major gave Derek a substantial banknote, saying 'The lawn. And a bit extra. Don't suppose you've got much dough.' Derek's face went rosy with unexpected pleasure. 'Our secret?' queried the Major, with an interrogative lift of the eyebrows.

'Good grief, sir, what do you take me for?' said Derek.

The Major laughed and said 'Call me Vernon.'

Pam was in the kitchen preparing dinner. She was growing somewhat fatter than she liked to be – and she'd been neglecting her exercises. With Derek here, they'd been having full meals when she and Gordon might have made do with snacks. Gordon hadn't put on weight of course; he always stayed the same – lean, economical, alert, boney. She, however, blew up at the mere sight of anything *extra*. But she hadn't been lazy. Since Derek's arrival she'd been fully back in the saddle of family life. Cooking, cleaning, washing, worrying, collapsing, forgetting. She'd passed the menopause, but now colour once again came easily to her cheeks. At times she felt frothy and turbulent inside. She was more easily moved by events than in recent years, not saddened, but touched, so that her eyes moistened and even though tears usually didn't form she felt that they easily might and that if they did it was because of something wonderful, not something terrible. Not that there weren't terrible moments, moments when she wondered what the HELL was going on – but when hadn't life had such moments? Furthermore, in her inmost recess, her most recondite sanctuary, there was no longer that sense of a platform onto which she could drop in moments of crisis. Just a deep hole which went down and down and down to the very depths of . . . . . of what? She didn't know that one yet. And every day brought her something she didn't know. And this sense of existing in a state of not knowing was exciting. It implied that life was much larger than she was, that life was full of possibilities. Always to be living within the limits of the known, the predictable, the practised – this, she now felt, was not living at all, but merely functioning. That reliable platform had been a blockage, had blocked profundity. She had been happy enough with the blockage; her whole life indeed had been dedicated to its construction. But she knew now that the blockage was a cop-out, a settling for less, the closing off of an insupportable truth. The blockage had gone. And she felt more alive. *More* functioning. More vulnerable – but less precarious. Oh God, these paradoxes!

Derek was in the dining-room, bored, a bit low, having a casual look at Gordon's 'bumf'; letters, documents, solicitor's stuff. Derek was glad it wasn't his stuff. He'd never wanted to be a solicitor or anything remotely like that and, in the presence of the bumf, he knew he'd made the right decision. For example, a company called International Pink, head office Finsbury Circus, had written: *Dear Sir, With reference to our further meeting on the possible sale of Hogarth Parade, hereinafter called the property, on which occasion we begged to remind you that the siting of the dual carriageway extension, construction of which is scheduled to begin the year after next, will not interfere with the access road to the property except insofar as greater access will be provided and the value of the property thereby enhanced, and your subsequent offer, we beg to inform you that at the meeting of the board of International Pink Blue (Sales) Incorporated the aforementioned offer was held to be unacceptable, except insofar as the subsidiary properties, hereinafter called the subsidiary, may be excluded from the sale, the subsidiary having been delineated, at the afore-mentioned meeting, as . . . . .*

It droned on . . . Derek drifted into the kitchen and Pam said 'If you're bored, go and feed Gordon's fish.'

'Don't you fink about anyfing but fooood?'

'Think. Not fink. T-H. Ththththink.'

'Fink.'

Pam went hot, without deviating from her task at the kitchen table. When Derek was in a mood he sometimes exaggerated his cockney accent. She knew it was best to ignore this. But sometimes it got *right* under her skin.

'What are you doing?' he asked.

'Stuffing a chicken. Cooking tip, Derek. Always put an apple inside the chicken – it keeps it moist. Chickens can get very dry, you know.'

'I don't think I'll be stuffing many chickens in the immediate future.'

'Why not?'

'I don't cook.'

'Learn.'

'Not innarested.'

'What are your interests?'

'Films. Travel.'

'I see.'

'Yeah. Lots and lots of travel.'

A thought flashed through Pam's head. Italy. Gordon's sister's husband's cousin's wife's uncle was a man called Sir Glorian Jones. Pam and Gordon had once visited the bachelor knight's famous villa in Tuscany – for tea. Pam loved it but Gordon found the experience distasteful. 'Did you see what the butler was wearing? Swimming trunks,' was all he said of the occasion. When Pam later suggested that Derek might enjoy the experience of Italy, that perhaps Glorian Jones could find the boy a summer job, Gordon's reply was an emphatic 'No! And don't say anything to Derek.' Pam never mentioned the idea to Derek because she knew he'd go for it like a shot and this would lead to terrible problems with Gordon. Gordon was an unemphatic man but a man of principle. When he decided on a course of action he saw it through – in this case they had decided to take responsibility for Derek and would continue to do so until Derek was in a position to look after himself.

'But Gordon, a couple of months in Italy in the summer – he'd love it – surely it's worth a try?'

'Pam – no.'

And Pam knew better than to pursue the argument – but she never understood why Gordon was so set against Glorian Jones. This belief of Gordon's, that having made a decision one should carry it out, had enabled him to plough through all the problematic arrangements of life rather well. But the flaw in it was stubbornness. There was from time to time a brittle, artificial quality to these courses of action, a failure to respond to changing possibilities. And this was because Gordon's emotions weren't properly expressed by such decisions. His emotions were often repressed or indeed disconnected altogether from his actions. This case was more complex, however – Gordon was afraid that Jones would steal Derek from him.

Back to Pam and Derek in the kitchen. Pam said 'I don't suppose you'd travel as far as the shops for me, would you? I forgot the fresh basil for the salad.'

'We having salad? It's freezing out.'

'I thought it would make a change. But if you don't want to go—'

'No, no, I'll go. D'you want anything else?'

'Yes, I'll make a little list. Well, don't look so wretched about it.' She stopped what she was doing, rinsed her hands under the sink, and took up pen and paper, but before starting to write she looked at him and said 'Let's go into London this week. The West

End. I can do some shopping. We can get Gordon's birthday present, something from you, I know it's early, but it would be fun. Then we could see a film, have something to eat, pick up a hamburger.'

'Can't stand that American crap.'

Pam sucked in one cheek with a glitter in her eye. 'I give up. You're in one of your moods.'

At the shops, Derek, on walking past the butcher's, saw Marilyn Dashman queueing there for meat. She was wearing green silk trews, brown cowgirl boots, and a blue skiing jacket. Her hair was fluffed out in a burnished bell-shaped bonnet. She waved him over.

'Long time no see. How *are* you, Derek?'

'Great.'

'Sorry Cordelia couldn't come at the week-end. I bet she didn't telephone. She's terrible. But I bet you're just as bad.' She touched him coquettishly on the tip of the nose with her long gamboge fingernail. Derek screwed up his face and smiled bashfully without parting his lips. 'Anyway, you must come up to the house and say hullo. How about next Wednesday? Is that a good time for you? About 3 o'clock? I think she has a half-day holiday from school.'

Back at the house Derek said to Pam in as off-hand a way as he could manage 'Who's this Cordelia then? What's she like?'

'Did you get my basil?' asked Pam, going through the shopping.

'No. They'd run out.'

The Rape of Europa by Boucher. She and her mother had alighted at Baker Street, gateway to the world, and visited the Wallace Collection. She'd liked this painting, bought a postcard of it, and stuck it in the corner of her dressing-table mirror (a modern powder blue Louis Quinze-type dressing-table). Above it was another picture, of the international tennis phenomenon Rot Gurke. She loved him. He looked so easy to play with. Her mother teased her about it – then the mother confessed that as a girl she'd been secretary of the Brandon de Wilde Fan Club –

Brandon, oh Brandon, so compulsive in *Blue Denim*, 17 years old – I need you, Brandon! – He was dead at 30 after a car crash. It was a tragic story – let her mother have it! Cordelia yearned for Rot Gurke, *brilliant* NOW – therefore, tragedy to come – tragedy in the future is much more exciting than tragedy in the past – it really wakes you up! Also Rot struck her as being quite unlike her father, a definite plus point since she was finding her father a pain in the neck. Perhaps it was only a phase – she was slightly guilty about it. She knew girls at school who were really pashed on their fathers – the desires they confessed to, enough to make yer crewcut drop out. She'd had a crewcut – adored it in the mirror and gone *right* off it the moment she'd walked out of the hairdresser's. But it was already growing brilliantly . . . . .

Cordelia, the Princess of Rorke's Drift, and one of the most beautiful girls ever born, slid the Boucher postcard back into the mirror frame and, deciding not to think about Daddy (who was such a bloody peasant sometimes, said such rude inconsiderate things to her in front of other people, passing it off as a joke, but she knew he meant it, oh yes, he was simply using the joke justification in order to humiliate, be horrid, embarrassing – why did he like to insult her in this way? did he get a sick thrill out of it? did he have to show off in front of other people at *her* expense? pure Freud fodder), she let herself fall onto the bed as if cut down from a gibbet, so that her legs flopped into the air and went thunk down onto the eiderdown again. She clamped a pair of light-weight earphones over her head and pressed a button in the navel of a tiny tape recorder. Pop music in 2 jets from left and right spurted through her eardrums, splashed together and flooded her brain – *Something Smells Good* by the Hooters from their hit album *Doers Are Sexier Than Dreamers* – a series of chord changes did something painful and gorgeous inside, the punching brass coming in from God knew where gave her goose pimples, the heavy tugging bass – obscene – it got into her – obscene . . . and the voice went down her back like hot lemonade. Anal Mucus, the lead singer, was so . . . no, she preferred Rot . . . Oh God, her father pissed her off. What did he do? Make kitchen gadgets – this wasn't nearly romantic enough for her – right now Daddy was 'bad news'. Cordelia was at the age when the world, the universe, life itself, was divided into 'good news' and 'bad news'. Her brother Ward was 'good news'. One day when Cordelia was fretting about why couldn't Daddy be a Painter or an Ambassador or even a Theatrical Agent (the father of one of her schoolfriends was a theatrical agent – they were very poor and would soon have to sell their house because of the theatrical agent's alcoholism, but Cordelia didn't know this), Ward had calmed her by saying 'The father of Sophocles was a factory owner. He made armaments.' That was what a posh school did for you. Taught you how to handle the difficult equations simply by rising above them.

– I wish I was away at school, she thought. The music crashed in her head. *Love Boot* –

> *Oh Love Boot*
> *You're so cute*
> *Give me a kiss*
> *Splash me with piss*
> *It means so much to me*
> *Ah . . . Love Booooooooooooooooooooooooooooot*

With the music fixed to her head, the fair Cordelia rose from the eiderdown, skimmed over to the dressing-table mirror and shimmied at her reflection in it, floating on the driving beat, lost to the world . . . . .

Derek was lying on his bed, absent-mindedly playing with his foreskin. It was a week-day, he was half-dressed, supposedly going to the Job Centre. He'd been a few times, jobs as waiters or cleaners. Nothing with travel in it. Maybe he'd have to take a job as a waiter or cleaner eventually, to get his hand in, but the pressure had yet to reach that point of desperate need and . . . and anyway his thoughts drifted not in that direction but in the direction of Jervys O'Jimminy's *Here To-day, Gone To-morrow* . . . Now Derek was not a book boy but he was far from illiterate and he was at that age when the urge to discover is strong and generalised and might follow anything which crosses its path. So Pam was surprised but not staggered when he said 'I'm going on to the Library after the Job Centre.'

'But aren't you assuming there won't be a job interview to go to?' she asked.

'I've been thinking, Pam. If nothing interesting [he pronounced the 't's so deliberately that it was almost like spitting] turns up soon, I'll be a waiter or a cleaner.'

She was sewing a button on a shirt, put it down, went across and gave him a hug. She didn't feel awkward about this any more, though Derek was always a bit flustered by it. Pam saw this but knew it was good for the boy to be hugged. She stroked his neck and behind the ears where the hair curled, while he remained stiff, allowing it to happen. The neck at the nape seemed so powerful and so vulnerable. She kissed it where the loose collar drooped and felt a surge of emotion which wasn't quite the same as the emotion she'd felt with Mark. She kissed his ear to make it ring, as a jocular way of breaking the hold upon her of this rich emotion, and said 'Perhaps we should have a family conference in a couple of weeks – when you feel it's the right time. See if we can be more systematic and at the same time more imaginative about your future. You're a bright boy, Derek. But brightness dulls through lack of use.'

'Is that a line from a poem?'

'I don't think so. I think I just said it.'

'I'd like to talk about the future.'

'Good. In the meantime, if you're going to the Library, can you take a couple of books back for me?'

'OK.' But he said it with ill-grace. He was beginning to get the hang of women. He was irritated by the fact that if you told a woman your movements she always managed to lumber you with doing something for her too, always managed to wind a little bit of her business into your business. It was one of the ways women trapped men – with these little entanglements – so that when you did something for yourself, you'd be doing something for her too, and you'd continue to be aware even when alone that you were part of a relationship with *her*. But sometimes you want to go cleanly your own way. It is important for a man to be able to do this – but if you complain that you don't want these teensy little ribbons of her curled round your day, she complains that you are selfish, unreasonable, and that they are such small things and can be accomplished so easily at the same time as you are doing what you are doing. And all this is perfectly true, which is the cleverness of it. Yet it is the very triviality of these nagging intrusions that is so irritating, this constant fiddly hankering of the woman to be remembered in *your* day as if her own day is insufficient reason for her to be alive – and all you want to be is disengaged for a while – clean and free for a while – why don't they understand this without getting all upset and insulted?

But with repressed anger he put Pam's 2 books into a plastic bag: *On She Swans*, the autobiography (volume 2) of Una, Dowager Marchioness of Prestonpans, and *More Puddings* by Veronica Kilderkin (Pam had got Gordon's Ms Harding to photocopy the desirable recipes at the office and they had been returned to her in a smart clear plastic folder neatly labelled).

The Job Centre wasn't very life-enhancing. He chatted to a girl he'd chatted to on his first visit but hadn't seen there since. She'd been in a car crash and had lost an ear. She was quite phlegmatic about it and had very short hair. Also she was ugly.

'I freak them out,' she said.

'Who?'

'Employers.'

'No, I'm sure they understand,' said Derek.

'That's even worse. I don't want sympathy and charity. I just want a job. When I sense that they might offer me one merely out of pity, I run a mile. I couldn't work with pity round me. It's disgusting is pity.'

'But you gotta start somewhere. You can always find objections if you look hard enough.'

'What about you? You're good-looking. It should be easy for you.'

'Only up to a point. After that it's harder.'

'Why's that?'

'Because if you're good-looking, no one takes you seriously. Or they might even distrust you.'

'I think, mate, you're having yourself on.'

Derek felt put out by this and the conversation stopped. He thought about life as a railway-train and wondered whether Jervys O'Jimminy had hit on that notion. Looking down the list of jobs, he felt that those on offer weren't good enough for him, didn't do justice to his amazing potential, so he moved on . . . . .

The Library was a redbrick Edwardian building, with white stone dressings, and a green-capped cupola at either end of the main façade and a complex central doorway in which all the elements of classical architecture and a few new ones jockeyed for supremacy. Derek said to the youngish woman at the desk who wore her hair in a fat brown plait down her back and whose complexion was the colour of suet, 'I'm bringing these back'. Then he took a deep breath and said 'Have you got *Here To-day, Gone To-morrow* by Jervys O'Jimminy, a study of death, wanderlust, the psychology of change and movement, tot. . .er, totemism, iconoclasm, freedom?'

She flicked her small green eyes at him and said 'No.' Her surprise at a boy like this asking for a book like that almost animated a countenance on which indifference had gone very deep.

'He's one of the Comic Philosophers,' added Derek by way of completing what he'd learned.

'And the reason I know we haven't got it,' went on the youngish woman, pulling a tiny ball of fluff off her brownish jumper, 'is because someone took it out 10 minutes ago. It's one of those surprise hits.'

'Oh,' said Derek, nonplussed. He didn't know what to do next, and had the sensation of being on alien territory. He thought his request had offended the woman's sense of what was proper – she thought him unworthy of the Comic Philosophers and this made him plunge inside.

In fact she was thinking – What an interesting young man.

A short old woman in a black coat brushed past him, dumped her books on the counter, and went on in. Then inspiration struck and he said 'Have you got any of the other Comic Philosophers?'

She didn't reply even with so much as a glance but came out from behind the counter and marched off in the direction of the stacks. On the brave assumption that it might be what he was supposed to do, Derek followed her, and eventually both of them arrived at a wall of colourful tomes with titles such as *Wittgenstein's Shame* and *Kierkegaard: One Man's Problem* and *Getting On Top Of Kant*. The woman sank onto her heels, fingered books down there, then stood up and said 'No.'

'Oh,' said Derek.

'They're very new,' said the woman, knocking back her plait which had intruded over one shoulder. 'And they're very few. Do you want to reserve something? The other good one is *Notes on Secrecy* by James Thorne. He was blown to bits by terrorists. Not very comic.'

She grimaced hideously and Derek became alarmed. He suddenly felt he was getting in too deep – they'd ask for his name & address next. He looked about and seemed to be surrounded by smelly weirdoes in grubby clothes. In this particular section of the Library he now became aware of a revolting odour and saw a tramp in pebble spectacles buried in *Plato: Another Man's Problem* – Derek could read the title because it was a specially printed king-size edition for readers with bad eyesight. The rancid smell of an unwashed body in unwashed clothes in an unventilated space swirled oppressively round him. The library assistant sniffed and said 'I hate my job sometimes', poured over the tramp a look of extreme disgust and marched away. The box vent in the derriere of her skirt opened and closed to the beat of her steps.

Derek was about to leave too, feeling an urgent want of fresh air, when the short old woman in the black coat touched his arm and said 'You're the boy next door.'

He stared down at her. She wore a pair of National Health spectacles in pink frames Sellotaped together over the bridge, and a plaster which had once been flesh pink but was now heavily soiled covered one lens. 'Am I?' he said nervously.

'Yes. We've seen you. We see most things. Even in bad weather.'

'Really?' said Derek, edging away.

'Oh yes. It's not difficult. When you know how,' continued the old lady, adjusting her spectacles on her nose. 'Have you found what you want?'

'No.'

'Do you know what you want?'

'Yes.'

'Well, that's something. You know more than most people your age. But perhaps you've been looking in the wrong place.'

'No, they've got it. But it's out.'

'It's elsewhere. That's always maddening, isn't it? You've got a better colour than when you first arrived in the Rise. Things get easier, don't they, with time?'

'Yes,' said Derek, beginning to feel upset. 'But I haven't met you before.'

'That's right. My name's Eunice Chivers. I live next door.'

'Hullo. I have to go now.'

'I can tell that. But listen. Pop in for tea one afternoon. And Sibyl will read your tea-leaves.'

'Tea-leaves?' asked Derek much more loudly than he'd intended. A number of heads on long necks looked up and looked round from chairs and cubicles like shocked flamingoes. Ill-humour beamed from their eyes before they returned to their print.

'Tea-leaves?' questioned Derek again, in an intimate hush.

'Yes,' replied Eunice in a like manner. 'She's good at the tea-leaves is Sibyl. She'll probe your depths, elicit your innermost secrets past *and* future. She's highly intelligent. She studied at university. Probe your depths she will.'

Derek was now extremely nervous. It was as if thousands of insects were crawling between his skin and his clothes. 'OK. Thanks. Good-bye,' he said.

'And I'll tell you why you'll find it interesting. Because—'

But Derek had fled.

Next Wednesday afternoon at 3, Derek, washed and combed and brushed, made his way up the road to call on the fair Cordelia and pay his first visit to Rorke's Drift. The drive seemed to be ages under his feet. He reached the door and pressed the bell. There was a ding-dong within, followed by an incredible racket as a dog launched itself in frenzy against the door from the other side. Derek automatically drew back. A voice said 'Stop it, Albert, you big softie'. Marilyn opened the door and glancing at his white trousers, said 'Hullo there. She's not here. But come in anyway.' Marilyn was wearing a green silk dress flared in the skirt and buttoned up the front and high heels in royal blue silk. Derek entered the hall and immediately found himself in a vast space that was threatening, opulent and incomprehensible all at once. The threat came specifically from Albert who bristled dangerously and bared his teeth in snarls of mindless Pavlovian hate. 'He won't hurt you,' said Marilyn matter-of-factly. She addressed the dog in a deep voice. 'Albert, this is a friend.' Albert calmed down, sniffed and admitted the newcomer, who became a friend – of such are morons made.

The hall, which was very large, was cream and white and gold. It went the whole height of the house and from the ceiling hung a large cut-glass chandelier on a thick gold chain. Ahead of him the staircase swept up in a curve of cream carpet and gilded banisters; and beneath him the carpet felt soft and enveloping, gave subtly to his tread, so that he felt he was treading in the fur of a mysterious beast. The hall shone and told of an existence altogether out of this world. Tall windows looking onto the drive carried full-length golden curtains festooned and draped and caught at the waist with brocade tassels. It was *light* – there were no net curtains, just a view of the garden, pots of geraniums along the drive, and the small fountain of Cupid standing on one chubby leg which Bob had picked up from a demolished vicarage years ago when he was still interested in things other than making money and the weekly bang. Yes, it was *light*. Marilyn knew why people in small houses had nets – she too liked her privacy. But she knew they looked silly in big houses. Marilyn had left nets behind in her gilded glide upwards. 'Sorry about the mess,' she said.

– What mess? thought Derek. He was dazed.

'And very sorry about Cordelia,' she continued. 'Silly me, what a silly creature I am, I simply forgot – she's gone riding. She normally has Wednesday afternoon off – they go to school on Saturday instead. But she'd arranged to go riding. Miles away. Mill Hill. With a friend. She won't be back for ages. Still, all is not lost.'

She gave Derek a fruity look, full and luxurious like the house, and it shocked him because he didn't expect such fullness and luxury from Mrs Dashman's look. He was reminded of a look once given him by Joy, his mother's friend, but he couldn't have specified the resemblance since both women were very different in every way but this.

'Come into the drawing-room,' she said . . . . . A vision of blue and gold and white opened before him, with big chunky

110

glass bits and chunky gilt bits and china bits dotted about in it. 'Sorry about the mess.'

Derek thought – What mess? – what's this mess she keeps on about? – it's a dream of perfection as far as the eye can see and she keeps calling it a mess. He felt transcendentalised.

'Mary doesn't come to-day,' she said. 'Wednesday is the only day she doesn't come. Apart from week-ends of course. Because I like to have some time alone – and if Cordelia's here we can be alone together. We enjoy that. I'm sorry she's not here to-day. But I've got a gateau from Plummer's. A big one – with fruit – and cream. And a sponge so light it's like eating, er, God, it's like eating—' Her mind had unaccountably gone blank and she couldn't think of a simile which sufficiently conveyed the experience. So she said 'I must watch my figure. I could get fat. But I'm lucky – I burn it up, that's what I do, *burn* it up.' She gave him another fruity look which made Derek look away into the logs of an artificial gas fire flickering cleanly in a fake Adam fireplace. 'Do sit down,' she said, 'and tell me all about yourself.'

Derek chose a remote armchair. She sat down in one corner of a very long blue and gold sofa and it exhaled a voluptuous breath as she did so. Now she crossed her legs and Derek noticed out of the corner of his eye that the bottom 2 buttons of her skirt were undone. Through the opening in the green silk, a lightly tanned knee obtruded. She touched her hair at the back with the delicate tips of her red fingernails and said 'The important thing is – are you liking it here?'

Derek nodded and said 'I think so' but there was a croak in his voice and he coughed, putting his fist up to his mouth, and said in a clearer voice 'I think so, yeah.' Derek now sank back into the armchair and he thought he'd never stop sinking.

'Lovely woman, Pam,' she said.

'Yeah.'

'And Gordon's very clever. You could learn a lot from Gordon.'

'Oh yeah. I can tell that.'

She sighed deeply, and her bosom rose and fell like the sea. 'But I suppose you get a little bored.'

'Nah.'

She smiled indulgently. Such a polite boy.

111

'Well, yeah. A bit,' he confessed.

'No girlfriends?'

'Nah. Not yet.' He blushed deeply. His lips too seemed to turn a richer raspberry red. Hot moisture prickled on his brow. He sat forward in the armchair, leaning further forward between his knees, as if to escape the predatory bear hug of padded blue and gold upholstery. If he sat back, it was like being drunk – he had the sensation of sinking endlessly backwards in a nauseating marine roll.

'Plenty of time for that,' she said, while Derek held on tight to one of his little fingers. 'And I'm sure you won't have any trouble finding one.' A couple of inches of flesh now appeared above the knee as, miraculously, the skirt seemed to rise subtly of its own volition. 'A good-looking boy like you,' she added, softening her gaze, curving her smile, tilting her head forward ever so slightly . . . . . ever so slightly. Derek's finger slipped suddenly from his grasp and at this moment she rapidly crossed over her legs the other way (simultaneously straightening up her back) so that one lightly tanned knee was replaced by a flash of golden inside thigh only to be replaced in the green silk aperture by the other lightly tanned knee. In straightening her back the ample breasts were pushed forward and lifted up, firm milky breasts divided by an expert cleavage which now came into view because, Derek noticed, the top button of the dress had – astonishingly he hadn't seen it happen – come undone. A royal blue high-heeled shoe wagged slightly in mid-air. It was connected to the knee by a smooth shin and a curved calf muscle. She reminded him – except that the hair was a different colour – of Elizabeth Taylor, his favourite actress. At which point, with a shock that was like a grasshopper leaping in the pit of his stomach, Derek noticed that Mrs Dashman wore no stockings.

'We can have tea. But would you like to see the house first?'

Derek nodded. His expression was one of utmost seriousness, as if one of the Eleusinian Mysteries were about to be vouchsafed him. The tour began, of course, upstairs. They ascended in silence to a half-landing which had 2 chairs on it, a table and a vase of multicoloured silk flowers. Derek wondered why such an amenity should be available halfway up a staircase but was not disposed to mention it. They continued to the top where, with a sensual rush, the vista of the landing, perhaps Marilyn's most sublime creation, opened before them. It was galleried round 3 sides with golden banisters but had a large space of its own beyond where hung a second cut-glass chandelier. Marilyn switched it on and rainbows shot across the walls. To the basic cream, white and gold theme of the hall below were here added daring strokes of red. The cornice was painted geranium red. 2 vases of red silk flowers stood on matching wall tables and their reds went all the way from deep dried-blood maroon, through crimson and scarlet, to the palest pink. A mock Chippendale chaise-longue upholstered in geranium velvet stood at the far end beneath a round-topped window which carried maroon velvet curtains opulently draped, and trimmed with gold and vermilion taffeta; on either side hung huge gilt baroque mirrors. Undoubtedly, here, sheer force of character, backed up by money, had won through in a brilliant *coup de théâtre*. Indeed the commitment of the whole had gone beyond questions of good or bad taste and powerfully redrawn the rules on its own terms. Vulgar? Perhaps. But to say so would miss the point, as if one had attempted to describe an ocean by calling it wet. Some chunky glass bits were dotted about. On the left an artificial log fire like the one in the drawing-room was flickering in a real marble fireplace. Such a fire on an upstairs landing with a gilt and magenta velvet chair on either side of it produced an effect of almost royal sumptuousness.

'Do you want to use the bathroom?' she asked.

'No thanks,' he replied before the question was finished.

'If you do, there's one there,' she said pointing to a pair of double doors in front of her. 'And another one there,' she said, turning to a single door on her right.

Derek was dying for a pee and realised with a twitch that this was probably what she meant and that he'd better stop being silly and take advantage of the offer if he hoped to get through the next 5 minutes, let alone tea and gateau, so he said 'Yes, I think I better.'

She barged ahead through the double doors and he found himself not in a bathroom but in an enormous lilac and lemon satin bedroom with chunky glass bits and porcelain bits. One whole wall was cupboards and there were French windows with curtains covered in baby bows giving onto a wrought iron balcony. 'The bathroom's through there,' she said. It was her bathroom. Her's and Bob's. There were 3 bathrooms in the house, 2 upstairs and one downstairs, and 2 separate loos. But she wanted him to use hers. He went into it and as he brushed past her she caught the sharp odour of nervous sweating in his armpits.

Derek found himself in a bewildering, mirrored space of inde-terminate size. It had a round bath in the middle in avocado and black stripes, plants, cane chairs, a cork floor, and of course various chunky glass bits filled with things. Firstly he had his pee – the odd-shaped walls were completely mirrored and he saw dozens of Dereks slashing into dozens of avocado and black striped pans. 'Cor,' he said, shaking off the last drops.

'Fun, eh?' she said behind him. He hadn't put his cock away and now did so quickly, startled, turning quickly round, and catching his forehead on the corner of a mirror-fronted wall cabinet he'd not noticed because of the multiple mirrored perspectives.

'Ow!!!' he yelped, clutching his head.

'Oh God!' she expostulated, wincing and screwing up her face empathetically. She drew him into the bedroom and sat him on the bed and said 'Let me see, sweetheart'.

Derek was seeing stars and let her see, burbling 'Cor . . . my head . . . my . . .' He felt weakened, humiliated, sick, and swal-lowed deeply the saliva which welled up in his mouth. She was gone and she was there again, standing over him with cold water in a black flannel. She soothed his forehead coming up in a lump, dabbing it with coolness.

'Better?' she asked.

'Yeah . . .' he murmured, opening his eyes again, and in doing so he saw cleavage. She was leaning over, dabbing his brow and (he hadn't seen when it was but presumed it was only a moment ago) a second top button had come undone, giving greater freedom to her breasts which rolled heavily against each other as gently she plied the cold flannel.

'Is that better? Is that better?' she was saying softly, smoothing the hair off his brow, very sweetly stroking his temples, very delicately blowing on his bruise, and with her other hand she was stroking the other side of his head with such caressing attention that he began to melt warmly inside in the most curious and wonderful way. The surface of his skin and the circumference of

114

his perception were simultaneously dissolving into a warm vapour. Demarcation between the inner world and the outer world wobbled and gave way. He felt drunken and dreamy – but not at all tired. And he felt a distant autonomous pressure which was his penis rising against the cloth of his trousers. He didn't want it to – he wanted it to stop. But the more he said no, the more the penis said yes. He was trembling – very gently – trembling.

'Let's kiss it better, kiss it better,' she murmured, leaning further forward to kiss his brow and he saw that a third button had somehow come undone and her left breast was almost out – he wanted to see the nipple, he had to see that fucking tit out, he wanted to touch the breast, grip the nipple, feel with his fingers what the nipple was like – but he dared not move – and at this moment he saw Marilyn lift red nails to the fourth button and deftly untwist it. Her left breast swung slowly free of the bra and came to rest weightily against his cheek and nose making a booming noise in his head – it smelt wonderful – it smelt like *everything* – and he moved his cheek backwards and forwards over it. She brought the teat against his lips and he started licking at it with curls of his pink tongue and tenderly chewing it . . .

Her eyes closed in pleasure as she held the boy's face against her exposed breasts where he licked with relish, sucked like a baby, chewed, kissed, and lost himself in a world of plenty. 'Lick it better, lick it better,' she whispered from afar, like a goddess, while Derek's face became wet with his own saliva and he made snouting noises, slurps and grunts. Part of him, a rapidly diminishing part, was still alert to events in the objective world and this part registered her green silk dress floating softly to the floor with a faint hiss; it stopped diminishing and started increasing when she started to pull off his jumper from the waist upwards but he obediently raised his arms. He was disconcerted when she unbuttoned his shirt and was aware of an intense heat suffusing his face. She unhooked her bra, which was the barest support, and shook her shoulders forward. It fell into his lap. This made him downright self-conscious, as if the sight of the full breasts, complete, unobscured, free of all impediment, surging mightily before his eyes, was too much to swallow at one sitting. He was embarrassed – but the embarrassment contained no thought at all of escape. He was flustered – but she saw this and proceeded.

'Take your shoes off,' she said. He looked aghast, as if the door had spoken. But being thankful for a familiar task to do, he bent down, undid the laces and slipped them off. 'And the socks,' she said. 'I can't stand it when the socks are last.' He thought she was speaking a kind of personal gibberish but did as he was told. The blush had descended down his neck to his chest. She drew him to his feet, undid his trousers, and pushed – he promptly sat on the bed again and she said 'No, no, take them off.' Gauchely he stripped off his trousers and pants and stood up, his arms hanging cluelessly at his side, his penis sinking before him. But this coincided with Marilyn's removing the royal blue high heels which reduced her by many inches, making her altogether less intimidating. And when, finally, she took off her white lace panties, Derek was mesmerised. A furry prospect held his attention and his penis started up again.

Her first thought on seeing the naked boy was – It's bigger than Bob's one. She pushed him backwards onto the bed.

'Hey, watchadoing?' he croaked weakly, overbalancing onto his back. He stared down his belly to see her crawling up the lilac counterpane towards him. But she stopped at the point where his member emerged from a clump of fur, and his whole apparatus now disappeared beneath the gyrations of Marilyn's hair-do. Derek, who'd never been treated like this before, threw his head back among bed cushions – Christ, the sensation had to be filed under pleasure but it was too much, it wasn't comfortable – he whined. Aaaaaaaaaaah . . . She assumed he liked it but he liked it more when she stopped working on the knob of his penis, which was too crazily tingly, and like aah . . . moved about. Her mouth and tongue explored the fruitful jungle of his loins – the loins unclenched – relaxed – undulated – drowning in electric bliss . . .

She loved the musky, ferny smell of him. She raised her head up from her business and said 'You're beautiful. You smell of you. Not of soap. Not of yesterday. Just you – clean – to-day,' and leered towards him along the fine line of hair which grew up to his navel. He looked down towards her with an expression of utter horror and terror on his face, his mouth pulled back from his teeth as if he were in pain – he shot out a mass of spunk, wailing

116

. . . he wailed . . . and she wailed, she was wailing. He'd shot a dollop of it into her right eye and she was wailing 'Oh God, it stings, it *stings*, oh God! My contact lens!' She ran into the bathroom and swilled her eye. 'God, I didn't know it could sting so much.'

'I'm sorry, I'm sorry, I'm sorry,' beseeched Derek from the bedroom. 'I'm sorry, I'm sorry, Mrs Dashman.'

'For fuck's sake call me Marilyn,' she requested. 'I've lost my sodding contact lens.' In a minute she came back into the bedroom, with one eye screwed up and a black towel in her hand with which she mopped at the sperm.

'It's made a mess,' he said.

'It's supposed to,' she said, giggling.

His feet were drawn towards him, his knees were apart, and his hand covered his genitals. This hand she removed, replacing it with one of her own. 'It's hot enough to cook eggs between your thighs,' she said, adding 'Your strong hairy thighs.'

The description of his thighs as strong and hairy caused him further embarrassment – he didn't know why – which became not less when she took his member between red-nailed thumb and forefinger and said 'Cootchy-cooh'. This however soon became a minor aspect of his hotness, and by the time she had hauled her whole body on top of his, embarrassment had been entirely swallowed up by a concern for breathing. A significant weight was on his chest and a great face, tasting of everything except humanity, was on his face. They were kissing. He was inside her. Yes, he could breathe. He started to get the hang of it. But he was thrown out of gear when she started to bounce up and down on top of him in a manner which became more and more furious, clawing at his shoulders, making death rattle noises, gurgles, and sharp roars. He uttered short gasps of pain as she clawed at his back in frenzy, bounced and pushed at him. Then the phone rang . . . She froze in mid-air, came down on him with a mighty crash, rolled over and picked up the receiver. Derek bellowed unstintingly as his balls, between his strong and hairy thighs, were crushed.

She put her hand over the mouthpiece, whispered 'Quiet', and said into it with weird composure 'Rorke's Drift.'

'It's only me, darling. Did I interrupt you?'

117

'What? Oh Bob. *Darling*. God, no! Of course not.'

'You sound out of breath. Been at the yoga again?'

'God, no. Yes! Of course! Phew-eeeeee . . .'

'Don't overdo it. You'll pull something. Just to say I'll be back a bit earlier. I've got to go through some papers with Gordon Drake.'

When the receiver was back in its proper place, she gazed at Derek for a little while and broke into a soft beautiful laugh. It wasn't a giggle or a chuckle, it was a laugh, but short, intimate, sweet, and it enchanted him. The intrusion of the husband had freaked him.

'Is my back bleeding?'

'Only a little,' she said, stroking him, reassuring him, thinking – He's young, clean, inexperienced, uninfected, and I can do what I like with him. Awkwardly he touched her too. And now she drew him on top of her, drew him down, and their necks twined and she enclosed him within her centre which clasped his penis and with her arms which enfolded his body and ran over his buttocks and slowly he started to move within her. They rolled over and over. He was quite dizzy – one moment on top, the next beneath. His motions became freer, more extreme. As he rolled from beneath to on top, he held her there, pinned her down. His haunches moved upon her with freedom, fucking her. He didn't give a damn about whether he was satisfying her or not. He was using her, having her.

And she didn't give a damn about whether she was satisfying him. She was using him, having him. She was having her first teenage boy. It's great – he's screwing me – SCREWING me – I'm pulling him, PULLING it OUT of him – PULLING PULL-ING – be my boy, my juicy rotter, yeah, be my juicy rotter – bite your neck – smell your hair – rough legs against me – hard chest heavy on me – young bristles rubbing my face – moving hot, hot, hot, hot! – they both felt the Great Spasm rising in them – and he went at her, knocked her whole body with a crude aggression of his centre and her tits were knocked up towards her chin and fell back, knocked up, fell back, knocked up, fell back –

ooooooOOOOOOOO – aaaaAAAAAAAAAHHH!!!!!!!!!!! – !!! . . . . !!! . . . . . . !!! . . . . . . !!! . . . . !!! . . . . . . !!! . . . . !! . . . u . . . g . . . h . . . . . ! . . ! . . ! . . .

118

```
. . . . . ! . . . . . . . . . . . . ! . . . . . . . . . ! . . . . . . .
. . . . . . . . . . . . . . . . . . . . . ! . . . . . . . . . . . . . .
. . . . . . . . . . . . u . . . g . . . h . . . . . . . . .
. . . . . . . . . . . . . . . . . . . . . . .
. . . . . . .
. . . . . .
. . . ! .
. . . .
. . .
. .
.
.
.
mmmmmmmmmm . . . . . . . . . . . . . . . . . . .
                      .
                      .
                      .
                    m
                    m
                    m
                      .
                      
                      .
```

Afterwards she went and clothed her nakedness in a fetching, floating ensemble. Derek wrapped a towel round his middle. 'This is silly,' she said laughing. She took off her ensemble and dragged the towel off him. They lay against each other on the bed, cooling. She leant across and kissed him long and softly on the lips and afterwards he smiled at her, a smile which just came, without any thought.

But eventually cogitation and motive returned. She said 'You were rough – I loved it. Have you ever done this with Pam?'

He looked at her, shocked 1) by her assessment – surely he hadn't been rough, *she* had; and 2) by the crudeness of her question, the inanity of it, and said almost under his breath 'Cor . . . blimey . . . Yeah, Pam and me, every night.' Then he gave a laugh which was a cackle.

119

She was put out. 'Well, I don't know what you do . . . . What do you like best?' She wanted sex talk, she wanted more . . .

But he replied 'Liquorice Allsorts'.

'No, no . . .'

'And films. Some films. I saw a great one on the box the other day, *X, Y & Zee*, Michael Caine, Elizabeth Taylor, Susannah York – brilliant, from another era – really, you know, *open*. People were less afraid in those days. Did you see it?'

'No . . . . .'

'And I like this house,' he said.

'Silly boy.' She pushed him playfully in the ribs and he giggled. She went on, floundering somewhat (to her own surprise), 'I mean – what do you want?'

'I don't want money or anyfing,' he said, exaggerating his accent and adopting a mock-earnest expression which squeezed his eyebrows together.

'Cheeky bugger,' she said, forcing a smile, but offended inside that he'd thought of such a thing, however jokily, during the *après*. She slapped him lightly on the cheek. An uncertainty flickered in his eyes. She was sorry she'd done it. He was young and the young often took the wrong things seriously. Besides, they didn't know each other. Many uncertainties flickered in the wings. So she ran her face over his face and said 'You smell gorgeous.'

'So do you,' he said. 'Bloody gorgeous. Fancy . . .'

'Fancy?'

'Fancy . . . . . fancy you thinking I might do it with Pam.'

'I expect she wants to.'

'Don't be daft.'

'Are she and Gordon still in love? I mean, are they still lovers?'

'You're asking the wrong bloke there. All I can say is – it's dead silent after the Ovaltine.'

'It can't be easy for her,' said Marilyn, running her forefinger down Derek's belly and playing with him gently between the legs. 'Your belly's so flat . . .' she said dreamily. 'Would you like Bob to help you with a job?'

'Bob a job!'

'Be serious.' She continued to play with his genitals but this didn't lead to major arousal. In fact he was beginning to feel embarrassed and out of his depth again, was eager to get dressed and into a less demanding, more social role. He was unable to think of anything to say and so said 'I've got to go now.'

He picked his clothes up, took them into the bathroom and was about to close the door when, irritated by his fastidiousness, she said 'There's no need to close the door . . . Do you know the last time a strange man used that bathroom? It was an Arab, a business colleague of Bob's. You know Arabs have loos which are holes in the ground and they squat over them. Had to do it once on a business trip with Bob – horrific, absolutely *horrific* . . . Presumably this Arab thought our loo was some kind of hideous trap which would infect him with germs or swallow him whole. Anyway I happened to go upstairs and barge in here, not knowing, and there he is up on the seat, with his business jacket and collar and tie on and nothing else—'

Her bra had become mixed up in Derek's clothes and he handed it out to her. 'Thanks, love,' she said. He felt peculiar. Doll used to call him 'love' in that way. She went on 'Nothing else at all, not even his socks, squatting up there in the air, blinking like a bewildered eagle. God, I was embarrassed. "Sorry," I said and walked out. But not as embarrassed as he was – when he came down, which he had to do of course, he left immediately with his family, unable to look me in the face as he said good-bye. He felt unmanned, you see. Pathetic innit. God, I can't stand that machismo unmanned honour crap, can you?'

Derek came out of the bathroom and said it again. 'I've got to go now.' He was famished but didn't think it right to mention tea and gateau. He didn't find it too easy to look Marilyn in the face either. Now that passion had had its discharge, he was lost. He felt immediately better when the bedroom was left behind them. On the way downstairs Derek glanced at the half-landing with its little chairs and said 'I suppose that's for them who don't want to go all the way up.'

She smiled but this remark, like the other, about money, didn't please her sense of romance. She wasn't sure why but felt that within it there lurked a sliver of disrespect. In the hall she kissed him on the mouth and cheek and said 'Come again', and closed the door on him. She stood awhile, listening to the crunch of his steps receding on the gravel drive, looking at his receding figure through a window beside the door, but he didn't look round. He skipped and was gone.

– God, the arrogance, she thought. She went upstairs to recompose the bedroom, stared at the creases in the sheets where they'd been only minutes ago. A terrific sadness overcame her. . . . . . and then a sudden shocking sense of the enormity of what she'd done blew like a great wind into the room – it was the first time she'd been unfaithful to Bob in nearly 8 years – and she went downstairs and poured herself a stiff drink.

When 2 days later, in the afternoon, Derek knocked again on the front door of Rorke's Drift, it was opened by Bob Dashman who said 'I know who you are. Come in. Come into the lounge.'

When Derek walked into the room Marilyn flinched, she had no idea Derek would return so soon, and uninvited, but caught herself at once. 'Oh good,' she said. 'Bob, I want you to meet Derek because maybe you can help him find out what he wants to do. Get him a job even.' Derek, still embarrassed at finding Bob at home (but Bob often came home early on Fridays), was staggered by her aplomb. 'Now I have to go to the shops.' She left in an aggressively smart Burberry mackintosh, velours hat at a jaunty angle, and high-heeled boots. Derek knew he was being given a lesson in something – but didn't know what.

'Would you like a beer?' asked Bob. He was a big man in his late 40s, thinning on top. He'd once played rugby and although now turning to fat, he still had a strong physical presence.

'No thanks.' Derek stared at a pile of drawings on the floor.

'I'm dreaming up a new line of kitchen gadgets. Does that interest you? Do you think people can be persuaded to eat square eggs?'

'On a regular basis?'

'Yes.'

'No.'

'Oh . . . So what does interest you?'

Derek thought – Everyone wants to know what my interests are – it's an impossible question right now – I've only been here a few weeks – I used to know what my interests are – he's a silly git, this one – does he know what *she* does?

Derek said 'I'll probably go and work on one of the oil rigs in the Arctic.'

'You're too young.'

The phone rang. Bob took it in the hall and Derek heard him say 'Listen, Jim, I can smell the shit in your pants, so don't put that big act on with me.'

When Bob returned Derek said 'I've got to go now.'

'Oh, all right. Maybe I can get you a job in the factory.'

'I'd like to travel,' said Derek helplessly, knowing that the Great Conspiracy was blocking his real desires and fixing him up for a factory. Would he have the courage to withstand the fix-up?

'There's many who'd like a job in my factory. You'd have to join the union. But that's no problem.'

Derek edged towards the door with a clutching sensation at his throat, 'Really, I have to go now.'

'But er, what did you come for?'

'Nothing, a mistake, right? Please, Mr Dashman, I've got to go.'

As Derek clutched at the front door and escaped into fresh air, Bob shouted after him 'Some advice, Derek. Fuck and the world fucks with you; wank and you wank alone . . . Good-bye.'

It was tea-time. It was raining. The phone rang. She put her college cream biscuit back in the saucer, hauled her heels off the pouffe, placed both hands on the arms of the chair and, summoning slackened energies, pushed herself onto her feet – feet which now carried her with puffy reluctance into the hall. Not voomphy – not in the slightest. She felt dreadful. Gordon hadn't been sleeping at all well lately and accordingly neither had she. Why in heaven's name did he suddenly have to give up sleeping-pills and upset everything? Simply because Derek had said they were bad? What did Derek know of it!? Gordon should ignore the voice of youth, return to his routine, let her get some sleep. She didn't want to move into the guest bedroom but . . .

'It's only me, Pam,' said a voice on the other end of the line.

Pam couldn't for the life of her fathom who 'only me' was and she replied weakly 'Sorry?'

123

'Vernon Playfair, you know, neighbour, all that stuff.'

'Major Playfair – I am sorry. I was dozing in a chair.'

'Having a siesta? Never take them myself, not in England. But in Malaya – always. It's the heat, you know. Fags one out. But in England, never take them, I don't.'

– Why doesn't the silly bugger say what he wants so I can get back to my chair? she wondered.

He went on 'When I was in India, which was only for about 6 months actually, during the revolt of—'

– Silly old fart, she thought.

'In India I'm sure you had siestas coming out your ears, Major.'

'. . . Not exactly,' he replied in an odd tone – he was convinced she'd said 'coming out your arse', almost convinced.

'And what can I do for you?'

'Ah. What can you do for me? Nothing – exactly. Is Derek there? My lawn needs a bit of a go. He does such a good job on it.'

'Your lawn does grow very fast.'

'Yes, doesn't it. Doesn't yours? At this time of year everything shoots up, doesn't it.'

'Oh – shoots up. I must get Derek to do ours, bless him, only Gordon likes to do it actually. It would be lovely if Derek developed green fingers and became a gardener.'

'That would be very lovely,' agreed the Major, thinking – She must be mad, she doesn't know the boy at all. 'But I don't think I can help him there. Pruning roses – one simply hacks at them as far as I'm concerned.'

'He's gone swimming.'

'When will he be back?'

'Later. He's going to the sauna with Gordon afterwards.'

'What?'

'Yes, it's become one of Gordon's things.'

'Has it, by Jove.'

'Yes. Recently. And now he thinks it'll be good for his insomnia. So he's going to go more.'

'Insomnia?'

The conversation had already gone further than Pam had intended and she didn't want to start thrashing out Gordon's problem with a mere neighbour, so she said 'Gordon's having a small party the week after next. Can you come?'

'I know he is. It's his birthday. I'm already invited.'

'I did tell him not to say it's a birthday party. It's almost like, well, asking for a present. It's going to be very casual. Please don't bring a present or anything.'

'Might I bring an old chum of mine called Vincent Quayle who's going to be in this part of the world then? He's an extremely good mixer. An army chaplain – used to be, anyway. Will you tell Derek I've got a little job for him?'

'Little jobs, big jobs, anything to keep him at it. Yes, Major, I'll tell him.' She put the phone down and thought – I must get Derek to redecorate this hall.

She returned to the chair with a flop, closed her eyes, and felt her head to be a mass of crackling fuzz and interference. She stood up, went and sat on the sofa with her back to the door, played with the pearls round her neck staring into a vase of big daisies beside the fireplace. A tremor moved through her. She shivered and looked over her shoulder. But there was no one there.

Derek and Gordon changed in the changing room. Derek said 'With your long legs and square body, you look like a radio on a stand.'

Derek tweaked Gordon by the nipples and Gordon said 'What are you doing? That hurt, leave me alone, you little bugger!'

Gordon shoved Derek away and the boy stopped laughing. Derek said 'Aw, I only pinched your nipples. I wanted to turn you on, Gordon, like a radio.'

Miss Wimbush popped her head round the door and said 'Can I have your ticket, Mr Drake? I didn't hear you come in. Oh, you're with your young friend again.'

'Hullo,' said Derek, nodding at her.

'We've got a new masseur,' she said. 'You should give it a try. You might like it.' She gave Gordon a good solid professional smile and he felt uneasy. He was feeling raw, vulnerable. His lack of sleep was getting to him. Yesterday morning outside the front door of his office – the door was on the street but the offices were on the first floor – he'd baulked. He couldn't go in. Everything started bending as if the world were made from Plasticine. His skin had prickled and the whole world looked strange and hostile. He had a sense of a tremendous energy dangerously trapped in his joints and muscles. He'd walked round the block (a most unpleasant experience), taking deep breaths, then gone into the office at the second attempt (after which the world soon settled into its familiar groove – but he was left exhausted).

'See you in the sweatbox,' said Derek and when Gordon joined him in there, the boy was throwing water on the coals to send up clouds of scalding steam.

'Good heavens,' said Gordon, slamming his hands against his face.

After a while Derek said 'I went to the Dashmans' house the other day.'

'Yes, Pam said.'

'They're very rich, aren't they. Their son's going to university. Did you go to university?'

'No. I could've gone but . . .' This was a sore point with Gordon – not having been to university. In his heart of hearts he felt forever a sense of inferiority because he hadn't gone. 'But I chose to enter a solicitor's office instead. Thought I'd get on with things.' Why hadn't he gone to university? Because *they* wouldn't let him. 'What do you want to be doing with university for?' said his father. 'Don't know where the lad gets his ideas from,' said his mother. And he'd joined a solicitor's office as an articled clerk. '. . . I'd have liked to have gone to Oxford,' said Gordon, the heat now slowing his thoughts and softening his body. 'I'd have liked Mark to have gone. I always thought it the most wonderful place. I'd've liked Mark to have *tried* at least. But he didn't want to. That drunken idiot next door filled his head with the army.'

Derek was surprised by the tone. Gordon was not given to strong personal insults. 'The Major's all right. I like him,' he said.

'I feel sorry for him, I suppose. He's got no family life,' said Gordon.

– Neither have I, thought Derek. And is family life something I want? Seems a bit of a minefield to me – back-stabbing, greed, machinations, mistaken motives, confusion, guilt, love & hate and the inability to recognise the difference between them – and money of course, this often screws up families, too much, too little, using money to control people, using the absence of it to

126

threaten people. Fiendish things grow in family life, like cancers burgeoning in a blocked corpus . . . But I'd like someone to love, to hold onto, to push my cock into and hug, and wake up with. Is this what I want? Yes but . . . I also want to be FREEEEEEEEE. Don't want to be tied, obliged, fixed. Don't want to be trapped – but want someone to love – don't wanna be trapped – but want someone to love – don't wanna be trapped – but want someone to love—

'Uuugh, I've gotta have a breather,' said Derek and he lolloped out of the cabin and dropped into the plunge pool and bellowed 'Arrrrrrrrrrrrrgh!' to a man sitting opposite who was contemplating whether to plunge or not. This person, who was very fat with yellowish skin and looked as if moulded from uncooked pastry, oozed a sweat which smelled acrid. He said 'You're a braver man than I.'

Derek experienced an intense ache as the cold penetrated his muscles as if he were turning hard, like water into ice. He jettisoned out, vigorously rubbed his thighs, belly and arms, and went back into the cabin where the heat struck at him. But the heat seemed to stay at a distance, was held at the barrier of the skin where the combination of heat and cold produced a powerful glow which rendered one weightless, evanescent and concentrated all at once, a glow such as Christ might have experienced on his ascent to heaven.

Gordon was standing up with bright red face, hands and feet. His grey hair stuck out in damp tufts above the ears. He was lank, hot, dripping. His face hung off his skull like an old rag. 'Let me out,' he mumbled, stumbling past Derek. His elbow caught the boy's flank as they passed each other and Derek thought what a boney, deathly thing this elbow was. Derek climbed to the upper deck for maximum heat and lay on his back with his hands behind his head, his knees raised up and his legs apart. He felt the relaxed weight of his genitals sag between his legs, the pull of the muscles in his chest and up his sides as he pushed his elbows back, and he felt good.

Gordon came back in and said 'We're on the upper deck now, are we?' Derek grunted, a soft deep blissful grunt, and Gordon thought – These young ones can take anything, can do anything. They're made of rubber. How is it that one becomes so fixed and brittle so soon? How is it that one so soon becomes capable of doing only a few things? I wonder if he's happy – he seems fair enough but you never know – they hold back a lot at that age – Mark at that age, we could hardly get a word out of him. Pam seems to be taking it in her stride. Am I addicted? I must break the reflex of not being able to sleep until I've had the pill. It's silly . . . but the silly can be very powerful . . . . .

'Cor, my bloody eyes,' said Derek. 'The sweat's pouring into 'em. Stings like hell.' 2 sturdy legs came down across Gordon's vision and Derek was off to the plunge again.

When he returned Gordon said to him 'Have you lost weight? Your body seems a bit tighter than when we first came.' Gordon wanted to touch him.

'It's the swimming. I'm going to do it regularly, get in training.'

'Training for what?'

'Don't know yet. Just training.'

'How are you getting on with Pam?'

Derek looked at him and said 'Why do you ask?'

'You see a lot of each other and . . . well, I just wondered.'

'OK. No complaints, Gordon. What I like about her is – she's straight up, you know where you stand with her, she's quite, you know . . . gutsy.' Derek smiled. He felt easy with Gordon. Taking your clothes off together and sweating and showering together does that. Doesn't create a depth – but something very similar to depth: ease. Derek felt words were easy under such circumstances because the essential communication or contact was non-verbal – the words were just a tincture, a confirmation, a bit of play on the side. Most things happen in the non-verbal universe, he thought, and most lives would be happier if people didn't allow themselves to be trapped in the verbal universe. Marvellous things happen in the non-verbal universe. This is because, being non-verbal, it is unrecorded. It exists in freedom and spontaneity, in which the past cannot choke the future, in which the present is unafraid of retribution. The verbal universe can create a model of the real universe. But the non-verbal universe is closer to the real universe. Sometimes his thoughts were quite complicated. Then curiosity mixed with mischievousness made Derek say 'You still do it with her then?'

Gordon was wrong-footed. His thoughts had been adrift in an

unusual aunty/mummy/baba world – he was in something like a pram but was strapped down at ankles and wrists under a sky of scudding purple clouds and was trying to work out why. Also, being a solicitor, he could be flummoxed by the direct question. They were both stretched out opposite each other on the lower decks. Gordon looked across at Derek, then up at the pine slats of the ceiling. 'Oh, well . . . Yes, sometimes, but you know, after a thousand years of marriage one ceases to be quite so desperate about it as when one's, well, 17.'

Derek who was already red, especially at his tips, went redder and said 'Yeah.'

'What about you? Have you had any experience?'

'Oh yeah,' said Derek with forced nonchalance. '. . . But not so much . . .'

'There's plenty of time.'

'Is there?' questioned Derek. 'Are you sure about that?' Gordon looked across and Derek grinned at him. The boy's penis was lying across his thigh and the red knob was poking cheekily out of the foreskin. 'They're all a bit posh round here,' he continued. 'Shouldn't think they're much interested in a bloke from the East End. It's all a bit Rodney and Nigel, innit, and Cordelia and Ward. Harrow and all that fucking mullarkey, innit.'

'Not really,' said Gordon. 'There's some of that. But – well, yes, maybe there's snobbery, maybe it's unjust – but . . . You have to make something of your life whatever the circumstances. And we're all much closer to the East End than we admit. Did you know that Queen Anne's grandmother was a barmaid of unknown parentage? That Richard III's illegitimate son died a bricklayer's labourer on parish relief?'

'Relief, that's what I need, relief,' and Derek exited fast, dumped himself in the plunge, jettisoned almost at once, popped his head out of the door and asked Miss Wimbush for a dry towel, collapsed face downwards onto one of the loungers. His body felt wonderful and he himself was nothing. It was so good to be nothing – an alert nothing. He dozed in clarity, felt cooler air on his buttocks. A man was saying 'We may have won the war but we certainly lost the peace.' It sounded far away but clear as a bell. It was the fat man with the acrid smell.

– Silly pillock, thought Derek.

Drifting, he heard Gordon say (and it sounded even further

away) 'This really is ridiculous. Only someone motivated entirely by material greed could agree with that statement. Traditional German culture can never hold its head up again – because of what it led to. Is this winning the peace? But Great Britain has the most glorious history of any nation – and one reason for that is we have rather little to be ashamed of.'

– Silly git, thought Derek.

'I'm going to have a massage,' said Derek and nipped off. He returned within the minute. 'That kills that idea. It's incredibly expensive.' He smelt the man again – and saw that the man had very hairy ears.

'I'll treat you,' said Gordon.

'But it's bloody expensive, Gordon.'

'Don't argue. I'll treat you.'

'Really? . . . Thanks.'

Behind nylon curtains the masseur told him to lie on his tummy, began with the neck muscles and went cleverly all down the back and sides to the feet. As the brilliant fingertips pressed, slid and rubbed over the buttocks, Derek got an erection and thought he was going to come. He thought of Marilyn Dashman – no, not of Marilyn exactly, but of her wet squelchy hole. He wanted more of it. That hole. But not necessarily more of its owner. And Cordelia, the daughter, the tantalising daughter – what was her hole like? What was her face like? The erection was still there when the masseur told him to turn over. 'I've got the horn,' said Derek, bright red. He'd been bright red a lot lately and although it was agonising, as if one's very soul were cringing, it did not impede the forward motion of his experiences because his curiosity was greater than his shyness. He'd also discovered that going all red, though torture for him, a horrible betrayal of the self by the body, nonetheless delighted other people and put them in a good mood. 'Seen that before,' said the masseur, blankly dropping a white towel over Derek's horn and starting on neck and chest. It's fabulous, his first massage. Conceivably the most incredible thing he's ever experienced. Not as intense as *coming* but the pleasure of massage is a pleasure unravelled, taking its time, and goes on and on and you floating and rubbish uncoiling in the muscles and dream dream – you dream – ugh – fingers plunge into stomach muscles and pull out rubbish. There goes the rubbish like ash floating off in the wind, like black ash floating off into a grey sky above a blue sea, like the ash of death, like the ash of the past, like the ash of memories, and a light breeze disperses it into a darkening sky over wavetops, speeding over wavetops into a dark sky and approaching night – night-time – already night-time laps over you like a wave. Night is here. Here and there a star. But mostly no stars. And no moon. Very black close night and Derek walks and walks and walks at a steady even pace as though coming from nowhere, and going nowhere, walking only the walk-in-itself. But he's not doing the walking. His body's doing the walking. He has nothing to do with it. His body's doing it all by itself. And what Derek is doing is – nothing – he's doing nothing while his body walks around in the night, along the dark street, turn left, along the dark street, turn right, along the dark street, the street with no buildings on the right hand side but a great space swooping off into darkness and the twinkling lights of distant buildings. And on the left side too there is unexpected space and intermittent low houses and distant blocks of flats, far away on the far side of demolished expanses dim in the night. All this black unexpected space. And on the left the church of St George rises up like a castle in the night, a castle on the moors, for it has towers, battlements, turrets black against blackness and the body goes on walking all by itself, so easily – dreamy and sharp at the same time – autonomously – and a sharper coolness falls across his face. He notices this as the body carries him effortlessly along. And with the coolness, a sharper smell as of something alive and perhaps vegetable and Derek found himself beside water. Slurp, slurp; black oil heaving in the darkness. Lights twinkled on the far side of the great river which seemed very wide here. He couldn't remember it's being so wide here. Perhaps it is an optical illusion. The twinkling lights of the buildings on the far side seem so far away, so impossibly distant, another continent, another planet, separated by the limitless black divide of flexible water. Derek puts his hands in his pockets. He takes an object from his pocket and looks down at it. It is a knife. He opens the blade and it catches a spark of light and flashes it to him in the blackness, like a friend saying hullo. He turns the blade this way and that, trying to find the spark again, to make the blade flash again. But it doesn't. Just the dead weight of the knife in his hand

131

He stands at full height, then leans backwards and his arm eases back behind his head then shoots forward with tremendous force and a flick. The knife flies from his hand – rises in the air – higher, higher – turning over and over, head over heels – and it catches something in its escape – the moon edges out from behind a cloud – and the knife catches several strands of moonlight and flashes them at Derek as it somersaults – flash – flash – flash – flash – then down – in a great curve – down – flash – down – and it strikes the water and is gone as the great river hungrily draws the knife down into its breast. Derek shouts 'Take it with you, Mum! . . . . I'm sorry!' It is a dry shout, empty of feeling, empty of power, because this is the dead long night after the afternoon of his mother's death, and Derek carries on walking and finds himself in a street he doesn't recognise – he thinks it's – but no, no, because there should be 2 exotic doorways at the far end and to-night there is nothing there. The doorways have gone. A black hole is there. Derek approaches the site and his toe kicks lightly at rubble. He climbs across the shallow mound of rubble searching for something, anything, but there is nothing. The lights of the street are far away. He sits down in a dark corner of the rubble. It is damp. After a while he starts to tremble.

From the kitchen window Pam stared into the back garden and thought – Summer is beginning . . . . .

A voice behind her said 'What are you doing?'

A shock shot through her and claws clutched at her innards. 'Derek, you made me jump. I'm making a fruit salad for the party.' She turned back to her business, thinking – The party, 2 days to go – I'll never get it all done in time – I'm a bag of nerves already.

Derek came up behind her, stuck his chin out and dumped it on her left shoulder. 'What are you doing?' she asked. He tickled her waist, as sometimes he used to tickle Doll's. 'Derek . . .' She rearranged the waist-band of her track-suit top over her hips, fumbled at the fruit and an unsteady tone entered her voice which made him move apart from her. He thought Pam was weird sometimes. And since he knew that fruit salad came out of tins, he thought the fruit salad weird too: no bright colours in it. She said in a voice that had an artificial sheen 'Cooking tip, Derek. When you're making fruit salad, put in lemon juice. It stops the fruit going black. This has to sit in the fridge until Saturday.'

'Are we having caviar?' he asked.

'No we are not having' and she added the word 'caviar' in an undertone. 'Did you know that 17% of the world's caviar is eaten aboard the QEII?'

'Yes.'

'You knew that, did you? You know everything, don't you.'

'You told me. That's great.'

'What is?'

'Your track suit.' He'd never seen her wear it before.

'It's only a track suit.'

'But you look dead good in it.'

'Do you think so?'

'Amazing.'

'Now you're exaggerating.'

'No, really good. I like those things. *Relaxing*.'

'Yes . . . Would you like one?'

'What, a track suit?'

'I'll buy you one.'

'No, I don't expect—'

'Yes, I'll buy you one.'

'What, really?'

'Of course.'

'I'd really love one.'

'When this party's over, we'll go and get one.'

'Really? I'd love it.'

'A blue one.'

'Yeah, blue . . .'

Derek wanted to know if the Dashmans were coming to this party, especially if Marilyn were coming, more especially if Cordelia were coming. *Vis-à-vis* Marilyn he wasn't sure what he wanted – but he didn't want to get embedded in her. And he didn't want to reveal his interest in this family by a direct reference, so first he said 'Are the funny ones coming from next door?'

133

'You mean the Chivers sisters? I couldn't not invite them. Eunice may come.'

'I met her at the Library.'

'Nobody sees Sybil any more,' said Pam. 'She's gone funny. She stays indoors. Reading.' She added 'reading' as if to hint at a dark and unsavoury practice. Pam read. Of course she read. But she kept books in their place.

Then Derek said 'What about the Dashmans?'

'We couldn't very well have a party and not invite the Dashmans, could we?'

'Couldn't you? So I'll get to meet this Cordelia.'

'She may come,' said Pam, huffily chopping another apple into small cubes. 'Do you know, she didn't even phone me? She used to be such a nice girl.'

This made Derek much more interested, but he said 'Their house is amazing.'

Pam said 'Derek, I want you to redecorate our hall after the party. I wish I'd asked you before but it's too late now. It'll have to be afterwards. Have you done anything like that? Decorating?'

'No,' said Derek blankly, hoping the idea would go away.

'It's easy. And we'll pay you. Have you bought Gordon's present?'

They'd gone into the West End but hadn't found anything which satisfied Derek's fastidious taste for Gordon. Derek said he'd see to it himself – and he had done. 'A pocket video player.'

'What?' said Pam, half turning towards him, her chopping knife frozen in mid-air.

'That's what I bought him.'

'But you can't afford that.' She resumed chopping with forced alacrity.

'Don't worry. That's my present. He'll love it.'

'I'm sure he will but . . . the expense, Derek. You can't *afford* a pocket video player.'

'Who says?'

'I says.'

'It's none of your business.'

'But Derek . . .'

'What did you buy him? You never told me.'

She was worried about where the pocket video player came

from but could see that he'd dug in his heels. 'I bought him a beautiful jumper from Marks & Spencer.' Derek's face dulled over. Glancing at him, she said 'Well, he needed it.'

His face went duller and he said 'It ain't gonna make him leap for joy, is it?'

She put down the knife, turned right round from her business and looked him full in the face. Derek was smirking at her with his hands behind his back. One part of her adored the smirk, another part of her absolutely loathed it. 'We're in a cocky mood to-day, aren't we?' she said in a voice that was disapproving but not 100% disapproving.

'Bit voomphy, am I?' he questioned, raising his eyebrows in mock innocence.

She noticed for the first time that he was standing in an unusual way, his feet well apart and his hands, as it were, tied behind his back, like a soldier at ease. Suddenly he said 'For you' and held towards her a coloured box in Cellophane he'd been concealing behind his body.

Pam was taken completely by surprise. 'For me?' she murmured with a petite frown. He nodded. She waved her sticky hands in the air. 'But my hands . . .' She rinsed her hands under the tap, wiped them on her pinafore, and feebly took hold of the proffered gift as if it might be a booby trap and explode custard in her face.

'Hope you like them . . .' he said, getting embarrassed.

'But . . .' she said in a voice that had shrunk to a quarter its normal size and was continuing to shrink, so that it disappeared from her body altogether.

Derek panicked and blurted out 'If you don't like them!'

This panicked her in turn and she blurted back 'No, no, I—!' Her sentence ended there, on an exclamatory uprise.

'Oh . . . .' he said, weakly, feeling horribly uncomfortable and realising in a remote part of himself that giving is an emotional act, giving without return, and that it is difficult to do because it makes one feel opened, exposed, revealed, vulnerable. He felt incredibly light, as if he were hovering like a soap bubble. – How is it that the act of giving does such strange things to the body? he thought.

'Derek, you shouldn't've. They're so expensive . . .'

135

'For fuck's sake . . .' he murmured.

'Don't say that. But you mustn't spend your money like this. You mustn't.' She too had been physically affected by this act of giving and her immediate response was to rebuke him for having done it. As if she were saying 'How dare you expose my raw like this?' Then she said 'I'll put them in the fridge.' She was touched to the heart. She wanted to cover her confusion and putting them in the fridge became the stop-gap. Stop-gap to what? Closing up again? to composure? to not reacting? to not being invaded, touched, changed? to being aloof, capable, armoured? to being touched only within the acceptable limits of habit and expectation? to not being surprised? to not being refreshed and renewed? to hiding from new experience? to being DEAD NOT ALIVE? Oh, let the outer thing die a little, let the inner thing breathe a little . . . Pam, oh, Pam, don't rush so fast into the strategy for concealing the fact that you were touched. Don't be ashamed of being touched . . . . .

Rebuking herself thus, Pam's eyes filled with water. Having popped the box in the refrigerator she stood looking at the floor and if one could have seen her face one would have seen its features held in a grip. Her face was gripped by the determination not to express her real emotion. The effort demanded all of her and for the time being she was unable to do anything except stand there.

Derek stood there too, like a soldier ill at ease, his hands dangling at his sides, worry in his eyes. 'Really, don't you like them then? They're hard centres. But I could change them . . . Have I done something wrong?'

Pam realised that she was causing Derek to misinterpret the situation *totally*. This woke her. She embraced and kissed him, saying 'It's the loveliest present, they're my favourites, the loveliest present, I love them, I love!' The sentence ended there as she kissed him again.

'It's only chocolates,' he laughed, writhing, holding his hands into his breast in an attempt not to be overwhelmed by Pam's physical and soulful effusions. But he enjoyed refusing in this way her excess. It made him feel secure, as though the bank account marked 'Love for Derek' was well in credit.

She pushed her hair back and touched his face, saying 'Derek, you're so lovely . . .'

136

He felt gawky and helpless and said 'Thanks' pronouncing it 'Fanks'. And having said it he thought it a pathetic thing to say and managed to construct a whole sentence. 'With Gordon getting all the attention, I thought it would be nice for you to have something.' What a number it had turned out to be.

Pam's head tilted to one side. Her eyes went dreamy, soft focus and watery again. She felt as though a warm tongue were firmly but gently licking all the right spots inside. She felt it was all worth it. Oh God, how she felt right now that it was all *worth* it!

'Let's have a drink!' she said. 'Let's have a gin & It!'

'Can I have beer?'

'Dearest, you can have whatever you like. But I'm going to have a gin & It. It's *years* since I had a drink in the afternoon.'

They drank in the kitchen and talked and when Pam had finished her gin & It, she realised she'd enjoyed it enormously. And so had another. Derek had another beer and they moved into the sitting-room, lit the gas log fire, and talked more. 'Isn't this lovely?' said Pam, interrupting the flow of conversation. Then they carried on.

Derek said 'A woman sent a blind man a birthday present of a cheese grater. She never heard anything. So when she saw him, she said "Did you like your present?" And he said "Oh yes, thank-you. But it was the most violent book I've ever read." '

They giggled like 2 jellies on a plate, giggled helplessly. But after a while of helpless giggling, Pam suddenly threw her head back and, showing all her teeth and a bared throat, gave issue to a mighty full-bosomed howl of laughter. A long cackling laugh poured loudly from her body in jagged waves. She looked like a hyaena in a dress and Derek couldn't keep abreast of her laughter. He saw her objectively and thought she looked over the top – OK, Pam, it was just a joke, don't overdo it.

Eventually Pam closed her mouth and covered her teeth with her lips. 'Let's have another,' she said, wiping the tears of hilarity from her eyes.

'I've got to go now.'

'Go? What do you mean, go?'

'I'm going to give the Major's lawn a go.'

'Oh, don't go, not yet.'

'I could do with the money.'

'You seem to have more than enough.'

'One can always use more.'

It was the first time he'd used the expression 'one' to her, and she said 'Can one?' with a touch of mockery that wasn't wholly good-humoured. 'Oh, don't go.' Now her voice was maudlin, almost plaintive, which made Derek want to go immediately.

'See you in a bit,' he said, vanishing.

By the time Gordon came home from the office, Pam was completely drunk.

'Oh, it's you,' she said, throwing him a ghastly sneer with a toss of her head. 'It's Gordon,' she mumbled to the empty arm-chair opposite. 'Hullo, Gordon. Give me a kiss. A *real* kiss.' Her hair was sticking out. She leered up at him so that the whites beneath the pupils of her eyes showed sinisterly with the ludicrous emphasis of a vamp in a silent film. 'I'm feeling wonderful,' she declared hopelessly from her chair, flinging her arms wide and knocking over a glass which didn't smash but dribbled its contents of gin & It down the legs of a small tripod table and onto the carpet. 'Mary can, I think—' She mislaid what she was going to say and pushed at her hair with the palms of her hands. 'There's chocolate and – my favourite – er, my favourite . . .'

Gordon was shocked, distressed. Pam wasn't *like* this. Stability had become instability. This *wasn't* her – this was . . . someone else. 'You're incoherent!' he said in a voice that was low but aggressive, a subdued snarl.

Pam looked at him – she wanted to glare but had drunk too much for that – so her eyes emitted a soggy fury. He'd called her incoherent and the strain of piety – that he was so bloody coherent, so bloody coherent he was! – enraged her! Why shouldn't she be incoherent now and again? Why shouldn't she have a holiday from so much bloody coherence? What was so sodding great about coherence all the time? She was sick to death of coherence year after year after year! 'Yes, that's right!' she bellowed, drawing energy from the primal source. 'In fact I'm gincoherent, that's what I am, quite gincoherent, and I'm loving every damn bloody second of it, so why don't you *piss* off, you *boring old* FART!'

Gordon walked out of the room. Then walked out of the front door. And Pam looked groggily at the armchair opposite and –

she didn't start to cry, that would come later – she started to grunt at it, long low grunts, and this was accompanied by a rhythmic nodding of the head, as much as to say 'That showed him, the complacent old bore', which was a dazed attempt to approve of herself. That night in bed she apologised to Gordon, said she had a splitting headache, and in fact slept very well, although she paid for it the following day. Gordon did not sleep well and had a bad dream – a large black ball thwacked into the brick stomach of Hogarth Parade, just where his office was, and made a frightful hole.

The black limousine edged slowly through the suburban streets like a great ship looking for a dock. It turned left at the traffic lights at the end of Hogarth Parade, passed under a bridge for the underground railway (which was entirely overground in this district) and found itself on a smooth stretch of dual carriageway with oblongs of lawn down the centre and mock-Tudor semi-detached houses on either side. The front doors of these houses had oval glass panels let into them at eye level, leaded with pictures of galleons, plants or old-fashioned aeroplanes in coloured glass. Here the black limousine picked up speed, devouring the mile or so of dual carriageway in moments, and finding itself in an area where semi-detached houses mingled with factories for light engineering. Some of the factories were quite old, built in a theatrical Egyptian style or with windows which were wrapped round corners. Others were modern with walls of suspended glass or walls seemingly made from coloured rubber. Here the black limousine turned right onto a small industrial estate, felt its way circumspectly past the various establishments proclaiming their business in large plastic letters, stopped, then drove through a pair of factory gates at the end. The building was new and 'The Dashman Group' was spelled out in orange letters across one of the matt grey gable ends. The black limousine turned in the forecourt and pulled up languidly beside Bob Dashman's hard ice-blue Rolls-Royce. A driver got out, went round, opened the car door, and an elegant Arab – the same one Marilyn had surprised in aerial defecation – emerged in Savile Row grey and walked across the tarmac into the building. This time there was no family with him.

– Rock – Rock – Rock – How wonderful to rock – rock – rock – one can do it for ever . . . I've been doing it for years – seems like for ever – I'll do it for years yet . . . rock . . . rock . . . in the room where Time is *stilled* . . . Diddums and I, we don't do much – but we don't have much to do! The world does it all for us . . . The tulips in the vase are beautiful, drooping so gracefully, full of grace . . . But I'm tired. Some days I feel very very tired. To-day is such a day and on such a day one needs an intrusion from outside – every 7th day or so, something should impinge from outside. Intrusions keep one fresh. Keep it fun. Do I hear someone calling? Is my wish to be so conveniently granted? Or is it that the wish arose in the knowledge that something is out there, waiting to impinge? Rock . . . rock . . . rock . . . How very pleasurable sometimes is abstract conversation . . . It's like playing chess . . . Not that I play chess . . . But abstract conversation with oneself is idiocy . . . And on tired days one's bum aches, always plonked in the rocking-chair. I had the bum-ache to-day, certainly did, but now it is gone and this because lo! someone approaches. Who is it that approaches?

'Guggums dear!' shouted Eunice up the stairs. 'Are you there?'

– Am I here? thought Sybil. That is a ridiculous question – when haven't I been here? I've been here for centuries in my dark blue cardigan and black dress printed with large blue cabbage roses which are of a blue we call Mayan blue – the blue which the Mayans painted on the faces of victims singled out for sacrifice.

'Yes, Diddums,' Sybil shouted down from her room. 'What is it then?'

'Oh Guggums, good, you're there!' Eunice shouted back.

'I'm always here, you great haddock!'

'There's someone to see you!' returned Eunice from the bottom of the stairs. 'Shall I send him up?'

– Someone to see me? How fascinating, thought Sybil. Even she, so deeply gone in the sublime grasp of things, could not renounce the vanity – or was it self-respect? – of taking up a

140

diamond-shaped hand mirror and tucking loose strands of hair behind her ears. She had straight tough hair which had been bobbed as a girl and been bobbed ever since, with a square section cut out for her face. It fell in a fringe down her brow to her eyebrows and the short side curtains she usually tucked behind her ears when visitors came, to expose the refinement of her earlobes. But the most extraordinary thing about this hair was its colour. Sybil dyed it an impossible red. Not ginger; fruitier than that – crimson.

'No, Diddums,' shouted Sybil, '*bring* him up!'

– What's happened to her manners, she thought.

There was a muddled clatter on the staircase (which had no carpet) and Sybil caught a young voice saying 'Are you sure it's OK?'

'Yes, yes, she *loves* people,' said Eunice. 'I've squared it with her, we're *expected*. I'm coming too.'

The clatter approached the front bedroom where Sybil lived and rocked. The door was ajar and Eunice tapped it with a knuckle. 'Enter,' said Sybil.

Eunice poked her head round the door, blinked through her taped spectacles and said 'Here he is.' She stepped back and pushed Derek into the room with a delicate fist in the small of his back.

He paused nervously in the doorway. In front of him a wizened ancient, like an iguana in red wig and cardigan, rocked hypnotically back and forth in a rocking-chair. The net curtains were discoloured and grimy and let only a soiled light into the room which was furnished with heavy dark furniture. There were bottles and jars everywhere, strings of beads and strange totems, mottled yellowed newspapers, pictures and photographs – but a row of silver frames standing in pride of place along the mantelpiece had no photographs in them at all – just blank silver-framed spaces staring out at the world like a challenge. And there were books. Not like the Major's books, everywhere, colourful, paperbacks, hardbacks, brand new ones with older ones. Nor like Gordon's books, kept tidily in the large dining-room bookcase or in the box-room. Sybil's books were all very very old, with frayed leather bindings. They were large, seemed much-used, and there were only a few of them. The bed was covered with a thick

141

patchwork counterpane that looked too heavy for it. And the floor was covered with a carpet which looked too lightweight for it and which twisted underfoot. Chests of drawers had cloths spread over their tops. The mantelpiece had a complicated cloth on it with tassels – a vase of tulips stood in the centre precariously (the ledge was so narrow). All these coverings had been made from fragments – Sybil made them and they were collectively known as her rag rugs. She did it to prevent her hands seizing up. Seized-up hands were one of her few dreads. She was proud of her hands, as well as her earlobes, and drew attention to the left hand by sporting an electrum ring bearing the device of a diamond lozenge bisected by a horizontal line thus: $\longleftrightarrow$ On the wall behind her was a dark cape pinned up like a fan. And a desk at her rear right carried more silver frames, only this time bearing photographs of people. The room smelled of eau de cologne, cigarettes, and old age.

Eunice poked her head out from behind Derek, pushing him forward a little more, and said 'He's so like Cuthbert, isn't he?' She was bent 45° off the vertical which was quite upright for her.

'He's a boy, if that's what you mean, you donkey.'

'Oh Guggums, don't be such a cross-patch. He's *just* like Cuthbert. And do you know, Jennifer didn't even bark when he came in.'

'Well, the poor creature hasn't barked for 10 years.' Sybil looked Derek up and down and softening said 'He is a little like him.' When she came to his green eyes, which gleamed with keenness, she paused and looked right into them, swam right into him via the eyes, and said 'Cuthbert was our brother.'

Derek's eyes widened. 'Was he, Mrs Chivers?'

'Yes. And it's Miss Chivers.'

'He was killed, you know,' said Eunice dolorously to a corner of the rag carpet.

'Don't start on that,' said Sybil.

'In action,' added Eunice at the verge of tears.

With unexpected suppleness, Sybil twisted round to her right, threw her arm behind and picked up one of the photographs from a raggy surface. This was accompanied by a curt sound which could have been the squeaking of the chair but was in fact Sybil breaking wind, an odourless baby one popping out. As the rocker tipped back and forth she held the photograph towards Derek. It

142

bobbed up and down hypnotically but he stepped forward, took it and looked at the picture of a blond young man with jolly face in army uniform who bore no resemblance to Derek that he could discern.

'Killed in *lots* of action,' Eunice went on. 'Not very nice. You see, the order was to send the armies at each other until no one was left.'

'Diddums, shut your trap. We don't want to know.'

Eunice looked petulantly at her sister and said 'You never let me talk. I'm not going to stay if you're going to be such a cross-patch.' There was a slow clatter as Eunice made her way back down the stairs, her body bent at the waist.

'I have to discipline her sometimes or she goes all to pieces,' said Sybil with a sigh. 'Where did she find you?'

'My name's Derek. I—'

'I know all that stuff. You're the boy next door. What I want to know is – how did you get over to this side of the fence?'

'I was in the garden and saw Miss Chivers and—'

'Yes, that's her area of operations, the garden. But any chance to stop doing it she grabs at. Was she *doing* it? The garden? Or just fiddling about?'

Derek had been in the back garden, heard a scuffing noise, looked through a narrow gap in the fence and come face to face with Eunice who stood up at that very moment and said force-fully to him through the chink 'I'm slugging.'

'Sounds nasty.'

'You get used to it.'

'Slugs and snails don't do any good, I expect.'

'Snails are all right. They're hermaphrodites.'

'Are slugs?'

Eunice had thought a bit and said 'Don't know. Let's ask Sybil . . . . .'

'So she invited me in,' said Derek.

'Oh yes, she would, she's very sociable,' said Sybil. 'Says hullo to anything in trousers. Man-mad. Years ago there was a terrible business with – mmm, well, do you smoke cigarettes?'

'Sometimes.'

'We can smoke one now. One each.'

They lit up and Derek said 'Are they then?'

'What?'

'Hermaphrodites. Slugs.'

'Goodness gracious, I don't know. Pick one up and have a look'
. . . She mused and said 'It all seems so recent . . .'

She didn't add anything, just rocked a little, so he asked 'What
does?'

She looked at him with impatient grey eyes and said 'Everything. Civilisation, names, products, buildings, culture, everything. All so very very very very very – recent. And already we're
on the way out! Ha! What will they say about humankind? They
crawled out of their caves and blew themselves up! How very
sapiens . . . . . Are you going with girls yet?'

'I've had girls.'

'Didn't ask you that. I'm sure you've put your little dickie in a
hole.'

'I haven't got a girlfriend. Not regular. I don't seem to meet
many round here.'

'There's plenty of everything round here. You have to make an
effort. Meet people. Look at me when I'm giving you advice.'

'I've met people. The Dashmans. Major Playfair. I'm going to
take up some activities.' He sat down on a chair and crossed his
legs in a grown-up manner.

Sybil laughed. It sounded like an old car starter turning over
but failing to ignite. 'The Major's a rascal,' she said. 'But he has it.
He's got it. But the others . . .'

Derek wanted to ask her what 'it' was but was rather uneasy
about pursuing a Major Playfair conversation with a woman who
seemed to have her finger on the pulse of things.

'What do you want to be?' she asked him with a jocular growl.

'Dunno. Are you going to . . . interrogate me?'

'Perhaps. But what I'd like to say now is – it's perfectly possible
to be more than one thing at a time, because what one is pre-
empts the description of what one is. Descriptions unfold sequen-
tially. But what one is – experience – this is many things at once.'

'She said you'd been to university.'

'Quite so. But I left it after 18 months to get married. Then I
changed my mind. About getting married.'

'Confused were you?'

'No, I wasn't. I was decisive.'

'So what do *you* want?'

'What do I want?' echoed Sybil. 'The kid has spirit. What do I want? I want to die. Have you been to the National Gallery yet?' She held Derek in her gaze as, hypnotically, she rocked back and forth.

He shivered and said 'How do you want to die?'

'How? He asks me how . . . Like tulips. I love tulips. Tulips die so well.'

She looked across to the vase on the mantelpiece and Derek followed her eyes. The stalks of the dying tulips came out of the vase and bent over in serpentine curves and the petals had opened out almost flat. The tulips were red and swayed there in a mist of diffused cigarette smoke which showed bluish in the half-light. The vase had squeezed itself onto the narrow ledge but seemed on the point of suiciding by hurling itself into the abyss below.

She said 'Tulips die effortlessly. They let the other do the dying.' She looked extremely old and wrinkled at this moment shrouded in the bluish grey of cigarette smoke, a wraith, a fragile idea only.

'Will it be soon?' he asked.

'What a rude question!' she exclaimed. 'We were going to talk about paintings. Are you a rude boy?'

'No, no, but I—'

'You want to know how old I am. It's very rude to ask a lady her age – a lady or anyone else for that matter.'

'I didn't mean that. I just wondered if you could feel death approaching . . .' He petered out, dropping his eyes onto the rag carpet.

'Age . . . time . . . numbers . . . science . . . death . . . Science is a terrific thing. But it does get it wrong – ultimately. Because science believes that something exists only when it can be measured. But what is measurement, eh?'

'Don't know,' said Derek. He understood that his role was to be Sybil's rhetorical egger-on. She liked to be egged-on. But she preferred to be understood.

'Then I shall tell you. Measurement is arbitrary. The ruler floats in mid-air. Even Euclid understood that.' Sybil blew out some smoke and farted discreetly. 'Think about numbers too much and it drives you MAD!!!' She emphasised the word 'mad' by vibrat-

145

ing her head and pushing out her eyeballs in an impressive imper-
sonation of that condition. 'It is absolutely essential to escape
from all superstition before you die. The tulips advise us that. Do
you know what vril fluid is?' Derek gave a slow nod of negativity.
'It's a big joke, that's what. What is the purpose of man's life? The
escape from superstition. All art, all science, all endeavour is just
that.' She rounded off her statement with a flourish of the ringed
hand.

'That's a beautiful ring,' said Derek, hoping to bring the occasion down to more solid things.

'And it's a beautiful hand too. The ring's electrum. It comes
from . . . I forget where. From some wonderful place. Our father
was an explorer, you know, Daddy was.'

'Really?'

'Really . . . You see this dark brown thing behind me?
Batskins. A cloak of batskins. From Peru. It's said to come from
the wardrobe of the Last Inca. And looking at it I can well believe
it. Smelling it too. A very *superstitious* smell.' Derek made as if to
get up and smell it but Sybil said 'No, no, not until we know each
other better. I don't know where your nose has been.' Derek
screwed up his nose coquettishly for her. 'And this funny whatsit
over here,' she said, pointing to a stone stump with a horrid
leering face, 'is a god. Ixtab. A not-very-nice god. None of their
gods was very nice. "Nice" isn't a god word.'

'It looks so old,' he said. 'I can tell you're a religious person.'

She grimaced in an agitated way, as if her face were a mass of
itches she couldn't scratch. 'Religious! Oh *do* me a favour please.
Religions – there's not one that's not a heap of bird droppings. I'm
not religious *at all*, not in the slightest degree, not REMOTELY.
No thank you. Religion is' – she looked him right in the eyes –
'BALLS. That's what religion is. Men's testicles. Some silly
women fall for 'em.' She looked back at the statue and stroked its
head. 'Old. Yes, it's old. But there's older. Oh my word, there's
much older than this. It belongs to myth and that's always old.'
She stopped for a moment, stubbed out her cigarette, and
resumed with a pedagogic air. 'Myth is life cleansed of time. The
sense of myth is the sense of discovery. The end of living is to
know it all . . . Right. All that should've softened you up. Shall I
ask Diddums to bring in the tea now?' Sybil reached down,

picked up an Indian club (which came from Africa), and banged the floor with it 3 times.

Derek was relieved. The conversation had made him claustrophobic – he asked 'Do you ever open a window?'

'Ugh . . .' Sybil glanced at him with contempt. 'The door's quite enough thank-you. Are you trying to kill me before my time? The air is cold and poisonous. I'll not have it directly off the road, I won't. It must come the long way round. Through the house. Up the stairs. By the time it reaches me I want it nice and sluggish. Fresh air at my age. Are you mad?' She emphasised this word 'mad' in the same way as before.

'How old are you?' He truly wanted to know. He'd never met anyone this old. She seemed prehistoric.

'What a persistent . . . You'll go a long way – if you can find your rails. Let me see, when Tolstoy was my age – he'd been dead 6 years!' She burst out laughing.

Derek asked 'Who's Tolstoy?' and stood up.

She stopped laughing abruptly and looked at him with a gentle, loving expression tinged with sadness. This distressed him considerably.

Eunice arrived with the tea and set the tray up on a table in the corner. Derek stood on one leg and scratched the raised calf muscle of the other leg.

'You didn't drop anything this time,' observed Sybil drily. She nodded in the direction of Derek and said 'He keeps going on about how old I am.'

'I'm sorry, I didn't mean to,' said Derek, apologising to Eunice.

'Our cousin Minerva—' began Sybil.

'Minerva Cox,' interposed Eunice.

'Yes, our cousin Minerva Cox—' Sybil began again.

'We don't see her very often,' said Eunice.

'No, but our cousin Minerva—'

'Because she lives in Bath.'

'Eunice!' Sybil only called her Eunice when she was really angry. 'Eunice, please . . . . . Thank-you . . . . All I was going to say, with my dear sister's permission, was that Minerva is a good few years older than I am. Built like a tractor she is.'

'We last saw her when she came up to town for that show at the Palladium, do you remember, Guggums?'

'*Between the Cheeks*. I didn't go.'

'Of course, you wouldn't't've. I'd like to see Minnie again. Milk and sugar?'

'Both please,' said Derek. Suddenly he felt good. 'This is a very interesting room,' he said, looking round it.

'Why don't you sit down?' asked Eunice, handing him a cup with a few dark leaves floating on the milk-brown surface.

'Yes, sit down,' said Sibyl, 'drink your tea, then hand me the cup.'

'That's why I haven't used the strainer. It's tea-leaves time,' said Eunice.

Derek swallowed his tea quickly, burning his throat somewhat, draining it to the dark stodge at the bottom. With another burst of gruesome laughter Sibyl took the cup and, looking down her nose, began to turn it in the weak afternoon light. Eventually she muttered 'Wonderful things . . . terrible things . . .'

'She always says that to begin with,' whispered Eunice.

Sybil gave Eunice an admonitory glance and went on 'But not yet . . . Not to-day . . .'

'She often says that too,' whispered Eunice.

'Diddums!' Sybil released a pert little fart at the same time as if to underline her resolve.

'Sorry, Guggums.' Eunice gave Derek a small shrug and raised her eyebrows, implying 'Naughty me'.

'Terrible things . . . wonderful things . . . not to-day but . . . soon . . . . . yes, soon . . . very soon . . .'

Derek's mouth hung open but he didn't know it. Eunice pushed her spectacles up her nose and waited.

'. . . Terrible things . . . and soon, very soon, too soon—' At this point Sybil's voice lost its clarity and underwent a transformation. It wobbled and cracked, and an unpleasant sound, a combination of croak and growl, filled the spaces between the words Soon-soon-soon, like a sulphurous lava forcing itself out between fissures. Sibyl's eyes stared straight into the cup with an intensity oblivious to all else. Grey eyes – but a lurid and horrified light emanated from them. Then they came slowly out, like snails' eyes on stalks – it was revolting – and as they did so, Sibyl extended the arm holding the cup to its full length, riveted all the while by the tea-leaves. Then her head started to vibrate, wagging the bangs of her hair which had dropped down over her ears.

'Dear me,' said Eunice.

Derek was sweating in groin, feet and hands, and small of back. He looked at Eunice nervously.

'Dear me,' Eunice said to him.

'Soon! . . . Soon! . . . Arrrrghhurrrummm!' gibbered the wizened ancient, popping farts from her bottom.

'Dear me, she's having one of her fits,' declared Eunice between sympathy and annoyance.

– Fuck me, she's oozing something dreadful – what on earth is that disgusting stuff? thought Derek.

What indeed. Was it pus? Or vomit? Or bile? Or lymphatic fluid? Or vril fluid?

Derek ventured a tremulous enquiry. 'Is she all right?' It was only tea-stained saliva but he thought it prodigious and had real anxiety.

'She's having one of her fits,' said Eunice; then addressing her sister, she shouted aloud 'I'm getting your pills, dear. Hold on. Hold on to your ragwork. It'll be all right, you've got your ragwork. Don't want seized-up hands, do we. Hold on to your ragwork!'

'Arrrghummphrrrurrghhllysssglooooogshshshlluppp!' replied Sybil, clawing and kneading the ragwork which Eunice had stuffed into her hands.

'But is she all right?' repeated Derek as Sibyl now began to swing violently back and forth on the rocker like a naughty chimpanzee, swinging it up to its very extremities, foaming yellow saliva, waving ragwork, farting generously.

'She's having one of her fits,' repeated Eunice, rooting in a drawer for the pills. 'Better leave, Derek. We'll do the tea-leaves another time. Yes, dear, hold on to your ragwork! Hold on to your ragwork!'

Derek wasn't sure he wanted another tea-leaf time. He backed away towards the door, giggling in horror.

Washed, brushed and combed for Gordon's birthday party, Derek lay on his bed, looking up dirty words in the 2-volume

149

Shorter Oxford English Dictionary. He was beginning to enjoy this literate culture he'd found himself in. The fad for finding a copy of *Here To-day, Gone To-morrow* had lasted no longer than the duration of the day on which he had failed to do so. But Gordon had been impressed and gratified when Derek asked to borrow the dictionary. 'It's beginning to rub off on him, Pam,' he said to his wife.

Derek looked up all the obvious words – cunt, prick, arse, fuck, bollocks. He hadn't found bollocks. Why had they not included a beautiful word like bollocks? Anyway this exercise gave Derek a fine hard-on but he wasn't going to have a wank because he was washed, brushed and combed for Gordon's party – and he'd wanked a couple of hours ago. This wanking business – sometimes, there was no 2 ways about it, you had to wank, had to get shot of the stuff. So that you could get on with other things. Otherwise the cock gave you no peace. Otherwise you couldn't think straight. He couldn't think straight anyway half the time – sometimes, wank or no wank, it was sex, sex, sexy things, everything was a sexy thing. Clitoris . . . *A homologue of the male penis, present in the females of many of the higher vertebrata*. Aw, juicy one. *Homologue – That which is homologous . . . Homologous – Having the same relation, proportion, relative position, etc.; corresponding*. His penis, which wasn't a homologue of anything, which was purely itself, strained at the fabric of his best white trousers. He'd insisted on wearing the whites, even though Pam had bought him new dark blue ones which were now official best, because Pam had suggested that white trousers, except on hot afternoons in high summer, or overseas (where anything goes), weren't quite the thing for a man, and this had caught Derek on the funny bone – he'd been flattered by being called a man but offended by 'not quite the thing'. Shove it, grandma! He decided that if he were a man, then it was a man's right to wear what the hell he liked! And although he'd've quite liked to wear the blues, he was wearing the whites on principle. And another thing: the whites showed off his genitals more. They weren't tight but they bulged in the right place. Pam's new blue ones didn't. And dark trousers, bulge or no bulge, disguised the genitals. In the whites his fly got glanced at, his bum got glanced at, the shadows in the white told a story . . . But in dark trousers – just darkness, blackness, nothingness. Nothingness where there should be muchness – what a tragedy . . . . .

Birthday presents had been presented that morning at breakfast. Being Saturday, this was at 10 a.m. Gordon told Pam he liked the jumpers enormously. (Piqued by Derek's disapproval of the first, Pam had gone out and bought a second and given both.)

'I like them enormously.'

'You need them, don't you,' she said with encouraging eyes.

'Oh Lord yes, I really need them.'

Gordon had been genuinely moved by Derek's gift. It would be truer to say genuinely shocked by it. Like Pam, he wondered where the money came from. It was one of the good pocket video players, made by the Yushomi Corporation of Korea (slogan: 'Information technology is freedom – undermines tyranny and censorship'). Gordon said 'My God, it's one of the good ones, I can see that – all I need now are some video cartridges.'

'I couldn't afford those as well,' said Derek, at which point Gordon wondered – What do I do in return? – buy him a car?

'Derek,' said Gordon, talking eye to eye, 'you mustn't spend your money on me like this.' Derek didn't bat an eyelid and Gordon, reassured that theft hadn't been involved, went on 'But insofar as you have – I'm very pleased with it, very very pleased.'

Derek broke out in a grin, the remains of which he eventually passed on to Pam.

That was this morning. Now he was waiting upstairs. He dreaded this party but was excited by it too. He'd never been at the centre of such a party before – not that it was for him – but Gordon, Pam and he, they lived here, they would be at the centre of it. He would be part of the centre, wouldn't he? They wouldn't push him off to the side, would they? Mark, the son, was coming. Would he resent Derek? And Gordon's sister and her husband – they sounded a right pair of harriets. Quite suddenly he missed his mother. It was like a skewer going through him. He opened the dictionary again. *Bumf* . . . It was in the Addenda. *Bumf – slang. 1889. Short for bumfodder (BUM sb.[1]). Toilet paper; hence, paper (esp. with contemptuous implication), documents collectively.*

Meanwhile, below in the living-room, the clock said 7.30 and

151

Pam said 'Nobody's going to come! I know it. Nobody's coming. All the food will be wasted. All that time I spent on it. Nobody'll eat it! Gordon, do you know what time it is, it's 7.30! Where are they? Nobody's coming, I know nobody's going to come! And where the hell's Mary?'

Gordon stood in front of the fireplace, wearing one of his new jumpers (the green one with the yellow dragon on the chest), while the bogus logs cast an artificial flicker across the back of his grey trouser legs, and he rather hoped Pam was right. Parties and such-like weren't really his thing. And he always hated this bit, the just-before bit. He tried another clue in the *Daily Zoo*'s weekend crossword – *Mad prelate eats carpet for lunch* – 8 letters. No good. He couldn't concentrate. Or do the opposite – lateralise. He wanted to get on with this party, get it over. He'd do it charmingly – for Pam's sake. He hadn't seen Marjorie [his elder sister] for ages – and that pathetic husband of hers – Harold – retired – he'd been 'high up' in the Electricity Board – now he did nothing – Harold had 6 months ago had a nuclear-powered heart fitted and afterwards he'd still done nothing. They were driving down from Solihull and staying. The guest bedroom would blossom for a night.

– Thank God we've got a guest bedroom for Marjorie and Harold, thought Pam. What a pain they are! But I won't let the side down, for Gordon's sake. But then it'll be Sunday lunch – perhaps we can drive out to the Pigsy Arms [a mock-Tudor steakhouse they'd been intending to take Derek to ever since he'd arrived]. No – leftovers – we can finish off the leftovers – oh God, then we'll be stuck in the house all bloody day – and if we go to the Pigsy Arms Gordon'll end up paying – even if I tell him not to, he will – actually, Harold's not too bad, but Marjorie! The most selfish woman who ever drew breath. And that stupid shop in Solihull – the Giftique! – I bloody well hope that—

Pam's private hopes were cut short by a knock at the door. The electric chimes weren't working.

'That'll be Mary,' said Pam. 'She's $\frac{1}{2}$ an hour late.'

'It's me,' said Irish Mary. 'I'm $\frac{1}{2}$ an hour late.'

'We know that,' said Pam. But since Irish Mary wasn't offering any excuse, Pam continued 'Let's get out the nibbles. They're all ready in the kitchen.' When they'd dotted bowls of nuts and

152

crispy curlies about the sitting-room, Pam said 'Right! I'm going to shut you in the dining-room, Mary, until we need the food. I'll do the drinks. You'll help me, won't you Gordon? I've put some magazines in there, Mary, so you don't get bored.' The dining-room to-night had to do service as the servants' hall – until it was time to eat when Irish Mary would be permitted to wheel round the canapés, stray into the kitchen to help with the hot food and stack the dishwasher. When she'd been safely shut in, Pam said to Gordon 'I told her to put on a black dress but of course she didn't, did she. I've had to lend her one of mine.'

There was another knock at the door. 'That'll be *somebody*! I told you to repair those chimes, Gordon. Honestly, do I have to do everything myself?' said Pam, fiddling with her composure as he went to answer the door. He opened it and looked bleakly out at the world.

When he seemed not to recognise her, Tina Harding said 'It's me, Gordon.'

Indeed he hardly had recognised his secretary without an office round her. 'Tina, of course it is, of course it's you, come in.'

'This is Craig,' she said introducing a man in his late 20s. They were both in their late 20s, both short, but where Tina was petite Craig was ratlike. They had identical smiles, identical mid-length hair-do's, and similar over-fashionable casual clothes. Craig had 2 crowned teeth at the front which didn't match any of his others (which were smaller and darker). As Gordon shook his hand he noticed that the man was wearing a gold bracelet. Tina and Craig had met last year at the Club Mediterranée in Tunisia.

'Is he your beau?' asked Gordon as they came into the hall. He was trying to be jolly but Craig gave Tina a funny look.

Tina didn't answer Gordon's question but pushed a parcel at him as if she were ashamed of it and said 'Happy birthday, boss.'

'Oh Tina, you shouldn't've. Look what Tina's brought me, Pam,' he said as he led them into the living-room. He almost said 'bought me' but corrected it just in time.

'Ti-na. How *nice* to see you,' said Pam with slow emphasis, with an accent plummier than usual, tilting her head to one side, with a grimace of grinning welcome fixed on her face like a big scab – scratch and surely the whole thing would come away.

'Hullo, Mrs Drake. This is Craig.'

153

'Cr-aig. How *nice* to see you. Do come in.' Since they were already in, Craig gave Tina a funny look. 'What will you have to drink? I think we've got everything.'

'Look what Tina's bought me, I mean brought me, Pam.'

'Tina *and* Craig,' said Tina. 'It's from both of us.' She giggled nervously as though confessing a titbit on their sex life.

When Gordon at last got it undone, out rolled a jumper from Marks & Spencer, a dark blue one with a light blue horse on the front. Gordon said with a serious frown 'Great. Really great. I really needed this, didn't I, Pam?' Tina was after all the best secretary he'd ever had – and they don't come 2 a penny.

'Super. Really useful,' said Pam. 'He always needs things like that. I don't have to tell you, Tina, how fast he goes through at the elbows. How sweet, Tina.'

'Tina *and* Craig,' said Tina with another nervous twitter.

'I'd like a beer,' said Craig.

'I'd like a gin & blackcurrant,' said Tina.

'Have we got any blackcurrant, Gordon? No, no blackcurrant. Gin & orange, Tina, would that be all right? Gordon, where's Derek? Tell him to come down and say hullo to Tina, and Craig. Do sit down.'

'Thanks everso,' said Tina sitting down and receiving her drink simultaneously. 'Oops,' she said, spilling a few drops on a cushion.

'Do have a nibble,' said Pam, indicating a bowl of bits. 'I'll get Derek down. Gordon, put on some music.' She went into the hall and shouted 'De-rek! Would you like to join us? Tina and Craig are here!'

– Who the fuck are Tina and Craig, Derek wondered.

'Coming!' he shouted down.

Another knock at the door. It was Joan and Ronny. Joan was Pam's 'best friend'. The fact that they hardly ever saw each other didn't alter the other fact that Joan occupied the slot 'Pam's best friend'. She was a big, capable woman who lived much further out now – in Buckinghamshire – almost in Oxfordshire. But she'd always come in for something important. They'd been at school together, and didn't see each other for whole stretches (even when Joan was further in, for that matter), but if Gordon ever left Pam, God forbid, but, well, Joan was the person Pam'd

154

phone. As for Ronny, he was a bit dropped off Joan – overweight and amiable – but shorter, smaller, less masterful. He was a dentist, and a day spent looking down people's throats left him with no fight by the evening, just a number of unfulfilled appetites which Joan fulfilled. He drank to excess.

'I'm dying for a g & t,' said Joan.

'So'm I,' said Ronny.

'Of *course* you are,' said Pam. 'Joan, you're looking terrific.' Pam felt a gesture indicative of best friendship was called for (it was always a bit stilted with Joan at first perhaps because the significance of their relationship suggested an ease and intimacy they rarely had time to establish) and this remark was it. Joan usually looked like the back of a bus. To-night was no exception – except that to-night it was a very colourful bus.

'So are *you*, Pam. Years younger. What's been going on here?' By contrast Joan rarely felt stilted with anyone.

'Nothing at all. We go on just the same. Derek of course is living with us now.'

'Derek?' asked Joan, lifting 2 eyebrows pencilled about an inch above where her real ones would have been had she not pulled them out with tweezers.

'Yes, Derek,' replied Pam with an affected nonchalance tinged with obstinacy, as if Joan should know all about it. 'I'll get him down. Derek, would you like a drink?' she shouted up from the hall.

'Coming,' came a faint response from the heavens.

'Let's go in. He'll be down.'

'Gordon!' proclaimed Joan. 'Here you are – I'll tell you right now, they're socks.'

'Hullo, Ronny,' said Gordon. Ronny smiled decently and looked round for his g & t. 'You shouldn't't've.'

'Don't be silly, Gordon, it's nothing,' said Joan with perspicacity.

'I really needed them, didn't I, Pam?' said Gordon.

But Pam had gone off for the drinks, some of which were in the kitchen, so Tina stood in for her and said 'Yes, he really needed them.'

Joan was rather surprised by Tina's knowing whether or not Gordon needed them, socks, which Joan classified as underclothing, and when Gordon said 'This is Tina my secretary' Joan said 'I don't doubt it for a second, Gordon.'

Ronny honked laughter and looked round again for his drink which was now borne down on him by a Pam grimacing with *bonhomie*.

'Are those nibbles?' asked Joan.

'This is Craig,' said Tina. 'We met in Tunisia.'

Joan thought – What a horrid little creep Craig is. Bet he's got damp palms. And he's wearing a gold bracelet. I could never trust a man with a gold bracelet. Or any bracelet.

Ronny slurped at his glass, wetting his neat ginger moustache.

And Gordon said 'Where's Derek?'

Pam was about to reply – but the door went. 'I'll go,' she chirruped, abandoning Gordon with a pair of snot-green socks on his hands like dead fish.

It was Major Playfair and the Rev. Vincent Quayle. The Major was wearing a dark blue blazer and custard yellow cravat with skulls & crossbones on it – his 'going out for a bit of fun' dress. He was already well-whiskied. The Rev. Quayle ambled in behind him in a black outfit tipped with dark red silk – he was muscular High Church with a face both sensual and controlled. His tough white hair was cut in a crewcut (convict/monk).

'I bought you this,' said the Major, handing Gordon, unwrapped, the paperback of Tatlock's *Legendary History of England*. 'Hope you haven't got it.'

Gordon was overcome – he'd been overcome ever since the first guest arrived. He *loathed* being the centre of attention. And to be called upon to express emotion while being the centre of attention was almost more than he could bear. Therefore he did it charmingly. People found his discomfiture endearing, a sign of genuine feeling, which it was, though not necessarily a sign of genuine love for socks and jumpers and their company.

'Where's the bog, Playfair?' enquired the Rev. Quayle in a rich fruity voice which penetrated brick walls.

'Same blasted place as mine,' said the Major, 'only the other way round.'

The Rev. came back in a second and in a voice which could have been heard in the African Desert said 'There's no bog paper.'

Pam reacted as if physically struck, and said '*Isn't* there? Isn't there really? Hang on a mo.' She disappeared into the kitchen, took a secret slug from the gin bottle, found a couple of toilet rolls and returned surreptitiously – it didn't look good, flaunting loo rolls at your own party – to the loo, but the door knocker went. She left one of the toilet rolls on the bottom of the stairs, stuffed the other in the loo, and opened the door. It was Eunice from next door.

'Sibyl couldn't come.'

Pam wasn't surprised by that. But she was surprised by Eunice's hair – aquamarine, dyed for the occasion presumably. And her dress – faded red wine colour with mustard splodges on it.

'But she sent this present for Derek,' said Eunice.

'You mean Gordon, dear,' said Pam. 'It's Gordon's birthday.'

'Is it Gordon's birthday too?' said Eunice. 'But this is for Derek. Specially for him, Sibyl said. It's not for Gordon. Don't go giving it to Gordon. Sibyl will be very angry if you give it to Gordon. It's specially for—'

'Yes, dear, what would you like to drink? Derek!' she shouted up the stairs.

'Coming,' was the faint reply.

Eunice and Pam went into the living-room, passing the loo from which loud and complex farting noises came which was the Rev. Quayle getting into his stride. In the living-room Tina and Craig were nodding and saying to the Major 'We met in Tunisia.'

'No, my dear, unless I'm very much mistaken, we've never met before,' replied the Major.

Craig gave Tina another funny look and the Major said to him 'You know anything about Rileys?' while Pam barged up with a gregarious swagger and said 'Anyone for a fill-up?'

'Wouldn't mind, Pam,' chipped in the Major who'd only just received his but miraculously it had vanished from the glass.

Joan said 'Aren't those the new nibbles from Marks & Sparks?'

'Major, you remember Joan, don't you,' said Pam.

'I suppose we met in Tunisia too,' said the Major.

Ronny honked laughter and Joan looked annoyed – she didn't like tipsy men – her husband was one. She said 'You're the man from next door who got Mark in the army, I remember you.'

'Is Mark here?' asked the Major, his face lighting up. It was pretty well lit now.

157

'He's coming,' said Gordon.

'They're both coming,' said Pam. 'I mean – Derek's coming too. I mean, Derek's already here, but he's coming. Coming down, is what I mean. I – that is – when is Mark coming, Gordon? He should've come earlier. Gordon—'

Gordon was listening to Craig who was saying how great, how really great Tunisia was. Pam pulled Gordon by the elbow and said quietly 'Why didn't you tell Mark to come earlier?'

'Didn't you tell him?' asked Gordon.

'I spoke to him – when you did. But I told you to invite him – I thought it was right coming from you. You are his father. It's your birthday.'

'I know I'm his father. But I thought you'd arranged it all with him, the time, the day—'

'No! I thought you had! But he knows it's your birthday. You had a card. It said "Prezzie to follow".' Pam was aghast.

'But I didn't tell him about the party. I thought you told him.'

'Gordon! . . . . . .' She went hot and cold in her feet, hands, neck and crevices. 'Oh God, I must ring him now!' She was in a panic. They were having a birthday party – and they hadn't invited their son! She clambered desperately through the air with her arms and reached the hall as the Rev. Quayle was emerging from the loo – he was wiping the back of his hand across his lips as if he'd just eaten something tasty.

'Ready for anything now, Mrs Draper,' he said with a smile of big square yellow teeth – he'd given up smoking but still had the teeth.

Pam didn't hear him, she was saying frantically down the phone 'Mark darling, Mark, is that you, darling?'

This is Mark Drake here. Sorry I'm not in. But please leave a message after the tone and I'll get back to you as soon as I can. . . . . . Beeeeeeep!

'Mark darling, it's Mummy. Oh God – what do I say? I hate these bloody machines. No, no, Mark, I didn't mean that, darling, would you ring home *immediately*!' She slammed the phone down. 'That *bloody* machine!' she said to the opposite, in-need-of-redecoration wall. There were hot tears in her eyes. 'How could you, Gordon, how *could* you!' Then she screamed up the stairs 'Derek, for God's sake!' And went into the kitchen, stared out of the window at the twilit garden, bit her lips.

Aloft meanwhile, Derek decided that he couldn't reasonably hold out much longer without causing himself more trouble than the trouble involved in going downstairs and doing his duty. He didn't want to go down. Suddenly it was for him a descent into Hell. Those people. And the new ones. He was terribly shy of it all. He readied himself for the plunge by getting off the bed, going to the mirror and playing with his hair.

Gordon went into the kitchen and said 'Did you get him?'

'No, just that sodding machine.' Her back was to him.

'I'm sorry, Pam.' He was no more to blame than she was but on such occasions he was quite willing to accept the whole burden of error. Pam was also quite willing for him to do this and turned round with red eyes. 'How *could* you, Gordon! Our own boy. Our only boy. Our only child.'

'Pam, I said I'm sorry. We'll try again later. Now let's get Derek down.'

'Oh Derek yes,' she said petulantly. 'Derek is all you can think of. Whereas Mark, our own flesh and blood – you never had much time for him, did you? You never took Mark to the sauna!'

'But I didn't go to the sauna in those days.'

'That's not the point!' She turned back to face the window, gripping the draining board, biting her lips, as the tears threatened to overbalance.

'Come on, pet. It's just one of those unfortunate things.'

'The sheer injustice of it is what gets me. Mark – fruit of our loins. Here we are having a party – and he's, he's – he's not even . . . Gordon, it's so cruel. We're like a couple of monsters in a Bette Davis film. And Marjorie will kill you for this – you know how much Mark means to her . . .'

It was the first Gordon had heard of a special relationship between his sister and his son. He blinked helplessly in his new jumper and said 'Come on, pet' again. He wasn't his most talented in a situation like this.

At which point Mary in the borrowed black dress (which was too big because although Pam was not a large woman, Irish Mary was tiny) came into the kitchen. Pam shouted 'Not yet, Mary,' and Mary said 'Just checking,' retreated back into the dining-room and closed the door.

'Come on, pet.' Gordon's needle had stuck at this phrase.

'For God's sake, stop calling me pet! I never could stand it. It always makes me feel . . . *pathetic*.' There was a dull rage in her voice and Gordon thought she was going to get hysterical.

Now the Major came into the kitchen and said 'Haven't got another spot of whisky, I suppose?'

Pam span round and glared. Without saying anything, she snatched the whisky bottle from the kitchen table, found a straw, put it in the mouth of the bottle, and handed it to Major Playfair with an expression that was both wild and rigid.

'I say,' he said, 'what an extreeemely good idea. Is Derek around?'

Pam snorted and stamped like a Spanish horse, folded her arms across her heaving bosom and stared off left (biting her lips).

'I'll get him down, Vernon,' said Gordon thinly.

At that very moment there was a loud tumbling noise like an avalanche. A blood-curdling yell. And a crash which shook the whole house. Everyone went to the hall doorways to find Derek on the floor, clutching his head, surrounded by the debris of Gordon's mother's vase and the flowers, water and sludge it had contained. 'Who left a bloody . . . toilet-roll on the stairs . . .?' he wailed.

Pam, who gave no indication of having heard this question, leapt forward like a springbok and took Derek's head in her hands saying 'Let me look, let Pam look.'

Gordon appeared with a cold flannel which Pam applied to a purple lump rising like a plum beneath the skin. The Rev. Quayle appeared with a glass of brandy which he applied, like a communion chalice, to Derek's lips, saying 'Do you the world of good, boy. Let it slide down. Down red lane.' Derek didn't need further encouragement, swallowed and coughed – as he recalled people always did in films when brandy was administered medicinally.

He looked up and saw these faces staring down and felt he was lying at the bottom of a pit in the jungle and that a tribe of natives were deciding on the best way to roast him.

'My mother's vase . . .' mouthed Gordon with a haggard look. For a moment he too was in another world – in the dining-room of his boyhood – dark wood – heavy curtains – glimpse of trees through the French windows – the beautiful vase glowing in the centre of the dining-table on a silver mat . . .

'No more of that, Rev.,' said Derek as Quayle came again at his lips with the glass.

'Pam, where's your dustpan and brush?' said Joan. Stout sensible Joan. Never frightened to get down on her knees if the occasion called for it. She had plump fleshy kneelers of knees.

'This is Derek, everybody,' said Pam. She was smiling. The incident, especially the breakage of the vase, had, at a primitive level beyond connoisseurship, made a fresh start to the evening. She felt it was a serve-you-right, Gordon. The Pam of 5 minutes ago, wanting to murder the whole world and weep over the crime, was reborn as Florence Nightingale. She helped Derek to an armchair in the sitting-room.

'I'm OK,' he was saying. The door knocker went.

'Gordon, the door, that'll be Marjorie and Harold!' shouted Pam from the sitting-room or hospital bedside as it briefly became. She started dabbing Derek again with the flannel.

'Honestly, I'm OK,' he kept saying.

It wasn't Marjorie and Harold. Gordon blinked cluelessly. It was Helen Crack from the Library. 'Oh,' she said. 'You've got people in. I was passing and I thought – someone left Pam's library card in the Library and I thought I'd drop it off.'

'Are you a friend of Pam's? You'd better come in and have a drink.' Gordon shouted from the hall. 'Pam, someone for you!'

Pam absent-mindedly dumped the flannel on Derek's face and went to see who it was. 'Helen, what a nice surprise. With my library card. That'll be Derek.'

'But you're having a party,' said Helen Crack. 'I'm not dressed for a party.' But she was never dressed for a party, so that didn't matter. Mrs Crack was in her mid 30s and had been married, but 4 months after her marriage, her husband had been knocked unconscious by a swingboat at a funfair and died from a brain haemorrhage. She took off her duffelcoat and headscarf and a sausage plait fell down between her shoulderblades with ugly weight.

Meanwhile Eunice crept up to Derek and handed him the small packet. 'From Sibyl,' she said in a conspiratorial whisper, looking round as if expecting police arrest.

'I hope she's better. What is it, drugs?' asked Derek, only half joking. Eunice cackled and pushed her spectacles up her nose and wound a lock of aquamarine hair round her finger while Derek had problems with the bands of Sellotape. The packet contained a Bisto box, inside which was a small roll of paper. On it he read the following.

The removal of conflict in the human is the equivalent of entropy in the universe: the increasingly even distribution of energy through a system. This leads to peace of mind and inertia. Since man as a species is characterised by the opposite of peace of mind and inertia – by an astonishing mental, physical and emotional activity – we must assume that he was programmed for this – that nature, or whatever, designed him not for inertia but for activity. The next question must be: why?

Derek's next question was: is the old bat off her rocker? It was the oddest present he'd ever received. He looked up at Eunice from his chair and said 'Thank her very much. But what's it all about?'

Eunice chuckled and said 'I expect it's one of her important presents' and chuckled again.

– They're both off their rockers, Derek thought.

Major Playfair came up and said 'Quite a shiner on yer forehead [he pronounced it "forrid"]. You really went for a burton. All right now? Have a cigarette.'

'I keep telling everyone I'm all right. It's the vase that needs help.' Derek clambered to his feet and wobbled. 'The brandy's great.'

'This is Vincent Quayle,' said the Major. 'We were in the army together.'

'We've already met,' said the Rev. Quayle. 'On the floor.'

'What idiot would put a toilet roll on the stairs?' asked Derek.

'Some fucking idiot,' said the Rev. Quayle in his deep fruity voice.

Derek gave him a double look. He hadn't expected those words from the Rev., from any Rev.

The Major sucked at his straw and said 'You can mow my blasted lawn any time you want to, *any* time.'

'Dirty bugger,' said Derek with a smirk.

162

'Derek does a wonderful lawn, Quayle,' said the Major tilting his head back and blowing up a cloud of smoke towards the ceiling. 'Extreeeemely, er . . . wonderful.'

'I've got a lawn too. Do you want to come and do that?' asked the Rev. Quayle.

'Where is it?' asked Derek.

'Hartlepool,' said the Rev.

'Where's that?' asked Derek.

'West Hartlepool. The North. You could stay the week-end, couldn't he, Playfair – tell him how pleasant it is up there. We could have a little party.'

'I like parties, I've decided,' said the Major. 'We should have *more* parties, *lots* more parties. We used to have *such* parties, didn't we, Quayle? Remember those corkers in Singapore? Hollier-Chopping always put on women's clothes and sang

It was a nancy from Nancy
And a lulu from Toulouse . . .

He must be dead now, wouldn't you say, Quayle?'

'Very probably, Playfair. Drink, opium dens, brothels, boys, girls, *animals* – was there anything he resisted? I heard he made a fortune in rubber afterwards – but I can't believe it.'

Helen Crack, nodding to the Major whom she recognised from the Library, said to Derek 'You're that interesting boy. Did you buy that book?'

'Can't afford to buy books,' said Derek.

'Nonsense,' said Gordon. 'He bought me a pocket video for my birthday – much too generous!'

'Did he?' asked the Major. 'Can we try it out?'

'I haven't got any cartridges,' said Gordon.

'Get *I'll Never Forget What's His Name*, *Take A Girl Like You*, *Otley*, *The Italian Job*, *What's New, Pussycat?*, they're great ones,' said Derek.

'The things they can do now,' said Gordon. 'My brother-in-law's got a nuclear-powered heart. He's coming to-night. I can't think where they've got to. Helen, what will you have to drink?'

'An orange juice.'

'You must have more than that. Now you're here.'

163

'Really. An orange juice.'

'Let me put a touch of vodka in it.'

'I'll have more of that,' interposed the Rev. Quayle. He'd asked for a teeny vodka but Gordon had given him vodkatinis and he'd gone quite high on them.

'Just orange juice for me,' said Mrs Crack. At the Library, she was, for many reasons, known as 'the Crack'.

There was sadness in Gordon's eyes as he padded off to get the orange juice. A noise came out of the kitchen which was Gordon blowing his nose without restraint. He missed Jack. And Pam had been so bloody mean.

Joan expertly swept up the bits of vase, stopping to chat to anyone whose legs happened to go by. She was on her way into the kitchen when, passing the dining-room door, she heard a curious noise. Pssst! Pssst! it went. She looked round and saw a little face peering between the door and the doorpost (artful black curls above blue eyes and red cheeks, pointed chin and nose, about 60).

'Pssst!' repeated Irish Mary, beckoning her over.

'Who are you?' asked Joan.

'I'm Mary.'

'Why don't you join the rest of us?'

'It's not my business to be joining the rest of you.'

'What *is* your business?'

'The food. The nosh. Yes. The grub. That's where I come in. That's a jolly nice dress you're wearing. I'm fond of pillar-box red. She's got me in black, you'll notice. I swore she wouldn't get me into black. But when the moment came, all m'fortitude deserted me. Now it's hanging round me ankles like a right ol' rag. I can look better than this. Much better. That was a terrible tragedy.'

'Oh, you don't look *tragically* bad.'

'No. The vase,' said Mary, indicating with a nod the dustpan and brush in Joan's hands. 'It was his mother's, you know. A delectable piece. I used to love dusting it, bringing it up like. Well, thanks for the conversation. It gets a bit lonely in here. But what I wanted to say was – would you ask Mrs D if it's time for me to come out yet? Possibly it's slipped her mind, the nosh, you know, what with all the goings-on.'

The telephone rang in the hall. Pam was on it in a second. Irish Mary sharply withdrew as if she didn't fancy coming face to face with her mistress right now. 'This'll be Mark,' said Pam to Joan. 'Mark! Darling! I'm so glad you called. You're—'

'Hold on, Pam,' said a voice on the other end. 'It's me, it's Marjorie.'

'Oh Marjorie . . .' said Pam, collapsing like a punctured tyre, a sick expression coming over her.

'Look, Pam – we've broken down, the car's broken down, it's a whacking great bore.'

'Oh Lord, Marjorie, get a taxi, where are you?'

'Well, that's the point. We're not far out of Solihull actually. They've been trying like *billy-o* to fix it up. We've been here *hours*. And Harold's getting cold. They say the car'll have to go in. So we have to get a taxi back. So we're not going to be able to make it. Isn't it the most *wretched* bore? Doesn't it drive you *absolutely mad*?'

'Oh Marjorie . . .' said Pam, looking sicker. Joan, who'd put the dustpan and brush on the floor, was, (mindful of her message from Mary) making waving motions with her hands – they looked like uncooked doughnuts flying about. Pam made a rapid little wave back to say 'Not while I'm on the phone, Joan'. Every few moments Pam said 'Oh Marj . . .' and looked sicker. By the time her face was on the point of touching the floor she took a grip on it and said 'I'll get Gordon.' She went into the sitting-room, got Gordon, and said 'Anyone for a fill-up?'

The Major and Ronny simultaneously made a movement towards her. Joan, who'd been following, said 'Ronny, no more. Until we've eaten. Which reminds me, Pam – your woman wants to know if it's time to come out.'

A decision was forestalled by 3 loud knocks at the door. Irish Mary's head popped out and shot back in again. Pam pushed past Gordon on the phone – he was saying 'Oh Marj . . .' every few moments and his face was getting longer and longer – and opened the door. It was the Dashmans, Marilyn and Bob.

'Cordelia couldn't come and Ward couldn't get the week-end off school,' said Marilyn, gliding into the hall and twirling off a champagne mink jacket. She was wearing a dress of silver sequins with purple rhinestone collar and cuffs and high-heeled shoes of silvery grey kid. Her hair had become a luminous prune colour. Bob who loomed in behind her was more plainly attired in jumper and trousers. His jumper had neither dragon nor horse on it but instead a small motif in the region of the left nipple which cognoscenti would have recognised as the device of Hermès. Every so often Marilyn would roar up and down Bond Street on a ravaging expedition, armed with credit cards – this had come back in the bag of such a day.

Gordon was saying 'How's the Giftique? Oh good. Marj, I must go now. Some people have turned up. You're missing all the fun. Give my best to Harold. And tell him I'm sorry to hear about the heart. I'm sure it'll settle down.'

'Happy birthday!' said Marilyn and Bob together, handing Gordon a beautifully wrapped parcel. Such a wonderful sense of occasion they had.

'It's a shame to undo it,' said Gordon. 'Come in and get a drink.'

In the sitting-room, where there was a hubbub which Pam found gratifying and Gordon found threatening, he said 'You shouldn't've.'

'Yes, I always think it's such a shame to undo them,' said Pam while Gordon pulled feebly at the red and blue wrappings, trying to delay the moment of response for as long as possible.

As glossy bows fell one by one to the floor everyone gathered round to see what the treasure might be. Marilyn began to get nervous. She hadn't expected a public unveiling. 'Really, it's nothing,' she said, and added, as a diversionary tactic, 'God, Pam, I'd love a Campari.'

Pam didn't budge an inch. But she did say 'Marilyn, your hair looks gorgeous.'

'It's supposed to be Titian red,' said Marilyn, 'but I don't think it is. But I *have* discovered this great conditioner. It's got this *penetrating* formula based on armadillo foetuses. Costs the EARTH. But I always take a tube of it along to Florian's.'

'Is Florian good? I've heard mixed reports.'

'Judge for yourself, Pam,' said Marilyn, turning round like an automaton.

'Come on Gordon, the suspense is killing me,' said Derek, and Marilyn gave him a tight narrow smile, about ½ a second long.

166

Finally Gordon arrived at a box with lots of colourful writing and designs on it. He turned it this way and that but couldn't understand what it was.

'Open it then,' said Bob.

Gordon opened it and took out several bits of plastic contraption which he looked at, nonplussed.

'It's a new line of ours,' said Bob.

'Thanks . . . thank-you very much,' said Gordon. 'But er, I mean, what is it – exactly? I mean, it looks *marvellous*.'

'It's for making square hard-boiled eggs. Convenient,' said Bob.

'Convenient for what?' asked the Major.

'Oh, for packing . . . . on picnics . . . er, they fit in corners and . . .' As Bob's spiel went on, the commitment went out of it. Funny, he'd worked out the whole sales pitch on this one; but with everyone staring at him as if he were a flasher exposing himself, he suddenly felt terribly alone with his gadget.

He looked at Marilyn and she said 'Great!' Good loyal Marilyn. But couldn't she expand a bit?

'How intriguing,' said the Rev. Quayle. 'An American cousin of mine sent me a gadget for turning the television on its side so one can watch it lying down in bed – I never use it.'

'Intriguing my arse,' said the Major. Tina gave Craig a look and tittered.

'What is it?' bleated Eunice from an armchair.

The Crack said 'I can't eat eggs. They repeat.'

'And they're terribly bad for you, regardless of shape,' said Ronny.

'But they're not bad for the teeth, Ronny,' said Joan.

'I didn't *say* they were *bad* for the *teeth*,' said Ronny with a twitch of his ginger moustache.

– Drink always makes him uppy, Joan thought.

'It's square *balls* we have to worry about in this place! God save us from square balls!' declared the Major.

'I'll drink to that,' said the Reverend.

Ronny honked laughter and Joan gave him a dig, saying 'Pam, listen – Mary wants to know if it's time to come out.'

'Oh Joan,' said Pam. 'Do you remember Marilyn Dashman?'

'God yes,' said Marilyn with a solid plastic smile.

– What *is* she wearing, thought Joan.

– What *is* she wearing, thought Marilyn.

'What will you drink, Marilyn? There's everything,' said Pam.

'I'd love a Campari. Oh you've got one of those log gas fires like ours.'

'Yes, Gordon *finally* got one.'

'They're *so* authentic,' said Marilyn.

'*So* authentic,' said Pam. 'And no heat, absolutely none. Perfect with central heating.'

'Pam – Campari?'

'Marilyn – what *can* you think of me? Let me see, Campari, oh, I don't think – no, I *know* we haven't got that one. I *think* so anyway. Gor-don!' she hallooed across several heads to where her husband was bending over Eunice, trying to bring her out a bit, but Eunice was very content where she was, not quite out, not quite in. 'Gor-don . . . Campari – do we have it? . . . Just as I thought – no. Try again.'

'Dry Martini?' tried Marilyn.

'Yes, we do have that one, I know.' Pam came back from the kitchen. 'Someone's finished it all up. Third time lucky.'

'I'll just have Perrier water.'

'No water in a bottle, I'm afraid. I just don't see the point of bottled water in England. On the Continent, where things go *off* so quickly, yes. But here – well, we've got tap water. Plenty of that,' said Pam with a jocular left-right movement of her head. She was bloody fed up with getting drinks for people. That Quayle man whom she didn't even *know*, she'd seen Gordon pouring him pints of vokdatinis. Trust Gordon.

'Whatever water you've got, Pam.'

'But you can't have a glass of water from the tap. It's Gordon's birthday.' Pam was distinctly put out by the fact that on this festive occasion Marilyn was prepared to participate in the general voomph to the extent only of a glass of tap water. 'Have a sherry. There's *bags* of sherry.'

'But Pam,' said Marilyn, flinging a luminous prune lock back over her shoulder, 'sherry makes me so drunk! So *quickly*.'

'Go on. We've got some lovely old sack. It'll match your hair.'

'That sounds rude. Oh, all right. A glass of old sack for the old bag!' And Marilyn smiled all round the room, confident in her wardrobe, in her orgasmability, in her moreness and her lessness and her oneness, that is, her number oneness.

Beside her the Rev. Quayle was saying to the Crack 'Were you at Oxford too? What college?'

'L M H. What was your college?'

'Teddy Hall.'

Marilyn leaned in and said 'You're so lucky. Education's a wonderful thing.' And she thought – Number One maybe, but one can go higher – I'll never be Absolute Zero – you can't reach that by effort alone – maybe Ward and Cordelia will reach Absolute Zero – rich, beautiful, intelligent *and* educated.

'I never found my education the slightest use,' said the Crack. 'I wanted to be an opera singer.'

'What went wrong?' asked Marilyn with a pained look.

'Didn't have the voice. But I go a lot.'

'Go where?' asked Marilyn. The pained look had become the lost look.

'Well, where do you think? Covent Garden.'

'Do you know, it's the most extraordinary thing, but we've never been. I keep telling Bob we *must go* to Covent Garden and he agrees – but we've *still not been!*' She stamped her little silvery kid foot and laughed.

'But if you don't like opera . . .' suggested the Reverend.

'Opera schmopera! I love an occasion! I want to see what it's like! Life's so short! It's over so fast!'

'Go to the new production of *I Pagani*,' commanded the Reverend. '*Mind*-blowing. And the music, ugh – that aria at the end of Act 2 . . . "My twat is aflame" . . .'

'I beg your pardon?' queried the Crack, not believing her ears.

'Well, I can never remember the Italian,' confessed the Reverend, 'but that's what it means . . . "My twat is aflame", it would melt Siberia.'

Meanwhile, Irish Mary sat on a hard chair under the unflattering light in the dining-room, reading an article in *Me Woman Jane* magazine. It was a questionnaire. *Are you a slut?* Many of the questions she hadn't understood. She was pondering one – Do you and your man share any clothes? – when the call came.

'Right, Mary,' said Pam round the door. 'Bring out the bits and I'll shove the hot stuff in the microwave.' Bits were what came after nibbles. Mary picked up a large oval platter of them and toured the appetites in the sitting-room.

'Good,' said the Rev. Quayle, 'I'm too pissed by half.' Though the observation was addressed to the Major, the Reverend gave Derek a big fruity grin as he said it. Derek was learning how to handle big fruity grins and trotted off behind Mary, eating bits.

'Are they fishy?' said the Crack as Mary staggered into her *lebensraum*.

'Don't know,' said Mary glancing at the greyish brownish pulp smeared onto pieces of toast and topped with a sliver of green olive and sliver of pimento. She gave them a sniff and said 'Probably.'

'Can't eat fish,' said the Crack, and she went across to stare at the aquarium.

'No thanks, Mary,' said Marilyn. 'That's an interesting dress you've got on – is that what they're wearing now?' Irish Mary tutted, moved on, and Marilyn thought – What did she mean, match my hair? – it doesn't match my hair at all.

'That's yer turd or fart already, Master Derek,' said Mary. 'You'll have no room fer yer stoo.'

'Don't call it that,' said Pam. 'It's Boeuf Bourgignon.'

'Oh Mrs D, you can't expect me to get me tongue round that at my age,' said Mary.

'Thanks everso,' said Tina, taking a bit off the platter.

Irish Mary stared at her dreamily and said 'Well, we share that balaclava. As long as we're not both going out the same time. There's only the one 'clava, you see.'

Tina gave Craig a funny look which Craig returned.

'Marjorie's broken down,' Gordon said to Eunice. 'Isn't it sad. She can't come.'

'I am sorry,' said Eunice. 'What was it? The strain of married life I expect. But there are splendid clinics these days. Was it a strait-jacket job?' But Gordon was helping Ronny into a chair – he'd had too much.

'Hullo, Derek,' said Bob. 'That's a nasty bruise on your fore-head.' He pronounced it fore-head.

Derek stood up – Bob always seemed to loom over him. Standing up didn't make much difference to this actually. Then he remembered and said with a smile 'It's not the first time I knocked it.'

'What did the Man Mink give to the Lady Mink for Christmas?' asked Bob.

A soft interest entered Derek's eye. 'Dunno,' he said.

'A full-length Jew.'

Derek laughed aloud. So did Craig who said 'I'll use that.'

'Marilyn hates it when I tell that joke. Her mother was Jewish. But it was told me by a Jewish bloke I know on the Council.'

Gordon came over. 'What are you laughing at?'

'Gordon, the very man I want to see,' said Bob. 'I'm having a meeting with a couple of Councillors on the Redevelopment Plan – you know, those 2 we met before. It's Monday afternoon. My place. You'll be there, won't you?'

'Yes, of course, but please, Bob, not now,' muttered Gordon and an observant eye would have seen that the hand which held his sherry was trembling. Gordon went to another part of the room.

'Can't stand my own parties either,' said Bob. 'So, Derek, are you going to work for me too?'

'Pardon?'

'Don't say pardon. Say what,' said the Rev. Quayle.

'He can say pardon if he likes,' said the Major.

'You know, what do you want to be when you're old,' said the Reverend.

– Fuck this for a laugh, Derek thought. Which rallied him. 'Oh when I'm old . . . I want to be a dirty old man.'

They laughed. He felt good.

Pam appeared in the doorway of the sitting-room and said 'There's food in the dining-room. Come and eat while it's hot.'

'I'm starving,' said Craig to Tina. 'Let's eat and go.'

'Ooo, Craigie – I know where you want to take me – and what you want to do,' giggled Tina, pulling his gold bracelet.

'Don't, you'll break it. If you want to pull something . . .'

'Oooo, Craig, you're vile!' she giggled.

As they moved into the dining-room, the Major said to Eunice 'It's a buffet, Diddums. You know what to do?'

'Gordon's sister's had a nervous breakdown, Vernon,' she said. 'They carted her off in a strait-jacket.'

'I say, that's bad luck. What'll happen to her boutique?'

'Has she got a boutique?' replied Eunice. 'That's what's done it, then. That and her husband. The conflict.'

171

Gordon said to the Crack 'Won't you come and eat?'

She was examining an Italian plate on the wall. 'I can't eat red meat,' she said.

'There's bound to be something you can eat. Derek, take Mrs Crack into the the dining-room.'

Derek ostentatiously offered his arm and winked at her and felt her arm stiffen at the elbow. 'Have you known Pam long?' he asked.

'Only through the Library,' she said. 'Er, I find you quite unusual. Where do you fit in? Are you their son?'

'No. I'm the boyfriend.'

Derek didn't know why he said this but smiled to himself as he saw curiosity fight with discomfort in the Crack's demeanour. 'Boyfriend' was for her one of the power words. She'd hardly got into the swing of marriage when . . . And she should have a boyfriend. Everyone said so. Everyone who dared. Just a mention of the word caused her consternation, a defensive tightening of her surface, a plunging sense of inadequacy and worry. But curiosity – that curiosity which had won her a scholarship to Lady Margaret Hall – had the upper hand. She couldn't resist saying 'Whose?'

He left it a second, then said under his breath 'Both'. Then he turned to Marilyn, who was talking to the Rev. Quayle in a jam by the door, and said 'Hi.'

'Hi,' she said and turned immediately back to the Reverend. 'Yes, my granddaddy was Raven Master at the Tower of London. And wore one of those costumes, you know, as a Yeoman of the Guard which is the oldest military corps in the whole world!'

'How intriguing,' said the Reverend.

'The Yeomen of the Guard *are* the oldest in the world,' chipped in the Major, 'but they do *not* operate at the Tower of London. They're Yeoman Warders at the Tower of London, which is different. The Raven Master is one of the Yeomen Warders.'

'God, you know *all* about it!' she expostulated. 'Tell me *everything*.'

As they edged towards the food, Marilyn managed not only to conduct this conversation on her ancestry but also to bring her leg against that of Derek who was shuffling behind her – he went hot and a stream of tingles poured out of each of his temples.

172

While the guests made their way into the dining-room, Gordon stood in front of the fire and stared into the middle distance which was occupied by no one, thinking – Why doesn't Bob get off my back? – I don't want to be involved – but I am involved – I've got no chums here – I feel unhappy. A terrible desolation claimed his heart. He wanted to join the guests but wherever he looked he saw only a babbling emptiness, a devastating papery thinness of experience, a grimacing vacuum that was horrific. He wanted to withdraw and weep behind a newspaper. But withdraw where? His house had been taken over by monsters.

'You remember the Major, don't you, Joan?' motioned Pam.

The Major thought he ought to make more of an effort with this Joan in a red evening dress and asked 'You know anything about Rileys?'

'Oh good. Stew!' said the Reverend very loudly, with a beam of his carnivorous-looking yellow teeth. 'And heaps of veg.'

Pam, who felt her *répas* deserved better, said 'Mary, dear, perhaps you'd serve the Boeuf Bourgignon. Plates this end, everybody. I thought a buffet would be more relaxed.' She pronounced it in the English way, emphasising the first syllable (likewise 'gateau' and 'garage'). Gordon came up to her blowing his nose and Pam said under her breath 'For crying out loud, Gordon, not near the food.' Unfortunately this coincided with a general lull in gratifying hubbub, so that Pam had to raise her head and laugh curiously at her guests.

Derek went back into the sitting-room with a plateload and sat down. Marilyn followed him with a more decorous helping. 'Have you been avoiding me, you sod?' she said quietly, and her eye could not avoid skimming over that place where his penis bulged in white trousers, a place on which he now spread a napkin and plonked his plateload.

'Thought you didn't want me round any more,' he said.

'Did I say that? You've got a girlfriend, is that it? And how did you get that lump on your head?'

Bob came in – he suspected nothing but nonetheless noted intimacy worthy of resentment. 'Derek's going to work in my factory,' he said.

'I'm not. That's definite,' said Derek.

Marilyn said 'What *are* you going to do?'

'Something where I meet *young* people,' said Derek.

She turned her head away and looked the curtains up and down.

Derek said 'I'm going to get some more of the sauce' and left.

Bob said to Marilyn 'You miss Ward, don't you?'

She stared at her husband as if he weren't there and said 'If you like, Bob. If you like.'

Pam came in, looking harassed, followed by Gordon, Derek, and most of the others. 'I'm going to put on some music,' she said.

'Sorry to hear about Marjorie,' said the Major.

'It's a real shame, isn't it?' said Gordon.

'Should I eat something? I haven't eaten a thing,' said Pam, as a big band version of *(You'd Be) So Easy To Love* swam round the room.

'Ooops,' muttered Ronny, as he dropped half his stew on the sofa.

'Here's to Mary,' said Bob. Mary was in the dining-room trying to find out if she were a slut and so didn't hear this. 'Delegation is the heart of the matter. I hand-pick all my assistants, Derek.'

Derek said 'Your fingernails must be disgusting.'

Marilyn squealed with laughter. So did Tina who was next to her. It sounded like 2 steam trains rushing into a tunnel. Marilyn felt disloyal.

'But I did the food, Bob,' said Pam.

Craig came across, took Tina's plate from her, put it on a side table, and started a slow smooch with her to the music. Tina's eyes closed dreamily on his shoulder as she finished off a slightly tough piece of meat.

'Can I get you some more, Eunice?' asked Pam.

'No thanks.'

'That's a lovely dress, Eunice.'

'No, it isn't, it's dreadful. It's my dreadful dress.'

'How about some pudding then?'

'No thanks.'

It was past Eunice's bedtime.

'Splendid, Mrs Draper, splendid!' said the Rev. Quayle.

'There's pudding too, vicar.'

174

'Yes, that's what I'm eating.'

– Greedy pig, she thought.

Joan went into the kitchen where the Crack was getting herself a glass of water. 'Can I have that? And a damp rag. Ronny's messed up the sofa.' She went back and said 'It's nothing, Pam. It'll come right out, you see.'

Pam said 'I thought dentists were meticulous types.'

Joan didn't reply. She didn't quite like references to her husband's profession in public, as though she knew that looking into people's mouths all day wasn't a very classy act to have.

But Marilyn was onto it like a shot. 'Dentist? God, don't get me going on that subject. Crowns? Bloody nuisance they are. I'll never have them again. Just because my dentist persuaded me! I didn't *need* them! He just wanted my money!' She was serious about it. The purple rhinestone cuffs were zipping about in the air.

'But you have beautiful teeth, Mrs Dashman,' said Joan, on her knees, working at the sofa with the damp rag.

'Shouldn't you've used salt first on that stain?' asked Marilyn.

'That's for red wine,' said Joan tightly.

'There's red wine in the sauce,' said Pam. 'Bags of red wine. And garlic.'

'Is that what that smell is?' asked Craig, still smooching.

'We had garlic in Tunisia, Craig,' rebuked Tina.

'I've never been to Tunisia,' said Marilyn. 'Do you know Sardinia? Let me recommend the Costa Smeralda – the Hotel Plonka, run by Greeks, just great for a getaway.'

'Sardinia – where the sardines come from,' said Derek. He was at the brandy again.

'You better sit down, Ronny,' said Joan.

Ronny was staring groggily at the Rev. Quayle who was saying to him, as best he could while opening his mouth wide and pointing into it, 'Look, here, this tooth here, I'm sure it's rotten, can't you see?' Ronny thought he saw lots of meat and bits of trifle clinging to lots of teeth – but he couldn't be sure. 'Look, this one at the back, don't you see it? I'm sure it's *totally* rotten.' Ronny saw the waggle at the back of the Reverend's throat looking like a large pink tear ready to drop. Then Ronny passed out. He corkscrewed to the floor like a ballerina. And was out.

'I told him to sit down,' said Joan. 'Roll him into the corner.

175

Hang on, I better take the plate out of his mouth – sometimes he champs on his plate. I'm driving – as usual.'

'You're not going yet, are you?' asked Pam frantically – because there was a lot to get through yet.

'No, I was just saying, I'm driving – as usual.'

'I'm lucky, I live next door,' said the Major.

Joan looked him over with loathing – the man who had drunk far more than her husband and who was still on his feet, the man who imagined she might know something about Rileys.

Derek said 'Major, why isn't "bollocks" in the Oxford Dictionary?'

Joan took a couple of steps backwards, let out a scream as the raised torch of Mercury on the coffee table went up her bottom, and decided to go and be nice to Eunice.

The Major said 'It's supposed to be spelt "ballocks" and the Oxford of course doesn't include the far more widespread alternative "b-o".'

On hearing 'b-o' Marilyn turned round with a little pained look, then turned back to the Rev. Quayle, saying 'And God, do you know, there he was, sitting up on the loo, not a stitch on below the waist, like a great bewildered eagle!'

The Reverend guffawed heartily while the Crack bit non-committally into a peach she'd unearthed among the foodstuffs. – I should've peeled it, she thought – there's probably all sorts of muck on the outside, fertilisers, insecticides, strange viruses from outer space.

'I'm told,' said Marilyn, 'by a friend of mine who went to bed with a few when she was a nurse in the Emirates that Arab men are neurotic about having their bums touched. You mustn't, apparently. They feel unmanned by it.'

'Is there anything they *don't* feel unmanned by?' wondered the Crack, knocking back her plait.

Craig started to say 'They seemed OK in—'

'Tunisia,' said the Crack for him.

'Where's Gordon gone?' asked Tina to Irish Mary who'd emerged again and was sitting on the sofa with her knees apart, sipping a glass of whisky mixed with sherry, her special poison.

'This is very warming,' she said to Tina.

Gordon was in the kitchen. He was feeling smothered – the

176

drink, the smoke, the chatter had got to him. He felt as he felt in childhood when his mother pushed hot kaolin poultices onto his boils – smothered, uncomfortable. He opened the back door to admit fresh air.

'Hullo, Gordon,' said Derek, coming quietly in. 'Happy birthday. I'm very sorry about the vase.'

'Thanks, Derek.'

'You can blow your nose if you want to.'

Gordon smiled and looked at Derek with something like love in his eyes. 'This weird world,' said Gordon. 'And we all pretend it isn't weird. The conspiracy of silence on the world's weirdness . . .' He'd picked this word up from Derek but didn't realise it.

'Gets pretty creepy sometimes . . . Can I get you another drink? Might as well get a bit squiffo, eh?'

'In a minute. I had cider. On top of sherry. It hasn't mixed very well.'

'Oh, go on,' said Derek, pouring himself a brandy and one for Gordon too.

'Oh, all right,' said Gordon. It was a mistake.

Marilyn came in, glittery and *louche*, and said 'So this is where you 2 boys are hiding. Derek, show me the garden.' She stubbed out her cigarette on a dirty plate on the kitchen table, and her egress into the leafy outside somehow sucked him out too.

'Why have you been avoiding me?' she asked. 'I want you to visit me again, I want you—' She made a motion towards him of her whole mind, body and soul, and he shot back indoors. She pulled angrily at a lilac tree, tearing the blossoms, saying 'Blast blast blast.'

Pam gave Mary a screwed-up look and said 'There's work to do, Mary. Look at all these plates.'

'Bejaysus!' said Mary. 'I'm just sitting down fer a second. Is it blood yer wanting?' As she spoke, her dentures shot forward out of her mouth but were immediately rescued and drawn back in again by sleight of lip and tongue.

'Ah, Major,' said Pam, 'have you had any pudding? Tina, Craig, pudding? There's still some left.' With every phrase she put space between herself and Irish Mary. 'Helen, pudding? Oh, go on, *of course* it won't spoil your figure.'

177

'I haven't had any yet,' said Bob. 'Marilyn says I've got to try the Hollygog one.'

'B-o-b,' said Pam with kindly emphasis, laying her hand lightly and coquettishly on his Hermetic breast, 'follow me . . .' She led him into the dining-room and served him a large helping. She knew that, despite everything, Bob was very voomphy.

He lifted a spoonful, his lips closed on it, he withdrew the spoon, a little syrup and cream bubbled out of the corners of his mouth, and his eyes closed in slow rapture. 'Am . . . az . . . ing,' he said at last.

'I do know my puddings,' said Pam, visibly excited. She gave her mouth a crooked smile which was her way of being raunchy.

'Where's Mark, incidentally?' he asked.

'Ah!' she replied, choking. 'He's, er, he's abroad. That's where he is. But he might be back now. I must ring him.' She rang again and got the machine again. Ruddy fiddlesticks! Then she heard a clapping noise in the sitting-room and a voice. It was Gordon's. But strained and crackly.

'. . . . . your attention only for a second, ladies and gentlemen and, er, what I'd like is to, er, thank, er, you all for coming and for the presents and for having me, I mean, making . . . making my birthday a really . . . *super* . . . one, and—'

As she stood in the doorway she thought – This isn't Gordon – he's been drinking.

'. . . and it's not every day one has a day like to-day . . . I mean, this evening, a *super* . . .' The skid on the first 'super' had been sickening enough; this second was very nearly a crash. '. . . one – although earlier to-day was good too. And *finally* . . .' Gordon, weak with emotion, confusion, indigestion, drink, held on to 'finally' the way a falling man grasps air. He righted himself. 'I'd like to thank Pam for this . . . super party and ask you to raise your glasses TO PAM.'

'To Pam,' went the rumble. Pam undulated, twitched, put on her crooked smile, dropped it, put it back on the wrong way round, and generally disclaimed the honour.

'And all who sail in her!' declared Bob.

Now Tina stepped forward and said 'And I'd like to say to Gordon – Happy birthday to a wonderful boss. And Gordon, I'd like to tell you now that you've been *everso* good to work for but that Craig and I are going to get married and I'm going to have to

178

leave you because I'm going to have a baby but it's been everso good having you for a boss and I'm very happy and, well—' At this point she started a chorus of 'Happy birthday to you' which they all joined in while Gordon, stunned that he was losing the best secretary he'd ever had, sank pathetically into a chair with his mouth hanging open.

'That reminds me!' exclaimed Pam feverishly as the chorus dragged itself along. 'I've forgotten the cake! It's still in the freezer!'

'Again!' shouted Bob, starting the chorus again. They sang it all again while Gordon suffered a second torture. Bob had done this not only from enthusiasm but also to give Pam extra time. But she hadn't reappeared. So he said 'Again!!' and they all joined in for a third time, giving way to their drunkenness, sloshing the room, and Bob felt back at the rugby club. The third time caused Gordon to twitch hideously round the mouth as inane grin and panic fought each other to the death. 'Again!!' bellowed Bob – it was too much for Gordon, panic won, but the panic was too much too, and he buried his face in his hands in sheer distress and started crying for the first time in ages, probably for the first time since Mark left home – as Pam triumphantly bore in the cake, frozen rock solid, flaming with candles.

'Again!!!' bellowed Bob, and the room sloshed it out again. If they noticed Gordon's tears they thought them tears of laughter, pleasure, inebriation, anything but tears of tears, but they didn't notice much.

'Blow out the candles!' said Pam as if he were a bashful 5-year-old.

Gordon had nothing left in him and expiated air through his blubbing face and not one candle went out. Everyone groaned and the cry went up – 'Pa-the-tic, pa-the-tic!'

'Do better than that!' yelled Pam in the noise.

He looked up at her in desperation and perhaps only Derek saw how anguished he was, because the boy stepped forward and blew out all the candles. 'Pa-the-tic' turned into cheering and applause. Derek gave Gordon a 'silly old thing' type hug, though this was difficult with Gordon cringeing in the chair. Pam broke a knife trying to cut the cake. The handle came clean away without making a dent – the icing was cold concrete.

'Here's some chocolates instead!' she yelled.

'Oooooh yes!!' yelled Marilyn.

'Derek bought them for me,' said Pam. Her hair had gone awry and she tried with one hand to return it to cohesion while offering the box with the other. 'Hard centres. My favourite.'

'Are they?' said Marilyn acidly. 'Are they really? God, how fascinating, how utterly enthralling. Don't we all love hard centres! You're trying to get me fat! You've put on weight, Pam, recently.'

Pam gagged on the caramel and thought – You cow.

'Gordon looks dreadful,' said Joan.

'Haven't you heard?' said the Crack, opening somewhat under festive influences. 'His sister was carted off in a strait-jacket. This sherry's good.'

'Was she? I met her once,' said Joan. 'Mad as a hatter. Gift shop in Solihull. Husband high up in the Electricity Board.'

Derek was feeling dizzy. The Rev. Quayle who'd taken a proprietorial interest in him all evening, now had his reward – Derek approached him unsolicited, the worse for brandy. 'Wanna mow my lawn?' said Derek. The Reverend was confounded. 'What do you make of this?' Derek asked, handing him the paper from Sibyl.

The Reverend perused it for a few moments and replied 'Such shit. What has programming got to do with it? Man is not the slave of what nature might have intended him to be. And it seems to me that in seeking God, seeking to know whether God exists, we have all been guilty of a grave error of perspective. The question is not whether it is possible for men to know God. We know this is perfectly possible, we have the testimony of thousands of individuals in every culture to personal religious experience. No, the crucial question is – IS IT POSSIBLE FOR GOD TO KNOW MAN? This is the crucial question. Every other question is a fucking waste of time.'

The last 3 sentences he had addressed to Pam and she looked round for help and said like a creature lost in space 'Derek, more to eat?'

Derek belched handsomely.

Quayle grabbed her arm and brought his big face up close and gritting his large teeth with strange passion he said 'If it weren't for the prohibition of paganism by Theodosius I in 391 AD we might have discovered the answer to this most important fucking question by now! Of course we want a unitary god! But to say that there is only one possible human expression of that god is a lie! Look at Freud's desk!' The Rev. Quayle had recently been much impressed by a visit to the Freud Museum in Hampstead.

Pam whimpered and the Major said 'That's something to think about, Derek.'

Derek felt sick. He'd overdone it. Marilyn said to him 'Didn't know you were interested in' – here she rolled her eyes – '*theology*.'

'I'm interested in cosmology!' he answered with an extravagant gesticulation.

'Is that what you're going to be when you grow up, a cosmologist?'

'No, he's going to work in my factory!'

'I'm not!'

'Got a girlfriend yet, Derek?'

'What are your interests, Derek?'

'How old are you, Derek?'

'17!'

'Why, when I was 17—'

'How much do you get on the dole, Derek?'

'Let me pull your pants down, Derek!'

'Touch me here, Derek.'

'Feel this, Derek!'

'No, Derek, feel *this*!'

'What do you like, Derek?'

'Derek, can I feel your derek, Derek?'

'What do you want, Derek?'

His head span with brandy! What were people saying! Leave me alone! He looked in desperation out of the bay window, saw 3 boys coming up the path, and gasped 'Oh Jeeesus! Not now! I don't need this now! What are *they* doing here?'

He fled through the house, out the back door and down the garden. He forgot to close the back door and cool air blew in to fill his absence. There was a knock at the front door. Pam answered it and saw an alien face staring at her.

'Hullo, Mrs. Does Derek Love live 'ere? We're friends of 'is,' said a fat boy in a black & white striped canvas suit. There were 2 dark boys in the crepuscular dimness behind him.

Pam blinked uncertainly on the threshold, nervous, trying to focus on the outside world. Then she called over her shoulder – insofar as this was compatible with keeping her eyes trained on the 3 boys – 'Derek! I think it's someone for you . . .'

Part Four

Derek ran down the garden and down the garden and down the garden which wasn't so very long but he had the sensation of gliding down a tunnel – he wasn't doing the propulsion – he was simply sliding forward at high velocity. There was a fence at the bottom of the garden. He was lifted up and floated over it with a wind whistling in his ears and he floated into the spinney, several feet off the ground, but descending, descending like an aeroplane coming in to land, descending towards the earth, and as he struck it, he tripped, fell, the dark trees span fanlike around him and he drowned in murk. His face was buried in long dewy grass and the damp fragrance of earth glided up his nostrils, clearing his head, and he stopped floating and felt the whole weight of his own mass pushing stubbornly against the curve of the earth. He didn't move. He lay still, with heart beating fast and heavily like a solo drum. A breeze, mild and feathery, stirred the leaves about him with a noise which sounded like small waves rushing up a shingle beach, a soft seductive rush made up from thousands and thousands of individual voices, overlapping, moving forward, overlapping. He didn't stir, so restful were the natural sounds, so undemanding was his position, so heavy and happy his belly against the turning earth . . . . .

. . . . . Something delicately touched his bottom here and there . . . so delicate. It felt nice . . . . . What? He sat up with a start. It was Albert, the Dashmans' dog, giving him a friendly sniff-over . . . . .

'Albert . . .' whispered Derek. 'What are you doing here?' He ruffled the dog's ears and rolled onto his back, stretching out his limbs, looking up at the sky through the trees. Twilight was fading out of it on the western side. A rich violet glow and some large untidy clouds held the dying light the way a mother clings

185

to a disintegrating family, passionately, hopelessly. Elsewhere stars had appeared, and behind a black filigree of leaves and branches a moon shone ferociously white. It was a warm night, but he had been indoors for some time and the damp teased him with a chill. Albert came up for another sniff. Derek lifted his knees, embraced them, and the dog vanished. The stars twinkled. The breeze moved with a seigneurial grandeur through the domain, stopping and starting wherever it chose, without explanation.

'I knew it would be like that,' said a voice behind him.

As if electrocuted, Derek let go of his knees and span round on his bottom all in one movement. Standing a little way off was a girl. She wore trousers and a shirt. She glimmered in the moonlight which reflected silver in her pale hair, obscuring the face in darkness. Derek stared hard at her but could not develop much from the shadows. She was half illuminated and seemed covered with a spangled darkness which was velvety deep. He knew she was young. And he felt she was beautiful.

'What?' he said from the grass.

'I said I knew it would be like that.' She came a few steps closer and stopped. There was a hush.

After some moments he said 'Knew what would be?'

'The birthday party.'

'Oh . . .' More silence. She said nothing. He asked '. . . Would be like what?'

'Like how it was.'

'I wanted some fresh air,' he murmured down at the earth.

'Don't blame you.' She came a few steps closer and he saw her trousers were tucked into soft leather ankle boots. 'Anyway,' he said eventually, plucking at the grass, 'who are you?'

'I thought you'd know that. I know who you are.' She laughed like a silver bell. 'Where's Albert gone?'

'Are you Cordelia?'

'God, you're brilliant. Are you studying nuclear physics?'

'You are, aren't you?' He wanted the assurance.

'I suppose I am.'

'Your parents are in there.'

'Oh God. Them,' she said with a groan.

'I like your parents.' Derek was surprised to hear himself say this, since it wasn't precisely true. Perhaps it was the politeness

186

reflex. Perhaps it was the brandy. Maybe it was to arouse her by being contrary.

'I saw my father undress once. He knew I could see. He did it on purpose. Do you like your father?'

'Er, yeah, well, I dunno.'

'Why not?'

'I dunno because – I dunno who he was. I didn't have a dad.'

'Lucky you.' She sat down beside him. He caught a whiff of shampoo from her hair. He loved that and sat closer to try and catch it again but not so close as to seem pushy. He was shy. 'But I like my brother. He's good news,' she said.

'Ward,' said Derek.

'That's right. Ward. You seem to know a lot about my family. You even recognised me without having met me before! You're not at all like Ward. He's got fair hair – like me. He's thinner than you.'

Derek was pleased that she'd observed him to this extent. Her face came closer to his. If such a thing be possible, a dark light emanated from Cordelia's face. Patterns of darkness swam over her. She looked beautiful but not in a fragile way. Her presence was in no way ethereal and yet she sat very lightly on the earth. She had nerve, warmth, levity, a curious and enthralling combination of elements. Streaks of silver flashed from her hair.

'Would you like a Polo?' she asked.

He said yes and took one of the white mints. They sucked in silence. A dog barked in the distance. Albert growled from several bushes away but they could not see him. They sucked on, while 2 aeroplanes in succession droned overhead, lights flickering. Then silence.

– How strange we are able to sit in silence like this, thought Cordelia.

'Have you got a brother?' she asked.

'No,' he said. There was a short interval before he said 'But I've got a sister.'

'Have you? How old is she?'

'A baby sister.'

'Where is she?'

'Where is she? Oh she's . . . I think she's . . .' Then Derek realised with an uncomfortable, sucking jolt, which always

187

happened when he realised this, that he didn't know where his sister was. Doll hadn't told him. How would he ever find out? There must be a way to find out. There must be records. His mind blurred, his heart raced.

'What's the matter?'

'Nothing's the matter,' he replied. But the Fear had broken over him like a cold Atlantic wave. He stood up.

'You get foxes here,' said Cordelia.

'Where? Here?'

'Yes, here . . . They're very cunning.'

'Really?' he said curiously, gently.

'Ya. They like it here. It's safe for them. Was it really dreadful?'

'It had its moments of total dreadfulness.'

She giggled. 'You going back in?'

'I spose I'll have to.'

The breeze picked up. The sky was clear now and shone with stars above the tangle of trees and shrubs and bushes in the spinney. It was dark. The stars made the sky blacker. The odour of vegetation stimulated him like a tonic. Cordelia fascinated him. He became aware of the touch of his clothes all over his body. Cordelia stood up too. She was 3 or 4 inches shorter than Derek. He saw clearly the glint of her eyes and the soft faunlike line of the eyebrows above. He desperately wanted to pee but now was not the moment.

'You don't have to go back in,' she said. 'There's no law which says you have to.'

'No, but . . . . .'

'That's a nasty lump on your head . . . .' She reached forward with her hand but didn't touch it. He hoped she would but she didn't. Instead she asked him if he wanted to come to the Psychoplasty with her. 'I'm meeting some friends there,' she said.

'Is it good? What sort of friends?'

'OK.'

'I dunno . . .'

'OK, don't.'

'All right – yeah.'

'I want to change first. I'll meet you on the corner of the street in 20 minutes – the walk will do us good.' She gave out a low whistle, like a Red Indian signalling to another of the tribe, and

Albert reappeared. She looked at Derek. He was nervously rubbing his chest with one of his hands. She took this hand, slowly examined it and said 'You've got nice hands.' He didn't say anything. Then she prised up a tiny sliver of flesh from the back of his hand with her sharp fingernail. Just before the blood began to flow, he gasped. Then she was gone . . . .

Derek stood there, licked the back of his hand. The moon shone fiercely into the spinney, marking it with ghostly fluorescent paint. A breeze stirred the curls on his head and he stared at the place where she had been. Then he stepped behind a tree, pulled out his cock, and let the bladderful of urine – a whole partyful of drink – pour out in a thick straight stream which frothed joyously against the bark of the tree.

At the entrance to the Psychoplasty, a man in black shirt and trousers, both of which were too tight for him, said 'What do you want?'

Derek said to Cordelia 'This is just along from where Gordon works.'

'We want to come in,' she said. She was wearing yellow dungarees and a black tee-shirt cut off just below the breast, and nothing else except shoes.

The man looked them up and down and said 'OK. Go over there.'

They went through to where another man, in a black tee-shirt and white trousers, said 'I'm going to search you.' Which he did.

They went through again and down a narrow flight of stairs to where a woman with a man's haircut, wearing white shirt and white trousers, sat on a stool. Cordelia stood back and let Derek pay. The woman winked at her and they went through again, through a door, into a luminous blackness.

'Can't see a fing,' said Derek, heavying up his Cockney accent, from nerves.

Cordelia pushed through numbers of oddly dressed people in the direction of the dancefloor. It was small, with orange plastic walls, floor and ceiling, like a cube with 2 sides missing. The plastic panels were lit from behind and the colour throbbed.

'Ward says orange is the most neurotic colour in the spectrum,' said Cordelia. 'He's read about it. They've done tests 'n' stuff. The nerve endings go all funny when they see orange.'

'What?' said Derek. The music was very loud, he hadn't heard her. 'Do you wanna drink?'

She said 'You paid entrance. I'll get them,' but she pushed forward to the dancefloor and on attaining it, started to dance. She tried to dance cleverly and Derek was annoyed with her for being pretentious. A few others were dancing. A group by the dancefloor looked as though they were dying to dance but for some reason couldn't bring themselves to do it. They were blocked. The vibrating speaker which thumped above their heads was both a command to move, to *do something*, and a terrible constraint. The big freeze was stiffening within them. Inhibitions had been drawn out of their hearts by the music, like worms out of a cheese – only to snap back in at the last moment. So close to freedom of action, so far from it! One male was dancing with his shoulders and his hands thrust hotly into his pockets – he couldn't let himself go. He was horribly bashful. Every moment that passed made it more impossible to move. The idea of dancing! The idea of dancing assumed monstrous proportions as of some obligation way beyond possibility. The idea of dancing – why, it was tantamount to flinging oneself over a cliff! Drink did nothing to help. Drink simply increased this group's ability to reinforce each other's inhibitions.

'I don't feel like dancing to-night,' said one, trying to be nonchalant about it but feeling a pathetic worm inside.

'Neither do I,' yelled back another, with relief. The relief lasted but the length of a sentence. A deeper sense, of inadequacy, reasserted itself. The inability to dance, to overcome the immobilising gravitas, turned into a hate against those who could.

'Some of these people are pathetic,' said one of the males.

'God . . .' said one of the females. She'd been feeling 'wrong' all evening. The music crashed ever onward, making all but a dash of yelled conversation impossible.

'What did you say?'

'I said – God!'

'I thought that's what you said! What do you mean?'

'What?!!'

'I said what do you mean!!!'

'Do I what?!!'

'Doesn't matter!'

'What?!'

'I said it doesn't matter!!!'

'What doesn't matter?!'

'Nothing, nothing! For Christ's sake, nothing!'

The ice closed again over this attempt at communication. Each became resealed into their cocoons of inadequacy while the body continued its appeal to be heard – 'Do let me dance, oh go on, let me have a dance, *please,*' squeaked the body's yearning voice from the extremity of a little toe. Inhibition glowered down from where it sat enthroned in granite and said 'Dance? You must be joking, mate. Dancing? Simply not on.'

But unexpectedly one of the girls mumbles down into her tits 'Oh, fuck this.' She moves forward. What madness is this revolt? She trembles fearfully before the invisible wall, thinks again, clenches her fists, and throws herself onto the orange dancefloor like a woman committing suttee on a pyre. This unexpected boldness lands her squarely in a tub of anguish and torture. She dances woodenly, alone on the edge of the gyrating dancers, and feels herself burn, roast, tortured under 1000 spotlights of self-consciousness. 6 eyes beam sneery astonishment from the group she's abandoned. Her embarrassment is excruciating, she feels her valour fading fast, an awesome magnetic power trying to suck her off the dancefloor and back to the group standing by their table. 'No no no!' she cries. 'Let me dance, let me dance!' She forces herself to hold on, fighting the order to fade away. Her body is stiff, afraid. It has in it no feeling whatsoever. It lumbers feebly, cut off from the music by an anxiety of nerves, motorised solely by irregular detonations of willpower . . . However, after a few minutes of heroic perseverance, something begins to change, to soften, to slide, even to enjoy. The anguish of embarrassment and nerves begins to dissolve like impacted ice in a warm medium. Pleasure arrives. Followed by self-forgetfulness. Followed by felicity. The girl smiles as she moves. My God, she's dancing! Yes, yes – dancing! To-night is a success! O dancers! Throw off your gaolers in East and West, North and South! The miseries who trample you down, who ridicule you, who despise you, who hate

191

your delight, who interfere with your soul, throw them off! Throw them off, throw them off! Don't stand for it! Let your dance fly in its beautiful curve! The miseries who search you with cameras, finger you with robots, twist you with lies, throw them off, throw them off! Arise from their swamp of fear, tricks, interference, arise in a beautiful curve! Or if you want – an ugly curve, a silly curve, any shape you like! The miseries, throw them off! Or, if it's easier, sidestep them with your dancing step! They are hungry for your energy. They need your energy to survive. They slip leather thongs round your testicles, slip hand grenades into your vaginas – oooooooooooooooooooh. Dancers, the clarity of freedom is yours! You don't need permission to dance!

Derek felt hunkered in, as the above girl had done. He was shy of dancing in front of Cordelia. Cordelia had felt the initial embarrassment too, which is why she had thrown herself in at the deep end to forestall more thinking. Thinking nearly always tripped her up. She'd overdone it but eventually found her balance. She was rather a show-off anyway. Derek decided to join her. He went onto the dancefloor and moved awkwardly in her vicinity. Then he forgot about her and lost himself in movement. It was hot in the orange cube. He unbuttoned his shirt and sweated freely. After nearly an hour of dancing Cordelia came and pulled him off the floor. They'd turned on harshly flickering strobes and these always upset her.

'Let's have a drink,' she said. 'Oh, you've got muscly bits on your chest, but not too muscly.'

'What do you want to drink?'

'I dunno,' she said. 'Something. I'm going to the loo.'

Orange plastic walls lit from behind gave way to aluminium walls lit from below. Light coming up under the chin made everyone look vile. At the bar Derek's foot was stamped on. 'Watchit mate,' he said.

A burly back facing the bottles began to turn and a voice came out of it saying 'I know that sound'. And by the time the figure had fully turned, Derek realised it was *him*. 'Greetings, comrade,' said Dudley Dennis. 'We thought we'd find you here. Apparently it's the only place to go.'

192

'How'd they let you in?' asked Derek morosely. 'Wanna drink?'

'Very civil,' said Dudley. 'Shake my mit.' Dudley's right hand was bandaged and the bandage was very grubby. 'But I'm learning how to do it left-handed – like you.'

'What happened?'

'Went to the football. We had a party afterwards. Some cunt stabbed me through the hand.' Dudley now waved his bandage in the air and the 2 others came over. 'Derek wants to know what you're drinking.'

'Wotcher, lads. Maurice, you're getting very huge.'

'I'll stick to whisky,' said Dougal Gupta.

'Tho'll I,' lisped Maurice Hampton. 'I'm on a diet.'

'So'll I,' said Dudley. 'I'm on a binge.'

'She gave us whisky,' said Dougal.

'She let you in?' asked Derek.

'You knew we was there then?' observed Dudley.

'I guessed,' said Derek.

'Dangerous practice. Guessing,' said Dudley. 'Of course she let us in. Very pleasant landlady you got. When we said we was friends of yours, she had us in, sat us down, fed us whisky. Malt whisky. Single malt whisky. 12 year old single malt whisky. They got any of that 'ere?'

'And fed us food,' said Maurice.

'Cut us some sandwiches. Special. Said all the other stuff'd gone. Said she was hoping for leftovers – but it'd all gone. Totally congenial she was, weren't she, Maurice?' said Dudley.

'Yeah, totally con – totally what you thaid, Dudley.'

'Quite a party they was having,' Dudley continued. 'Some religious geezer in a collar offered Maurice a job in Hartlepool.'

'*Odd* jobbing,' said Maurice with a smile. 'Maybe I'll go up there, give it a whirl.'

'Hang on, Maurice,' said Dudley. 'There's lots of weirdoes in this neck of the woods. Take every precaution. Maybe he was after your dong.'

Maurice shrugged. He had dong to spare.

Derek peeled a banknote from several to pay for the drinks.

'You been selling your body?' asked Dudley.

'Fuck off,' said Derek.

'Such a welcome we're getting from this boy,' said Dudley to the others.

'He's just missing his mum,' said Dougal.

'Your mum had a great pair of hooters,' said Dudley.

'I ain't settled in 'ere yet,' said Derek. The whole evening was making him very confused.

'Yeah, well, don't freak out. It's only us,' said Dudley.

'We drove over in Dougal's car,' said Maurice.

'Nipped round on the London Orbital,' said Dougal.

'We're staying with some of Dougal's cousins in Hendon,' said Dudley. 'Or would be if they were there. They've gone away for the week-end. They're week-ending away – like us. Thought we'd look you up. Nipped out the back, did you?'

Cordelia returned from the loo and said 'I can't find my friends.'

Derek said 'Meet mine then. This is Cordelia.'

'Ooo . . . Charmed,' said Dudley, extending a fat black and white striped arm with a dirtily bandaged hand on the end. 'Very charmed.' But Cordelia didn't touch it.

'What you drinking?' asked Derek.

'What are you drinking?' asked Cordelia.

'Whisky.'

'OK,' she said. Cordelia was excited. She'd never met a Cockney boy before, not really, not to *be* with. Now she had a whole group of them. She wondered – Where does the word Cockney come from? – it's got 'cock' in it – I like that.

Derek gave Cordelia her drink and said 'Just going for a pee.' He needed a breather.

Cordelia said to Maurice 'There's a black girl in my class at school. Her father's at the Embassy of the Ivory Coast. She's very friendly.'

'Oh they're a very friendly race,' said Dudley, taking Cordelia's hand and pressing it gently against Maurice's fly. A gameness in her let it happen. She was hypnotised by the action. Her heart started to beat fast, she felt something squirm there, the penis coming alive and twisting beneath the cloth. She went 'Agh' and pulled her hand away.

Maurice said to her 'Right joker, innee?'

Derek came back and Dougal Gupta said to Cordelia 'Would you dance with me?' They went off.

194

'You working yet, Maurice?' asked Derek.

'Only in the gym. What about you?'

'Just looking. I might be going to the Arctic.'

'You're not in your right mind,' said Dudley, taking one of Dougal's cigarettes which were on the bar. 'That woman's dead keen on you.'

'You think so?' asked Derek. It was as if Dudley had switched on a light inside him. 'She's not bad looking, is she?'

'See what a git we got on our hands, Maurice. Not that Cordelia whatsit. That, er – *Pam*.'

'Oh,' said Derek.

'She thinks the sun shines out your arse. Good job someone does,' said Dudley.

Derek was surprised to hear this. He always imagined that in some way he fell short of Pam's expectations and that – no, his head ached, he didn't want to think, tired . . . suddenly tired . . . the plug had been pulled, tired . . . he wanted to leave. How could he talk to Cordelia with the boys here? How could he talk to the boys with Cordelia here?

'Is, er, *Pam* . . . Is she putting the squelch on you?'

'Whadyamean?'

'It's obvious, she fancies you rotten.'

'Rotten,' agreed Maurice.

'Bet she's a right squelcher,' said Dudley. 'Whereas that other one – the Lady Cordelia – that's a snapper for certain. A right strangler. Bet she can crush balls at 50 paces.'

Cordelia came back and said 'Dougal's a great dancer. Weird great. Indian style.'

Derek said to her 'I'm going to have to call it a day – you coming?' Then he turned to the boys and said 'Let's meet up tomorrow.'

Dudley said 'She, er, that is, *Pam*, said we was to come to tea to-morrow if we wanted to. Sunday tea.'

'Er . . . Good! See you then, then,' said Derek with a smile which made Dudley very happy.

'Bye love,' said Dudley to Cordelia.

There were a couple of taxis outside the Psychoplasty.

'We can walk,' said Cordelia.

'I'm knackered,' said Derek.

'Who were they?' asked Cordelia in the taxi.

'Friends.'

'They were interesting. Especially the fat 'orrible one. God, he was gruesome!'

'You wanna come round too to-morrow?'

'Can't,' said Cordelia.

'Why?'

'Promised my mother I'd go to Chorleywood with her and take the dog.'

'Why didn't you come with us last time?'

'With who? Where?'

'With Pam, Gordon, and me. To Chorleywood. The other week.'

'Didn't know you were going.'

'But you were *invited*. Pam asked your mum to ask you.'

'Did she? First I've heard of it. God, the bitch! She never told me. Just wait, I'm gonna ask her about this. That's *really* bad news. Not nice, is it? Not passing on invitations.'

The night of the party Pam had had no sleep. She was worried to death about where Derek had gone. She was roused at 2 a.m. by Mark – he was worried to death by the message she'd left on his machine. He'd thought Dad had died or something. Then she was woken up again at God knows what hour by Derek letting himself in. And between being woken up she hadn't really been asleep. Over-excitement. A nasty throb in one of her toes. She couldn't work out which one – it seemed to jump from toe to toe – very exasperating. Gordon, exhausted, managed to get off but was tossing and turning most of the night, giving out distraught emanations, but saying nothing, drifting (presumably) in and out of nightmare. So on the Sunday morning when Mary arrived at 9 a.m., bright as a button, complaining about the world, and ready to start on the clean-up, Pam just let her get on with it for a change. She let Gordon and Derek sleep on. Gordon came down at 10.30 with an awful headache. She woke Derek at noon for brunch and they all ate omelettes in a spaced-out wuzzy silence that was in fact rather comfortable and pleasant. These days they could sometimes be silent without an atmosphere building up. Pam and Gordon napped fitfully after brunch in the sitting-room while Derek watched television. Pam stirred herself and said 'You should've said you were going out. Your friends were very disappointed to miss you. What time are they coming?'

'You told them tea-time.'

'Then I must get something ready in a minute.'

Gordon groaned in his armchair, opened his eyes and closed them again.

'I'm glad you all met up in the end,' she said.

'I met Cordelia,' said Derek. 'In the spinney. She was taking the dog for a walk.'

'Did you? She's a strange girl,' said Pam.

'I like her.'

'Oh yes, I didn't mean . . . That Dudley's a funny one. When I asked if he wanted anything to eat he said "Yes, please, porridge and chips with cream and vinegar on" . . . So you all went dancing. That's nice.'

Pam turned towards the television on whose screen pictures of devastation were being presented. A nuclear power station had exploded in India, killing $\frac{1}{4}$ million people and reducing a large part of the Deccan to a radioactive deathscape.

'The Major's good value, isn't he?' she said.

'Yeah . . .' said Derek, wondering if perhaps another lawn-mowing expedition were called for after last night's expenditure.

'I couldn't swallow his friend though,' said Pam. 'That awful vicar. And he kept using those awful words. God knows, I'm not a prude, but it really wasn't necessary. I suppose it's his attempt to get down to the common level. Are you ready for a cup of tea, Gordon?'

Her husband, momentarily roused, shot forward as if a bucket of water had struck him. She repeated the question and, calmed again, he sank back into the embrace of his armchair, saying 'Whenever you like, pet . . .'

'I'm afraid I neglected Eunice – did you talk to her? And I hardly spoke to Helen Crack either – did you talk to *her*? Marilyn looked very well, I thought. But doesn't she always? I must say I do like the way Bob and Marilyn always put their best foot forward. It's so nice when people *bother*. But that *dress*. Whatever next . . .'

At this point Derek was distracted by a kerfuffle through the nets. The boys were out there. Dudley's voice came through the window and presumably the windows of surrounding houses: 'What's wrong with this fucking gate?!'

Pam blanched and said 'Gordon, the boys are out there. Let them in, Derek. Gordon, if I have to tell you *again* about that gate . . .'

Gordon stirred in his turbid soup, rubbed his eyes, and muttered 'I thought I fixed it . . .'

'Fixed it be blowed,' she said.

The next moment 3 big boys, whom Gordon vaguely remembered from somewhere, were standing in his sitting-room, vaguely trying to shake hands with him. He had a powerful desire to sink below the surface of his soup but Derek was saying 'You remember, they're my friends from where I lived before.' And the politeness reflex forced Gordon groggily to his feet. 'They're visiting the countryside,' said Derek jokily.

'This ain't the countryside, ya silly pillock,' said Dudley. 'I've been to the countryside. There's cows 'n' stuff.'

'I know that,' said Derek hesitantly. 'But you do get foxes here.'

Maurice was looking at the aquarium and said 'Look at these.'

'They're tropical fish,' said Gordon.

Dougal and Maurice looked at each other as if to say 'Poor old soul'.

'I remember a school visit to the countryside,' said Dudley, settling himself into the room the way one would into an overcoat. Actually he was standing in the middle of the carpet. Gordon was standing by the fireplace, looking across with tension creasing deeply round his eyes, bent at the knees, terrible posture. 'One of my mates peed on an electric fence. There was a fault, the charge was too powerful, it travelled up his piss and electrocuted him. He weren't killed or anything. But he'll never be daddy.'

'De-rek!' Pam ululated from the kitchen.

'She's calling you,' said Dudley. Derek glanced at him uneasily and went out. 'Mr Drake, thanks for having us in. There was no time last night, so I'll take the opportunity now, on behalf of

198

Maurice and myself and Dougal here, to wish you happy birthday.'

'Oh. Thanks. How kind. Won't you sit down?' asked Gordon, collapsing into his own chair with evident relief.

'Too much booze?' suggested Dudley with a knowing frown.

'Oh, well, it's not often,' said Gordon.

'That's good,' said Dudley. 'Because – this isn't meant unfriendly like – you look really terrible. Absolutely butchered.'

Gordon was so astonished by this impertinence that he could say nothing. He was gagged. Derek came in carrying the tea-tray.

'This is a nice house,' said Dougal.

'Very cosy,' said Dudley. 'Don't you concur, Maurice?'

'I bet you vote Conthervative,' said Maurice to Gordon.

'I don't actually,' said Gordon with a quick smile of self-satisfaction.

'I vote National Front,' said Dudley. 'No messin' about, that's me.'

Pam came in with sardine and cucumber sandwiches and a sponge cake on a pedestal cakestand. The corn on her right little toe was throbbing painfully.

'My uncle's got a house like this,' said Dougal.

'Really?' said Pam.

'Only his is bigger.'

– Isn't your uncle a clever dick! thought Pam and she made an ostentatious clatter handing out plates.

'How can you vote National Front when you have a black friend and an Indian friend?' asked Gordon.

Pam looked at him and said 'Oh Gordon, not on Sunday, please.'

'I'm curious, pet.'

'Easy,' said Dudley. 'You put a cross in the appropriate place. I get my first chance next General Election. Can't wait. Should be a right dust-up. Can I have some more sandwiches, Mrs Drake?'

'You've got quite an appetite,' she said, offended by his glut-tony. The sandwiches had simply vanished from his plate.

'I was raised on cardboard boxes fried in old diesel oil. I tend to overcompensate,' said Dudley with an oleaginous smile.

Derek was less than himself in this situation. He felt constrained by both sides and thought it best to keep his head down, but he

199

wasn't permitted to because Maurice asked him at point blank range 'What'th it like living 'ere?'

'It's great.'

'Not much thtreet life,' said Maurice, having as he always did a real problem with the word 'street'.

'Plenty of house life,' said Derek. He felt an idiot.

'Any prejudice?' asked Dougal.

'I expect you inherited this place, Gordon,' said Dudley. 'That's one of the things we'll get rid of in the National Front – passing on the shit.'

'Watchit, Dudley,' said Derek, sweating.

'Pardon my French,' said Dudley; 'Watchit, Dougal,' he said as Dougal dropped some cake on the carpet.

Gordon sat there, dazed and uncomfortable, not knowing what to do. But Pam knew what to do. She was furious. She turned heatedly towards Dudley and said 'Gordon worked hard for this house. He earned it. He didn't just sit around grunting and whining! He didn't think how he could steal or destroy or—' Her fury jammed her thoughts at this point.

Dudley took the opportunity to say 'What's that, granny? Destroy?'

'And as for you,' she said, turning towards Dougal and Maurice, 'you should know better. If you expect to get anywhere in England, learning how to eat properly would be an excellent first step!'

Dougal was needled and said 'I know how to eat! And I've never been to India. My grandparents came from Zanzibar. The nearest I've been to India was where I was born, just off the East India Dock Road.'

Gordon wore his 'interested' expression and tried to calm Pam but she went crashing on. 'OK, you know how to eat – that's not the point! You boys think you're *entitled* to things. But life's not like that. No one's entitled to anything. We all make the best of it we can. And if you don't put your back into your life, and your intelligence too, you only have yourself to blame. There's prejudice, of course there is – so what's new? When wasn't there? Don't use prejudice as an excuse to avoid responsibility for your own life. You can waste your whole life stuck in the prejudice trap. Because Gordon hadn't been to university he thought he could never be a *real* solicitor. But I told him to stop being so bloody stupid. And now I'm saying the same to you boys, you men – stop being so *bloody* stupid!'

'You finished, granny?' asked Dudley. She had said her piece and was breathless. But Dudley had gone hot in the face. He wanted to hit Pam, smash her silly prattling face in, to shut off her pious babbling noise, to still her babbling brain with a violent blow to the skull. His skin was tingly and his heart thumped. But he didn't smash her head in. He looked down and said in a voice that was low and trembling 'What's this bit of crap?'

'It's Mercury,' she said. 'The messenger of the gods.'

'Is it now. Well, here's *my* message.' With his unbandaged hand, Dudley picked up the bronze statue by its head and, with a scream such as Samurai would utter at the killing moment, and a force which drew all his spiritual energies into one act of physical commitment, he swung it at the aquarium. As the bronze struck the glass flank, there was an awesome shudder which shook the room and the bowels of everyone in it. Then the glass caved in, shattering into triangular shards, and water, green weeds, fish rushed out into the air, were grabbed by gravity and splashed across carpet and furniture.

Pam screamed too, a girl's roller-coaster scream. Gordon made an in-breathing, throttle noise. Fish twitched in death spasms on the floor. Dudley did a Red Indian war dance. Dougal said 'I'm getting outta here,' and rushed to the door, followed by Maurice and Dudley.

It happened so fast. Derek couldn't move. He'd gone completely numb. His whole world had suddenly risen up on right and left and crashed together, obliterating him.

Meanwhile Gordon went for a bowl of water and started to pick up dying fish. Some revived quite quickly, others never did. He picked up pieces of broken glass which cut his fingers but he didn't notice it – saying 'Oh God, oh God' in a masculine wail. And Pam – she was in a fever of distress, shaking, dry sobbing, but not clueless. She went next door and bashed on it. The Major answered and saw a frantic face atop a palpitating torso. He drew her in, sat her down in the hall, and gave her whisky from a bottle by the telephone. 'Sip this, calm yourself. Tell me all in good time . . .'

'Those boys,' she burbled. 'The police . . . phone . . . I want to phone the police, I've got to phone the police.'

'Give yourself a moment. That's it, calm yourself, Pam, c-a-l-m . . . yourself . . . Has anyone been hurt?'

What a lovely afternoon it was up at Chorleywood. A breeze rolled out of the Chilterns cleaning the sky which was blue and fresh, holding a few small clouds and one glider plane. Albert disappeared and reappeared, joyfully testing the limits of his freedom. The warm sun poured a rich yellow light upon warm leaves of brilliant green. Marilyn loved this time of year – early summer – fully out but still fresh – like herself. She was in country gear – jeans, jumper, Wellington boots. They'd thrown wellies in the back of the shooting brake because it was often squelchy up here. Cordelia was in combat gear – black jeans, 3 tee-shirts one over another, camouflage jacket and wellies. There were a few other walkers with dogs but it was surprisingly quiet for a Sunday afternoon.

'I see Rot Gurke won again,' said Marilyn, squelching happily through a mud patch and jumping aside as an unknown creature shot into a bush.

'Who cares,' said Cordelia. It was a flat statement.

'I see, it's like that, is it?' said Marilyn. 'I thought he was the love of your life.'

'Mummy – for God's sake . . .'

'You haven't had enough sleep, Cordelia. Did you enjoy yourself last night? Derek's a nice boy. But . . .'

'But what?' asked Cordelia.

'It's not for me to say, but . . .' Marilyn wanted to say – Don't go getting involved, he's a nice boy but he's not good enough for you, he's just a common boy.

'I'm not going to marry him or anything,' declared Cordelia.

'No, no, I'm not talking about marriage, darling. Watch out! Cow pat . . . You're a beautiful girl. You can have a fabulous life if you want. Did Daddy tell you we met this prince in Sardinia who—'

'No, he didn't. I don't want to get married – ever,' Cordelia

202

went on. 'The whole idea of marriage strikes me as gruesome—'

'Hang on,' said Marilyn.

'No, Mummy, people stop trying when they get married.'

'God, that's the *point* of it, darling!'

'There's cow shit everywhere.'

'Marriage enables one to stop trying. One can't spend one's whole life merely *trying* something. It wears one out. A trying relationship is too . . . frangible.' She'd come across the word this morning in the *Sunday Zoo*. 'Marriage is about accepting the other person entirely, getting beyond that ego thing, that trying it thing, and moving forward into life. Marriage is not a passion. It's an arrangement with someone you love. Marriages of passion are the unstable ones.'

'Don't you have any passion with Daddy?'

'Yes, but . . . . help me, darling.' One of Marilyn's feet had conveniently stuck in a boggy patch. She extended her hand to her daughter who took it and pulled. There was a loud schlupping noise as Marilyn righted herself, and they continued across the open turf, skirting the woodland.

'Derek's got a beautiful mouth,' said Cordelia. 'I think he would be a nice person to live with.'

A current shot up Marilyn's insides and she said 'You're too young for that sort of thing.'

'I could leave school now if I wanted to.'

'Stop it, Cordelia,' said Marilyn, her voice sliding upwards on the last 3 syllables of her daughter's name.

'I'm not going to. But I could.'

'Don't you *want* to go to Drama School?'

'Ya . . . But I might not get in.'

'Look . . .' said her mother. 'If you . . . well, do anything. You're too young and it's not right, but *if* you do – do take precautions, won't you, promise me, darling, promise me, will you? Not only for babies, but also for disease. I know I've mentioned this before, but I get worried for you. If you get a boyfriend and start . . . anything, do go to the doctor about contraception, do make the boy use a condom, and do—'

'Don't worry,' said Cordelia. 'I think sex is boring.'

'You know nothing about it,' said Marilyn, trying to disengage the arm of her woollen jumper from a gorse bush. 'Anyway, sex isn't the point. Love is the point. True love.'

'True love sounds boring too,' said Cordelia. 'Sounds like prison. Always fretting, always worrying in case something comes along to wreck it.'

The breeze rose to a wind, then fell. 'Albert!' shouted Marilyn. He was burrowing in a shallow ditch, making himself filthy.

'Mummy,' said Cordelia.

'Yes, darling?' Marilyn still had a pained look.

'Derek said the Drakes invited me out with them. Why didn't you tell me?'

Marilyn had another minor seizure. 'Ah – oh, *darling* . . . I'm *sorry*. Yes, they did. How stupid of me. I clean forgot. I *am* sorry.' She was panicky.

'Thanks, Mummy.'

At 7 in the evening of this same Sunday, 3 policemen – 2 in uniform, one not – appeared at the Drakes' front door. Between the 2 uniformed ones was Dudley Dennis. He was chalk white. Gordon, who'd answered the door, said 'You better come in.'

As they entered the sitting-room Pam, who'd had several shots of brandy in the interim, as well as the Major's whisky, said 'Yeh, that's him, that's the little bastard, officer, he should be shot!'

'All in good time, Mrs Drake,' said the un-uniformed one. He began to ask her questions and take notes and when he appeared to have finished with her she said 'I'll make some tea. I can't stand the sight of him. Gordon, can you deal with the rest?'

Dudley hadn't spoken. Sweat soaked right through the armpits of his black and white striped jacket. The sharp odour of nerves came off him in incisive whiffs.

The un-uniformed one said 'Anyone else present?'

'There's Derek,' said Gordon. 'He's upstairs. I'll get him. But it won't be necessary for him to make a statement.'

'I'll be the judge of that,' said the un-uniformed one.

Pam brought in the tea. And soon after Derek followed Gordon downstairs. He stood in the doorway and said nothing.

'What you looking at me like that for?' asked Dudley with a feeble show of resentment.

204

Derek didn't reply, carried on looking.

'Where are the other 2?' asked Pam.

'We haven't found them yet – but they'll be picked up soon,' said the un-uniformed one. The uniformed ones sipped their tea in silence, relaxing on the job.

'They had nothing to do with it,' said Derek unexpectedly.

'No, they had nothing to do with it,' echoed Gordon.

Pam said nothing, Dudley said nothing.

'I think we should be the judge of that,' said the un-uniformed one.

Derek turned a curiously wistful expression on Dudley and said 'You smell disgusting.'

Dudley seemed to sink further into his fat and start steaming anew. He was in a state of intense humiliation and had dealt with it by going blank. It was not moral humiliation, not contrition, but the deeper, more primitive humiliation of having been caught. To have dared – and lost. A humiliation which can only be expunged by some greater daring, some larger winning.

'I don't understand it,' said Gordon.

'I do,' said Pam. 'The trouble with you, Gordon, is you refuse to believe in evil, plain evil!'

The 3 policemen sipped, holding their cups in one hand and saucers in another, observing.

'That's it, Dudley,' said Derek. 'The . . . End.'

A quiver ran through Dudley. 'Ha!' he said, trying to be amused. 'You – Maurice – Dougal – all left me now.' His lardy bulk quivered with conflicts: anger, hate, self-pity, fear, understanding and ignorance, frustration and desire. He didn't need Derek. He looked at him in the consternation of love/hate. Had the chemistry been only a little different Derek might have been the great love of his youth. Perhaps, even so, was that. But always the rivalry and belligerence, Derek's refusal to submit. This refusal was what attracted Dudley in the first place, arousing anger and respect which comes very close to love. And now? Now . . . I'm frightened, he thought – and I'm trapped. Look at them with their fancy sofas and silly little garden – look at goody-goody Derek, posing as the son – look at it all! . . . . . I can't look at it all – it hurts my eyes – my eyes are prickly – and my skin is burning—

This burning sensation of the skin became much stronger as Dudley realised, to his utter horror, that he was going to cry. He had seemed quite stable in his present blankness. Then out of the blue, tearfulness . . . . . He felt it begin in his centre, as if the heat of his heart, his fury and self-pity had melted something there. He had a melting feeling in his centre. It might have been the shits or pissing in his pants, that helpless melting, loss of control and involuntary abandon in the centre. But in this case the melting manifested as tears. He'd have preferred to shit his pants, it seemed to him more appropriate to the situation, but the matter was out of his hands, the choice was made elsewhere. And tears started to come, like coming, like orgasm, of their own accord, all by themselves. He didn't want to cry, he had no need to cry. His body was doing this without his permission. He was crying – Oh fucking hell! it's awful – I'm crying – Dudley *doesn't* cry – stop it! – in front of fucking Derek too, in front of *him* – why, why, why, why? . . . I don't want to cry, please let me not cry, PLEASE . . . But the relevant stopping muscles were inoperative. His body carried on regardless, producing these tears which came slowly out of his piggy slit eyes and ran elegantly down his round white cheeks and dropped off the jaw in pairs. As one pair dropped off, there would be a build-up in the eyes, and another pair would start on down. He realised that there was nothing whatsoever he could do about it – Dudley was in meltdown! He had to accept it, it drove him wild but he had to accept it, crying here in this posh room surrounded by strangers who wished him ill and no one in the whole world to turn to for help and his only real friend standing in the doorway saying 'You smell disgusting . . . This is the end.' He hadn't the strength to fight it any more, so he had to accept it . . . . . and once he'd accepted it, the tears stopped being slow and elegant and precious. The meltdown rushed ahead! A shattering sob broke out of him. The noise startled him – like a dinosaur disengaging itself from a bog – a complicated slurping sob came out of his chest and throat, and as it came out it grew so that it came out of his whole body like another form of himself undergoing noisy and painful birth. And he started to sob and heave and weep in the most heart-rending way – blubbing, really blubbing. So many years denying it, fighting, choking it, had only made it stronger and here it was tearing him apart as it escaped from him, tore its way out into the light of the world, his terrible terrible heartache.

Pam couldn't stand it – she detected compassion rising in her breast and had to leave the room in tears saying 'Oh God, it's pathetic' and feeling all shitty inside for having said it in that sneering way.

The policemen sipped on. Things had to run their course.

Gordon and Derek looked painfully into the carpet.

And Dudley's woe rolled out of him and heaved and mounted and reached its tragic climax of shuddering sobs and – finally – began to abate.

Which being so, viciousness now had its opportunity and in due course entered Dudley's being. If Derek was breaking free of the past, so would he. If Dudley were to survive, folly would have to become a serious business, controlled and systematic. From delinquent to right bastard, from hooligan to nasty piece of work, from crazy boy to real weirdo – the transformation was under way. He sat there damp and sullen, red eyes glowering at Gordon's slippers, sniffing.

Derek looked out of the window . . . examined the privet hedge in obsessional detail.

The un-uniformed policeman said 'I think that's all for now. We'll phone you to-morrow, Mr Drake, with details of the charges.'

Gordon looked up at him and said firmly 'There'll be no charges.'

'But, Mr Drake, we have a lot of material here.'

'I'm not bringing any charges,' reiterated Gordon, flushing red.

'This kid Dennis needs a good dose of medicine, if you ask me – but you're not bringing any charges?'

'That's right, officer.'

'Mr Drake, we could bring charges without you.'

'Of course, but you'd find it very difficult in this case.'

From beneath a baleful, downcast head, Dudley listened.

'Mr Drake, this kid starts smashing up your house for no reason, your wife phones the police, we pull him, and you're not bringing any charges?'

'You haven't wasted your time, gentlemen. It's given him a deep shock. That'll do. No charges – so long as we never see him again in this area.'

'Well, it's your choice, sir, but—'

'Oh I won't be back, I won't *ever* be back!' burbled Dudley, oozing complaisance. 'I've learned my lesson, honest. It was a dumb thing I did. I've been unhappy. I'll try and get a job, honest.'

'I advise you to drop the National Front as well,' said Gordon.

'Yeah, don't need it any more, just don't need it,' said Dudley, nodding and shaking his head in violent agreement with any remark made by anybody.

'Then we'll have to let him go. And get back to the station. I'm very disappointed, Mr Drake. But listen, Dennis. Don't think you've got off Scot free. We've details on all this. And they'll be in the Big Computer *for ever*, along with anything else we've got on you. Just remember that. And remember too – this part of London don't exist for you any more. All your maps, from this day on, have a big hole in them, right?'

'Yeah, officer, right, certainly. I'll remember it. Always. Thanks, Mr Drake. I won't ever forget what you did. Never. And tell Mrs Drake I'm very sorry for what I done.' Dudley adopted postures of nauseating obsequiousness all round. And he nervously approached Derek who turned round from the window with a face that was colourless, drawn tight by tension. 'No hard feelings, mate,' said Dudley. But Derek read there 'Just you wait, you fucking wanker.' And Dudley left with the policemen.

This Sunday evening had not quite finished. Derek felt low and thought of Cordelia – she'd think him a rough and dangerous peasant now, the whole street would know about it and . . .

Gordon felt, more than anything else, relief.

Pam, who'd been lying on the bed, getting her anger back, came downstairs and said 'What happens now?'

'I'm not bringing any charges,' said her husband.

'What!' shrieked Pam.

'What's the point? It's only an aquarium.'

'But that evil boy . . . If he thinks he can get away with it every time!'

'I don't want to put Derek on the spot any more, Pam.'

'Derek!'

'I can handle it, Gordon,' said Derek.

208

'What about *my* spot, Gordon?!' she exclaimed. 'This ugly maniac starts smashing the place up and—'

'Pam, that's an end to it. Besides, I'm told the black boy's on a suspended sentence. He'd go to prison and I don't want that. Because it wasn't anything to do with him.'

'You can *tell* them that, can't you? We've got *tongues* in our heads, haven't we?!'

'Pam – listen. No charges. All this has gone far enough. I want it to stop here. Otherwise there's no telling where it'll end.'

'But Gordon—'

'Oh *shut up!* I've made my decision!'

She was shocked by the vehemence of his reply. Blocked and hurt by Gordon, she turned on Derek and said 'I hope you're bloody proud of yourself, bringing people like that here!'

Derek was stunned. 'I didn't invite them!'

'You didn't exactly get rid of them!'

'*You* invited them!' he shouted.

'Just because of you! If you'd been here in the first place instead of running off with that stupid girl! Look what's happened!'

'It was only a bloody aquarium. I'd've bought a new one. You didn't have to call the police, you fucking cow!'

Pam hit him across the face. Derek hunched and his hand flew to his own face to protect it. But too late. The ring on her finger caught his lip and cut it. Blood flowed between 2 of his fingers and fell. Aghast, Pam was mesmerised by the red liquid which dripped between his fingers and down the white shirt front. The shirt she'd washed. Derek's eyes were closed tight in pain and grief and his hand remained over his mouth as he said '. . . don't hit me. You're not my mother. You'll never be my mother . . . . .' Pam bit her knuckles. Unable to bear it, she ran sobbing from the room.

Monday morning broke like an egg. Bob Dashman was sunny side up. Very centred and contented, enterprisingly relaxed, optimistic and full of ideas – he was his own man. He stared up at the ceiling of his office which was a transparent dome of plexiglass letting onto the blue blue sky. It wasn't always blue, the sky, but when it rained he liked his transparent domed ceiling just as much. The run-off made beautiful patterns. And when it snowed, it was like being kissed by the sky – and the warmth from the room below kept it from settling. On his left a bank of computers clicked, blinked and chattered, resembling a row of agreeable aunts at a wedding. On his right a desk shot away into the distance. He never sat behind it, always to the side of it – the relaxed approach. Besides, sitting out here, on the 'pitch', he could stretch out his legs and reveal his rugger-bugger bulk to whoever was visiting him. The walls of his office were also transparent. He had nothing to hide. Only occasionally was it a bind – when he fancied a flirt, for example, canoodling on to a fuck. But this wasn't often, one could always go elsewhere, and it was a small price to pay for the great trust he imagined flowed to him from all sides through the transparency. Not that he was always in the office. Sometimes his 2 secretaries never saw him for several days at a time. He smiled inwardly and outwardly and thought – You jammy cunt! Successfulboots!

Bob picked up the phone and spoke the number into the mouthpiece – the number then dialled itself.

'Hullo? Is that you, Gordon? You sound dreadful. Just wanted to say what a great time Marilyn and I had. What time did it finish? Those boys looked all set to stay the night . . . What do you mean don't mention it? . . . Why do you keep on saying don't mention it? When you say don't mention it, do you mean to say – it was nothing, old boy, glad you could come. Or do you mean, well, do you really want me not to mention it? . . . . What? . . . . Oh no . . . . Oh no . . . . Really . . . . I see . . . . [Clearly Gordon was pouring something out at the other end because this was the longest Bob had been silent in a telephone conversation for about 5 years – the previous long silence had been when Marilyn was telling him she was going to leave him and why (luckily that had turned out to be no more than a severe attack of dyspepsia follow-

ing her morning coffee)] . . . .
. . . .
. . . . Poor Pam . . . .
. . . . Well,
look, sorry to hear about this and all the rest of it. But I wanted to
mention something else . . . . . No, I'm not going to mention it.
You're the one that's mentioning it! I said mention *something else* .
. . . .
. . . .
. . . . yes, Gordon, OK, fine, I've got it, you already
went through that, but look, there's other things happening in the
world, and at least nobody was hurt . . . OK, apart from the fish
then, but it could've been MUCH nastier – no, I said much *nastier*
– but look, I have to change the subject for a moment. Yes, it is
about International Pink . . . Well, it can't wait, Gordon . . .
Gordon, *it can't wait*, you get my meaning? Anyway – the Council
are about to approve the plans . . . What do you mean what
plans? *Any* plans I give them of course . . . Yes, I've got the
architect's plans here. Oh just the usual sort of thing. Nothing
fancy . . . Of course we'll use them. I have shares in that construction company . . . Can you come to-morrow? OK, Wednesday . . . Now go and have a drink . . . Well, have a pill. And
listen – love to Pam. Right. Wednesday. Here. 10 a.m. . . .
Gordon, stop messing around, I'm not joking . . . OK, 'bye.'
   Gordon put down the receiver, leant his head back in his chair
and stared at the light in the centre of the room, a 5-pronged
modernistic claw which hung on a chain from an Edwardian
plaster rose much clogged from overlays of paint. The sun slanted
across his desk. He stood up and walked to the window. The
shoppers were out. Gordon observed them with bleary eyes. He
wasn't sunny side up. His yolk was running everywhere. His soul
had drained right out of him. How dare Bob tell him to take a pill
in that cheap way! He'd finished with pills. He had a headache.
Damn this International Pink business! Dammit, dammit! And
why had he gone on and on about the trouble at the house
yesterday? Perhaps because he'd not had a man to talk to since
Jack died. Some things only another man can help you carry.
Fowler, he could never talk to Fowler. When Fowler died it was
as if the silence merely deepened in the other room. Professionally

211

it had worked well. They'd both become lazy, called a halt to ambition. Fowler liked the boring stuff. Positively gorged on it. The more boring the better – conveyancing, property management, civil offences, motoring offences. Banality satisfied and reassured him. The small cogs of documentary life, turning at the same pace day after day, lulled him into an almost mystical repose. But Gordon preferred less predictable material. Most of the wills had been Gordon's, and any divorces or property disputes which passed through the office, and the commercial accounts among which Bob Dashman's was the biggest. Gordon couldn't afford *not* to be interested in International Pink. Bob had made that plain. Bob wanted a decent suburban solicitor to deal with it, a trusted local fellow – and Gordon had been muggins. For a fee, of course. He should've stood out for a higher fee. If he was laying his neck on the line, he should get *more* . . . . . As Gordon turned back from the window and looked wearily about him, a corrosive sense of grievance, of having undersold himself, was now added to his burdens – he felt he was a fool and had to go on being a fool because the alternative was . . . the alternative was not possible. Ha! He scrutinised the room more closely . . . Was this all there was? Had it all been just for this flimsy mess? Instead of the domain of a man of the law, it looked more like . . . more like? . . . yes, that was it, it looked more like the office of a seedy private detective. Too few clients, too little money, a definite lack of the necessary . . . Bob had grasped this. Clever Bob. Oh so bloody rich and successful fat arse Bob. That Indian boy's uncle had a bigger house, did he? It's so pathetic – the ratings game, it's so pathetic . . . Gordon was tired. So very tired . . . He felt himself in a lift descending. He stretched out a hand to stop himself descending and it touched the intercom.

'Yes, Gordon?' answered Ms Harding.

'Oh . . . The International Pink files, please, Tina.'

'Yes, Gordon.'

5 seconds later, as if they had been at her elbow, Ms Harding came pertly, petitely in, and slapped them down on Gordon's desk with, he thought, perhaps overmuch sharpness. He blinked and she smiled nervously.

'Is anything the matter, Tina?'

'No, of course not.'

212

'I wish you weren't leaving.'

'Well, I am,' she said – again with more force than was called for, as if she were afraid that she might not be.

'Yes, I know. And I wish you weren't. How'll things be?'

'What do you mean?'

'I mean – will things be difficult with the baby, loss of income and so forth?'

'I was going to talk to you about that.'

'Well, don't worry – I'll give you a bonus. But I wish you weren't leaving.'

'Craig and I have got a lot to organise before the baby comes.' There was a disembodied look in Tina's eyes and the rest of her face wasn't exactly festive. In fact she looked as if she were coming on to vomit. 'It's an expensive business having a kid, getting married, not working.'

'Is there anything I can do to help?'

'Perhaps I could work part-time.'

'No, Tina. I want a full-time secretary. I can't fiddle about.'

'I see.'

'Well, don't blame me. It's your own fault.' Now it was Gordon's turn to use more sharpness than was necessary.

Tina bristled at once and at the same time seemed to be unhooked. The vomitous visage vanished to be replaced by one that was firm and sombre. She said 'The International Pink file makes very interesting reading. Is all that stuff legal?'

Her remark caught Gordon on the raw. He knew how an oyster felt when lemon was squeezed onto it. Tina's vomitous visage returned. Obviously something within her was having a painful parturition.

'What do you mean – interesting?'

'Just what I say. Not interesting to me particularly. But in other hands . . .'

'Tina, I don't catch your drift. That'll be all, I have work to do.'

'Not all, no. As I said, bringing up baby is an expensive business.'

'Tina, as you well know, the things you see here are strictly confidential.'

'Oh yeah, I know all that.'

She had gained in confidence. Although the firm and sombre

213

look did not return, something else almost as disquieting did, a sluttish innuendo in the voice. Gordon knew that pregnancy could do bizarre things to women. Then the truth of it dropped into his awareness, softly, surely and completely, like a turd dropping from a rectum into a pan. And the plop of it sent hideous coruscations through his soul. He was being blackmailed.

All that week there was a very strange atmosphere in the house. Pam moved into the guest bedroom because Gordon's insomnia was driving her to distraction – she was getting no sleep – and she discovered, after moving to a solitary bed, that she was getting no sleep anyway. She was apprehensive, glanced uneasily at mirrors, and one afternoon while in the guest bedroom had to tell herself to stop being so bloody silly when she fancied she felt a shaggy presence breathing in the corner – she quickly left the room and tripped downstairs, a terrifying sensation on the back of her neck as if hostile eyes rested there . . .

The weather was sunny, mild and breezy, very pleasant, but Derek kept a great deal to his room, reading, thinking, eating bits, playing music, not thinking, not feeling, occasionally in a sluggish manner peering into the Jobs section of the *Evening Cry*. Once he laughed aloud. *Writer seeks secretary. Typing not essential.* For the first time since he'd moved in, he took his photograph album out of the drawer, from beneath a couple of jumpers, and opened it. Doll stared back at him, from another world, chattering to him with a happy faraway voice, like the sunshine in an old newsreel – Clacton. He stared for ages and ages at the photos of the 2 of them at Clacton. Life churned in his brain like the heavy, sultry waters of a tropical river and he began to dislike it. He was depressed, didn't feel comfortable anywhere in the house except in his room and even here he didn't feel secure, felt the room was merely on loan to him. Derek and Pam hadn't referred to the face-slapping incident and this made the air brittle between them. Derek came down in the evenings to eat, to watch television, when Gordon was around. Once he went to the Chinese Take-away for them – Pam paid – it was hardly a thaw – the man said

'Funny wevver for de time ob year' and Derek heartily agreed. He felt OK with Gordon who hadn't taken sides – Gordon was fair, Derek judged. There was a television documentary one night about young people who'd died strangely or committed suicide – Sir Francis Laking, Raymond Radiguet, Otto Weininger, Jacques Vaché, Sid Vicious, Olivia Channon, Antinous . . . It was the one possible programme which could engross them all. Derek felt better afterwards. At least he was alive.

One afternoon over the garden fence the Major said to Pam 'Is Derek all right? I hope he's not taking it too badly.'

'He's a bit quiet.'

'Tell him to pop round – I've got a book for him.'

Derek went next door, round the back, poked his head in the kitchen door and shouted 'Hullo?'

The Major shuffled into the kitchen. 'Come in, dear boy. I've got that book for you. The Jervys O'Jimminy. How are things?'

'OK . . .'

'Really?'

'Not really . . . I have to *do* something, Vernon. For myself. But I don't know what it is.'

'When are you 18?'

'Not long.'

'Get out and about. Find a job. Anything. Make a start. Don't brood.'

'Bob Dashman says I can work in his factory. But I don't want to.'

'Then don't. Go to the centre of London. Start there. It'll wake you up. Remember, it's your town.'

'Ha!'

'I've got some new magazines. Do you want to come upstairs and have a look?'

Derek shook his head. 'Not to-day, Vernon, if you don't mind.'

'That's all right,' said the Major. He ruffled the boy's hair and kissed him on the cheek.

Derek said quietly 'Thanks, Vernon. Thanks, you know . . . for everything.'

'Thank *you*, Derek. You're a very loving boy. Believe me – thank *you*,' replied the Major with a twinkling smile.

215

A couple of evenings later, a Friday, just after Gordon had arrived home early from the office, Derek heard music downstairs. Faraway it floated in a cloud of infinite sadness. He went to investigate, appeared in the doorway and looked at Gordon. 'What's this?' he eventually asked.

Gordon looked up from his armchair, startled, gaunt. 'Rachmaninov's First Piano Concerto . . . A young man's concerto . . . . .' The slow movement was drifting to its close. It was shockingly beautiful and sad to Derek. The cloud of sadness enveloped Gordon and was impenetrable. Derek swallowed and said 'I'm on my way out. See you later.'

Pam came out of the kitchen as he was going out of the front door and said 'Dinner's on the table in half an hour.'

'I'll get something out,' he answered, not looking at her, and slammed the door.

Pam went into the sitting-room as the happy third movement began. She sighed deeply and said 'Turn it down a bit, dear.'

Gordon turned it off. And they both sat there, staring into space, into different spaces.

On leaving the house Derek walked up Wildwood Rise, straightened his back, and ran his fingers through his hair. He was wearing the blue track suit which Pam had bought him and feeling a mixture of guilt, anger, despair. He turned into the drive of Rorke's Drift. Though late in the day it was still fine. Red admirals fluttered in the drive. Bees buzzed among the roses. Green and copper trees made beautiful shapes against the blue sky. But it was rather humid.

He knocked on the door. Marilyn answered. 'Is Cordelia in?' he asked.

'No, she isn't. And, Derek, listen. I don't want you going out with her, OK?'

'But—'

'She's working hard for her exams and although she wouldn't

216

tell you herself, she's not really interested. So there's no point in coming to the house, is there?'

Marilyn closed the door in his face. He saw a flash of red – of his mother – of Marilyn's cunt – of Pam – and he left the place. It was horrible. He wasn't surprised by Marilyn's action and so she hadn't hurt him, but he was bruised by what she'd said about Cordelia. 'Fuck this hole,' he muttered to himself, making his way towards the recreation ground. He was suffocating in a hole. He felt breathless and trapped. It was Friday evening. An evening not to be wasted. But what to do? He'd almost reached the rec. when he heard the sound of running behind him. It was Cordelia with Albert. She'd been standing on the upstairs landing, picking her beautiful nose when Derek called.

'I saw you from the window,' she said, out of breath. 'I heard what Mummy said. She's getting quite strange – I don't understand it. It must be her menopause coming on or something. God, how gruesome! I'm sorry about what she said to you.' She was beautifully flushed. He could feel the heat coming out of her. She was wearing jeans and a baggy tee-shirt with *The Race Against Time* printed across the front. He couldn't help reading and re-reading her breasts. 'I got you these,' she said, pressing a box of Liquorice Allsorts into his hands.

He stared into her eyes with astonishment. One minute, nothing, desolation; the next, all this. His astonishment relaxed and he saw that her eyes were quite relaxed and open to him, were alive to him in their centre. They held each other gently in each other's eyes and emotion rocked between them back and forth in wavelike pulsations, dissolving their separate identities. Then Derek became embarrassed and said 'What you giving me these for?'

'That's not very gallant,' she said. 'I'm not giving them to you to apologise for Mummy. It's because you like them.'

'How do you know I like them?'

'Mummy said.'

– They've been discussing me, he thought – Christ, what else did her mum say? – did she tell her about . . . *that*? Derek, to cover his worry, opened the box and said 'Do you want one?', steeling himself to throw a frantic glance at her to see if she knew what he'd done with her mother. He suspected Marilyn was quite

217

capable of saying anything to stop her daughter . . . yet he perceived that Cordelia knew nothing.

They walked along the road eating the sweets, along another road, into the recreation ground. He gave 2 to Albert.

'Don't give them all to him,' she said.

'I'm not. It's only 2. We didn't have a dog. We had a cat. Phyllis. She's at my auntie's.'

'What was it like where you lived before?'

'It was OK.' His voice swerved up and down on 'OK' which made it a positive statement meaning 'Not at all bad actually'.

But she wanted more. 'What sort of OK?'

'You know, East End style.'

'Where does the word Cockney come from?'

'What's this? *Brain of Britain*?'

By the time they reached the Spinney almost all the sweets had gone. He sat on a log and said 'Will you come swimming with me one day?'

'Yes,' she said, sitting beside him. He extended his hand towards her. The trembling middle finger came within an inch of her left nipple which was causing a bump through the cotton of her loose tee-shirt.

'You've got a spot on your chin,' she said.

His hand dropped onto his knee. 'I expect I've got several,' he said.

'No, only one. Only one that's ready. Shall I squeeze it for you?'

'Cor blimey, do you have to?'

'I will if you like.'

'I wouldn't like.'

'You're that type, aren't you? Self-conscious.'

'No, I'm not.'

'Shy and awkward.'

'No, I'm not.' He had the sensation of having sunk rapidly out of his depth.

'And good-looking.' She was flushed, her nipples pert beneath the cloth.

'Yeah?'

'Mmm. Good-looking. It's a good job you are, coz you aren't anything else.'

218

He plunged inside and didn't say anything.

She was smiling a vicious smile at him.

'Why did you say that nice thing then that nasty thing?' he asked, pulling a piece of bark off the log.

She fiddled with the buckle on her belt and said 'Perhaps because I feel all shy to-day too. I get shy days. Anyway I prefer older men.' She succeeded in catching his attention. His eyes flashed at the buckle. 'Older men are more interesting,' she said.

'You're a bit of a cow, aren't you,' he said, standing up and turning away to conceal his hard-on which pushed out his track suit, but not so fast that she couldn't catch a glimpse of it. Her nastiness had aroused him, broken the barrier of reserve between them.

She said 'You only say that because you want to milk my tits . . . I have pretty breasts. I don't wear a bra, you know.' He knew. He could see that. He'd been seeing that for some time. 'Mummy said I should or my breasts will sag when I'm older. But they'll sag anyway when I'm older, so what's the point?'

His mouth had gone dry. There was a tense bitter taste in it. He swallowed hard. His heart was thumping. A faint tremble ran through his thighs, doubling back at the knees and making them rather uncertain. Despite this he turned gracefully on one leg, so that she could witness his erection, and walked away to sit beneath a tree, drawing his knees up with his legs apart.

Cordelia looked across at him, pushed a few loose strands of golden hair behind her ears. Her colour had mounted and stayed there. She stood up from the log with a certain petulance and, slipping a hand into her waistband, said 'Have you seen Albert?' Albert had disappeared.

'What's the matter with you?' he asked with a frown. 'You're so stuck up you can't be yourself. Try having no money for a bit. You'd improve.'

'Don't be so classist,' she said. 'Just because I've got a rich dad doesn't mean I'm a horrible person.'

'I'm not into a hot pursuit scene,' he said.

She walked towards him pouting.

'You're a cock-teaser,' he said.

'I'm not. I gave you those sweets, didn't I? You wolfed the lot in 5 minutes. I couldn't believe it. Don't they feed you?'

He screwed up his courage and said 'Your mouth was made for the madness of blow-job.'

'What?'

He repeated the line, more cockily.

'What do you mean?'

'You know,' he said. 'Lick my thing, my derek. Like a lollipop.' He went crimson.

'What? You're revolting! People like you should be tortured to death!' He laughed thinly and she sat down in the grass a few feet away from him.

He said 'That Psychoplasty's not bad,' joining her in the grass where Albert too was panting.

'Do you know My Place? It's in the West End. It's fantastic. I went with some friends at Easter and we got drunk and had cocaine and stuff and it was brilliant.'

Derek looked at the dog and saw that Albert's penis was sticking out of its sheath. The pink prong gleamed wetly in the evening sunshine. He said 'Look at Albert'.

She said 'He's often like that.'

He said 'Just like me.'

Cordelia looked at Derek and rolled onto her back.

'You should give him a wank.' Derek hardly knew what he was saying, he was so excited. Cordelia was feeling very spaced-out. She glanced up at him again, tilting her eyes back in her head. She was the colour of roses. Derek wanted to cherish her and screw her out of existence at the same time. She looked susceptible to force (which was far from always the case) and this drew the force out of him. He was drowning in warmth and rolled closer to her. He could feel the prickle of sweat at certain points on his body and his heart beating heavily within. They were both on their backs looking up at the early summer sky. It was very quiet. Albert trotted off again. They looked at each other. It was dreamy. The edges of the personality had dissolved away. They were points of awareness – all else was *else* – and the awarenesses overlapped, melted together, danced apart, drifted, swooped, melted, rocked and span, overlapped . . . Cordelia felt a compulsion pushing forward through her lips which lifted and very softly touched the lips of Derek and all 4 lips, in the conjunction, pushing together, gave pneumatically under the pressure, swooned and moved apart

220

again. They looked into each other's eyes and the beyond, were warmly moving there, gone in the look that was searching, restless, uncertain, enveloping, of limitless extent, infinitely fascinating and insecure . . . . .

Derek slid his arm over her and she said 'Not here'. He looked desperately about, as if being hunted down by something, and pulled her into nearby bushes – pulled off Cordelia's tee-shirt and his track-suit top and they hugged, pressing against each other, feeling and smelling the gorgeousness of it, but hardly seeing it, too many pictures, too close up, and he fumbled at her buckle, fly buttons, pulled everything down, her jeans were tight, jammed at the hips & bum, difficult to get down, her pants were easy, his track-suit bottom and pants were dead easy, made for it, they pressed their furry parts together, hot, hugged, his cock stuck up between them like a bright flower, he fingered her pussy too desperately, she went 'Agh', he pushed the stem of his cock down to get it up inside her, trembling, too desperate, he came immediately, groaning 'Oh God, oh fucking Christ, oh fucking Christ . . .' Hot sperm dribbled down her hip – they were half sideways on in the grass – he stayed hard and slumped over on top of her and mounted her, managed to put his cock inside her with his hand, she wasn't helping, he looked at her profile against the grass, she was staring out sideways with a grimace of some sort on her face, sweat glued strands of gold hair to her forehead, he slid in, she groaned, he slid in and out of her, in and out, swooning against her face, rummaging over her young rubbery flesh, her pussy was tight and oily, and he suddenly stopped and focussed. 'You on the pill?'

'Yes,' she said, sharp as daylight, rubbing her hands nervously over his hard rubbery bottom.

'You done this before?'

'Once.'

'I'm inexperienced too,' he said, swooning against her again, hugging, writhing, pushing, sliding, sweating, hot wetness sweet between them. It went on for ever and ever and ever – sliding sweet and kissing – he licked her breasts, bit them, swooned against her face – and Cordelia thought – This is fucking . . . This is what dogs do . . . And Derek's so heavy and he's knocking the breath out of me and a stone or something is digging in my back and I'm not feeling very much heavenly stuff and I think I'm

221

supposed to have an orgasm and if only he'd stop bumping up and down on top of me perhaps I could think myself into an orgasm but it just feels like I'm jolting over cobbles in a cart and it's like the weirdest dream because I can think straight but everything's too close up and I wish he'd bite my breasts again because it sent a big tingle right through me but now I've got his hair in my mouth and it smells/tastes shampooey and sweaty and although I like to smell shampoo on a boy's hair I don't think a mouthful of hair is what it's all about and the last time I did this it wasn't like this, and Derek thought – I am . . . getting the ram-ram-ramming movement right, I am . . . gouging around in her, gouging around in her with my cock, and Derek didn't want to think of anything else and it wasn't thinking anyway, it was doing this.

Derek drew his head away from Cordelia's and said 'Lie on top of me.'

'What?' she asked.

'. . . get on top of me.'

'I don't know how to.'

He rolled onto his back and pulled her onto him and said to her 'Squash me a little bit.'

She said 'I feel naked up here, exposed. I can feel the air on my back,' and before long Cordelia had managed to slide under him again and thought that the last time she did this, which was also the first time, it was all over in 5 minutes which was with that Adam friend of Ward's from school with his white skin and yellow hair and pink cock and blue eyes and I don't quite know why I did it then and I don't quite know why I'm doing it now and what if he's slept around? but one *must* have experience and I – oh God I'm so dizzy and trembly and uncomfortable – is this an orgasm? is this it? why doesn't he nibble me again? is this an orgasm coming? is this an orgasm?

Derek clenched and came inside Cordelia with a not quite involuntary ramming of his loins, trying to ram a hole right through her, discharging into the heart of his possession. He slumped on top of her, feeling the supreme success – the young ease – ease in Technicolor – and love in electric lights.

Eventually he sensed a chill on his back, felt apprehensive and vulnerable, and rolled off her. His cock was puffy and red.

'You're very gentle,' she said.

222

He was upset by this but didn't say anything and thought – She says I'm gentle, Marilyn said I'm rough, it was different both times but not in that way, and so I conclude that women must have something different from me in mind when they talk about it. Did Marilyn mean we had a fucking situation? Does Cordelia mean this is a loving situation? What have I got myself into? Should I use a rubber next time?

Thought, shyness, complexity returned. They readopted their clothes.

'God, anyone could've seen us,' she whispered.

'Not in the bushes.'

'They could look through. Peeping Toms.'

'Yeah,' he said with bravado, deriving pleasure from the possibility.

She laughed at him and he was unnerved. Laughing women frightened him. He wanted romance, not comedy. Yet he was drawn to the laughter as to a superior power. It subsided into a smile he'd seen before on women – loving, predatory, knowing, inquisitive. The Mona Lisa smile.

'You've got the most wonderfully shaped head. It's a sort of cube,' she said.

'Pardon?'

'You mustn't say pardon. And you mustn't say lounge. They're dead giveaways socially.'

'I don't mind being a dead giveaway,' said Derek.

She kissed him all over his face.

'You'll give me the horn again '

'The horn of life!' she said.

He got an erection and went 'Ouch!' The knob had stuck to the cotton of his underpants with a glue of love-juice and this now tore away painfully.

'What's the matter?' she asked.

'Nothing. A man's problem. Sometimes things get in a twist. There's a good film on TV to-night. Do you want to come to my place to watch it? Pam won't mind. She'd like it.'

'No, I'll have to go back.'

He kissed her and started feeling her and she said 'I don't want to start all that again. It's getting damp here. Don't you feel damp?'

'Yeah,' he said with a horrible leer.

She drew away. 'Sometimes men are just . . . revolting,' she said.

'What's the matter with you?'

'Nothing. I'm feeling chilly.'

'Come here.'

'Leave me alone.'

'There is something the matter with you.'

'Oh for God's sake, don't keep on. There's nothing the matter, OK?'

'OK.'

But there was. She felt she'd lost something. She felt less. She was not accustomed to sex. It disturbed her. She felt weakened, her power broken. She felt under an oppressive obligation to him. She was no longer in control of her life. And what if she got pregnant by accident? Such things did happen . . . . .

Derek felt a mixture of exhilaration and exasperation. He felt as if he'd been let loose in a great ocean and did not know which way to swim. He knew there was a lot more to it than ramming, but exploring this depended on dealing successfully with the opening and closing of the personality of the partner – and this, he surmised, could involve a great deal of work. He became abstracted, pensive, close to melancholy; and they didn't speak for some time.

'Do you read books?' he asked.

'Of course I do.'

'I don't mean for school. But just because you want to.'

'I like biographies of actresses. But I haven't read one for ages. I've got exams in a few weeks. I'm dreading it.'

'I've been reading a book *Here To-day, Gone To-morrow*,' he said.

'Yeah?' she said, imitating the upcurving way Derek said 'yeah?' which meant 'I'm interested. Please continue.' But she didn't realise she was imitating him.

'The Major gave it to me.'

'That old fool.'

'He's all right. One bit says: *It is the essential characteristic of desire that it can never know satisfaction.* What do you think about that?'

Cordelia was irritated and said 'What are you trying to say?'
'I'd say that the more you get the more you want . . .'

She became perplexed. He looked very beautiful to her – and she didn't want this. There was a noise and Derek turned his head round to see Albert approaching them through the undergrowth. Cordelia looked at the way the hair grew on the back of Derek's neck and felt a hot sucking pain inside.

Earlier, at Rorke's Drift, not long after she'd closed the door in Derek's face, Marilyn had shouted 'Cordelia!' . . . No reply. 'Cordelia! . . . . .' But no reply. She mounted the gracious staircase to the red and gold landing, knocked on her daughter's door and when there was still no reply, went in. The bedroom was empty. She knew immediately where her daughter had gone. She just knew.

– She's gone chasing after that boy – she must have heard him come to the door – the tramp! – at *her* age! Why can't she find a nice young man like that Adam? Oh no, not her, not Miss Smarty Pants. She's got to go after some twerp from the East End. What does she see in him? She could have anybody! That boy who hasn't the *faintest* idea what he wants to do with his life. Not a *clue*. Hasn't she got any self-respect? How could she do this to me? God, I'm not a snob – I don't mind that he's working-class, if only he had *something* going for him. That's not quite true. He's got Cordelia going for him and I expect he thinks he's damn clever. Well, we'll see who's clever! Oh, where did we go wrong, where did Bob and I go wrong? She's only showing off, only doing it to annoy. She's as hard as nails. He'll soon find out – she's just using him to get at *us*, Bob and me, using him to throw up 2 fingers at us – the tramp! She doesn't give a tinker's cuss about that poor boy. He'll emigrate to Australia or somewhere, if they'll have him in – what if she goes to Australia too? – we won't be trekking over to that dump just to gawp at their howling brats! – we won't see her *ever again*, oh God. No, she won't go to Australia, not her, she'll hurt him, he'll get hurt. Poor kid – no family, no one to look after him – or he'll get her pregnant then piss off, yes! – she doesn't understand – oh, Cordelia darling, I'm not trying to interfere, but you just *don't understand*. An abortion, I can't stand it, so squalid – my poor darling on the slab with needles up her – no, no, they're very tender these days but Cordelia, psychologically you'll be scarred for life – for life! And Derek's so alone – he's just a boy – he's so young damn him! Why is he so young, so fresh, so warm, so clear? How could he mess me around like this! How could he do this to me! Damn them both! Damn them TO HELL!!!!!

Marilyn cried hot, hysterical, angry, frustrated tears, frustrated by Time which she felt was leaving her behind, frustrated by . . . everything. She was STUCK. Shedding tears relieved the awful pressure on her brain and she decided to call Pam. She asked how Pam was and Pam said she had a bit of a headache.

'Oh Pam,' she said with slow emphasis, 'I'm so sorry to hear it. Have a good cry.'

'I don't want to cry, Marilyn.'

'Well, I wanted to have a quiet word with you, off the record, strictly *entre nous*, about, well, about – about Cordelia and Derek. Before, you know, before things get out of hand.'

'Are things getting out of hand?' Pam wanted to know. 'I thought they hardly knew each other.'

'You know what young people are to-day. They feel they've got no time. It's the Bomb or something. They can move very fast. They don't have the long run-up like we used to.'

'Don't they?' said Pam who remembered her and Gordon's long run-up almost with despair. Is he never going to do anything? she'd often thought. Marilyn on the other hand was being disingenuous – Bob had had her on the third week-end, a nice ½ Jewish girl like her.

'But I don't think Cordelia and Derek are right for each other, Pam.'

'Don't you? I must say, I find young people rather cautious to-day, rather hangback on life. What happened to voomph?'

'I hope you're right because I mean, well, you know, God knows I'm not a snob but the difference in their background, really it's—'

'Marilyn, are you suggesting that Derek's not good enough for her? Because if you are, I'm not going to agree with you. Derek's a fine young man. I know there was that terrible business recently with those boys. But Derek tried to protect us, you know. He behaved wonderfully. And besides, it's all over now.'

'Oh I know, I'm *not* saying that. I wouldn't blame Derek for what happened and I must say, Pam, do get some security fitted on your house. We have *total* security here.'

'They didn't break in. We invited them in – like idiots.'

'You can't be too careful. The world's not getting any quieter. Do get someone round to fit you a *system*. I'm not saying Derek is violent but, well – it's not fair on Derek. He'll get hurt. Cordelia's going away to Drama School and—'

'Marilyn, do you really think it's any of our business if they want to see each other? And don't you think all this is a bit premature?'

'Maybe . . .' said Marilyn with a deep sigh. 'But I may as well tell you, I've told Derek he's not to see Cordelia any more and shouldn't come to the house again. Perhaps I was a little hasty, and God knows I don't want to be unkind, but well, I was frightened by what happened at your house, and what's said is said and I mean it – so I'd be very grateful if you'd support me on this one.'

'Marilyn, I'm finding all this rather strange. Are you giving me the whole picture? Do you know something I don't? . . . Well, I know there was an unpleasantness here. But to blame Derek for it is extremely cruel of you and in fact, Marilyn, I thought you had more – more . . . I thought you had more soul, quite frankly. I'm very disappointed to hear you getting it so wrong. So I'm going to suggest you think about it and ring me again if you reach a more intelligent and Christian position. Otherwise there's no point in discussing it. Now, if you'll excuse me, I have to get Gordon something to eat.' And Pam put the phone down. She felt drained.

– The bloody nerve of that *bloody* woman! she thought. That common tart coming on superior with *my* nephew! I'd be very grateful if you'd support me on this one indeed! I bet she would! . . . Heavens, my neck's stiff . . . And my shoulders . . . Why? Tension? I haven't done my exercises in yonks – Marilyn Bloody Trashy Nouveau Riche Dashman indeed! . . . I'll have a quick run-through the exercise on the video, before dinner, while

Gordon's going through his bumf in the dining-room.

She went upstairs to the tallboy in the back bedroom to change into her keepfit clothes. The back bedroom, the guest room, was her bedroom now, for the time being, until Gordon was himself again. At first she could hardly sleep alone. It was like sleeping on the edge of a cliff, of a hungry emptiness which would devour her. She'd had a couple of nightmarish flutters. But she'd adjusted, was beginning to enjoy solid sleep . . . She looked out of the window. The trees were in full, luminous leaf. It was a fine sunny evening. The garden was lush. The peonies and corn-flowers were out, the dahlias and snapdragons, the lilac, the laburnum, lobelia, gypsophila, glowing and whispering. She saw a flicker. The gold cross on top of the church spire flashed a cute wink at her as a cloud passed, then sustained the beam of its exotic message. She saw the flicker again. No, it wasn't the cross. There was a dog in the spinney, an alsatian – and something else. People. A person. Was that Derek in the grass? She recognised the track suit. Who was that with him? She screwed up her eyes but couldn't make it out. Pam went for Gordon's field glasses in the cupboard on the landing and flitted back in for a closer look. The focus came and went – she got it . . . Derek and Cordelia . . . A lead ball plunged inside Pam. She didn't know why. She was riveted to the scene. Derek was sitting under a tree, part of him obscured by the leaves of a bush. Cordelia moves across, lies down in grass. Derek rolls into grass. They are kissing. One of Derek's hands is under the girl's top. Pam can't see what Cor-delia's hands are doing. They move crouchingly into bushes. Pam loses sight of them.

Pam Drake felt sick to her stomach. Dizzy, trembling, hot, cold. This reaction distressed her enormously. She did not know why she should be reacting like this. But she thought – That boy's going to get himself all confused just as things are beginning to settle round here.

But this thought left her unsatisfied. It insufficiently accounted for her reaction. She felt a bit of acidosis coming on.

– What if Cordelia gets pregnant? Has Derek thought of that? He never thinks of anything, just drifts from day to day. I've asked Gordon to get a few ideas mapped out with the boy but Gordon seems to be in a drift too . . . . He's getting old . . . I'm

228

getting old . . . But I don't feel old. That's what the young don't understand – old people aren't old – what's a lifetime? A squit. Nothing. They just have these old bodies to cope with. There are old souls and young souls and it doesn't much matter what age you are. Am I an old or young soul? I'm young! Gordon's an old soul, always was . . . And I've allowed myself to be brainwashed into behaving like an old soul – but I'm not – my body is old, that's all . . . And the place where body and soul meet, *there*, I've allowed that to become old too – I am old *there* . . .

On the word 'there' she pressed 2 fingers into her vagina, only a little way. It was warm. Surprisingly – moist . . . But in contradiction of her previous analysis she felt dry in her soul. Moist in her body but dry in her soul. Seeing 2 young people disappear behind bushes had made her soul seem terribly, terribly dry.

When on this Friday evening Derek returned to the house, Pam didn't know where to look. Gordon and she had eaten and he had stayed on in the dining-room with his bumf and to stare at the opposite wall for long stretches of tortured time. Pam meanwhile watched the 10 o'clock News, very convenient when you don't know where to look. At present the Pope was commanding the Faithful to breed breed breed breed breed. Pam was offended by it and was provoked into saying 'Derek . . .'

'Yeah?' There was not much upswerve on this.

'Derek . . .'

He looked at her and she quailed before the steadiness of his eyes.

'Derek, I . . . I . . . I just . . . wantedtoapologiseforslappingyoutheothernightitwasfoolishofmeIhavenoexcusebut . . . I was upset, I'm very sorry.'

'That's OK.'

'It was a terrible thing to do to you. I've felt ill with remorse ever since. I don't know how to make it up to you.'

Derek thought he'd settle for 25 quid but didn't say so.

'All I can say is, well, I'm not perfect, I've all the human faults, and I'm very very sorry because I love you and want you to be happy here and feel it's your home and I think I've set that back a long way.' She was not sad, but deeply and quietly moved by what she was saying.

Derek squirmed. Her sincerity was agony to him. 'It's OK, Pam,' he said, hoping this would shut her up, but also hoping she would go on caressing him with words in this way, sweetening him and drawing him into her with these words, but she didn't. But the silence could not rest there, it was flooded with emotion, the subject had to be changed before there could be silence, so he said 'There's a great film on after this.' The Pope withdrew into the South American palace from the balcony at which he had ordered the teeming, starving, penniless and diseased throng to love each other and avoid all forms of contraception and alternative sexual outlets and breed breed breed for Catholicism.

'Is there?' she said, giving him a powdery smile.

She and Derek sat at opposite ends of the sofa. *Charlie Bubbles* came on. Derek got up to adjust the picture from the remote control pack beside Gordon's chair and sat down in it which he sometimes did when Gordon wasn't there.

'Did you have anything to eat?' asked Pam after an interval long enough to allow Derek to become fully absorbed in the film, so that her solicitation became an interruption.

'I forgot.'

'There's some shepherd's pie left.'

'Yeah?' He was ravenous after his energetic mounting of the fair Cordelia.

'Yes, and some veg. No pudding though. I'll get it. You watch your film.'

The camera panned across scenes of urban waste and demolition in the North of England. Grim towers grew out of the rubble of redbrick streets. Or nothing grew – only a cold wind wailing across demolished wastes.

'That's what they did to the East End,' said Derek when Pam came in with the tray. 'The bits the Germans didn't get, *they* got.'

He ate and after another interval Pam asked in a casual way 'Where did you go this evening?'

He chewed for a time, not hurrying, swallowed and said 'I was with Cordelia.'

'You like her, don't you?'

'Do I?'

'You seem to. She's quite a tough cookie.'

'That's one of the things I like.'

'You know about contraception and all the rest of it, don't you? I'm not saying there's anything between you but I feel happier mentioning it. We're all old enough to be sensible about these things.'

'No, I've never heard of it. She'll probably get pregnant.' He looked at her with a look she hadn't seen before. It enthralled and disquieted her. It was the look of self-possession. Then she wondered if she over-credited Derek with self-possession. Self-possessed in that moment, he was no more what he was in *that* moment than he was what he was in any *other* moment. But it showed her one thing – that he was capable of self-possession. The sense of relaxed power in his face told her that. Then they both laughed, seeing he'd made a joke.

Gordon came in, saw Derek sitting in his seat, and said 'There's something I want to watch on the other side. You don't mind, do you?'

'But we're watching this film,' whined Derek, his self-possession gone.

'What is it?' asked Gordon.

'*Charlie Bubbles*.'

'Oh, I've seen that,' said Gordon. 'Haven't you seen that? It's always on.'

'I haven't seen it before, Gordon,' said his wife, 'and I'm enjoying it too.'

'We can get it from the Video Shop if you like. I just wanted to catch this special report on the other side on coastal pollution in Cornwall. I've a client with some property down there.'

'Let's record it then,' said Derek.

'Derek, I haven't time to fiddle about with all that. I need to watch it *now*.'

'Jeeesus,' said Derek.

'Do you have to watch that boring stuff, Gordon? We're enjoying this film.'

'*Were* enjoying it,' said Derek.

'Surely I'm allowed to watch an important programme in my own house?!' said Gordon raising his voice.

'It's my house too,' said Pam. 'Or had you forgotten?'

231

'And I don't think Derek should complain,' continued Gordon. 'He does very well on the whole!'

'What?' said Derek. 'Do I owe you something, Gordon?'

'Well, if you're going to live here, you might do more to justify your presence!'

'Gordon!' said Pam, shocked.

'I don't ask much, Pam, in return for my hospitality! Just a bloody TV programme now and again!' Gordon was shouting. He was in a rage and the wrath of a gentle man is a formidable thing. 'You 2 have it bloody easy! Neither of you has *any* idea!!'

Derek was white. He didn't understand this. Derek's understanding had limits. He went up to his room.

Pam tried to be soothing. 'You've been working too hard, Gordon.'

This drove him wild. 'Don't patronise me, Pam! I won't have it, I won't have it! It's just not good enough!' He was trembling. He had experienced that shattering moment when a person in control of a situation realises he is no longer in control. Not only that. Not that the control has given way to chaos – that would be bearable. But that the control, the decisive centre, has passed to others. In his domestic life this was to Derek and Pam. In his professional life to the likes of Bob Dashman and Tina Harding. It was a moment of decision. Either he reasserted himself – or evaporated.

Pam was shaken too. She'd seen Gordon angry before. But never . . . sulphurous like this. She got up and turned on his programme. 'I'm going to have a gin,' she said. 'I'll get you a whisky.'

'No thanks,' but he didn't refuse when it arrived. His trembling continued all through the programme on Cornish sea pollution, not a single word of which he took in, throughout the police thriller afterwards, throughout the late news summary & weather, and only ameliorated with *Goodnight*, a short talk by the Bishop of Durham on why God is a woman as well as a man.

Pam knew it was important for her to stay as normal as possible and so she said scornfully of the dark, collared figure on the screen 'The man's not in his right mind. Does he seriously think God is interested in being us?'

'I'm going to bed,' said Gordon blankly.

232

'Gordon, darling – listen – take a sleeping-pill to-night. You need a proper night's rest. You've got to get your sleep. You've been under a lot of strain lately. It's Saturday to-morrow. Have a lie-in. Take a pill to-night. Give yourself a break.'

'Maybe,' and he went upstairs without kissing her.

She tidied up downstairs, washed a few things in the kitchen, heard Gordon leave the bathroom and close his bedroom door. She was particularly glad on this night that she wasn't sharing a bed with him. They would've given each other no respite. She went upstairs, saw the light under Derek's door, and knocked softly. He said 'Yeah?' and she went in. He was in bed, a book flat on his bare chest. 'Don't mind Gordon,' she said. 'He takes you too seriously, that's all. He's going through a bad patch. It's what they call the male menopause, when a man gets upset because, you know, he has to take the back seat sometimes. But I know he loves you very much.'

'I've never seen him like that. Freaked me out.'

'But I've seen him like that.' She lied. 'Just occasionally. He's so placid by and large that it's shocking to see him in a temper. But don't worry.' She caressed the side of the boy's face and when she kissed him he felt her intensity. 'Funny, isn't it, how it so often takes nasty events to make people come close to each other. We're not doing very well, are we, Gordon and me?' She gave him a queer trusting smile as she said this and he felt sorry for her. When she left him, he turned out the light, drew back the curtain, and masturbated in the light of the streetlamp, staring down with relish at his penis but holding in his mind shifting close-ups of different parts of Cordelia's body, discharging into a towel which he kept at the back of his wardrobe for this purpose.

Gordon followed Pam's advice, had a sleeping-pill and a very heavy sleep. Indeed, although he got up, he didn't seem to wake up. Breaking the circle of his insomnia collapsed his alertness. From the moment he awoke he wore a twisting frown. Pam said 'Don't frown like that. It'll get stuck.' But he didn't hear her.

'I'm going for a walk,' he said. He didn't return until late. Pam grew worried. But when he came to her again he seemed, miraculously, much happier. To say he had recovered his old self would be wrong. Instead of tension and fog, a clarity seemed to have possessed him, a capacious calmness. He was both buoyant and serious. Yet he didn't talk intimately with her, explain himself, so that she was all at sea. It was as if he held a secret which strengthened him, and this was a challenge to her. But she did not meet this challenge. She busied herself. She let him be.

Derek was out most of the day, hovering on obscure corners, trying to catch Cordelia on her way to or from Rorke's Drift. At last he succeeded. She'd stayed at school on Saturday afternoon working in the library and was doing extra work that evening, but would meet him on Sunday evening in The Flying Fox where nobody they knew went. Derek nodded and moved off. He now realised how much he'd been kissing her yesterday. His neck muscles ached and the saliva glands under his tongue were sore.

On Sunday Derek was at the pub ½ an hour before the appointed time. It was fairly empty and had recently done itself up in what was supposedly the style of a 17th century manor house. She was 20 minutes late.

'Where've you been?' he asked.

'Have you got a plane to catch?'

He was silent, chastened.

She was brittle, said in a manner that was both imperious and dreamy 'Will you get me a drink?'

'What do you want?'

'Same as you.'

He went and bought 2 halves of lager.

'I've been thinking,' he said. It sounded ominous to her. 'I want to get a job. Anything. In a caff in Soho. Right in the centre. And somewhere to live, you know, where I can have people back. Shall we go to the spinney?'

'It's too cold,' said Cordelia morosely.

'I'll warm you up.'

'No thanks.'

– Here we go again, thought Derek. Closing time – why are there always these pissy little games? An answer to his question was not long coming.

'I had a terrible row with Mummy this morning. She was . . . revolting. And she said she *knew* things about you and I asked her

234

what she was talking about and she wouldn't tell me. What was she talking about?'

A strange expression settled on his face, a smile with the lips held firmly together and fear in the eyes. He wanted to tell Cordelia about that day with her mother. He looked at her. Marilyn hadn't said anything specific. He was afraid to speak, of what it might lead to. But he wanted to speak of it. He didn't want the weight of it on him. This weight was not in his heart – because in his heart he was immensely proud of having had both mother and daughter – it gave him the grit he needed to survive these trying times. The weight was in his head. He hated the idea of the world as minefield, never being free from the demands of deception, living in fear of letting the cat out of the bag, never knowing the clean strong line, the power of fully conscious abandon. He would have to tell her. But not to-night.

'I dunno,' he said with weary emphasis on the 'I'. 'She don't think much of me. She'd say anything to stop, er . . . you know. Do you feel . . . you know, a special feeling?'

'I don't know . . .' Her voice trailed away. She hoped he wasn't going to ask her to make verbal commitments to states which hadn't defined themselves. It wasn't that she wanted to keep her options open. It was that she didn't want to start killing things by nailing them down – it would be desperate and futile to do that – it would be *silly* . . . And she felt this because she felt that perhaps something serious was happening to her and it should be allowed to take its course and not be wrenched this way and that by the wailing ego. And she didn't trust him

2 middle-aged men came in wearing expensive country-type clothes, ordered whiskies, and started to converse in posh penetrating voices. The pub was quiet and their accents grated on Derek. 'I expect you want a bloke like that,' he said to her.

'I don't want any bloke,' she said.

'Have they got a jukebox here?' he asked.

'No . . . They've got one at the Dandiprat.'

'We should've gone there.'

'I know people there. Daddy goes there – now and again. They know I'm under-age.'

There was silence and he said 'I found out what Cockney means. In Gordon's dictionary. It means cock's egg. The egg of a

235

cock. But cocks don't lay eggs. And it didn't say why this should be used for, you know, a working-class Londoner.' She didn't say anything and he said 'I want to find my sister. That's important to me. I've been thinking about that.'

'She's your family,' said Cordelia.

He was quiet for a moment. Then he said 'If there's a nuclear attack on England, and we're not together, remember – I'll be thinking of you as it happens. And so if you think of me too at that moment, we'll be together – wherever we are.'

A dreamy look entered Cordelia's eyes. She felt a spasm, as a pod of tenderness burst within. It tingled and diffused through her like a coloured steam, colouring her experience, bringing it alive. Her eyes grew moist but not tearful. She turned to him in their quiet corner of the bar and put her mouth softly on his mouth. The delicate kiss made a click and she said 'You're so bloody clever.'

'No, I'm not,' he replied. 'I'm just not stupid. Which people like you mistake for cleverness.'

Cordelia struck against his chest with her fist.

The next day, Monday, Gordon arrived at work with a rare composure. The 2 clerks in the outer office said 'Good morning, Mr Drake' and stared at each other as he nodded and went breezily through. He spent a large part of the morning simply reading the newspaper, which was unheard of – he never opened it until lunchtime – and there was a glacial case to his manner which Ms Harding found intimidating.

This did not however prevent her from popping the question: 'Have you thought about it, Gordon?'

Gordon fiddled about and said 'About what?'

'Don't give me that.'

'How much do you want?'

'Enough,' she said with a thrust of her face. 'I'm not saying you're a rich man – but there are those involved in this who are. Don't worry, we're not going to be on your back more than once. Craig and I just want something to start with, that's all. Call it my golden handshake. A house will do. 4 bedrooms, 2 bathrooms. And we'll call it quits.'

'I'm sure something can be arranged . . . I'll give you your answer to-morrow. Now – are you ready to take a few letters?' he said, folding the newspaper and tossing it across the room with a flamboyantly careless gesture.

She was jittered.

Derek was out most of Monday. He walked around, paid a routine visit to the Job Centre, and came back at tea-time. He held a stack of newspapers and started systematically to go through their job sections while Pam brewed in the kitchen, listening to the local news on LBC Radio. *A man was drowned to-day when the small boat, in which he was ferrying a marble fireplace across the Thames, capsized and sank near Blackfriars Bridge . . . . . And now – Your Horoscopes!* She waited for hers to come up. It said: *As you must've already realised, this is YOUR year! Things are on the up and up in your life! Forget that old-fashioned reserve, because the planetary aspects are terrific!*

'Oh goodeeee!' she said, skipping over to the biscuit barrel and putting some fig rolls and squashed fly biscuits onto a plate. She took the tea-tray into the sitting-room and said 'Seems like a renewed burst of activity on the job front.'

Derek raised his head – he was lying on the floor. Pam looked more vivid than usual. She was wearing a white blouse with red flowers slammed across it and pale grey slacks. She had more make-up on – normally she wore very little.

'Reckon it's time I got my skates on,' he said. 'I'm looking for work in Soho.'

'Work as what?'

'In a caff. A bar. Anywhere.'

'Why Soho?' She didn't quite like the sound of Soho.

'Seems a good place to start. Lot going on.'

'But don't you want a proper job?'

'You got one to give me? Anyway it is a proper job. Any job's a proper job. Let's face it, Pam. It's too late for me to be an astrophysicist.'

'Now you're being silly.'

'I thought of the Navy too.'

'That's a good idea.'

'The Merchant Navy.'

'Oh.'

'Well, don't look like that.'

'Don't leave . . . I mean, don't feel you've got to. Leave when you've got something really worth leaving for. Of course you want your independence – and we'd always help you. You're a clever boy. Have you thought about studying something?'

'Yes. And I've come to the conclusion that I'm the more practical type. And another thing—'

The phone rang and Pam went into the hall.

It was Gordon. 'I'm popping into the sauna. It'll do me good. It's always very quiet there on Mondays.'

'Will you want something to eat?'

'No. Don't worry, pet.'

'All right then.'

'And Pam—'

'Yes?'

'Er, nothing. It can wait.'

'Enjoy your sauna.'

She put the phone down and returned to the sitting-room and the consideration of her young man's future.

'What other thing?' she asked.

'I want to find my sister.'

'Sister? I didn't know you had a sister.'

'Yeah. She's little. But I don't know where she is.'

'Does Auntie May know?'

'I dunno.'

'We'll ask her. If she doesn't, Gordon can help you. He's terrific at that sort of thing. Finding lost people, it's one of the things solicitors are trained to do.'

'Really?' he replied in surprise.

'Oh yes! We'll find her together!'

Derek curdled inside. It was good to have help. But he recoiled from the way Pam seemed about to claim his sister.

Gordon dismissed the clerks and Tina Harding $\frac{1}{2}$ an hour early, in a cool, efficient manner which did nothing for her equanimity.

238

a cool, efficient manner which did nothing for her equanimity.

– What's the old bugger up to? she wondered. I should never have listened to Craig, never have got involved in naughtiness and aggravation. (These were Craig's words – 'If you want to get ahead, poppet, you mustn't be frightened of a bit of naughtiness and aggravation. No one *ever* hands it to you on a plate.')

'Good evening, Mr Drake,' said Miss Wimbush in the sauna. 'Haven't got your young man with you to-day?'

'That's right. Quiet to-night, is it?'

'Just a couple of regulars.'

In the changing-room, towelling himself down, was the large burly man with beard and small penis all but lost in a forest of black pubic hair. 'You just come in?' he said.

'Yes,' replied Gordon, thinking this must be obvious since he was taking off his clothes and hanging them carefully in the locker. Some people just threw their clothes in but Gordon was more careful, wished to preserve as much as possible, in the damp atmosphere, their presentability.

'Do you know what time it is?' asked the burly man, making a great fuss of towelling between his legs.

'Just after 6.30.'

The man started putting on his creased-up clothes and said 'Do you know what day of the week it is?'

'Yes. It's Monday.'

'Rotten weather we're having.'

Gordon, who didn't think the weather was either good or bad, said 'I don't expect brilliant weather in England.' In fact, weatherwise, he was a Ruskinian, but thought it might sound pretentious to say so.

'You travel a lot?'

'No.'

'Do you know what year it is?' asked the man.

Gordon closed his eyes in petulance and said 'Next year', picked up his towel and went through to the showers to wash off the dust of the day. ''Bye,' he said. The man grunted. The red light glowed inside the pine sauna cabin. It sat there opposite the showers like a vehicle arrived from Andromeda, both primitive and futuristic. Gordon entered it.

The very fat man with flesh like uncooked pastry was in there, imparting his unpleasant odour to the hot contained atmosphere.

He was lying on his back on the upper bench with his belly rising like a steamed pudding towards the roof. He turned his head sideways and, recognising Gordon, said 'Hullo. You look well.'

'Can't imagine why.'

'Why do people always say that when I pay them a compliment?'

'Do you mind if I throw some water on the coals?' asked Gordon.

'No, I don't. The air gets very dry in these things, doesn't it. Very bad for the hair.'

This amused Gordon because the man was very bald. The water exploded in steam off the rocks. Gordon lay on his back on the lower bench, his little round pot belly almost ironed away as he stretched out. It would reappear magically when he stood up. The steam sizzled on his skin and his body began to loosen and deaden about him, redden and ooze. He let his eyelids collapse. He could feel himself sinking slowly downwards and sliding slowly backwards as if he'd just had in quick succession 3 glasses of port.

'Heard a nasty thing to-day,' said the fat man.

Gordon, collapsingly, grunted.

'Yes,' continued the fat man, 'my next-door neighbour in the flats – his brother choked on a peanut butter sandwich last night. Choked to death, that is. He gulped it down and it got all glued up in his windpipe like a bolt of clay. You know how that stuff can stick. He couldn't breathe. Choked to death.'

Gordon chuckled.

'*We* didn't think it was very funny,' said the fat man.

'I didn't mean to be rude,' said Gordon, 'but it is a ridiculous way to go, don't you think?'

'No, I don't. I think it's nasty. That's what I think.'

The fat man didn't speak more after this. Gordon continued to collapse undisturbed until the fat man clambered down from his bunk with much noise and difficulty and said 'That'll do for me.'

After a couple of minutes Gordon went out for a cold shower – he avoided the plunge pool – and went back into the sauna. He felt very loose, very relaxed, very nothing. His emotion had separated from his body. He didn't go all silly in the cold shower and he didn't go all silly in the sizzling heat. He registered these contrary states without reacting to them. This was composure – detachment – awareness – sanity. He knew that he breathed, that blood circulated. More than that . . . nothing . . . He was in readiness but not waiting for anything. He was completely disentangled . . . . He went out for a cold shower and then into the changing-room. The fat man was dressed now and banged his locker shut. 'I'm off home for a decent meal. See you soon.'

'Watch out for peanut butter sandwiches,' said Gordon.

The fat man snorted and left. It was very quiet in the sauna.

Gordon went to his locker, took out his briefcase and took from it the small spongebag he usually brought to the sauna. He unzipped it and took out the small brown bottle containing his sleeping-pills. He walked across to the water cooler, took a white plastic beaker, filled it with cold water and flushed down his throat all the remaining sleeping-pills in the bottle, almost 2 dozen. He put the bottle back in the bag which he returned to the briefcase which he returned to the locker which he locked. He had a splash under the cold shower and returned to the sauna cabin.

He threw some water onto the coals – it exploded off them in steam. He lay on his back on the lower bunk, stretched out, let his eyelids collapse, and waited . . . . . Time passed . . . . . . He was very very calm. Time passed. His heartbeat was slow and heavy. He collapsed voluptuously downwards. It was blissful . . . very . . . blissful . . . Suddenly his heartbeat revved wildly! His heart was like a bird in terror, trying frantically to escape the cage of his ribs. He poured with sweat – threw his head from side to side – one hand clenched the bunk, another jerked in the air – there was a sharp twinge in his stomach and stabbing pains – he knew he was going to vomit – the puke spasm began – he was going to vomit up the whole shooting match – here it comes – the puke spasm mounted – the vomit muscles twitched . . . . . . and nothing happened – a twitching passed violently through his entire body . . . . and passed away – he didn't vomit – the vomit moment passed away – the fluttering heart moments came and went like booming and passed away – many moments passed – came, swelled and passed away . . . He could hear swellings. *Tod und Verklärung*. Obviously that. It's obvious. They are above me, these Straussian swellings, swinging like balls, like

breasts, like buttocks, like . . . Oh, they are the flying saucers at the Royal Albert Hall singing above me, come to wish me well. They are descending in a sublime smother. I'm ready for that . . . But they don't smother. The flying saucers take off, one by one, swoosh . . . swoosh . . . the disengagement . . . yes . . . . a boy's voice is chattering in my ear . . . or is it a monkey's – chatter – chatter – very close – very loud – no – faraway – faraway . . . Is it a boy's voice? . . . No, I know what it is, it is the sound of sea sliding up the shingle! shshshshshshsh – shush . . . shush . . . hush . . . . shush . . . . . hush . . . . . the sliding shush voice . . . be quiet . . . . . who is the boy? . . . . . who is the boy? . . . . me . . . I am the boy . . . . . I am the boy . . . . . and I'm going on holiday . . . to the seaside . . . . . faraway . . . . the sea sliding up shingle . . . shshshshsh . . . boom of waves far out . . . . and the sea sliding up shingle close at hand . . . shshshshsh . . . . boom . . . boom . . . boom . . . of waves far . . . out . . . the heartbeat is very loud then faraway . . . very loud then faraway . . . boom – boom – boom – bbbbm . . . boooommm . . . . bbom . . . . bbbbbm . . . the heart beat is sliding . . . the heartbeat is smearing . . . . . what is that? smearing? what is that? is that a heartbeat? or a boy's voice going shshsh? Be quiet, hush, hushing me, touching me, hushing me up, hushing me down . . . shshshshshs on the shshsingle – on the shingle – the waves sliding in – one – after another – after – another – for ever and ever and ever – and everything smears – smears . . . out of cognition – out of identity – out – out – out of focus – out of cohesion – out – out of existence – for – ever – and – ever – and – ever . . . . . and . . . . . . ever and . . . . . ever . . . . and . . . . . . ever . . . . . . and . . . .
. . . .
. . . .
      . . . .
      . . . .
      . . . .
                                .
                                .
                                .
                                .
                                .

Pam was out. She'd popped next door with the leftover fish pie for the Major. Occasionally she liked to give him a treat. And if Gordon wasn't bothered, why should she let it go to waste? Derek was watching the Monday Film on television. A spy film. A man was being chased by Special Branch police through St Paul's Cathedral. There was an important service taking place. Choir, organ and orchestra were performing Bruckner's *Te Deum* which was at full flood, pouring out of the television set, while the Special Branch chased their fugitive, this dark figure, across the arched sepulchral space of the cathedral, down side aisles, into

244

secret corners, dodging, swerving, halting, firing guns, but the noise of firing was drowned away by the roar of the *Te Deum*. So in the middle of all this din and activity, it was some time before Derek realised that the telephone was ringing in the hall with a feverish clamour.

Then it all happened very quicky. Mark arrived, tall and thin like his father, and whitely colourless. He busied himself with the funeral arrangements. Can a suicide be buried on Christian soil? Can he be cremated? Yes, he was cremated – it all seemed so squalid to Mark, such an unhealthy rigmarole. He wheezed and frowned, doing his duty, desperate to get away from it all. Working on chemical weapons inured one to death, made a tidy abstract of it, so that he was ill-equipped to deal with the individual human reality. Mark's mouth hung open a good deal as he tried to be of use to his mother. He couldn't reach her emotionally, so he didn't try, and kept it down to practicalities. And therefore he was of great use, though he didn't realise this and merely felt ashamed of his inability to rise to the occasion in a more noticeable way. Pam had to make her own equations with grief and would have resented any attempt by another to steal her thunder here. She loathed parasitism in any form, especially emotional parasitism. And she knew that Mark had his own, different equations to work out. Beyond this jealous guarding of her personal grief, she felt nothing. She was under sedation from the doctor. She wished she were in India and could wail out her grief. But no. This would be considered at best unseemly self-indulgence, at worst insanity and the doctor in his wisdom kept her blotted out: the doctor headed this conspiracy to deny the facts. A thought strayed into her drugged miasma – I didn't know him, I didn't know my husband . . .

Then, 36 hours after that apocalyptic telephone call, the stabs of guilt started – this was the worst – the sense of having failed someone to such an appalling extent – stab – stab – no rest from the stabbing, pet – she heard Gordon's voice and was further sedated by the doctor.

On the third day she rebelled. 'I don't want any more of that stuff!' And threw the pills across the room. 'Look what they did to him!'

Mark said 'Mother, you must get your sleep. I'm staying with you.' He looked at the doctor. Mark was anxious lest she get out of hand. He wanted her back in her 'mother costume', not jerking around in this rude primal form.

Derek held her hand. She pulled it away. He took it again. She left it there.

Why? Why? This was Pam's question. Day after day. To Mark, to Derek, to the Major, to sympathisers, to helpers, to anyone who came through the door, friend or stranger, to find her sitting in Gordon's armchair beside the fire gazing out into the nothingness, a flabby stunned thing. 'Why? Why?' And then the stab – stab – stabbing – stabbing you, pet. 'What did I do wrong?' she asked of the dead air. 'Where did I fail him?' No answers forthcame.

Mark Drake planned to stay with his mother for an indefinite period, which he hoped would not be more than a month, and resented Derek as an intrusion. Mark had to use the guest bedroom and in his ashamed state felt the slight. He took his mother's hand as he'd seen Derek do – and Derek backed off. Occasionally Mark looked at Derek with suspicious interest as if Derek held the key to something. There was no easy conversation between them.

Derek once said 'Poor Gordon, he must've completely flipped at the end.'

Mark said 'You're the expert, are you?' Derek had nothing further to say.

Pam noticed this and thought – Oh God, we pushed him out! Derek and I pushed Gordon out! He thought there was love between Derek and me! He thought nobody loved him! And what does Mark think? Terrible thoughts! She went through bouts of hysteria, her imagination inflamed and voracious, devouring and altering everything.

The vicar from St John the Divine across the field came, a small dark man with (she noticed in the middle of all this) a surprisingly common accent. 'Don't accuse yourself, Pam,' he said, addressing her by her Christian name though they'd only met a couple of times before. 'He lost contact with God. Because God, you see, keeps us directed. Remember the words of St John the Divine.

246

Love one another. That is the Lord's command. And if you keep it, that by itself is enough.'

It was too soon for these words. It was the wrong thing to say. They went through her like cold steel. 'There you have it! He felt unloved! I failed to love him, that's what I failed to do!' She started to get hysterical again.

Mark said 'Please, vicar, don't talk religion at a time like this,' and hustled the Reverend out.

Coincidentally at this time Derek saw an ad for a job in Soho, working in a video shop with banks of coloured lights flashing on the front of it. The Manageress liked him and said 'OK' and said there was a spare room above the shop he could use for the time being.

'Do you live there too?' he asked, fearing the worst.

'No,' she said, laughing.

Derek was elated. And guilty. How could he ditch Pam in the present circumstances? He walked through Soho and Mayfair, enchanted, thoughtful, uncertain. He stared at a strange new building like a baroque cathedral in transparent glass and was angry with Gordon. He took the bus to visit Auntie May – she was well. It was his 18th birthday. She said 'Why didn't you tell me?' and took a banknote from a drawer.

It was 10 days after Gordon's funeral when Derek came home with this job. Pam blinked and smiled wanly. She was red-eyed and looked so tired, so very tired . . . There's a negative kind of placidity which comes with very great emotional fatigue and Pam was now entering this phase.

She insisted he took the job.

'But will you be all right?'

'Yes, I will. I'm over the worst. Mark's staying for the moment. And the Major next door is very very kind. He said I can lean on him and I probably will, a little, now and again. And you'll be back to visit me, won't you? You'll come and stay for the week-end sometimes?'

'Of course I will.'

'And bring your washing. I'll do it and iron it for you.'

Mark winced. – How nauseating this is, he thought.

Derek said to Cordelia 'Will you come and see me?'

'Yes,' she said.

The Major said 'Well done! I expect to see you at regular intervals,' and he wrote out a cheque for £300. Derek did all he could to refuse it but the Major's clear, guiltless certainty of purpose won.

Lying in bed, Derek thought – Oh Christ, how can I walk out on the old girl now? She needs me. Well, she needs someone. That jerk of a son, he can't be much compensation . . . but he is her son. He's in the guest bedroom right now. Like a corpse in a grave. I'm glad I'm not him – the living death . . . I'm learning to handle the death of my mother. Finally I'm coming out of that – not that I'm forgetting her, but I am surviving her. Beginning to accept that she's not around any more, that she won't see me grow up now. She won't be able to come and visit me in my first job – sometimes I can't bear that sort of thing and have to go right down inside myself until the feeling passes away. Don't talk about it much. I haven't reached the stage where I can talk easily about these things. Perhaps I never will. Perhaps I'll always laugh it off, maybe that'll be my way. But I hope not. Why are people so ashamed of feeling pain that they must always laugh it off – until it gets so bad that . . . . . Perhaps I'm not coming out of it yet. But it's good Mum encouraged me to be self-reliant. It doesn't stop you feeling bad. But feeling bad doesn't come as so much of a shock. And I do feel angry with Gordon and not too depressed by his death. It was – what did that Joan say at the funeral? Squalid, incomprehensible . . . Not much sympathy there. Poor old bloke. I was easy with him but not close to him. He wouldn't have that. Often it was less easy with Pam – but I do feel close to her. I feel I can be me with her. I wonder why he did it. His life weren't so terrible. A screw loose maybe. He was a bit weird. Anyway, what with Mum and everything, I can't get all upset about him too. Not enough room for that. But I feel guilty about walking out on her. Why should I? We all know I've got to take this job – am I supposed to pass it up because of what you did, Gordon? Fuck that. But I still feel guilty about leaving her like this. Maybe I love her a bit then. See how you've messed it up for us, Gordon? Yes, I'm angry with you, and it's not because I'm

hard. I hope it's not that. I appreciate what you tried to do for me
. . . but let's not exaggerate and get all sentimental here. You
didn't exactly put yourself out in any major way for me – or
for anyone else. Despite your deep and honourable sentiments
about life. OK, you agreed to let me come here and took me
to the sauna a few times, and I'm grateful, but it was Pam who
did the lion's share. Not you, you miserable bugger. Only a
miserable bugger would top himself. I'm not being very chari-
table, right? You think you deserve charity after what you did?
. . . . OK. I'm sorry. You must've felt like shit at
the end, and I know what shit feels like . . . . . Pam, I'm leaving.
I have to, for Mum's sake as well as my own. But I'll be back to
see you a lot. It's all London, innit. I expect I'll miss you. I'll also
miss the Major . . . And Cordelia. She can come and stay with me
overnight, snuggle up in my cosy little room in Soho. I think
she'll come there. I think she will because I think she likes me. I
don't think she did it just for experience. Perhaps she'll be my first
love affair. Ha! I'm already thinking of it as only the first, already
thinking of the end of it, and it hasn't even started, not properly,
well, it *has* started, I mean, I've put it in there, so . . . She's
beautiful. What can I offer her? She won't stay with me. Do I love
her? Do I just love her hole? Anyway, what is love? Well . . . the
horn has something to do with it. With real love you get a helluva
lotta horn. And then that click, like you always knew each other,
that feeling almost from the first moment of meeting, and missing
them a lot. Then it needs time to develop. Do I want to get
stitched up already? And I get a helluva lotta horn anyway . . .
My balls are all tight and tingly because I'm nervous and excited
about my prospects, about this incredible future of mine. I've got
quite thick pubic hair – thicker than Cordelia's sweet golden
. . . . . I'm going to have to give this a go in a minute or I'll never
get any sleep. The light from the street is coming through a chink
in the curtains. I didn't close them properly. This room – was it
ever my room? Yes, as it happens. It is my room. Funny. It just
happened. Mark looked very put out when he saw me in it. He
knew all about me of course but he definitely looked a bit
deprived. But he accepted it, everyone accepted it, and he
unpacked meekly in the guest room. Yeah, I expect I'll be back
here quite a bit for some auntying and to say hullo to Vernon and

the rest of em – cor, that geezer sure was quick off the mark
. . . . . I don't think it means I'm really queer, does it? I expect it's
the father figure thing . . . oh, what the fuck, who cares? And
what I liked in him was – he wasn't screwed up and guilty about
any of that stuff, but was really cool about it too and didn't
embarrass me. Let's face it, Derek, you seem to like a bit of
everything. Yes, I want lots of experience, I want to experiment,
have adventures . . . . I'll have to be on my guard a bit in Soho,
what with these diabolical diseases and weird murders and drug
addicts . . . I hope I'm doing the right thing. Perhaps I should try
for something safer round here where it's quiet. Now, Derek,
don't go putting yourself off it. You'll have a great time. It'll be
the making of you. Soho – that'll be my university. Sure beats
Saint Fucking Andrew's. So this is my *moment*. The door of the
world is opening at last . . . .

The day Derek left, Pam gave him a box of Liquorice Allsorts and
said 'I'm not giving you anything more special because I'm not
going to pretend you're leaving. This is your home, darling. It's
not much. But I want you to think of it as home, a place you can
come to whenever you like.' She stood up and hugged him. He
kissed her on her dry powdery cheek. 'Now don't get into
trouble.'

'I'll be OK. I'm 18 now.'

'When?' she asked, taken aback.

'The other day.'

'And we forgot!'

'Don't matter. There was plenty else happening.'

'In all my involvement with death, I forgot . . . about life.'

'Don't matter.'

'It does matter, darling. One isn't 18 every day. Give me a
week or 2. I'll make it up to you. I'll think of something.'

Mark thought – They gave me some shares for my 18th birthday – she better not start giving stuff away to this Derek. Why is
she calling him darling suddenly? She's going to have to budget
carefully. Dad left her everything in the Will – I suppose it was the
least he could do – the bastard . . . Why did he do it, why?

Pam and Mark followed Derek to the door. As he walked through the hall, he wondered if he were mature. Certainly he had the sensation of being more grown-up than when he arrived. He was sound in body and soul – but he was nervous. He felt that youth was over and that from here on, life would be lived, at best, with a vague sense of unease – is this what it is to be grown-up?

He went down the path, pulled at the gate and eventually got it open, turned, and waved – Pam had shrunk in the doorway and looked shrivelled and remote. Mark stood over his mother with an arm limply round her shoulder – he looked as if his thoughts were altogether in another place, although he was smiling. And as Derek turned into the street his eye caught a movement in the house next door. It was Sybil at the window of her bedroom. She was waving her arms in a buffoonish way, shaking her red hair about, laughing like crazy and jabbing her thumbs upwards in the air. Derek laughed too, put down his bag, blew her a kiss with both hands, and jabbed his thumbs upwards. He picked up his bag. And with the rooks wheeling in the trees and cawing to him, and a fresh breeze darting down from a cloudy sky, and the milkman coming up the street towards him collecting bills, he walked briskly away.

The following Thursday a scandal broke on the front page of the local paper under the headline *Bribery and Corruption*, subsequently making the national press:

> *Local solicitor Gordon Drake, whose suicide in the sauna at the Leisure Centre several weeks ago surprised all who knew him, was involved in a joint scheme by International Pink and the Dashman Group to demolish Hogarth Parade and part of the surrounding area in a major re-development of shops and offices. It is alleged that permission for the multi-million-pound scheme involved payments organised by Drake to certain councillors. In an extraordinary statement to-day the police have revealed that they possess a tape-recording sent to them by Drake on the day of his death, and they have arrested Miss Tina Harding, Drake's secretary, on charges of blackmail.*

However this is expected to be only the beginning of what may turn into the property scandal of the decade. The Mayor said he is very shocked by to-day's revelations and that the Council will cancel the Hogarth Scheme, pending police enquiries. Opposition councillors are demanding a public enquiry into the workings of the Town Hall's planning department. Solicitors acting for International Pink and the Dashman Group say their clients are unable to make statements at this time. See p. 5 – The Dark Horse Solicitor.

Pam was sitting by the fire alone. It was late. About midnight. Autumn. There were no lights on in the room – the strawberry iridescence of the faulty streetlamp flowed gorgeously into the room. Unnaturally bright it seemed to her to-night although it was hardly anything at all. It merely tinged the dim interior here and there. She was sitting on the sofa with her back to the door, gazing into the fire and absent-mindedly playing with the pearls round her neck. Mark had gone back several months ago, gone back to wherever he lived now, he sent the new address, back to whatever he does, I don't know, I don't even ask any more. If he wanted to tell me he would. Anyway I'm not as interested as I was. I suppose I've aged since Gordon went. I know I look older. And let's face it, my feet are getting lazy. But I'm much more objective than I was – it was objectivity or madness. It's been 5 months since the funeral. His suicide shattered me. There was nothing in my life to prepare me for it, to hook onto afterwards. He left me on the floor like a puddle, very low down, formless, thoughtless – like the way they found him in that sauna. The girl said they virtually had to scrape him out . . . Death – how grandiose the word, the fact; how squalid the manifestation. And the tape coming afterwards, the scandal and all the rest of it – that was rather heartless of you, Gordon. Oh yes, it was the legal thing to do; you sure *fixed* them the way they fixed you. But it fixed me too. Didn't you think of that? You were an intelligent man, Gordon. And I have to assume that you did think of that – and that's a very painful thing to be left with. Couldn't you have written me a note, apologising for what you felt you had to do? No, you couldn't face me. So you tried to ignore me. Or were you being exceptionally intelligent? Did you appreciate that your conduct would rouse me from my distress, make it easier for me to cope by making me FURIOUS WITH YOU? How could you have ended our life together in such a brusque manner? It absolved me a little from guilt. Everything caved in on you. You had to go. No goodbyes because goodbyes would've prevented it. I understand. You went mad, Gordon. But anyone meeting you would never have suspected it. Those clothes hanging in the locker so tidily. That was creepy, Gordon, my darling . . . . . I tire easily. I like to gaze at the fire. It soothes me. Derek visited me last week-end. Stayed over Saturday night. He's bought himself some trendy clothes. But not too trendy. He looked beautiful. He's found out where his little sister is, but her adoptive parents are putting up barriers. Poor kid. I love to see him . . . . . We need outsiders coming in to rouse us. It's no good thinking you can always rouse yourself. You can for a while, then you must have something from outside. All this self-winding stuff I read about. Just the other day, a quiz in *Woman's Monthly* – Are You Self-winding? Who cares? . . . All you really need is someone nice in your life. If you have that, you can do anything. I don't like living alone. I'm not one of those who are interested in themselves. That's a beautiful light coming through the window, a beautiful pinkish bluish misty November light. It feels warm and the fire looks up at me with orange eyes – my own little Sahara burning at my feet. But you have to keep the central heating on because these fires give out nothing. Cordelia visited Derek in Soho recently. I asked him if they were serious about each other and he said 'No, Map, not in the slightest' with a big grin across his face. He's started calling me Map which is Pam backwards. The arrest of Bob Dashman was big news. Marilyn has been fantastic, quite fantastic, that's the only word for it. I do admire her, despite everything. She's stuck by him. She refuses to drop her standards one inch. The house is in her name and she says she's going to keep it on. The trial will last a long time, she says. Bob'll need the security, she says. I should take a leaf out of her book and liven up my ideas, put the old exercise video on again –

oh Lord, how long ago all that *stretching* seems. I've allowed all these horrid things to be my excuse for being lazy – and now I'm *contracting*. Gordon's mind must have been a peculiar place at the end. I sometimes wonder what it was like, his mind at the end – a large green and purple grotto, oozing acid steam, dripping with blue stalactites, worms writhing in and out of yellow meringue-like fungus. There obviously wasn't a place for me there, not at the end. And I'm glad I've decided to move. A ground floor flat in a converted 18th century house at Harrow-on-the-Hill. Beautiful light rooms. Heavenly views. But I do hate packing. I've made a start. Given masses away to the jumble. It took me ages to decide to move. After all, this is the scene of the largest part of my life. Was I running away? Then I realised I just wanted to move somewhere more beautiful, more . . . idyllic. Derek said he'd come and help but I told him that the removal men will take care of most of it but he says he'll come anyway. And Joan's coming to stay at the new place for a couple of weeks. Everyone's being very kind. I don't want to live here any longer – seeing Gordon flit round corners, catching faded echoes of his smell from the backs of cupboards, hearing him snore beside me at nights – yes, I heard that once and came to and realised he wasn't there, and everything that had happened flooded over me like cold water. I'm lonely. Agonisingly lonely. You can take that for granted, my loneliness. I'm learning to be objective about that too – oh so *bloody* objective! I don't want to be objective about everything. Especially I don't want to be objective about loneliness. I want to be involved with people . . . Joan says I should marry the Major. Apart from the fact that he hasn't asked me, I find the idea of him beside me in bed at night faintly repellent. I suppose I could overcome that. He's been a darling neighbour these past months. I wouldn't want separate beds. I don't see the point of marrying unless you at least get a teddy bear out of it. Anyway, doesn't Joan realise he prefers young men? Is she that thick? It's dark in here, with just the firelight and the light from outside. This is how our ancestors must have felt sitting in their caves. I suppose Cordelia goes to Derek because . . . well, frankly I don't know, but perhaps these events have drawn them together – for shelter. I wonder if – oh fiddlesticks! Why are we always trying to marry kids off? 99 times out of 100 they just like to be with each other and it has nothing to do with wedding bells . . . wedding balls . . . Pam, don't be cheap. Why not? I can be cheap if I want to. Cheap is friendly. And if I can't be cheap in my own house, where can I be cheap? I'm not eating like I used to. My figure's quite neat again. Not that I was ever fat but I did put on a bit with all those meals before. You know, when Derek and Gordon . . . . . If I can survive this I can survive anything. I said that to Derek and he said 'Except the Bomb . . . And if the Bomb doesn't get us, over-population and disease will.' I was quite horrified. He sounded just like Gordon. I hope he's not going to copy Gordon's . . . Gordon's what? . . . I don't know what it was, Gordon's thing, but whatever it was, when it came to the crunch, there was no strength in it, Gordon buckled under. And I keep going over the questions, trying to work out *why* exactly and I get no nearer an answer which satisfies me, maybe because I would have to accept that I knew him so badly . . . Perhaps there is no solid logic behind it. Don't most people just drift from one thing to the next, piecing it together as they go? It's what I've done. And it doesn't add up to much. I brought up a son – who never comes home. I succoured a man – who killed himself. I was here – when Derek needed someone. Don't let me down, Derek, or I'll begin to wonder if I'm a jinx. Loneliness unsettles one, irritating, getting at one, frightening. Loneliness is a poetical word. To convey more closely what I feel it would have to look more like 'shit' or 'sick'. That long word, loneliness, fluttering forward like a romantic pennon, endowing one with interest, a figure on a rock, a figure on a heath, a figure on a deserted beach, a figure around which lightning plays in a wild night sky. This is not it for me. 'Shit' and 'sick' – this is more like it for me. My husband chose to oblivionise himself with a chemical. Damn you, Gordon, you selfish pig! Here I am going round and round on the planet Earth like an idiot strapped to a carousel, gesturing inanely, killing time, being brave; what sort of sodding holiday do you call this, Gordon? You cheated! You played the biggest cheat one person can ever play on another and if God forgives you, rest assured that I shall not . . . . except that I do, because I'm too feeble to do otherwise. I haven't the strength to maintain my righteous anger against you. I see you as the man I once loved and feel a terrible terrible terrible pain at the thought of the pain you must have felt in your last weeks, and this pain drains all my anger and strength into a sadness that is as vast as the desert, as inert as the desert, the desert which changes only when the wind shifts a dune from here to there in a slowly billowing sea of sand – but this is not action, this is not change, this is time-killing, this is listlessness, sadness, playing silly games. This is what God does with man – plays games. If God is all-powerful, then he's playing sick games with man. To-day we'll have a Jesus, he says. And to-morrow let's have a Hitler, to wake the poor things up, to get them thinking about Evil and stuff. This is sick. This is not very nice. One sometimes meets people who could teach God a thing or 2 about how to be nice. Now he's thrown the Bomb in the ring, to see if we blow ourselves up, sink or swim, tee-hee, what fun, how interesting. They call it free will. God is no better than the Roman Emperor watching gladiators tear each other to bits. What's happening in the great wide world to-day?

Pam decided to find out by switching on the late night television news and soon became lost in the familiar soothing parade of tank battles, workers' strikes, terrorist attacks, ecological disasters, and general international mayhem. Television sucked her unresistingly into the tribe. She stared into the pit of the screen which lit up her face with eerie brightness and she was held there.

At this point, unknown to Pam, and with dramatic suddenness, a black leather fist, from the outside, punched through a pane of glass in the French windows of her dining-room. There was a few seconds' halt. Then the black leather fist reached in, turned back on itself, and twisted the key on the interior side of the lock. The door handle descended. The door opened into the blackness of the dining-room. A black figure slipped noiselessly in from the garden, muddying the carpet.

Pam didn't exactly hear glass break. But she thought she heard something. She climbed wearily to her feet, went into the hall and stared at the dining-room door. Had something fallen over in there? Had one of the plates slipped inside the sideboard? She hadn't used the dining-room for ages. She'd check it in the morning. No, she'd better do it now. Something might get broken. Pam rested her hand on the door-handle, depressed it, pushed the door forward and went in.

As her left hand fumbled for the light switch, something shot out and struck her with terrific force on the side of the face. She was knocked violently onto the floor by this and in her immediate confusion registered nonetheless the metallic taste of blood in her mouth. The door into the hall was slammed shut. There was darkness. She froze. For a moment she thought she was alone in there, so cold and abandoned was the atmosphere. Her heart was crashing under her ribs. Then she heard breathing. Strange breathing. Not easy breathing – but excited breathing.

'What is it?' she cried out.

Silence.

Just the excited breathing.

'Who is it? Tell me!'

Silence.

She felt herself getting hysterical and as if the intruder too felt this in her, a voice said. 'Shut up. Not so loud. Attract any attention and I'll kill you.'

Pam was aghast. '. . . Oh God, I don't believe it,' she whispered.

'I want you to keep as quiet as the grave.'

A squeak of distress escaped her. She knew him.

'That's not quiet as the grave. That's noisy in my book. Fucking noisy. Like . . . loud-mouthed. Don't like loud-mouths. Never did.'

Pam was rigid with terror. A sharp odour arose from her body. She smelt it on herself.

He walked across to the windows and pulled the curtains completely shut. It was now pitch-black in the room.

– Please God, this isn't happening.

There was a carving knife in one of the sideboard drawers. It shone in her brain like the gate of paradise.

– Where is he? Where is he?

There was no movement, no noise.

– I can't hear his breathing now. Where is he?

Now there was a funny noise. It sounded as if a stationary car were revving up and throbbing at a house down the road. Oh happy people! Down the road! Down the road was another planet. Then with palpitating horror, she realised that the noise was not the sound of a car revving up down the road. It was the monster, giggling, quite close at hand. He was giggling. And trying to suppress his giggle . . . . . She was on the floor. A hand touched her shoulder, she started, gasped, wriggled away – but remembering to wriggle in the direction of the sideboard. She was going to stab him. There was a burst of low giggling . . . . . 'Very frisky,' he said.

She stopped, held her breath. There was movement. Where? On the other side of the room. A sliding, rushing noise. Odd noise – what's that noise? It was the noise of a black leather hand sliding over the embossed surface of the wallpaper searching for the light switch. He flashed the room light on and off very fast. She was dazzled. And at the core of that brief moment of surprise, like a stone within a stone, a hideous image. He'd shaved all his hair off. The dome of his head was yellowish, perfectly smooth and shiny. She thought of Japanese torture.

'Why?' she asked softly.

'Why not? Everyone should try something new.'

Ludicrously Pam imagined they were discussing his new hair fashion and she said 'Why have you come here? What do you want?'

'Want? I don't want anything. I'm not the possessive type. Want? Want?' he said, kicking her along the floor. She shrank against the sideboard and opened slightly the bottom drawer. There was another flow of blood in her mouth. When she thought of it her lip stung. It had burst open. And although she registered the pain it did not impinge. 'Want? Want?' he said, kicking her. 'Do you think I'm one of those types that want to *grab* things?'

There was silence. Nothing happened. She heard the sound of a zip. Zzzzz–ip. And his footsteps approaching her very slowly. She froze. Leather hands on her face. She held the carving knife behind her. She felt something damp and very soft move across her face and smelt an unpleasant odour. She was disorientated. What was going on? She understood. He was rubbing his penis across her face. Ugh! She convulsed. She stabbed at him. He screamed, withdrew. There was a sound of dining chairs toppling over and a man toppling over them. Pam advanced on the sound, stabbing hysterically into it, hitting wood, hitting flesh, stabbing, stabbing, stabbing. She was possessed with the stabbing lust. Reached the far wall. Hugged it. Listened. Silence . . . . .

She sobbed out her frenzy. She'd killed him, she knew it. And she sobbed.

· After an endless time the dining-room light went on.

'Just thought I'd give it a moment or 2 in case the neighbours heard anything. You had a nasty turn there, Pam. You might have done some damage.' Blood soaked into the black jeans from a gash on his thigh. The denim jacket was ripped. Otherwise he was intact. His penis hung limp out of his jeans like a thick white slug. The monster was smiling. 'You've attacked me with a weapon. You've drawn blood. I'll have to go to the bathroom and attend to it. Which means I have to tie you up and gag you first. You're putting me to more trouble than I'd planned. Still, one has to be flexible. Adjust to circumstances.'

He moved towards her. She was crouching on the floor, holding the knife. He kicked it out of her hands and grabbed her by the hair. There was a sickening tearing noise as a thick clump of it came away. He pulled her up onto a chair and slapped her in the face a few times for general discouragement. He tore the lace tablecloth into strips and bound her hand and foot to a dining chair.

'These are pretty,' he said, and ripped off her pearls. They spat everywhere and he said 'Oh dear . . . Now what can we use as a gag?' He looked about, saw the clump of hair, stuffed it into her lolling mouth and tied a strip of tablecloth over her mouth.

His eye was detained as he looked down on her. 'Oh dear, oh dear,' he said. 'You should've told me you wanted to go. We could've come to an arrangement.' She was wetting herself, though hardly knew it. 'Which reminds me,' he said. 'I want to go too.' With grim fastidiousness, which involved sticking his little finger out, he took hold of his penis and peed, splashing the urine backwards and forwards across the prisoner. This, instead of adding to his courage, made him nervous and he said 'I must do my leg.'

He went upstairs and brought down the First Aid box, went into the kitchen for a bowl of warm water, came back in and drew up a chair opposite her. He undid his trousers and pushed them down, wincing with pain, and delicately dressed the wound. It was bloody but not deep. 'See what you done? Hope you are proud of yourself. That was a shitty thing to do.'

He was wearing no underpants and with his trousers round his ankles he shuffled into a corner, squatted down and shat a pile of evil-smelling matter. Clearly he was nervous. He wiped his bottom with the remainder of the roll of lint. And when he arose from the squatting position he was sexually aroused. He looked manically at Pam and said 'You bitch! You turd! Getting me arrested!' His fingers writhed at her in the black gloves. He picked up Pam's carving knife and flicked it suggestively back and forth across her line of vision.

She started making ghastly noises. Her whole body, apoplectic, heaved against her bonds. Her convulsions excited him. He was delirious with excitement. He started coming as he slapped his member across her face. He grabbed her head, pulling it against him, working his haunches deliriously against her, coming in heavy jerks from which by degrees the energy gradually seeped away. Almost in concert with him, the ghastly noises coming from Pam grew weaker and weaker until she slumped senseless.

Silence prevailed for some time.

He said 'I'll have to kill you now. I just wanted to frighten you. But now you've seen me I'll have to kill you.'

He pulled up his trousers and fastened them. He picked up the knife where he had dropped it in ecstasy and cleaned the blade on the sleeve of his denim jacket. He lifted up Pam's head by the savaged hair. He cut the gag. 'You can say your prayers first if you like. Are you a religious woman?'

The gag fell away and with it came a nauseous smell; the clump of hair fell from her mouth in a repulsive clot. Pam had choked to death on her own vomit. Her face had frozen in a rictus, a silent scream. She was laughing at him. That screaming laugh ripped through his brain with a dreadful roar. He backed off, gurgling 'Oh Christ . . . Oh Jeesus . . .', aghast before the spectacle of Death – scrambled over to the light switch, flicked it off, stumbled out through the French windows. And via the back garden and spinney, pursued by the Screaming Laughter of Death bouncing after him in kangaroolike curves, Dudley Dennis ran frantically away into the night.